HAWAI'I RAGE

OTHER TITLES BY TORI ELDRIDGE

Ranger Makalani Pahukula Mystery Series

Kaua'i Storm

Lily Wong Thriller Series

The Ninja Daughter

The Ninja's Blade

The Ninja Betrayed

The Ninja's Oath

Stand-Alone

Dance Among the Flames

PRAISE FOR THE RANGER MAKALANI PAHUKULA MYSTERY SERIES

"*Hawai'i Rage* offers readers a fascinating deep dive into the ranching culture of Hawai'i's Big Island. Eldridge writes with passion and an insider's knowledge, her love of the state where she was born and raised shining through on every page. If you love Hawai'i—and who doesn't?—you'll love Eldridge's Ranger Makalani Pahukula Mystery series."

—Ellen Byron, *USA Today* and Agatha Award-winning author of the Golden Motel Mysteries

"*Hawai'i Rage* is a deep dive into this country's most beautiful and enchanting state. This well-paced, sweeping contemporary western transports readers into a vanishing and unknown chapter of island heritage. Tori Eldridge writes from firsthand knowledge of the people, history, and the land she loves. Her native legacy and grasp of the Hawaiian rancher's way of life is a breath of fresh air in a literary world looking for something new and invigorating. Tori Eldridge first puts the reader into the real beauty of the Hawaiian experience, then reveals a dark side of detective work and crime that makes readers wonder how something so extraordinary can be spoiled by only a few."

—Reavis Z. Wortham, *New York Times* bestselling author of *Comancheria*

"Eldridge vividly brings the Big Island to life in this compelling page-turner. When's the next one?"

—Jeff Ayers, bestselling coauthor of the A. J. Landau National Park thrillers

"An atmospheric love letter to Hawai'i's Garden Isle with episodes of action and mystery."

—*Kirkus Reviews*

"Author and narrator Tori Eldridge invites listeners into an entertaining and enlightening new series. Eldridge's engaging performance and immersive writing ensure that listeners remain captivated from beginning to end—and eager for the next installment in this promising series."

—*AudioFile Magazine*

"The book [is] an excellent tutorial in both human nature and in the history and culture of Kauaʻi."

—*Deadly Pleasures Mystery Magazine*

"Eldridge, who has Hawaiian ancestry, has crafted an emotionally riveting, multigenerational story with authentic characters who engage readers in what being Hawaiian means."

—Carole E. Barrowman, *Minnesota Star Tribune*

"A deftly crafted novel from start to finish, *Kauaʻi Storm* showcases author Tori Eldridge's genuine mastery of the mystery/suspense genre."

—*Midwest Book Review*

"In *Kauaʻi Storm*, Eldridge combines a story of a strong woman torn between family and duty with a pulse-pounding mystery. Steeped in Hawaiian culture, it's as beautiful and complex as the island itself. A fantastic read!"

—Rebecca Cantrell, *New York Times* bestselling author of *It Wants Us Alive*

"Anchored by a strong, capable park ranger reminiscent of Nevada Barr's iconic Anna Pigeon, this thought-provoking, engaging debut immerses readers in Native Hawaiian culture, language, complex genealogy and social issues while delivering a solid mystery with more than a few surprises."

—Paula Woods, *Los Angeles Times*

HAWAIʻI RAGE

RANGER MAKALANI PAHUKULA MYSTERY

TORI ELDRIDGE

Published by Thomas & Mercer, Seattle

www.apub.com

EU product safety contact:
Amazon Media EU S. à r.l.
38, avenue John F. Kennedy, L-1855 Luxembourg
amazonpublishing-gpsr@amazon.com

ISBN-13: 9781662525254 (paperback)
ISBN-13: 9781662525261 (digital)

Cover design by Ploy Siripant
Cover image: © Todamo / Alamy; © ninjapoy, © nednapa, © Neenpeen / Shutterstock

Printed in the United States of America

For my ʻohana, living and ancestral, me ke aloha nui a me ka mahalo!

PREFACE

Welcome to *Hawai'i Rage*. Welina mai iā kākou! After writing *Kaua'i Storm*, the first of my Ranger Makalani Pahukula mysteries, I felt pulled to write about Hawai'i's magnificent cowboy culture. Although paniolo (Hawaiian cowboys) have been ranching in the islands longer than cowboys in most of America, relatively few people outside the islands know about their renowned history, beginning with the Mexican vaqueros brought in from Alta California in 1833. I set my fictional Hiapo Ranch on Hawai'i Island, the heart of Hawaiian ranching, close to North Kohala where my own ancestors were born. I have included a Hiapo family tree at the beginning, and at the end you'll find a list of main characters, a glossary of 'ōlelo Hawai'i (Native Hawaiian language), Hawaiian Pidgin English (as used and sometimes simplified in this book), locations, and historical and mythical characters. As always, I have woven actual locations, history, and facts into my fiction and taken liberties where needed to tell an exciting story I hope you will enjoy.

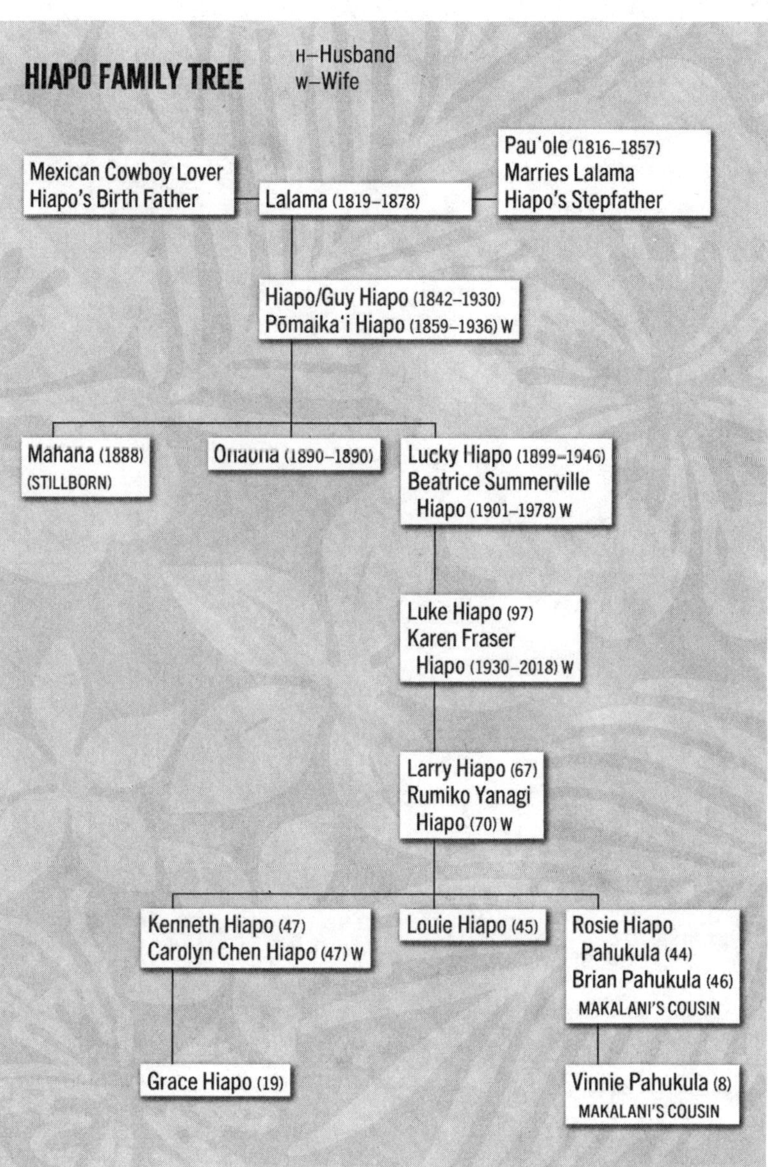
HIAPO FAMILY TREE
H–Husband
W–Wife
Mexican Cowboy Lover
Hiapo's Birth Father
Lalama (1819–1878)
Pau'ole (1816–1857)
Marries Lalama
Hiapo's Stepfather
Hiapo/Guy Hiapo (1842–1930)
Pōmaika'i Hiapo (1859–1936) W
Mahana (1888)
(STILLBORN)
Onaona (1890–1890)
Lucky Hiapo (1899–1946)
Beatrice Summerville
Hiapo (1901–1978) W
Luke Hiapo (97)
Karen Fraser
Hiapo (1930–2018) W
Larry Hiapo (67)
Rumiko Yanagi
Hiapo (70) W
Kenneth Hiapo (47)
Carolyn Chen Hiapo (47) W
Louie Hiapo (45)
Rosie Hiapo
Pahukula (44)
Brian Pahukula (46)
MAKALANI'S COUSIN
Grace Hiapo (19)
Vinnie Pahukula (8)
MAKALANI'S COUSIN

CHAPTER ONE

Ranger Makalani Pahukula gunned the utility quad and landed hard on the shelf of Palihae Gulch. Dirt sprayed from high-side tires as the sport three-wheeler ahead of her crested another mound and tipped, but didn't slow. The father was determined to reach his trapped son. If he wasn't careful, Makalani would have two people to save instead of one.

She sped ahead of him, cut down the slope, and forced him to turn. His tires dropped to the ground. Back in control, he followed her along the bank of the ravine.

Makalani's wavy brown hair trailed behind her like a cape. She hadn't felt this alive in months, certainly not since returning to Oregon and what she'd believed to be her dream job as a law enforcement ranger at Crater Lake National Park. But the echo of Hawai'i had beckoned her home. She had yearned to hear Tūtū chant in the kalo patch as morning sunbeams kissed her face. She craved the feel of the mud between her toes as she dipped her hands into water fed by Anahola Stream. Although protecting the Oregon forests filled her with purpose, caring for her ancestral land nurtured her soul.

Mālama i ka 'āina, mālama ka 'āina iā kākou.

Care for the land, the land cares for us.

She accelerated up the next rise of dried grass and colorless terrain.

"How much farther?" she yelled when the father's three-wheeler pulled alongside.

"I can't tell," he yelled back. "It looks different going uphill."

When John Tanton had skidded into the Puʻukoholā Heiau National Historic Site's management resources station, he was frantic and too dehydrated to speak. After chugging half a bottle of water, he had pointed toward the mountains and said, "The ground ate my son." More water and a tank of gas later, Makalani had pieced together the events.

Mr. Tanton had taken his ten-year-old son, Corey, off-road to try out his new youth ATV when the ground gave way and the boy fell into a hole. The stone mason at the station suspected the boy had fallen into a lava tube. Rather than wait for first responders to arrive, Makalani had grabbed her gear and hopped on the station's sole utility quad.

Should she have asked permission first? Definitely. Would it have been granted? Absolutely not.

Seasonal interpretive rangers gave presentations, led tours, and interacted with visitors. They did not jet off on search and rescue missions unless the rare emergency took place within the borders of their seventy-seven-acre property, as happened with the Akoni Pula brush fire that came down the coast. The Puʻukoholā rangers had to evacuate all the visitors and personnel from their land and assisted first responders to keep the community safe. Although still potentially dangerous, it didn't compare to the avalanches, forest fires, and cartel drug busts Makalani had encountered while working her Oregon job.

"No such t'ing as small kine jobs, Makalani," Tūtū had said over the phone when she had complained. "Only small kine people, and we definitely not dat."

Makalani pointed at the tread marks up ahead and sped into the lead. After three days of mandatory cultural immersion, she could finally do something more significant than study academic texts, open the visitor center, and raise the Hawaiian and national flags. Although she had applied for a transfer to one of the state's five national parks, the national historic site on the Big Island was the only opening she could find.

Mr. Tanton veered away with a shout and drove down a shallow dip toward a giant hole.

"Wait," she yelled. If Corey had jumped his ATV off a berm and landed in the dip, the impact could have caused a sinkhole. "This area is compromised. You have to back up."

He ignored her warning and jumped off his seat. "Corey, it's Dad. Are you okay?"

"Please, Mr. Tanton. Get back on your vehicle and drive it up here."

"But my son."

"I'll help him, I promise. But if you cause another cave-in, you'll make my job harder to do."

He stared into the gaping wound in the earth, then glared back at her.

"Let me help your son." When he hesitated, she added, "Everything will be fine."

But as the father did as she asked, she wondered if she had lied. Mauna Kea to the east had not erupted in 4,600 years. Elder Kohala to the north hadn't erupted in 120,000. None of the transcripts or historical documents she had read for her job had said anything about people falling into lava tubes in South Kohala. The only account she had heard was of a rancher in Kaʻu who had broken through the ceiling of a lava tube and fallen thirty feet with her horse.

If Corey had broken through the top of a fissure instead of a tube, he could be trapped a hundred feet underground.

Hurt. Buried. Trapped.

Makalani jumped off the quad, anchored the wheels with rocks, and brought out the climbing ropes, harness, and carabiner clips she kept with her gear. Having secured one end of the rope to the rear bar, she stepped into the harness and cinched the straps of her backpack into a snug fit. Choosing her footing carefully, she eased down the slope toward the hole. She lay on her belly and army crawled toward the edge. The depth of the cavern swallowed the meager sunlight from above.

"Corey? My name is Makalani Pahukula. I'm a ranger. Can you hear me?"

She pulled a headlamp from the side pocket of her pack, put it on, and shone the light into the hole. Twenty-five, possibly thirty feet below, she saw the electric-green fenders of a youth ATV. She couldn't see the boy.

"Is he okay?" Mr. Tanton yelled.

Makalani peered into the cavern, searching for some sign that Corey had survived, but it was too dark and obstructed by rocks and roots. She wouldn't be able to answer him truthfully until she planted her boots on the ground.

"I'm going down. Keep a lookout for first responders. When they arrive, warn them the ground's unstable."

She dropped the loop of remaining rope over a smooth rock that wouldn't chafe it. Then she lowered herself, hand by hand, into the damp, stagnant air. She dangled a moment to take in a sight no human other than Corey—assuming he hadn't been knocked unconscious—had ever seen. This lava tube was ancient, as if Madame Pele herself had coursed through the earth in a fiery rage.

I can do this. Focus on the details. Ignore everything else.

The cavern was roughly two car lengths across and deep. Stalactites hung from the ceiling where drips of lava had hardened into shiny spikes. Long shrub roots broke through the rock and descended several feet into the space.

Aside from lavasicles and roots, the ceiling swirled with glossy remnants of pāhoehoe lava. Unlike the more common ʻaʻā lava that burned hot and moved quickly in chunky avalanches across the land, pāhoehoe flowed like a river and dried in smooth, ropy patterns when the magma on top crusted and met the cooler air. Kept hot by the insulation, pāhoehoe continued to flow in a channel under the surface, hardening along the sides and bottom into what would eventually form a tube.

Makalani rotated her headlamp. Corey had fallen into a cavernous bulge that entered on one side and forked into two smaller tubes.

She climbed farther down the rope, watching above her as the ceiling of the cavern expanded and tons of rock and earth closed her in.

So much rock.

Dirt floated like snow flurries onto her face. She wiped it away and took a steadying breath.

Sweat beaded on her forehead.

Somewhere in the darkness below, a boy was trapped, possibly injured and definitely—hopefully—afraid.

Move, Makalani. Move!

She breathed in through her nose and exhaled slowly through pursed lips to calm her nerves and oxygenate her blood.

Unlike mines and other man-made tunnels, lava tubes and caverns were not airtight. Roots broke through the rock. Water seeped. Streams flowed. Insects and animals burrowed. Microbial mats flourished above geothermal vents. And with the cave-in, fresh air would circulate from above.

She took a deep breath.

See? More than enough air.

She uncoiled her ankle from the rope and continued her descent until her feet touched rock and the sky tightened into a discouraging disk. Just out of reach, Corey's ATV had pummeled nose down, crunching the frame and scattering shards of electric-green fenders on the rocky floor. She stepped out of her harness and swept her headlamp in a full circle, stopping when she found a crumpled figure in white riding gear, his electric-green helmet cracked and askew.

She hurried to his side. "Corey, can you hear me?"

His breath and pulse were weak.

"My name is Makalani. I'm a ranger."

He moaned in pain.

"Where do you hurt?"

When he didn't answer, she gently removed the broken outer shell of his helmet. The padded interior frame was intact. Blood had caked on his cheekbone where the rim of the helmet had hit. No blood flowed from his ears or his nose.

He moaned louder, then rasped in pain.

Although iron-rich dirt dusted his white armored jacket and pants, she didn't see any punctures or tears. She unzipped his jacket. No sign of blood. She raised his T-shirt and frowned. His abdomen was distended and bruised, indicative of internal bleeding from the impact.

She stretched him on his back, tucked a Mylar blanket around him for warmth, and rolled her jacket around the broken helmet to elevate his legs. To avoid aggravating whatever damage he suffered internally, she didn't offer him water. The boy needed immediate medical attention. There was nothing else she could do.

She shouted up to the sky. "Mr. Tanton, can you hear me? Any sign of help?"

"Not yet. Is Corey okay? Can I see him? I'm coming down."

"No. Stay on the rise. The ground could collapse again if you come into the bowl."

She looked from the dangling rope and harness to Corey. He needed to be moved more carefully than her simple harness would allow, not to mention the likelihood of knocking him against the lava if she tried to pull him out. Corey needed to be evacuated on a medevac litter. But even if a search and rescue helicopter arrived in time and lowered a medevac litter from directly above, the wind and natural movements of the chopper would still make Corey swing.

She stared up at the jagged outcroppings of lava as the all-too-familiar icy dread of failure crept toward her heart.

They won't be able to save him.

She had to find another way to carry him out.

CHAPTER TWO

Larry Hiapo loosened his reins so his mare could stretch her neck down to taste the kikuyu grass around his favorite wiliwili tree. He and ʻOpihi hadn't ventured this way up the mountain since he passed the daily ranch operations to his sons. It felt good to be alone on the upland plateau, big sky overhead, and the ʻōhiʻa lehua forest embracing the highest end of his ranch like a hug. Trees buffered most of the wind except for the trade winds coming up over the ravine.

Maikaʻi kēia, he thought. *This is good.*

Fine rain sprayed into his face. Although tourists and many other locals preferred Kona's dry heat or Hilo's humid warmth, Larry enjoyed his crisp Kohala Mountain air. The high plateau was cold compared to the temperate lower plains and arid steppe down to the west coast. To Larry's great fortune, Hiapo Ranch cut through them all, from the highest ridge down to the sea.

He rubbed his horse's neck, then looked up from under the brim of his hat at the overcast sky. A rainbow emerged above the sea cliffs below. Since it did not touch the land, his people called this kind of rainbow ala moku, meaning *broken path*.

Larry loved the poetically specific names that described a thing's purpose or how it looked or felt upon the skin. Some Hawaiian words drew context from a legend, an area, or a beloved person who had lived or died nearby. Was it a rain that roared with laughter, or one that pierced the eyes? Did it fall in Mānoa Valley on Oʻahu, or on the Hilo side of Hawaiʻi when the nehu fish ran up the streams? Or was it the fine spray that had now dissipated into a rainbow-hued mist? ʻŌlelo Hawaiʻi had a bounty of beautiful words and expression for a language with so few sounds.

He gazed over his ʻāina nui—his abundant land—that went back four generations of Hawaiian cowboys to the first paniolo days. Then and now, his family had cared for the ranch that, in turn, cared for them.

He asked his mare to walk on. When they had crossed the tree-lined plateau and descended into the next pasture, he encouraged her to trot. Although he would have loved to linger on this beautiful day, he was on a mission: One of his nine breeding bulls had drifted from the herd. He could have let his younger cowboy son, Louie, or another paniolo track down the animal. It wasn't Larry's job. Not anymore. But as he told his eldest son, Kenneth, who ran the business end of the ranch, he was still young and only *semi*retired.

"I give you boys freedom to take care of the ʻāina, but I still handle the reins."

Kenneth's jaw had tightened; he didn't appreciate the reminder that he wasn't in charge. "Maybe so. But this is an older bull—like you—out there all by himself. He's going to feel isolated, maybe even scared. He could give you trouble. What then?"

Larry hadn't liked Kenneth's tone or the way his eldest son went on about age. "Then I rope um, old-school style, like I did before you could walk. Besides, I remember this pipi laho. He stay plenny calm when he was young, how feisty could he be now?"

Kenneth had snorted as if Larry had been describing himself. *Snorted!* How could he have raised a son with such disrespect?

"You got something to say? Spit it out."

Kenneth had backed up like a skittish horse. What a disappointment. At least Louie would have held his ground.

But Kenneth hadn't given up. "You're not the only paniolo on the ranch. Why not let Louie and Malu gather this bull? They're young and strong. It's their job, not yours."

"Because I stay sixty-seven, not ninety-seven like your grandfather. I still get plenny cowboy years left."

Instead of persisting, Kenneth had only shrugged. "Whatever you say, Dad. You're the boss."

Larry had walked away smiling, but the satisfaction in his son's smirk had stuck in his mind.

Why he act so smug when I won the fight?

Larry urged 'Opihi into a lope. It didn't matter what any of them thought. He would lead this bull like a puppy back to the ranch and show all the young paniolo how it was done. He might even tighten the reins on ranch business to remind his headstrong sons who was actually in charge. Unlike *his* father, Larry wouldn't truly retire until he was dead.

Once below the tree line, his ranch land widened into rolling green plains to include the property his grandfather, Lucky, had purchased from the Reeds, another ranching family from back in the day. Only an old man and his son remained, living behind a barrier of eucalyptus trees on the highest portion of the property their ancestor had chosen to keep.

Larry slowed 'Opihi to a walk as they drew closer to the gulch. The jagged fissure provided a short but natural border along the upper south side of Hiapo Ranch, then widened and flattened at the mouth. Rainwater collected in the gulch and spread into the pasture for days after a storm. A sturdy woven-wire fence continued the boundary begun by the gulch, keeping Hiapo cattle on their side of the neighbor's easement down to the road. Although cattle could wander up the shallow mouth of the gulch, they didn't usually make the effort for the patches of grass and pooled rain when they had lush pastures and troughs of water so easy to reach.

So why was a distressed animal bellowing somewhere below?

"Eh, girl. You think that's our bull?"

'Opihi turned her head and gave him the eye.

"Yeah, me too." He guided her down the side of the gulch, but when she shook her bridle, he loosened the reins and trusted her to pick the best way down. "Okay, okay. No get testy with me. Just be careful, alright? I no like break my neck."

In horse years, 'Opihi was the same age as him. If he were being honest with himself, they both should have stayed home.

The bull bellowed again beyond the jagged rocks at the edge of the gulch, sounding frustrated and afraid.

As they progressed downhill, the sight lines increased, revealing a scramble of hoof tracks on the ground between rocks. It was as if the animal had banked up the sides, spun in the middle, then bolted away from the rocky opening and down the grassy hill. It didn't make sense. Cattle were lazy but smart. They avoided danger and stayed on the easiest terrain, following the paniolo's call to the next pasture for fresh supplies of water and grass. When droughts dried up the rain and the cisterns were bare, ranchers trucked in barrels of water to replenish the troughs. Breeding bulls lived the cushiest lives of all.

The bellowing continued.

Larry guided 'Opihi around the rocks, then brought her to a stop. The damn fool bull had fallen into a pit.

He spat in the dirt. "I should have filled it in."

He hadn't thought about the ancient bullock pit in decades, not since he discovered it as a young man before marriage, kids, and taking over the ranch. It had been dug more than two centuries ago to catch the cattle King Kamehameha I had allowed to breed wild and out of control. The wet slopes of Waimea offered shady forests with vines and ferns to augment the grass. When the horned menaces tired of that, they ventured into the coastal villages and fields. This pit would have been well placed for the hunters to catch the wild cattle as they drove them out of their forest home through the gulch.

"Is that what happened to you?" Larry asked as the bull turned for another lap. "Auwē, what I do now, 'Opihi? That laho covers forty-plus cows."

Charolais were among the largest and heaviest breeds. This one was as pure as they could get, 100 percent, not just the 31/32 Charolais blood in their genetics the USA allowed. As a result, his coat was a creamy white, with no hint of Red Angus or Black Angus to dull the sheen. Or it would have been if the agitated beast wasn't covered in grime.

The bull raced up and down the length of the rectangular pit and slammed the side of his creamy-white head against a dirt wall. Time and proximity to the water-dumping gulch had eroded the sides and raised the level of the bull's enclosure with silt. Even so, the man-made pit was too deep and slanted for the heavy animal to escape. His hooves had already churned the upland slope where he had most likely slipped after bolting out of the gulch.

"We gotta do something." He rubbed his horse's neck. "Whatchu think, girl?"

'Opihi snuffled in assent.

Larry nodded. It would seal his retirement if he went home for help. Louie—or was it Malu?—had practically goaded him into chasing this bull.

Practically, or had?

Larry couldn't remember when or why he had insisted on doing this alone, only that it had become a matter of pride.

"We may be old, but I'm still paniolo, and you still one of the best cow horses we get."

With that pronouncement, Larry unfastened the rawhide lariat from his saddle. He had made this kaula 'ili from cow hides he had cured, cut, and braided himself. Holding the coils in his left hand along with the reins, he extended the loop with his right. It had been many years since he and 'Opihi had roped a cow. Longer for a bull. Longer still for one as agitated as this. Domesticated bulls were not prone to aggression unless startled, threatened, or otherwise afraid. This one had scared himself into a frenzy and needed to be calmed.

'Opihi shifted nervously.

"Easy, girl."

He twirled the kaula 'ili loop overhead and tossed it while the bull pawed at the dirt. The loop settled loosely over the short, rounded-down horns, tips cut to lessen the damage they could cause. When the bull tossed his dirt-stained head, Larry tugged the loop tight around the neck. Rather than initiate a battle of wills, Larry gave the animal time to calm before he began the patient give-and-take that would eventually coax the bull up the eroded side of the pit.

'Opihi shifted nervously on the grass. Neither one of them was still in their prime.

"Give him time, girl. This laho will calm down when he stops being scared. Noho mālie," he commanded, but she wouldn't be still.

A loud crack startled them both.

Gunfire? Backfire?

The bull leaped into the air and landed with a yank.

Larry's lariat arm seared with pain.

Am I shot?

It all happened so fast, he couldn't tell what had happened first.

The Charolais jumped and spun, tossing his head to free himself from the loop, but the rope flipped around his eyes and irritated him even more. He lowered his horns and charged the dirt wall beneath Larry and his horse.

The ground shook from the impact.

'Opihi reared.

Larry leaned forward and loosened the reins so she wouldn't flip. At the same time, he tried to coil in some of the slack. But as 'Opihi's front legs descended, the bull tangled the rawhide in his horns and yanked the tightened lariat. The coil caught in a half hitch around Larry's wrist. 'Opihi's forward momentum did the rest.

As Larry slid off the saddle into the pit, his boot caught in the stirrup and pulled 'Opihi sideways toward the edge of the dirt slope. For one horrifying moment, Larry stretched in the air from wrist to boot, caught in a tug-of-war between the dangerous bull and the frantic scrambling horse.

He looked behind him at 'Opihi and saw a man standing far beyond her on the bed of a truck. Larry recognized him immediately.

Why?

Then his boot slipped off his foot, and he slingshotted toward the bull's curved-down horns.

CHAPTER THREE

Makalani tightened the straps of her pack as if tightening her resolve. The beam of her headlamp shone a mere six feet ahead. Beyond that was a blackness so heavy she could barely stand. Unlike the spacious cavern where she had left Corey sleeping fitfully on the rock floor, the offshoot lava tube was tight and cylindrical like a worm-bored hole. The confines disturbed her. The natural wonder of it kept the anxiety at bay. So did the ticking clock. She couldn't linger and take it all in while Corey fought for his life.

She focused on the details her headlamp allowed her to see and circumvented a crop of stalactites so silky she expected them to be wet. As the molten flow had subsided, these lavasicles had hardened mid-drip. Above them, the ceiling had cooled in smooth, shiny swirls, while the sides of the tube were marred by grooves and the occasional jutting rock. The pāhoehoe must have become more viscous toward the end because it left a chunky trail of rock as the molten river ran dry.

Three distinct formations in a tunnel thousands of years old.

Chicken skin rose on her arms.

Every space in this tunnel—where she walked, what she saw, the air that she breathed—had once been raging molten pele: the Hawaiian word for *lava flow*, *volcano*, *eruption*, and the tumultuous goddess herself.

Makalani shivered despite the mild, humid temperature underground.

Will Madame Pele sense my presence and take offense?

Not only was Makalani treading through her domain, Tūtū had always said Makalani was favored by Pele's nemesis, the snow goddess Poliʻahu, because she never minded the cold. Would that make her an enemy in the volcano goddess's eyes?

Makalani touched the smooth swirls of lava over her head and closed her eyes in prayer.

Aloha e, Tūtū Pele. I am Makalani Pahukula from Kauaʻi. I promise to show you mālama and respect. Please grant me your blessing and allow me to pass.

Makalani listened for a rumbling response. She had addressed Madame Pele as Tūtū, as she called her own beloved grandmother. Would the goddess respond with love and guide Makalani through her lava tube to an exit, or would Pele collapse it onto her head? Either way, Makalani had to advance. Corey's distended abdomen and bruising indicated serious internal bleeding. A jostling evacuation could kill him. He stood a better chance of survival with an outlet close to the cavern that search and rescue could use.

Although her mission seemed hopeless, she knew the Big Island had a plethora of cave entrances and skylights hidden among the ditches, rock formations, and shrubs. All she needed was an exit big enough for her—and therefore, most men—to pass while carrying Corey on a medevac litter. She set the timer on her watch for fifteen minutes. If she didn't find an exit by then, she would return to the cavern and check on Corey.

The ceiling sank lower and lower as she forged ahead. Five minutes later, the lavasicles combed through her hair. She stumbled against the wall, feeling dizzy from the oxygen-depleted air. She sucked in a deep breath and exhaled in a slow, steady stream. If she lost consciousness in this tunnel, she'd complicate the rescue mission even more.

Ten more minutes? More like ten more steps.

The tunnel expanded a few feet in all directions as if the lava flow that created it had pulsed here with added force. She raised her headlamp light. Was it her imagination, or did the outcropping above her look ready to fall?

She pushed off the wall and continued with more determined steps. She'd keep going as long as she could breathe.

Four minutes later, the ceiling spiked upward where large chunks of fractured basalt had broken free. She turned off her headlamp and peered overhead. When her eyes adjusted, she spotted a sliver of light. Although too small for her purposes, the skylight allowed a space for air and rain to pass. Yellowish-green microbial patches grew in the crevices and on the undersides of rocks. Roots broke through the ground above her and burrowed into the sides of the cleft, creating tangled mats for other microorganisms to grow. The sudden evidence of life felt like a mirage.

She breathed in the fresh air and the tangy scent of ocean. Not only had the lava tube moved closer to the surface, but it had also progressed closer to the shore.

Makalani switched on her headlamp and powered ahead. Fifteen steps later, she ran into an impassable wall of rock.

"No!" She had truly believed that, given enough time and determination, she would find a way out.

She reconsidered the skylight. Although she could probably climb up and squeeze through, the passage would be too vertical and precarious to extricate Corey on a litter. Her effort and optimism meant absolutely squat if it couldn't save a ten-year-old boy.

CHAPTER FOUR

Never in all Larry's years of riding and ranching had he ever been so violently jerked off a horse. Kicked, bit, rolled on, flipped? Sure. Charged, butted, and hooked by a bull? Several times, especially in his rodeo days. But he had never experienced anything as horrifyingly out of control as this. Although his boot had slipped off his foot as cowboy boots were intended to do, sparing him a gruesome limb-ripping death, the bull's forceful yank had him flying through the air like a fish on a line.

If Larry's life had passed before his eyes the way people always promised it would, he could have relived his first kiss with his wife, the births of their children, and the glorious ocean-view sunsets from his ancestral ranch. Instead of those blessings, he noticed every frightening detail on the way to his death: the way the bull's neck stretched to the side as he tossed his mighty head; the kaula ʻili tangled in the horns, pulling the rope taut; the rawhide cutting into Larry's bleeding wrist; ʻOpihi churning the slope as she tried not to fall into the pit.

Keep your eye on the bull, don't let him take you by surprise.

Larry strained his face forward as he sailed through the air. Did this adage, passed on to him by his father, apply to dying as well?

He slammed into the bull's body instead of his horns, dislocating his shoulder, and crumpled on the ground. Although stunned by pain, bull riding in rodeos had taught him to move when he fell to avoid being kicked, run over, or crushed. Larry scrambled to his feet, but he wasn't quick enough.

The bull ran over him, cracking his ribs and breaking his jaw. Blinded by the speed of the assaults, Larry floundered onto his dislocated shoulder, cried out in pain, and choked on a gooey paste of blood, cheek, and earth.

The spooked mare nickered nervously from somewhere above, where she had fled to escape the collapsing ground at the edge of the pit.

Larry backed against the slope, trying to avoid further attack from the bull. He freed his wrist from the half hitch. His shoulder and arm burned, his jaw throbbed, his busted ribs gripped his lungs in a vise. Drawing on his sixty-seven years of life and experience as a paniolo, Larry fought to stay calm and think.

The bull pivoted to find him, whipping the kaula ʻili still looped around his horns. The bull didn't feel the whipping lariat on his hide. He focused all his attention on the predator he now perceived.

Ignoring the imminent threat, Larry inhaled as deeply as his cracked ribs would allow and reached for his opposite shoulder until his joint popped into place. The relief was brief as pain from his other injuries filled in the void.

"Suck it up, paniolo. E hana i ka hana! Get up and do the damn work!"

He had done his share of tie-down roping, but this bull was no calf. In the prime of Larry's youth, even if he had wedged the kaula ʻili in the fork of a tree or had teamed with another paniolo who could rope the hind legs, he would never have been able to flip or wrestle this beast. The most he could hope for was to tangle the bull's legs and let the animal's own weight and strength knock him down and tie himself into knots. Although not much of a plan, it beat waiting to be hooked.

None of that was possible without an additional rope.

Upslope, ʻOpihi neighed and snorted with a rattling sound of distress. Despite her terror, she hadn't abandoned him yet. He loved her all the more, but what could she do?

"Noho mālie, ʻOpihi. Take it easy, stay calm."

That's when he saw his saddlebag lying open against the dirt slope.

In the same moment, the bull dropped his head and attacked.

Instinct overrode pain as Larry dove to the side and scrambled toward the bag. He yanked out the lead rope and dove again, this time rolling like an action hero into a crouch. Blood spewed from his crushed jaw, but he had twelve feet of hope gripped in his hands.

Who's the old guy now?

His triumph vanished as the dire reality of his predicament returned. If he didn't live to tell the tale, no one would know how youthfully he had fought.

As the bull circled the pit, Larry tied a lasso at the end of the rope. It wouldn't have the stiffness of rawhide, but it would hold its shape enough to possibly catch a hoof.

His vision blurred from his throbbing, crushed jaw. He could feel his strength draining like stormwater in a gulch. He couldn't keep fighting, but neither could he stop. He begged God to help. All he needed was one lucky chance.

But it was too late. The bull pivoted and charged straight at him.

Larry let go of the rope and scrambled toward the slope, trying to avoid the next move he had seen so many times—the lethal Kope Attack. If only his body wasn't so battered. If only he still had the strength. If only 'Opihi hadn't loosened the dirt with her hooves.

An engine rumbled in the distance. Although hard to hear over the noisy animals, he would stake his life—*was* staking his life—on the sound of that truck.

He's changed his mind. He's coming to help.

Larry screamed as the bull used his forelegs to rake him in. Once Larry was trapped beneath the animal's massive chest, the bull hooked him through the calf with his horn. Searing agony shot up Larry's leg and spine. Only sheer stubbornness kept him clawing toward the dirt slope to escape.

Help is coming. I have to survive.

He pictured the man standing on the bed of the truck.

Unless he's coming to finish the job!

Fire sliced through Larry's hamstrings as he flew into the center of the pit, landed in a heap, and stared up at the bull. Blood soaked his jeans. He tried to shove himself away, but his hamstrung legs wouldn't work.

The bull bellowed and stomped. Breaking his bones. Shaking the earth.

When the beast prepared to slam Larry again with his head, Larry knew he was done. He locked eyes with the animal he had bought three years before and wondered how he had missed the madness coursing through his veins.

I'm sorry.

He was too delirious to know to whom or for what.

The bull rammed his horns through Larry's pelvis and back. He pinned Larry to his beloved ʻāina nui and nourished it with his blood.

CHAPTER FIVE

Makalani had less than two minutes to find another exit or go back. Since the lava tube skylight wouldn't work for Corey, it was useless to her. She turned away in disgust and accidentally rammed her shoulder into a jutting slab of rock. The impact dropped her to her knees. When her hands fell onto something other than lava, she raised her headlamp and saw branches pushing in beside the rock ledge. Not just fuzzy patches of microbial growth or dangling roots breaking through rock, but actual soil-growing plants.

A way out!

Her phone alarm went off. Fifteen minutes had passed.

She grabbed on to the strongest branch and leveraged every inch and pound of her six-foot frame. The roots gave way and toppled her back. She rested a moment as sunlight streamed into the lava tube. She had found the exit, but was it large enough to get Corey out?

Only one way to know.

Shielding her eyes, she dragged the shrub through the exit into a shallow bowl. Since this was the leeward side of the island, the vegetation wasn't overly thick. It took less than a minute to clear a path to flat land. Although close to Route 270, also known as Kawaihae Road, she doubted anyone had ventured into or even known about the lava tubes belowground.

She breathed in the oxygen-rich air. The passage would work if she had found it in time.

Hang on, Corey.

His father's three-wheeler and the quad she had taken sat up the slope half a football field away. Although she had moved downhill in the lava tube, she was still closer to the cave-in above than the resource management station—with cell reception—below.

The *thrump-thrump-thrump* of rotary blades drew her attention to the sky, where a yellow-and-red medevac chopper was flying in from the southeast. She sprinted up the hill, wanting to tell them about the alternate route, and reached John Tanton as the chopper circled overhead. An HFD paramedic in a red jumpsuit leaned out of the open door to examine the cave-in opening. Although she tried to wave him off and pointed down the hill, the chopper lowered him and a medevac litter, in the upright position, into the hole.

"What's the matter?" Mr. Tanton yelled at her.

"There's an easier route in and out down the hill."

She hurried to her own dangling rope and climbed-slid down as fast as she could.

The paramedic watched her skillful descent with astonishment. "Who are you?"

She panted for breath. "I'm a ranger. That's Corey Tanton. His abdomen is swollen and bruised."

"You wrapped him up like this?"

"I did. And I found another way out if you can't lift him safely in the litter."

He checked Corey's vitals and examined his head injury and abdomen. He looked up at the jagged opening.

"How far is it to the other exit?"

"Five or six minutes, now that I know the way."

"You and me?"

She turned on her headlamp. "Got a better idea?"

He examined the hole again, unhitched the litter, and waved the chopper away. "Where will we come out?"

"Fifty yards toward the sea."

He relayed the message on his portable radio before they loaded and strapped Corey onto the litter. Makalani picked up her end with a backhanded grab and led them into sunlight in five minutes flat.

Corey's dad drove down the hill to meet them. He yelled his thanks to Makalani and climbed inside the chopper with his son. She waved as it lifted and flew toward Queen's North Hawaiʻi Community Hospital. Since the state's only designated level-one trauma center was in Honolulu, the level-three trauma center in Waimea would have to do. Makalani watched the helicopter vanish over the mountain and sagged with relief. She had done all she could for Corey. The rest was up to his doctors and God.

As the adrenaline pumping through her body finally drained, a deep sense of accomplishment took its place.

This is what I'm meant to do—helping people, not giving tours.

The momentary satisfaction fled as Supervisory Ranger Daniel Machado drove across the plains in the Puʻukoholā Heiau's 4WD truck. His strong features were fixed in a scowl. Although she hadn't asked about his heritage, she could easily imagine his ancestors storming beaches with war clubs in outrigger canoes. Whatever blood flowed in his veins was molten-lava hot.

A cloud of dust enveloped them both as he braked hard and jumped out of the truck. "What the hell are you doing out here? Patrick said you drove off with his quad before he could say no."

Whenever Ranger Machado lost his temper, the island lilt seeped into his voice. Not entirely, but enough to tell Makalani he was losing control. As for Patrick, he hadn't even tried to object. He had waved her off with assurances that he would make all the necessary calls. Makalani just hadn't realized that one of those calls would be to her boss.

Ranger Machado, who was several inches shorter, glowered up at her. "If that kid dies, the scrutiny will fall on us."

Makalani stayed cool. "The paramedic said he was stable."

"And how would he know? Is he a doctor? No. And neither are you."

"I never said—"

"*You* are a seasonal interpretive ranger for a national historic site. Not law enforcement. Not search and rescue. Not . . . whatever you did on the mainland at Crater Lake National Park. We educate the public and manage the most sacred heiau in the islands." He gestured around him. "This is not even our land."

"I know, but—"

"No buts." He took a breath and pulled himself together. All traces of local dialect vanished as he assumed his lecture mode and regained emotional control. "Return the quad to Patrick and get back to the visitor center. One of our volunteers is giving a talk later this afternoon on how King Kamehameha I unified Hawai'i. You will attend."

She stuffed down her emotions, but the rage inside her felt near impossible to contain. This ranger, who apparently valued his lessons over saving a child's life, would be controlling her work life for the next year. There was nothing she could do but swallow her anger and accept.

This is so unfair.

Despite the fact that Makalani was born and raised in Hawai'i, Ranger Machado treated her like a typical mainland transfer. He refused to cut any time off her six-week immersion period or reduce the volumes of oral transcripts, books, and documents about Hawaiian culture and history she was required to read or the demonstrations and lectures on Hawaiian crafts and traditions she was expected to attend. Learning about Pu'ukoholā Heiau and how the ancient Hawaiians built this and other rock temples made sense. Being tutored on her Native language, culture, and history like an ignorant malihini—a foreigner—grated her to the core.

At first, it had seemed as though Ranger Machado would reduce her immersion period to four weeks. But when he learned her Pahukula 'ohana came from Kaua'i, his attitude changed.

"Kauaians don't value the sacredness of this heiau," Ranger Machado had said. Then he sentenced Makalani to the full six weeks so he—and seemingly every other Native Hawaiian cultural expert on this island—could set her straight.

Tūtū had been furious when Makalani told her over the phone. "If you need pretend listen at work, go ahead, but I goin' teach you da truth."

Lucky me. More lectures.

If only there had been a seasonal ranger position opening at Hawai'i Volcanoes National Park, Makalani might have skirted this issue and seen a *little* more action. With two active volcanoes, there was always the danger of a life-threatening lava flow or visitors who ignored the warnings and ventured beyond the barriers. She could have been more useful. Then again, since she was a seasonal interpretive ranger, they still would not have called upon her.

Ranger Machado leaned his face into Makalani's. "The fire department and coast guard handle search and rescue, not us. We only help when it happens on our land or if they request our assistance. Right now, we have a hazardous sinkhole that needs to be barricaded and two stranded ATVs. You want more physical exertion? Run up that hill and clean up your mess."

CHAPTER SIX

Five frustrating days later, Makalani found her cousin Brian inside Kohala Burger & Taco, a Hawaiian-style diner near her work that served local fish and Hawai'i grass-fed beef. As one of his hands flipped through vintage comics, the other cradled a Captain America Pez dispenser and a yellow Toxic Waste container of "hazardously sour candy."

"Shopping for Vinnie?" she asked.

The older man laughed. "What makes you think it's not for me?"

Makalani eyed the green sludge supposedly overflowing from the candy barrel with disgust.

Brian laughed. "Nah, you're right. Only a kid would eat that." He picked up an issue of *The Incredible Hulk*. "I, on the other hand, have more discriminating tastes." He gestured to *The Mighty Thor*. "You want?"

"Already have it."

He gaped at her in shock. "Fo' real?"

She held a straight face for two more seconds, then broke down. "Nah. But I'll take a Jolly Rancher."

"Now you're talking."

Brian Pahukula was a cheerful man in his mid-forties with broad Hawaiian features accented by his father's half-Korean genes. She had always thought of him as a first cousin, until recent discoveries had taught her differently. Although he was eighteen years older, Makalani felt closer to Brian than to many of her other relatives. He was also the only family she had on the Big Island.

"Have you eaten here before?" he asked.

"Yeah, my first day of work."

Although the local hamburger joint was only a mile and a half up the road from Puʻukoholā Heiau, the food was too ʻono and expensive for her waistline and wallet to sustain. She'd have to start packing a lunch and find a shady outdoor spot on-site to eat, an easy task on fertile Kauaʻi but more challenging on the barren West Hawaiʻi coast.

"I'm usually stuck on the premises, so it's nice to get away."

Brian smirked. "You're stir-crazy already? You've only been at it a week and a half."

"I know, but the site is a lot smaller than where I was before—seventy-seven acres compared to over a hundred eighty *thousand* at Crater Lake National Park. I hiked in the mountains nearly every day, checked the trails, replanted hillsides, kept animals and visitors safe. Even when I was policing in the town where all the rangers and park workers live, I rarely stayed indoors. I burned off my calories and felt dog-tired when I went to bed. Now all I do is study like I'm in school."

They carried their food past the old-fashioned diner tables and spread out on the shellacked picnic table instead. Brian popped a pickled jalapeño into his mouth. Makalani followed suit, eyes watering as the fire slid down her throat.

"Gotta build up a tolerance," he said. "Maybe chase it with the fries."

Rather than take his advice, she took a long swig of pineapple shake. The cold pierced her brain.

Fire and ice. Pele and Poliʻahu strike again.

She dug into her messy burger as if she had done something more strenuous this morning than raise flags up a pole.

Brian noticed her frown. "It's only temporary, right? Until something else in Hawaiʻi opens up?"

She wiped off her hands. "Seasonal ranger is a one-year post."

"That's not so long. Vinnie just turned eight, and I tell you, the years fly by. It's already been nine months since I last saw you. How's your tūtū doing, anyway? Her birthday lū'au got kind of intense."

"Intense? More like a disaster."

He laughed. "Yeah, well . . . I'm trying to be kind." He nudged her shake. "Don't let it go to waste."

"The shake or my job?"

"Either. You're in Hawai'i now. Time to slow down and appreciate what's in front of you. The worth of a place is not measured by size."

Tūtū often said the same about her homestead and the islands as a whole. "We stay small, Makalani, but no oddah state has its own sovereignty and people. Kānaka maoli need control our own destiny. Like we do on dis homestead—all of our people should be permitted to live off da land. Mālama i ka 'āina, mālama ka 'āina iā kākou."

Care for the land, the land cares for us.

Makalani eyed her cousin. "You remind me of my grandmother."

"Thanks for the compliment. But seriously, after everything that happened on Kaua'i, couldn't you use a break?"

She sucked at her shake. This would make sense if they were talking about anyone but her. The greater the discomfort, the harder Makalani worked. It had been like that since she was a child, never fitting in but always a big help. At least, that's what she hoped. According to some of her relatives, all she did was intrude.

She sighed. The uncomfortable thought made her want to build someone a house.

Habitat for Humanity had helped calm her high school angst. Maybe she could find similar volunteer work in West Hawai'i.

"I don't take breaks," she said.

Brian shrugged. "Maybe that's why you're here."

"On the Big Island?"

"At your puny job."

"It's not puny."

"Eh, I'm just throwing back what I hear."

Makalani frowned, then adjusted her expression when Brian mirrored her embarrassing pout. "Are you always like this?"

"Like how?" He chuckled. "Just kidding. Once a parent . . ."

She waved him off, but she knew he was right. The more she fed her dissatisfaction, the bigger it would grow. She needed to focus on someone other than herself. Wasn't that why she became a law enforcement ranger? Not only could she protect people and animals, she could care for the land.

It also burned off energy and provided endless opportunities for hard work. Aside from her unauthorized search and rescue, the only assistance she had provided at Puʻukoholā was water for visitors and their dogs. Worse still, most of her hours were spent inside the NHS facility or walking on designated paths.

She stuffed a fry into her mouth, as if to stop the unspoken complaints. Her years at Crater Lake National Park were the happiest of her career. If her current position didn't provide an outlet, she'd have to find it somewhere else.

"Enough about me. You and Rosie still teaching at Hawaiʻi Prep Academy?"

"Yeah. Middle school social studies, going on twenty years."

"And Rosie's at the high school?"

"Yep. Teaches chemistry, AP chem too."

"Whoa. Vinnie doesn't stand a chance."

Brian grinned. "That's right. Nothing slides by us. I just wish he understood how lucky he is to attend a private school. We'd never be able to afford it without the faculty discount. HPA offers all these amazing activities, but all Vinnie wants to do is hang at his great-grandfather's ranch." His expression darkened. "But that's not such a good idea anymore."

"Why not?"

"Rosie doesn't want Vinnie in that environment. Her father passed away unexpectedly last week."

"I'm so sorry. How did he die?"

"He was gored and stomped to death by a bull."

"Oh my god."

"Yeah, it was pretty tragic. No one realized he was missing until his horse came back without him the next day."

Makalani couldn't imagine such a horrible death. "Who found him?"

"Rosie's niece. Everyone rode out to search, but Grace found him first. She snapped this picture before anyone else arrived." Brian passed his phone to Makalani. "It's gory, so feel free not to look."

A dirty white bull dominated the shot. He was resting in a dirt pit with his forelegs tucked in and his hind legs fanned to one side. Sleepy black eyes stared at the camera with mild interest. The alleged killer beast would have looked peaceful and cute if not for the bloody, mangled mess against the wall of the pit two yards away. If Brian hadn't told Makalani the body was a man, she wouldn't have known.

"Did Grace pull him out herself?"

"Nah. She rounded up her dad and uncle, who were searching nearby. Her Uncle Louie slid into the pit to check if Larry was still alive, even though it was pretty obvious he was not. Kenneth called the ranch with a walkie-talkie, and they called 911. Funny thing, though . . . Louie said the bull never moved until just before the firefighters arrived. Then it paced and snorted at the body, acting all distressed. Louie and another paniolo from the ranch roped and secured the animal so the firefighters could go down. HPD came later."

"What about the bull?"

"They didn't press charges."

"Funny."

He winked. "Well, you know, sometimes it helps to make light. Paniolo work is dangerous even in modern times. The cops know this. Even so, they had Animal Control pick up the bull. Rosie said they were respectful of her family, which is good. The last thing they need is hassle with the cops."

Makalani sucked the last of her shake.

Death by bull?

"How old was Rosie's dad?"

"Sixty-seven."

She chewed on her straw.

Old enough to retire but way too young to die.

CHAPTER SEVEN

Skip Una bought his ranch in Oregon the same month his wife told him she was expecting. By the time their son, Gordon, was born, twelve of Skip's fifteen heifers had delivered their calves and the rest of his fifty head of cattle were at different stages for sale. Meanwhile, his lone breeding bull had lived like a king. He had two bulls now, and they both lived more leisurely lives than him.

Lazy-ass studs.

Except when they fought.

Sometimes he wondered if they were more trouble than they were worth, especially since most of his profits now came from buying calves shipped from the Big Island, fattening them up on his green pastures, and selling them off when they reached their prime weight.

Hawai'i Island, he reminded himself. That was the new trend. Everyone back home was making such an effort to call things by their proper Hawaiian names, as if a resurgence of the language could empower the people and improve Native Hawaiians' lives. Skip had his doubts. No one had empowered *his* life except for him.

He stared out his office window at his flat, grassy land—cattle grazing in the distance, horses swishing their tails in the nearby corral. More cattle grazed in the feedlots beyond the two-level barn. His operation had expanded over the decades. Now that his son was thirty, Skip wanted to pass the Oregon reins to him and acquire a cow-calf operation of his own.

Gordon is ready. I need a break.

Not only could Skip increase his profits, he could retire in paradise while his hired hands did all the work. Most importantly, he would finally own a Waimea ranch.

He stared at his phone, wondering if six days was enough. He opened his contacts. Now that his obstacle had been removed, he didn't want to wait. When the rancher's son answered, sounding sad and exhausted, he turned on the charm.

"Hey, Kenneth, it's Skip Una in Oregon. So sorry to hear about your dad. How are you holding up?"

"Hi, Skip. I appreciate the call. It, ah . . . it's been hard, you know? We're all kind of in shock."

"Understandable. I mean, no one could see something like that coming, right?"

Kenneth Hiapo didn't respond.

Skip was losing him. He needed to get to the point.

"I'm sure you're all devastated by the loss. If there's anything I can do, please don't hesitate to call."

He bit his tongue on what he actually wanted to say. But what if another shark was circling the waters like him? He couldn't risk losing this chance.

"If it's any comfort, my offer stands. You could use the money to pursue your *own* dreams."

From what Skip had divined from watching Larry's eldest son on video interviews and reading articles about Hiapo Ranch, Kenneth seemed restless and might want to move on. Although Skip didn't know where that ambition might lead, he was more than willing to help if it would return Skip to the island he had never intended to leave.

"Well," Kenneth said. "If it was just me, I think I would. Honestly, though, I doubt my grandfather and brother would agree."

"I understand, but things often change after a death. Trust me, I know. I went through two major transitions in my life—once when both of my parents died when I was a kid, and again in college after my grandfather died and the Department of Hawaiian Home Lands took back his ranch. Both of those times, unexpected doors opened for me. I hate for you to lose what may be your only opportunity to break out on your own."

After a drunk driver killed both of Skip's parents in Kona, his grandfather had raised him on his small ranch in Kaʻu on the southern slopes of Mauna Loa. As the executor of their trust, he used the funds to send Skip to Hawaiʻi Preparatory Academy during his high school years. Skip fell in love with Waimea's crisp, clean air and lush pastureland, so different from Kaʻu's harsh terrain and the vog—volcanic smog—that frequently polluted the air. Hiapo Ranch epitomized for Skip how a cattle ranch should look.

The third major life transition that Skip failed to mention was when his beloved wife, who hated tropical weather, had died. Now that she was gone, he yearned to return home.

"I appreciate the offer," Kenneth finally said. "But we have the memorial tomorrow and, you know, it's just not a good time."

"I remember how it is. Take care of your ʻohana, and give me a call later this week."

He hung up before Kenneth could offer another excuse. Better to leave the young man with thoughts of Skip's offer niggling his mind. If Kenneth was anywhere near as ambitious as Skip, he would find a way to overcome his obstacles and succeed.

CHAPTER EIGHT

Hoʻolohe Reed drove up the dirt road in an ancient truck as tired and beat-up as he was. Up ahead, the peeling eucalyptus trees extended their gnarly arms like needy old men. He parked in their oppressive shade and unfolded his spindly legs out the door. If not for their unusual length, he would have had a hard time reaching the ground without help.

He leaned on his cane to shut the door and proceeded with care toward his childhood house. Remnants of past coats of paint hung stubbornly from the wood he and his son hadn't had the funds to repaint. Everything in Hoʻolohe's life had been sliding downhill ever since his father had sold off the prime pasturelands of their ranch.

I was ten. It's time to move on.

Flint met him at the door in his usual slovenly state—unbrushed and graying black hair, patchy whiskers along his gaunt cheeks and chin, that dreadful old T-shirt he refused to throw out. The only impressive attribute his son had was his height, or it would have been if he ever stood tall like a man. At forty-nine, he looked beaten and weak.

Flint pointed a butter knife at the bandage taped to the side of Hoʻolohe's head. "How much they cut out this time?"

"Half the damn ear."

Flint cursed and marched back to the kitchen with his smear of peanut butter on bread. Hoʻolohe shared his son's frustration. Between social security and Flint's paltry salary from Foodland, they barely had enough to eat beyond the free or discounted foods Flint brought home from work.

"Will Medicare cover it?" Flint asked.

"Not all."

"What the hell, Dad?"

"Eh, I told the doctor not to bother, but she said it could be more cancer and we need to be safe."

Flint smeared another slice for Hoʻolohe. "Well, I hope you like peanut butter bread, 'cause that's all we got."

The peanut butter stuck in Hoʻolohe's throat along with his gall. Despite his parenting efforts, his useless son hadn't amounted to squat. Hoʻolohe was no better, running their meager ranch into the ground. But what could he have done with the little land they had left? "Might be time to sell another cow."

"And leave us with three? We can't buy any more."

Flint was right. Without a bull or money to hire a stud, they couldn't replenish their herd. And with the poor quality of the beef, it made more sense to slaughter one a year for their freezer than to sell it for cull.

"I can't pay my doctor with ground beef."

"What about that guy in Oregon?"

"Skip Una?"

"Yeah. He could solve everything."

"Maybe so. We could move into a senior living place. I hear they're nice enough. We'd have enough so you don't gotta work. But he'll only buy our property if the Hiapos sell first."

"Have you talked to him now that Larry is dead?"

"I left messages."

"That's it?" Flint said. "I give you a golden opportunity, and that's all you got?"

"Since when have *you* given *me* anything?"

Flint's eyes burned with resentment. "Every damn day."

Ho'olohe scratched his dried fingers. He hated his dependency even more than the deterioration of age. "What you expect me to do?"

"Tell him I can help."

"By doing what?"

"Whatever he needs." Flint curled his peanut butter bread and stuffed it into his mouth.

"What's going on in your head?"

"Nothing. Just picturing Kenneth and Louie without their precious ranch."

Flint's resentment of Larry Hiapo's sons began in early childhood. Although he was two years older than Kenneth and four years older than Louie, the Hiapo boys were always so far ahead in everything that mattered horses, money, friends. All the kids liked and respected the Hiapo kids. No one liked or respected Flint.

When Ho'olohe was a boy, he had felt the same about Larry's father, Luke. Now they were old. If the Hiapos sold their ranch, Luke, whom everyone called Kupunakāne—Grandfather—would be put out to pasture like him.

Flint's eyes narrowed. "Now *you're* smiling."

Ho'olohe shrugged. "Their grandfather won't last one day off his land."

Flint chuckled. "You hate him even more than I hate them."

"I get more time, and more *reason* than you."

Ho'olohe had grown up worshipping Luke. He would ride his horse along the fence between their properties, watching from a distance, hoping to be noticed and invited onto their ranch. But whenever he spotted the teenage paniolo riding across the pastures or moving the herds, he was accompanied by his impressive family or friends. None of them acknowledged or even noticed the neighbor boy on the swayback mare. And why would they? The Hiapos had everything they needed within the confines of their ranch. They should have been contented with the blessings they had. Why did they have to take more?

"I'll call Skip again. But if I tell him you can help, you better follow through."

"I got this," Flint said. "I'm not as useless as you think."

"Well, that's a relief."

Flint sneered at the dig, but Hoʻolohe didn't care. His son was yet another disappointment to add to the list. Hoʻolohe was ninety-one years old. His son should be taking care of him.

Flint shook his head. "You have no idea what I do to keep you alive."

"You mean while you live for free on my ranch?"

"This isn't a ranch anymore. Hasn't been since I was a kid."

"Then you won't care if I leave it to someone else when I die."

"Like who? You don't have anyone in your life except for me. This guy in Oregon is our shot. I know people. You tell him I can help."

Hoʻolohe stared at his son, surprised by his authority and wanting to believe. If Flint could find a way to convince the Hiapos to sell, Skip Una would buy the Reed property too. Luke Hiapo would die without his land. And after eighty years, Hoʻolohe would finally get his revenge.

CHAPTER NINE

Makalani rode up the mountain slope with her cousin in a side-by-side UTV. It had rained up here overnight, but the wispy cirrus clouds in the now-blue sky signaled a shift in the winds. Although the clouds held no rain, the upland climate would stay cool throughout the day. It was the perfect weather to say aloha to a steward of the land.

A procession of horses climbed beside them, each bearing a rider bedecked in colorful flower lei and paniolo attire. Only a dark-gray Appaloosa with a blanket of white on her rump walked alone with a thick rope of tiny green pakalana flowers on the saddle where her rider would have sat.

Makalani nudged Brian with her knee. "You didn't want to ride with everyone else?"

"Not enough horses at the ranch. Rosie and some of the part-time ranch hands don't have their own. With all the paniolo and immediate family riding in the procession, I volunteered to drive and bring you."

"It was gracious of the family to invite me."

"You're 'ohana."

"Only by marriage."

"Same thing to Rosie. She insisted you come."

Brian's wife rode a chestnut gelding the same color as her shoulder-length hair. A pink rose haku lei encircled the woven straw pāpale on her head. A matching rosebud lei rested against the fitted bodice of her tan-and-white-checkered palaka blouse. Instead of jeans, she wore wide gaucho-leg pants and matching cowboy boots. The outfit showed off her Hawaiian and Mexican roots.

"How much vaquero blood does she have?"

"Only one sixteenth, but it shows stronger with her Hawaiian than the haole or Japanese."

"I don't see the Japanese."

"It's less than a quarter, but combined with my Chinese and Korean, that makes Vinnie three kinds of Asian." Brian widened his eyes. "Imagine what his great-great-grandparents would think of that."

Makalani understood what he meant. The Chinese, Koreans, and Japanese had a tumultuous history to say the least. And yet, the combination blended beautifully with the Hawaiian, haole, and traces of Mexican in Brian and Rosie's eight-year-old son. He rode behind his mother on a buckskin mare with a black mane, tail, and legs, broken up by three white feet.

"Vinnie sits his horse well."

Brian rolled his eyes. "Too well for his own good." But he said it with pride. "His grandfather gave him that horse for his birthday a few months ago. Schooled it himself especially for Vinnie. Unfortunately, Larry didn't ask his daughter or me if it would be okay. Said it shouldn't matter since he would board and feed the animal at the ranch."

Makalani shook her head. "There's more to ownership than basic care."

"Exactly. Vinnie wants Uila to love him more than anyone else, and that means putting in the time. This isn't just another horse to borrow at the ranch. Larry gave her to *him*. Now that his grandfather is gone, that horse connects Vinnie to his paniolo roots in a way his mother and I cannot."

Makalani looked back at Brian's wife. "Don't know about that, cuz. Rosie looks awfully regal on that horse."

"Yeah, she does." He grinned ear to ear. "She dressed up to honor her dad and remind Vinnie she grew up on the ranch so he'll give her more credit when she hounds him about school. Ranchers are struggling. Fewer and fewer paniolo are able to earn a living wage. But it's enticing, you know? Rosie wants Vinnie to broaden his experiences before his uncles and great-grandfather narrow his view."

From the pride in Vinnie's posture, Makalani wasn't sure her cousin-in-law would succeed. Every inch of the boy's body emulated the paniolo men—the cant of his head, the cock of his wrist, the relaxed dangle of his legs. He even wore the same tan-and-white palaka shirt as his great-grandfather and uncles.

The checkered woven print had become a signature local design ever since the sailors first wore it to Hawai'i during the early plantation days. The contract workers adapted the heavy twill jackets into light-weight, durable work shirts that protected their arms and chests while picking pineapple and sugarcane in the fields. After the vaqueros arrived from Alta California to teach Hawaiians how to cowboy, the paniolo adopted them as well.

Makalani could identify the Hiapo family members by their tan-and-white attire while their friends wore aloha shirts or their own variations of colorful palaka and jeans. Since Brian wasn't a cowboy, he had chosen an aloha shirt with a tan leaf print on white. Makalani felt honored to have been invited to dress in kind, although the only matching colors she had were a heavy canvas jacket, a white T-shirt, and rugged tan pants—good choices considering the chill. She had rolled her wild hair into a bun so as not to tangle in the purple, green, and white orchid lei.

As if on cue, the wind kicked up and parted the clouds, shining direct sunlight on a blooming wiliwili tree on the knoll. The bright-orange flowers of the coral tree matched the vibrancy of everyone's colorful lei, from the humblest sherbet-colored plumeria to ropes of orange ilima and white pīkake twined with fragrant maile vines. As the riders formed a semicircle in front of the tree, Brian parked his UTV in a shady spot nearby. Other attendees without horses did the same. Most were dressed in aloha wear, but some wore cowboy hats, palaka shirts in other colors, and boots.

"Those are part-time paniolo friends," Brian said. "Not everyone has a trailer or even a horse."

A blue roan stallion caught Makalani's eye as he tossed his black head. The white hairs on his black-base coat made the horse look slivery blue. The rider was equally striking, like an ali'i among peasants—regal, confident, and aloof. He had thick, straight brows, a prominent nose, and a stern mouth she would have liked to see smile. Even his open-ended lei of dense forest leaves commanded attention—not maile or tī, but twined forest vines that would have overpowered a less sizable man.

"That's Louie, Rosie's second older brother. He's one of the best paniolo on the island and a serious wrangler, as you can tell by that horse."

And gorgeous.

Makalani chided herself for the thought. Even if this weren't a memorial for the man's father, his looks were way out of her league. Makalani might be "stunning," according to her sister, but that didn't mean she was appealing to men. Unless a woman was stick skinny like a model, towering above others tended to intimidate rather than attract. Men saw her as a peer, competition, or a buddy who could help them unload a truck. Seldom did anyone ask her on a date. Although to be fair, she didn't put out those vibes.

"How much older?" She tossed out the question as if it didn't matter much. If Brian thought she was interested in his brother-in-law, she'd have to crawl back into that lava tube for good. When Brian answered quickly, she figured her future was safe.

"Their mom had all her kids close together. Rosie's forty-four, so that would make Louie forty-five. Their eldest brother, Kenneth, is forty-seven, one year older than me."

Makalani gratefully shifted her focus from one brother to the next. Unlike the other paniolo, the eldest Hiapo brother wore a tailored white shirt with tan palaka trim. Even from a distance, his delicate strands of yellow-and-white ginger gave off a sweet, intoxicating scent. Compared to his ruggedly handsome younger brother, Kenneth seemed almost genteel. His daughter on the dappled palomino, on the other hand, looked ready to rope a bull.

Brian smiled. "That's Grace. In all the time I've known her, I've only seen her in a dress two times: as a flower girl at Rosie and my wedding, and at the church service when her great-grandmother died. Don't let that blond hair fool you, she's local through and through." He nodded toward a mixed-Asian woman in a fitted, long Hawaiian dress approaching from the parked UTVs. "That's her mom over there." Her dark, straight hair was a stark counter to her daughter's wavy blond bob. But despite the strong Asian features, Makalani could see the haole in both.

"Her mom doesn't ride?"

"Nah. Kenneth met her in accounting class when he attended UH. Carolyn is the only member of the family who won't get on a horse. She's also the only one they trust with the books."

He inclined his head toward an older hapa-Hawaiian woman astride an apricot dun horse. "My mother-in-law, on the other hand, has deep paniolo roots."

Larry's widow looked about seventy, yet she wore a palaka work shirt, jeans, boots, and a woven straw hat. Although tiny like a jockey, she appeared equally agile and strong.

"Rumiko's 'ohana comes from North Kohala," Brian said. "Her grandparents on her mother's side were missionaries, but her paternal grandfather was one of the earliest Japanese paniolo."

"There were Japanese cowboys?"

"Sure. Two are in the Paniolo Hall of Fame. Rosie's family is hoping that, one day, their ancestor Guy Hiapo might be inducted posthumously as well."

He shifted his gaze to the elderly patriarch in the double red carnation lei as he carefully dismounted from a dappled gray mare. "Luke Hiapo is Guy Hiapo's grandson, ninety-seven and still rides better than most. He's grandfather to Rosie and her brothers, but everyone at the ranch calls him Kupunakāne too. Larry was his only child."

Kupunakāne dropped one side of his split reins to the ground and wrapped the other around his saddle horn loose enough for his horse to drop her head if she wished; then he untied his son's Appaloosa from his saddle and ground tied her rein as well. Trained to understand that dropping the reins on the ground was the cue to stand still, the mare pressed her forehead against his in a sign of great trust and sustained the connection as he stroked the sides of her neck. When she finally broke contact, Kupunakāne left the animals rooted in place and entered the semicircle of his family and friends.

Everyone was still. Even the other ranch horses stopped fidgeting beside their riders as Kupunakāne raised the pū ʻohe to his mouth. Although Makalani's grandmother used a conch shell for greetings and ceremonies, kānaka in the uplands blew through a sanded, hollow link of bamboo. The sound Kupunakāne produced was pure and clean. When the memory of it had dissipated, he turned around to the south and blew the pū ʻohe again. He repeated the process to the east and the west. When nā akua—the gods—had been welcomed in all four cardinal directions, he dropped his arms to his sides and turned his face up to the sky, took a deep breath, and began chanting "Oli Aloha" in an unexpectedly resonant voice.

Makalani's eyes teared as she pictured her grandmother standing, thigh deep, in the muddy kalo field, chanting her welcome when Makalani had finally and truly come home. Tūtū hadn't minded when her moʻopuna—her granddaughter—moved to Hawaiʻi Island because Hawaiian waters touched both of their shores. Makalani had returned, and that was all that mattered to her.

Kupunakāne extended his arms to everyone as he chanted. "A hiki mai nō ʻoe, hiki pu nō me ke aloha." *Now that you have come, love comes with you.*

Makalani's heart swelled as she joined in with the final words of greeting and love, "Aloha e, aloha e."

Everyone seemed to take a collective breath and let it out at once.

"Maikaʻi," he said. "It's good that you are here."

He returned the bamboo link to his saddle, and removed a framed photograph from the pouch. Holding this against his heart, he lifted the pakalana lei from his son's saddle and carried it to the wiliwili tree. Larry's horse stomped a hoof on the grass, as if in approval or farewell, as the old man set his son's photograph and the lei on a tree limb against the trunk. After a private moment of prayer, he removed his woven cowboy hat and faced his family and friends.

"Kakahiaka nō. Good morning, everyone. Mahalo fo' . . ."

He clenched his lips as emotions threatened to overflow. After a moment, he shook his head and tried again with attempted good cheer. Although hoarse with age, his voice carried in the breeze.

"Mahalo fo' joining us dis morning. Larry loved dis place. He stay come hea plenny time, take in da beauty, contemplate life. It's da highest spot on da ranch. We get Hāmākua Valley to da east, Kawaihae Bay to da west, Kohala Mountain and Mauna Kea to da nort' and da sout'. I like t'ink Larry will keep coming hea to take in our 'āina nui." He stretched his arms to encompass the abundant land. "If any you like visit wit' him, e 'olu'olu 'oe e hele mai—please, come anytime you like."

He cleared his throat, too choked up to add any more, and beckoned to a Hawaiian woman wearing an orange kīkepa over her long-sleeve shirt and jeans. The kapa-like fabric, stamped with leaf designs, wrapped around her stout body and draped over one shoulder. Her beautiful face was encircled by wavy silver hair, adorned with an orange blossom behind her left ear. The mea oli took a deep breath and dropped her arms to her sides, grounding herself to the 'āina before beginning to chant.

Chicken skin ran up Makalani's arms as the chanter's tremulous 'i'i vibrated in her bones. Although the ranger Makalani worked with always chanted an oli before entering the rock heiau, not since hearing her grandmother chant had Makalani felt the power of an oli strengthen her soul. As she looked around her, she could tell others felt the same. While Kupunakāne's chant had touched their hearts, the mea oli inspired them into action with the mana and intention of her voice.

As if directed by her call, Kupunakāne removed the red carnation lei from his neck and carried it to the tree, gazed at his son's face, then laid his gift on the roots. As he stepped away, Larry's widow, Rumiko, took his place, followed by her eldest son, Kenneth, his wife, Carolyn, and their cowboy daughter, Grace. Louie walked up alone. As Rosie stepped forward, Brian signaled his son, Vinnie, and Makalani to come along. All of them removed their lei and laid them around the wiliwili tree, followed by the rest of the ʻohana, ranch hands, and friends. Rumiko lingered the longest, staring at the framed photo and gazing into her late husband's eyes.

Throughout the gift giving ceremony, the mea oli chanted about the bountiful ʻāina, the sustenance it brings, and how it was everyone's kuleana—their sacred responsibility—to care for the land. She chanted about family and the passage of time, and the myriad ways every living thing was connected and blessed. All ears rode the waves of her undulating voice. When the mea oli lilted her final note up to the heavens, the roots of the wiliwili tree were covered with love.

An Episcopal priest, wearing a white stole over a tan aloha shirt and a clerical tab collar, stepped forward. His beard was neatly trimmed and his fair skin tanned from the sun. Although his jeans looked new, his cowboy boots were aged with hard wear, as if the kahu—the priest—had delivered the word of God through all manner of weather and rough terrain over the years.

He thanked the mea oli and laid a comforting hand on Rumiko's back. When she turned, they touched foreheads and noses in the traditional honi kiss, greeting one another and exchanging the divine breath of God. Having honored the Hawaiian traditions, the kahu recited the opening prayer and passages from Revelations, Corinthians, and the Gospel of John. He followed this with a homily on the theme and possible meanings of what he had read.

"At the very core of our humanity, we live our lives searching. We search for ourselves, we search for meaning, we search to find the right job. We are always searching. Because deep down, we know there is something more. A bigger truth we are meant to find."

His words struck a chord.

Makalani had journeyed all the way to Colorado and Oregon on her own quest for meaning and truth. Although gratified by the work, it wasn't enough to be in service to others. As the kahu's lesson suggested, she needed the deeper connection she had felt when she served others at home—the connection she imagined Larry Hiapo's ʻohana must feel.

After the homily, Rumiko came forward with a koa bowl. "Hiapo Ranch meant everything to Larry. He loved this land, and he was so proud that his sons were following in his path. He will rest easy in God's grace knowing that his ʻāina nui will be cared for by family and thrive for generations to come."

Having completed her brief eulogy, Rumiko passed the koa bowl to the priest, who recited the Prayer of Committal and sprinkled the first handful of ashes on the wiliwili tree's roots. Rumiko went next with Kupunakāne right behind. As Kenneth and Louie followed their grandfather, Makalani glanced at their sister, Rosie. Their mother had not mentioned their father's love or pride in her.

Maybe the family is not as close as I thought.

Rosie looked understandably hurt, but why did Rosie's brothers seem tense? Neither glanced at their sister to see if she was okay, so either they missed their mother's slight or they were too self-absorbed to care.

Or they were annoyed about something else.

If Makalani's mother had said so little about Pāpā at his memorial, she and her sister would definitely have been upset. Of course, that would never happen because Māmā loved and admired Pāpā with all her heart. Everyone did. When Kawika Pahukula eventually passed away, family and friends would insist on sharing kind words about him.

And yet, no one else spoke for Larry Hiapo.

The longer Makalani spent with the Hiapo ʻohana, the more convinced she became that something was not right.

CHAPTER TEN

Coming down the grassy slopes of Kohala Mountain from the highest point on Hiapo Ranch gave Makalani a better perspective of the family compound below. When she and Brian had arrived, all she had seen was the utility shed that stored the motorized vehicles, tractors, and other machines and tools needed to maintain a working cattle ranch. Now she could see an assortment of structures varying in size, function, and age. The largest was a two-story dirt-red house with a matching roof and white trim. The long stable beside it looked equally new, while the other small mismatched houses, barns, and sheds showed progressive signs of deterioration that documented the generations of Hiapo ranchers who had lived and worked on this land.

Brian drove on a well-trodden path in the grass alongside a low lava rock wall. A high-tensile-wire fence took over where it stopped. Black and Red Angus cows grazed in the pasture beyond with their calves. A small puʻu rose behind them in the distance. The little hill and the valleys around it gave texture to the beatific scene. Makalani breathed in the open space, so different from the dense upland forest they had left.

Brian stopped the UTV and hopped out to unlock the gate for themselves and everyone following behind. As he swung it open, Makalani scooted over to drive through.

"The fences are electric," he said. "Be careful not to touch."

"Got it." She had assumed as much since there was a wire running along the top.

After driving through, she scooted back to her seat so her cousin could drive while the procession of horseback riders descended from behind.

They rode in silence, enjoying the peace, before Makalani broached the subject that had been niggling in her mind. "Was Rosie pleased with the service?"

"I don't know. Maybe not so much."

"Her brothers didn't seem happy."

"They usually aren't."

"And yet, they work together?"

"From what Rosie tells me, they mostly do their own thing. Louie is the real cowboy of the family. Her eldest brother, Kenneth, cares more about business. That worked out fine while their dad was alive. Now that he's gone, I don't know how things will fly."

"What about the grandfather?"

"He still owns the ranch. But someone has to run it, yeah?"

"Which means Kenneth and Louie will have to work together."

Brian rolled his eyes, conveying the likelihood of that.

From the impressions Makalani had of the brothers, she was inclined to agree. Buttoned-down Kenneth was the polar opposite of his rugged paniolo brother. Their diverse perspectives and skills could work to their advantage as long as neither of them demanded to be in charge.

Makalani's father and aunties didn't have that problem with her grandmother's homestead because only her father and mother were willing to work the land. Although Aunty Kaulana and Aunty Maile lived in the compound with their husbands, they didn't do much to earn their keep, nor had they ever expressed an interest in taking over the farm. Neither had Makalani or her sister, Pua.

What am I thinking? It's not even Tūtū's homestead to give.

That revelation had come as a shock. But as Pāpā would say, "Every day is a blessing. We no get time fo' sweat da small kine stuff."

The Pahukula ʻohana had their own problems, to be sure, but it had to be hard on a family when two of the kids wanted the same thing.

"Rosie doesn't care about the ranch?" Makalani asked.

"She cares, but her passion is teaching. As long as no one harms the ʻāina or ruins the family's reputation, she's okay with whatever her grandfather and brothers want to do."

They passed through two more pasture gates before they arrived at the compound where the family lived and ran their cattle operation. Once Brian parked the UTV in the shed, they headed to the grassy area in front of the big dirt-red house where tables had been set up with foil trays of barbecued steak, shredded pork, and sautéed slices of pipi kaula—semidried strips of salted, seasoned beef. Trays of white rice, steamed cabbage, and macaroni salad were laid out along with a platter of fresh fruit.

Makalani's belly grumbled in anticipation of the feast.

Brian chuckled. "That's only what the family provided. The potluck table is over there."

"I didn't bring anything."

"No worries. Rosie and me brought crab salad and coconut cake."

"Then I'll make sure it doesn't go to waste."

The last time Makalani had shared a feast with Brian had been at her grandmother's birthday lūʻau. A celebration that had begun with immense joy had ended with despair. She hoped the Hiapos' feast wouldn't take such a bad turn. Their ʻohana didn't need any more trauma piled onto their collective plate.

"I'm gonna check in with Rosie. You good by yourself?"

"Go," she said, smiling confidently while, inside, her stomach turned. Why did every social interaction cause her so much stress?

I should have brought Tums.

As a law enforcement officer ranger in Oregon, she had interacted with the public from a position of authority. Every conversation, no matter how casual, was designed to keep the park visitors happy, respectful, and safe. But as an interpretive ranger at her new post, she would be expected to chat with people all day long. The constant extroversion could be stressful. If she didn't get a handle on her social awkwardness, she'd need to stock antacid by the case.

Without consciously deciding where she ought to go, she found herself beside Larry Hiapo's gray-and-white Appaloosa, running her hand along her neck. "Bet you miss him, huh?"

The mare nudged Makalani with her head. How easy it felt to exchange affection with a horse. If only her interactions with people could feel as easy and relaxed as this.

Kenneth's paniolo daughter chuckled as she came alongside. "Grandad's horse likes you."

Makalani stepped back. "Sorry, I didn't mean to intrude."

"No worries."

The young woman, maybe eighteen or nineteen, cradled the horse's face and gazed into her eyes. The moment held such intimacy, Makalani wondered if she should leave. Then the paniolo kissed the mare's nose and patted her neck.

"Nobody pays attention to poor 'Opihi since my grandfather died. Too close to the trauma, you know? Did she do something wrong? Did Grandad put her at risk? Nobody knows, but she was probably the last one to see him alive." She loosened the cinch. "I'm Grace."

"Nice to meet you. I'm Makalani, Brian Pahukula's cousin."

"Oh yeah, Rosie said she had invited you. Glad you could make it."

"May I help with the horses?"

"You kidding? I never turn away help."

Makalani sighed with relief. An affectionate animal, a purposeful task, and a human who appreciated her help—Makalani might survive this social engagement with her stomach intact.

As they moved from one horse to the next, removing the bridles, saddles, and blankets, Grace led by example and trusted Makalani to learn. The lack of instruction gave Makalani the freedom to observe, not only the Hiapo protocol of putting away horses, but the young woman herself.

Grace moved as her name described, with an athletic gracefulness born of lean muscles, confidence, and—Makalani assumed—a track record of being bucked, kicked, and nipped. She had slightly more height than her petite Asian-haole mother, with the straight-across breadth in her shoulders and narrow hips of the hapa-Hawaiian Hiapo men. Although Makalani could easily have carried her across the paddock, she suspected the cowgirl could have done the same with her.

They hosed down the horses, starting with their forelegs to get them used to the cool water and moving upward, ending with a careful wash of the face. They took extra care to make sure no water got in the ears. Then they moved to the back legs, the girth area, and rinsed the sweat between the horses' ʻōkole cheeks. Once the horses were clean, they toweled them off.

Grace handed Makalani a brush. "Start with ʻOpihi. She deserves to be first after all she's been through."

Makalani patted ʻOpihi's withers. "Brian said she came back alone?"

"Yeah, the next day." Grace knelt beside ʻOpihi's foreleg and ran her hand down the cannon bone below the knee. "We're not sure if she fell into the bullock pit with Grandad, but she has scratches on her leg."

Grace began brushing the dappled palomino she had been riding. Although the mare's flaxen mane was a few shades lighter than Grace's own hair, the cowgirl's suntanned skin made her wavy blond bob stand out like Marilyn Monroe. Nothing about Grace seemed soft or feminine beyond that.

Makalani brushed carefully down ʻOpihi's legs. "Do you have a lot of those pits on the property?"

"Shoots, I never knew we even had *one*. I mean, they're all over the island from when Kamehameha I lifted the kapu on hunting wild cattle, but I never saw one until I found Grandad and the bull. The pits were dug so long ago, right? Rain and mudslides filled them in. If I saw another one, I'd probably just think it was a gulch. They aren't like the pā pōhaku—the stone walls—our ancestors built to contain sheep and cattle. Whenever we find pā pōhaku on our land, we fill in the gaps with lava rocks and put the old stone walls to use."

Makalani thought back to her time with the stone mason before Corey's dad arrived in a panic at Puʻukoholā Heiau. The skill and manpower involved in dry rock masonry boggled her mind. All the lava rocks had to be chosen and gathered with care, then strategically placed without mortar or mud. Their construction was so sound that many of the property walls and cow walls still remained, disturbed only by new building developments, natural disasters, or people repurposing the rocks. Makalani had seen a segment of these ancient cow walls while riding with Brian up and down the slopes.

"The pā pōhaku I saw on your ranch today were in great condition."

Grace smiled proudly. "Kupunakāne passed down the art. Even now, he can choose the perfect rock and just throw it into place."

Although Makalani's younger cousins called *their* great-grandmother Tūtū Nui—an affectionate Hawaiian equivalent to great-granny—Grace called *her* great-grandfather Kupunakāne—Grandfather—like everyone else. She slurred *kupuna* and *kāne* together as if the title had become his actual name.

Makalani thought about the walls "Would ancient pā pōhaku also work for bulls?"

"Sure. Pipi laho are lazy and heavy. They can't jump over the walls like a horse. We keep them separate until it's time for them to breed."

"What happened to the bull that . . . ?" Makalani stopped, wishing she hadn't begun.

"The one that killed Grandad?"

She nodded apologetically.

"It's okay to ask. Animal Control took him for observation. We should get him back soon."

"Then what?"

"Put him in a pasture." She said this as if it were the most logical place to put a killer bull.

Makalani waited for signs of frustration or bitterness, but Grace seemed perfectly at ease. Makalani didn't understand.

If an animal had killed Tūtū, I would have butchered it for steak.

CHAPTER ELEVEN

Once Makalani had helped Grace finish her chores, she washed up and found Brian and Rosie watching Vinnie practice reining maneuvers in the arena.

"He didn't want to eat?" Makalani asked.

Rosie sighed. "Not until he spent more time riding his horse and working on his sliding stops. I told him to stable her, but he won't listen to me."

"Eh," Louie yelled from across the way. "Enough already. Give dat horse a break."

Vinnie reined her in quick. "Okay, Uncle."

"And no forget to cool her down befo' you put her up. I can see sweat on her neck from here."

"Yes, Uncle."

Louie continued on his way, confident his commands would be obeyed. If Makalani had been a kid, she would have listened too. Heck, even as an adult, she worried he might find some fault with her.

Rosie watched her brother with resignation. "Vinnie idolizes him."

"Is that a bad thing?" Makalani asked.

"Louie barely graduated from high school. He's smart enough. Just never did the work."

"Yeah," Brian said. "Whenever we bring up homework with Vinnie, he uses Uncle Louie as an excuse."

Rosie nodded. "It would be so much easier if he admired Kenneth."

Makalani could easily pick out Rosie's eldest brother from the crowd, not because of his striking appearance or commanding presence, but because he seemed so out of place. With his palaka shirt neatly pressed and his jeans a barely washed blue, Kenneth belonged in a boardroom or city council meeting, lobbying for cowboys who did all the work.

The metal gate clanked as Vinnie fumbled to get it open while still seated on his horse. Although not humongous, the animal could easily have supported a full-grown man, which meant eight-year-old Vinnie was up too high for his short arms to reach the loop on the latch. Instead of dismounting, he leaned over the saddle until his head hung near his knee. He might have caught the loop if his horse had remained still, or if his far-side boot could have reached low enough to give her a meaningful kick toward the gate.

Rosie muttered under her breath.

Brian stifled a laugh.

Louie yelled from the buffet table thirty yards away. "Eh, I told you plenny time, get off da horse befo' you try unlock da gate."

Rosie sighed. "He's up here every Monday and Wednesday after school and most of the weekend as well. I keep hoping he'll get bored, but look at him."

Vinnie clawed one more time at the latch's metal loop as the horse backed away. His finger caught. His torso stretched. The saddle's horn slipped out of his other hand's grip. What began as a comic interlude took a nasty turn as Vinnie slid off the saddle and flopped, headfirst, toward the ground. Instead of piledriving his head, his boot caught in the stirrup and stopped him with a jolt.

The horse spooked and skittered to the side, wanting nothing to do with the boy flailing between her legs.

Vinnie pinwheeled his free leg and arms trying to shake himself loose.

The horse snorted and jerked away from the threat.

Rosie and Brian ran around the arena toward the gate.

With the situation escalating dangerously, Makalani climbed over the galvanized pipes and jumped to the ground. She rose with her arms out, fingers spread, palms toward the horse. "Easy, girl. I'm here to help."

The mare eyed her warily and stomped her front hoof.

Makalani arced around her and advanced calmly from the center of the arena to press her toward the fence. If she spooked the horse into a run, her hooves could clip Vinnie's skull. Makalani didn't want to think about what might happen to the boy if the horse reared or bucked. Meanwhile, his hapless efforts to rise jerked his free leg against the horse's flank.

"Don't move, Vinnie."

Although he glanced at her in response, the urge to free himself was too great. Makalani was a stranger, not a mentor to be obeyed.

"I can help you, honest. You just need to be still."

It took a moment for him to trust her, and then he finally relaxed. He stopped flailing his free leg and let it split up and out to the side, hugged his torso, and let his head hang. His mouth quivered in fear as his eyes pleaded with her to be right.

When the well-trained animal calmed, Makalani exhaled with relief. "Good job, Vinnie. Let's get you out of this mess."

With the danger level lowered a couple of degrees, Makalani continued her approach. Everything seemed fine until Vinnie's parents finally barged through the clanking steel gate and startled the horse.

Rosie grabbed the back of Brian's shirt. "Not so fast. Lock the gate so Uila doesn't bolt." She nodded at Makalani, who was closer to her son. "Sorry. You go. Please."

Makalani nodded and turned back toward the mare, cooing the name she had heard Rosie use. "Eh, Uila. Easy, girl. I'm here to help."

The mare tossed her head and moved back. After proceeding with patience, Makalani made the mistake of grabbing for the reins. Uila startled from the sudden move and bounced the hanging boy as she skittered against the fence. Vinnie covered his head as her hooves kicked up toward his face.

"Whoa," a man said. "Geev um room. If dat lio feel cornered, she goin' bolt down da fence."

Louie walked up from behind and covered Makalani's hand with his own. "I got dis, wahine. You did good. Now let go."

The warmth of his breath and the heat emanating from his chest distracted her for a moment, forcing him to repeat the command. "Let go of da reins and move out o' da way."

When she let go of the horse and prepared to untangle Vinnie, he scowled and nodded her back.

Pigheaded man. You can't do this alone!

He's a paniolo, Makalani countered. *He knows what he's about.*

This wasn't her world, so she trusted him and backed away.

Louie slid the reins in the crook of his elbow, freeing both of his hands to stroke Uila's neck. "Pehea ʻoe, Uila? Maikaʻi nā mea a pau, yeah? E mālie. That's a good girl. Be calm."

As he soothed her in two languages, he scooped up Vinnie with his unencumbered arm and, while supporting the boy's weight, used the hand from the arm still clutching the reins at the elbow to free Vinnie's boot.

He swung Vinnie onto his hip. "You good?"

"Yeah, Uncle."

"Okay, den."

He set the boy down and returned his attention to the horse.

Rosie rushed to Vinnie and smothered him against her chest. "Are you okay? Are you hurt? What were you thinking? You could have been killed!"

Vinnie glanced at his uncle and squirmed out of her grip. "I'm fine. It was my stupid boot."

Louie snorted. "Stupid somet'ing."

Rosie whirled on her brother. "Seriously? Who do you think he was copying trying to open a gate like that?"

"If he had copied me, he would have done it right." He glared down at Vinnie. "Or bettah yet, he would have done like I taught and dismounted his horse."

Makalani glanced at her cousin. Although shaken and greatly relieved, Brian shook his head as if to say, this wasn't his fight. Rosie, on the other hand, needed someone else to blame.

"I can't believe Dad gave him that horse."

"Not'ing wrong wit' Uila. I helped Dad train her. Dis could have gone plenny worse on a poorly trained lio. You like point fingah? Look at yourself."

"What are you talking about?"

Louie waved over Vinnie. "Show me your boot."

As Vinnie tried to pull it off, Louie stopped him and glared at Rosie. "Cowboy boots are meant to slip off easy for dis very reason. You like know why dis happen? Because you too stubborn to buy your growing keiki a biggah pair of boots."

He handed Vinnie the lead rope he had untied from Uila's saddle. "Your foolishness frightened your lio. Give her a good bath and show her respect."

"Yes, Uncle."

Murmuring apologies to his horse, Vinnie led Uila past his parents without meeting their eyes.

Makalani considered following, but she didn't want Louie's attention on her. Rosie's intense brother was easier to handle from afar. Unfortunately, the arena was only large enough to put a horse through its paces, not nearly large enough to hide.

"I don't know you." Louie's eyes bored into hers, his thick brows furrowed into an angry ridge.

He knows I messed up. I shouldn't have grabbed those reins so suddenly. Vinnie could have been killed.

Makalani silenced her thoughts and fumbled for a response. "I'm Makalani Pahukula. Brian's cousin from Kaua'i? I'm a ranger at Pu'ukoholā Heiau, recently transferred from Crater Lakes National

Park, that's in Oregon, where I was living, now I'm here . . . on Hawaiʻi Island, I mean . . . not on . . . your ranch."

He widened his eyes as she babbled.

His lashes are ridiculously long.

He shook her off like a wet dog with water. "Whatevah. Good work jumping in da arena. It coulda been bad."

She sagged with relief, not at all sure she had helped as much as he thought.

Louie turned back. "Eh, I saw you kōkua Grace. If you evah like help out at da ranch, let me know."

"Wait, what?"

"That's a great idea," Brian said, rushing to Makalani's side. "You said you were bored at work and wanted something physical to do. You obviously know horses. Isn't that better than building a house?"

Louie's interest increased. "You one contractor?"

"No. My cousin exaggerates. I worked for Habitat for Humanity as a teen."

Louie shrugged. "Still."

Brian bumped her shoulder. "See? Win, win."

Makalani didn't feel anywhere near as confident about her abilities as both men appeared to be. Hadn't she startled Uila and nearly caused her to bolt? What if, in her ignorance, she caused a serious injury on the ranch?

Louie frowned at her delay. "Whatevah, yeah? Rosie can text you my numbah. We get plenny kine food and a bunkhouse if you need a place to sleep. No money, tho. Dat's not how it works. All da cowboys on dis island help everybody else."

He called me a cowboy?

Makalani gaped at the paniolo. Before she could sort through the firehose of feelings and input, he strode out the gate.

Brian crossed his arms and smiled at his wife. "See what I did?"

Rosie smirked. "What? Hired your cousin out for free?"

"No. Remember how Makalani helped her 'ohana sort through their problems? Maybe she can do the same for yours."

Makalani snapped to attention. "Hold up, cuz. That was a totally different situation. I grew up with those people. They're my family."

"And you're ours, right, Rosie?" Brian waited for confirmation, but his wife was lost in thought. "Makalani is a *law enforcement* ranger. She could also help with the other things too."

Whatever was going on, the pain in Rosie's expression hurt Makalani's heart. "What other things?"

Rosie checked around them to make sure they were alone. "I think someone is targeting our son."

"Vinnie? Why? Because of what just happened?"

"No. That was him trying to do more than he can. But there have been other accidents that are harder to explain. It began with centipedes in his boots, not in just one but in both. Then a car alarm went off and spooked Uila at the exact moment Vinnie was passing through the highway gate. Grace was beside him and kept his horse from bolting into traffic. I know that sounds like bad timing, but in all my years growing up on this ranch, I've never heard a car alarm. Nobody would need one, and Grace said there were no cars parked on the road. So where did it come from, and why did it go off at that moment? Then, a week before Dad died, the cinch on Vinnie's brand-new saddle broke while he was riding. He slid off into a ditch. He was okay, but he could have broken his neck." Rosie shook her head. "No one in my family will listen to me. They all think I hate this ranch and don't want Vinnie to be here."

Makalani asked gently, "Is that true?"

Rosie took a breath. "It's complicated."

From the uncomfortable silence that followed, Makalani could tell this wasn't the place or time for Rosie to delve into her feelings about the ranch.

"Do you have any idea who might want to hurt your son or why?"

"None I'm willing to share."

Brian leaned in. "A neighbor boy used to torment her, so her family thinks she's projecting her childhood angst." He took his wife's hand. "At least, tell her about your dad."

Rosie shook her head and stared off at the family and friends gathered to celebrate his life.

"It's okay," Makalani said. "You don't have to say more. Your concern for Vinnie's safety is enough."

"It's not, though," Rosie said. "I'm afraid whoever is targeting our son, may have also killed Dad."

CHAPTER TWELVE

Detective Rona Kim had zero knowledge about ranching and Waimea life. She had wanted a break from Honolulu, and Hawai'i County's West Criminal Investigations Section was the first opening that appeared. With no idea what to expect, she moved out of the Nu'uanu house she had shared with her ex, stored most of her belongings in Honolulu, and rented a studio apartment in Kailua-Kona, close enough to the CIS offices to walk. A week later, they transferred her to the Waimea substation, an hour away.

After a month on the job and a fortune in gas, her captain and the other three detectives—all locally born—still treated her like an outsider and stuck her with the junk cases no one wanted to touch. The Big Island Boys had all grown up on ranches, so why not pair one of *them* with Detective Daniel "Call me Dan" Lau?

Sniggering bastards.

What the *hell* was Rona supposed know about bulls? When she stepped in shit—as she inevitably would—the BIBs would never let her forget.

She folded the take-out carton of her plate lunch and tossed it into the trash. Although it pissed her off that her fellow detectives hadn't invited her to their butcher-deli hangout for lunch, the solitude gave her space to breathe. Even her lone speckled orchid had perked up with them gone. The other blossoms had died in the sudden shift from Kona's heat to Waimea's upland chill. Rona felt the plant's pain. Not once had she considered packing ski clothes for this gig. Then again, she also hadn't expected to be assigned on a possible homicide where a rancher was gored to death by one of his own bulls.

"Hooked," Detective Dan had said, smoothing his wisps of hair over his scalp.

"Excuse me?"

"I heard you muttering. We say hooked, not gored."

She had stared back in puzzlement, imagining Ferdinand the Bull crocheting baby socks with a plumeria behind his ear. To make the case even weirder, the rancher had been *hooked* to death in a pit that was apparently dug out by bullock hunters in the early 1800s during the reign of King Kamehameha the Great. *Bullock hunters.* Was that even a thing? How in the name of all that was holy was she supposed to distinguish herself with such a ridiculous case?

Everyone at the station had been making jokes about it all week long, even the detectives who knew poor Larry Hiapo, who by all accounts was a "true paniolo and a standup guy." If not for the mandatory observation time required by Hawai'i County Animal Control and Protection Agency, the case would have been opened and shut the next day. Instead, Dan had saddled her with reviewing the photos and testimonies even though he intended to lay the tragic accident to rest.

And yet . . .

As she leafed through the paperwork she was supposed to file that afternoon, things didn't quite add up.

Why was Larry Hiapo in a pit with a bull? And if the animal had actually killed the rancher, why would it be released? Although Animal Control had cleared the bull of any diseases or abnormally aggressive behavior, Rona didn't understand why the family would want it back.

"Shouldn't it be destroyed, or at least sold and slaughtered for beef?" she had asked her partner.

"*He*, not *it*." Dan had stuck his thumbs inside his belt, drawing attention to a rodeo buckle. "And to answer your question, breeding bulls are valuable, Rona. Everyone knows that." Meaning, everyone except for her.

"Okay. Then why not sell *him* to another rancher?"

"They wouldn't get a good price."

"Because the bull is a killer. Exactly my point!"

He had shaken his head as if she would never understand, which, in all honesty, she probably would not.

Her intercom beeped.

"Detective Kim, there's a Skip Una calling from Oregon."

"Don't know him."

"He says it's about Larry Hiapo. Detective Lau said I should field the call to you."

Of course he did.

"Thanks, Lani, put him through." A moment later, she said, "Mr. Una? This is Detective Rona Kim. What can I do for you?"

"Thanks for asking, Detective Kim. Please, call me Skip. I'm calling to see if you've made any headway on Larry Hiapo's murder."

Rona perked up. "What makes you think he was murdered?"

"Why else would Larry have been trapped in a pit with a bull?"

Although Rona had been asking herself the same question, she wasn't about to share that with him. "I can't discuss an ongoing case."

"Fair enough. But if you're still investigating, you should know that Larry was going to sell Hiapo Ranch to me."

"No one has mentioned this to me."

"Well, I don't know who he told, aside from his son Louie."

"Louie Hiapo?"

"That's him, the younger of the two sons—big bruiser, tough as nails—and from what I'm told, the best paniolo on the ranch."

"I'm sorry but, who are you, and what is your interest in Hiapo Ranch?"

"I'm the owner of Una Ranch in Oregon."

"Why do you want to buy Hiapo Ranch?"

"We finish their cows, so I—"

"Excuse me, you what?"

"Huh?"

"You said finish?"

"Oh." He chuckled. "We fatten them up on our nice green grass until they get big enough to sell." He said this as if talking story with a child. "I'm from the Big Island. I'd like to return."

Just what she didn't need, another smart-ass BIB.

"Did you know the Hiapo family when you lived here?"

"Not personally. But they have a good-size ranch."

"That you wanted to acquire."

"And that Larry wanted to sell."

"Do you have any emails or signed promises from him that would corroborate your story?"

"Afraid not. Larry was old school. He preferred talking on the phone."

"And that's when he mentioned Louie?"

"Uh-huh. Said his son was mad as hell about the sale."

"Anyone else not want Larry to sell?"

"Not that he mentioned."

"Do you think Larry's son had something to do with his death?"

"Beats me. Sounds pretty unlikely, though, don't you think?"

"That a son would kill his father?"

"Nah. That a rancher would be caught in a pit with a bull."

CHAPTER THIRTEEN

Makalani began every workday at Puʻukoholā Heiau by hoisting the American and Hawaiian flags. After performing this duty, she checked the visitor bathroom for cleanliness and scanned the national historic site's entrance for trash. No cars drove down the treeless access road or parked in the blacktop lot. No visitors wandered up the paved pathways to the black lava rock buildings, designed to resemble the stone heiau themselves. Everything was as stark and silent as the moon.

Where are the birds?

Back home in Anahola, she woke to a chorus of tweets, coos, and the incessant, yet pleasing, crows of Kauaʻi's red junglefowl. Although Hawaiʻi Island also had wild roosters, she didn't hear a single crow, not on this morning, not on this tree-starved expanse.

Makalani listened harder and caught the faint mew and honk of a seabird down the road. Only one bird, alone on the shore.

Are you missing your ʻohana, like me?

Although she had lived on her own in Oregon, she had grown accustomed to the constant presence of her family during her transition month spent at home. She missed laughing with Māmā and cooking with her aunties as they bickered about whose mango chutney was the best. She missed kayak fishing with Pāpā and hunting wild pig with Solomon and his friends. She even missed Uncle Sanji's silence and Uncle Eric's laid-back smirk. But more than anything, she missed her conversations with Tūtū as they pulled kalo—taro—from the muddy earth.

A bird chirped from a distant tree. This land wasn't as silent and lonely as she thought.

Determined to approach her new job with a fresh perspective, she walked onto the visitor center lānai, where displays of laser-cut metal art depicted scenes of ancient Hawaiian life. More displays and artifacts waited inside, including a vast library of books, all of which Makalani was expected to read. With so much to learn beyond her ranger and law enforcement training, it felt like a whole new profession.

"What's wrong wit' dat?" she could hear Pāpā say. "If a plant no can grow, it goin' die, right? Same t'ing fo' us." And whenever he taught her something new, she always had fun.

I can do the same here if I try.

Her newfound encouragement increased when she saw what Ranger Jamison Akaka was crafting inside the window nook of the room.

Makalani leaned over the counter displaying a royal red-and-yellow feathered cape. A KAPU sign sat alongside the artifact warning visitors this was a sacred item they were not allowed to touch. A similar sign was posted on the craft table where Ranger Akaka guided a curved needle around a tiny reddish-brown feather on the five-paneled netting for a cape. He selected a new tiny feather, measured the length, then clipped it to the precise size for his row.

He smiled at her interest. "All of the Puʻukoholā rangers have at least one cultural skill. Nā hulu aliʻi are mine."

"*Royal* featherwork? Is this cape a replica of one worn by a chief?"

"No. I'm making this for one of our *living* aliʻi, the descendants of our revered nobility from our ancient Hawaiian Kingdom who continue to serve as leaders to the people of Hawaiʻi today. Not many featherworkers are qualified for this work."

She walked around the counter so she could see the rows he had already sewn up close. "When did you begin this cape?"

"Yesterday, when you switched workdays to attend the memorial. I make the most progress in the mornings when fewer visitors are here, but I continue throughout the day in between other duties. Visitors get a better appreciation for nā hulu ali'i when they see me crafting a cape."

"Would that make you a kumu?"

"It would if I taught. I'm more of a *kahuna* hulu nui."

Makalani was puzzled. "A great featherwork *priest*?"

"*Kahuna* also means *expert.* In ka wā kahiko—ancient times—everything in Hawai'i had spiritual undertones. So if you had mastered a craft, the ancient Hawaiians believed you were blessed from your ancestors."

Makalani thought of the gifted professionals and artisans she had met in her life. Each of them seemed to tap into a deeper and more profound source. "My tūtū weaves beautiful shell hatbands and lauhala hats. My mother sews feather lei. She's still learning, but she's already quite good."

"Did they teach you?"

"Nah, I don't have the patience for intricate work. I was more interested in helping Pāpā cut, shape, and sand poi pounding boards."

Ranger Akaka's eyes brightened with interest. "Crafting papa ku'i 'ai is an important cultural art. You could demonstrate and lecture about that."

"I'm only skilled enough to help, not to teach. I've never made a pounding board on my own."

"Hmm. I'm sure we could find a community leader to help you improve."

Makalani didn't want to dash his hopes, but her main motivation for woodworking was to be close to her dad. Although she enjoyed the physical exertion involved, without that bonding element, she would likely grow bored.

"E ho'omanawanui," Tūtū would remind her. "Be patient. Not'ing wort' anyt'ing goin' happen as fast as you like."

Ranger Akaka sewed in the feather and rose from his chair, leaving his work in progress for the early-bird visitors to see.

"Aloha kakahiaka. E komo mai," he said to the local women who had just walked through the door, bidding them good morning and welcoming them into the space. "Let me know if you have any questions."

The older of the two women saw his cape-in-progress and walked into the nook. "Dis your work? You make ʻahu ʻula old style, yeah?"

"Yes, I'm making this cape on an olonā netting."

The woman nodded her approval, pleased that Ranger Akaka used the traditional fibrous shrub netting as a base for his feathered cape. As she waved her friend over to hear Ranger Akaka explain the nuances of his work, Makalani realized she wasn't the only local who wanted to know more. Observing a cultural craft in progress brought the displays of ancient ʻahuʻula and mahiole—feathered capes and helmets—to life.

Maybe I should *put in the time and learn the papa kuʻiʻai craft.*

Makalani was warming to the idea when her supervisor appeared. As always, Ranger Daniel Machado's stern face was fixed in a scowl.

"Ranger Pahukula, a word?"

She joined him at the bookshelves.

"Ranger Akaka can handle the visitors. You have transcripts waiting for you in the back room." He selected a book from a shelf. "When you're done with those, you can move on to this biography of King Kamehameha I."

"Yes, sir."

"And after lunch, one of our generational locals is giving a lecture on sacred caves in the area that should not be disturbed. Make sure you attend."

Eight days had passed since her lava tube rescue, and Supervisory Ranger Machado still held a grudge. Of course, she hadn't actually *apologized* because she hadn't done anything wrong. Corey would have died in that cave if she hadn't acted quickly and done what she was qualified to do.

"One more thing, Ranger Pahukula. Assuming no one else dies in your family, I expect you to provide at least one week's notice for any future scheduling requests."

He strode out the front door without waiting for her reply.

Way to go. Two weeks in, and I've messed up again.

She had to get on his good side, or the upcoming year would feel interminably long.

If she called Pāpā right now, he would say: "You like make amends? Focus on what your boss care 'bout da most. Actions speak louder, especially when you too stubborn fo' words."

As always, she knew he'd be right. When she fixed on an idea, she wouldn't let go.

Because I was right!

She sighed. Then again, maybe Ranger Machado had a point. If she wanted to do well at Puʻukoholā, she had to leave her former position and those expectations behind. Qualifications didn't matter if they didn't fit the job.

Feeling resolved, Makalani headed for the back room, but paused to hear Ranger Akaka explain the real story behind the paintings on the wall.

"Keep in mind," he said to the local women, "the information you read on the plaques was written in the '60s and '70s by non-Hawaiians attempting to summarize our history in a way visitors could understand."

Makalani glanced out the glass doors to make sure her supervisor had left. She would read the transcripts and biography just as soon as Ranger Akaka finished explaining what he meant.

"This is why heiau are described as temples or places of worship."

"They're not?" the younger woman said.

Ranger Akaka glanced at Makalani before he answered, as if pleased she had stayed. "Not always. Just like a kahuna is not always a priest, or a kāula is not necessarily a prophet or seer. A great example is Kapoukahi—who told Kamehameha he had to build a heiau on this land before he could conquer other chiefs and unite the Hawaiian Islands. Although the people called him a seer, Kapoukahi was actually a brilliant strategist. He saw how things needed to be for Kamehameha to achieve his political goals. He was even an architect who understood exactly how the heiau should be built."

Ranger Akaka pointed to another painting that showed Hawaiian men in white loin cloths passing rocks over the land and up the various levels of the heiau in construction.

"It took ten thousand men less than a year, in an assembly line thirty miles long, to bring rocks from Pololū Valley to this location. This tall figure in the red loin cloth is Kamehameha. He didn't just order this heiau built, he laid rocks with his own hands. This old man with the white hair is the architect and visionary Kapoukahi. Since the Hawaiians were spiritual people, they believed his mana was passed down from the gods—gods who are actually our venerated ancestors, right, because the Western idea of gods doesn't match perfectly with our own."

The older woman nodded in agreement.

"So you see," Ranger Akaka said, "the Hawaiians thought Kapoukahi must be kāula—a seer—but he was actually a kahuna, an expert, on so many things."

"He stay from Kaua'i, yeah?" the older woman said.

Ranger Akaka glanced at Makalani. "Yes, he was. So when people from Kaua'i brag that their island was the only one Kamehameha never conquered, they should actually be proud that their kahuna helped their own King Kaumuali'i negotiate with Kamehameha for a peaceful solution to war."

Makalani nodded thoughtfully, but doubted her grandmother would agree that Kapoukahi—no matter how great an expert or seer—deserved more credit than Kaua'i's former king.

Before Ranger Akaka could expand on his theory, the women took an interest in the ancient war clubs and wooden daggers with shark teeth roped along the edge. Concealing his disappointment, he politely allowed them to move on and greeted a mainland couple walking through the door.

Makalani, invigorated to learn, went in search of the texts her superior had assigned.

Eight hours later, her brain had officially fried.

She had used every trick in the book to keep studying in the claustrophobic office despite the overflow of craft projects and storage that encroached on her space. No matter what tricks she employed, the lack of sunlight and fresh air made it hard to stay awake. Like the shark form her great-grandmother had transformed into when she became an 'aumakua—a family deity—Makalani needed motion to keep her alert. An hour lunch in the hot sun and the ninety-minute lecture sitting in the visitor center lānai had drained her energy even more. She stared at the clock. Time to check the ground for litter and lower the flags.

Woo-hoo, the highlight of my day.

She closed Kamehameha's biography and stacked it on the transcripts she had read. After her final chores, she would go for a swim down the road at Spencer Beach Park. It was warmer on the coast than where she rented a room in a house up Kawaihae-Māhukona Road. She might as well enjoy it. Once at home in Waimea, she would have nothing to do.

Except daydream about Rosie's handsome brother.

Oh my god, Makalani. Enough!

Every time she had tried to imagine King Kamehameha, Louie Hiapo popped into her mind.

It's because he's tall, she told herself. But it was more than that. The paniolo also commanded others and inspired them to measure up to his high ideals. He carried himself like an ali'i, and yet—like Kamehameha—he did the hard work himself. Makalani had beamed with pride when he had called her a paniolo and invited her to work on his ranch.

Should I do it?

The thought of working with him was exhilarating and a little terrifying. Although she knew her way around horses and wasn't afraid of hard work, that didn't mean she could handle daily paniolo life.

She didn't know a thing about cattle. What if she spooked the herd, or injured a horse, or caused someone harm? Although Louie Hiapo believed she had enough skills, she might prove him wrong. She'd die of embarrassment if he told her to go home.

Her phone pinged with a new text from Brian, his third for the day. This one was apparently typed by his wife.

> Hi, Makalani. This is Rosie. I know it's a lot to ask, but will you please look out for our son and check into my father's death? They're shorthanded on the ranch, so I know my family would welcome your help. Here's Louie's number. He's waiting for your call.

Despite taking Tuesday off for the memorial, Makalani still had her regular Thursday-through-Saturday weekend coming up. Hard labor in the mountains would rejuvenate her for the sedentary study during her four-day workweek after that. It would also give her something more meaningful to do on her days off besides drive to Kailua Village in Kona and spend money she didn't have. Everything was so expensive on the leeward side of the island, and Hilo—on the windward side—was a ninety-minute drive. The used Explorer she had bought ate more gas than she had hoped.

She reread the last line of Rosie's text. A man as busy as Louie was definitely *not* waiting for her call. She texted him instead and let him know she could begin helping out the next day.

A minute later, he called. "We start at five a.m. wit' breakfast and work aftah dat. Come fo' dinner at seven if you like bunk hea tonight."

"Um, thanks, but I live pretty close."

"Okay, but no be late fo' breakfast, yeah?"

He ended the call before she could reply.

She texted her cousin.

> I start tomorrow, first thing. Tell Rosie I'll look out for Vinnie and see what I can learn about her dad.

CHAPTER FOURTEEN

Makalani smiled when Sandy Hall's face filled her screen. Her childhood friend, a Kaua'i firefighter, beamed in return.

"Eh, stranger. Long time no see," Sandy said.

"It's barely been a month."

"A month with you on the Big Island starting a new job. What's with the witchy hair?"

Makalani attempted to smooth her salt-frizzy waves, then gave up. "Just got back from a swim."

"Must be nice to have all that free time."

"It was a workday. The heiau's near the shore."

The sun-worn skin around Sandy's blue eyes crinkled as she smirked. "Let me guess, they're not providing enough hard labor, so you swam a few miles."

Makalani laughed. "Something like that."

"I'd tell you to treat it as a vacation, but I know you too well."

Sandy and Makalani had been best friends through high school, building houses for Habitat for Humanity and riding horses on her parents' ranch. They had grown apart when Makalani went to Colorado for university and ranger training but had reconnected when Makalani had come home for her grandmother's eighty-fifth birthday last January. They bonded again while searching for Makalani's missing cousins and suspicious paka lōlō growers living off the grid.

"I miss you," Makalani said. After leaving her ranger job in Oregon, she and Sandy had been hanging out several times a week.

Sandy waved it away. "No you don't. You probably have tons of new ranger friends to occupy your time."

"Ha! Not even close."

"Oh, yeah? Then why'd it take you so long to call?"

Makalani could see the hurt in her friend's eyes. She should have called, but their rekindled friendship had meant so much that Makalani hadn't wanted to dampen it with her bad moods and complaints.

"It wasn't for lack of caring. I was just waiting for something fun to share."

Sandy perked up. "Spill it."

Makalani smiled. "Tomorrow, I start work on a ranch." When Sandy's jaw dropped, she quickly added, "I'm still a ranger, I'm just doing this on the side."

"Whew, that's a relief."

"Why?"

"Because cowboys don't get paid squat." She laughed. "Besides," Sandy said, "you're the best ranger I know."

As a firefighter on the east side of Kaua'i, Sandy had interacted with several rangers during floods and rescue calls for people in trouble on or near Wailua River. But since none of them were also law enforcement, the expectations weren't the same.

Sandy smirked. "And the only ranger I know with a gun."

Makalani rolled her eyes. "You're as bad as Solomon's old football buddies."

"Da Braddahs?"

"Yeah. That's the only reason they invite me on pig hunts."

Sandy raised her brows skeptically. "And it has nothing to do with Pupule's massive childhood crush? Or the fact that you can patch up Da Braddahs if anyone gets hurt? Seriously, Makalani, just because I tease you, doesn't mean you should sell yourself short."

"Okay, okay. Thank you, but can we talk about the ranch?"

"Yes! I'm so excited you've found somewhere to ride. But, you know, ranching is a lot of work. Are you getting paid, or just doing this for fun?" Sandy shook her head. "What am I saying? Of course it's for fun."

"It's my cousin-in-law's ranch. They need extra help, and I need something physical to do."

"And you start tomorrow?"

Makalani nodded. "At five a.m."

"They're feeding you I hope."

"Three squares."

"You'll need them. Trust me, they'll work you to death. Which ranch?"

"Hiapo."

"I know them. My dad bought me a horse Louie Hiapo trained. The gelding I had in high school, you remember him? Gorgeous animal."

"Louie's not so bad either."

"Right?" Sandy waved the imagined heat from her face. "I had a major crush on him as a kid."

"You went to their ranch?"

"Yup. I got to pick out my horse. Louie was a lot older, so he treated me like a kid. I, on the other hand, practiced writing *Sandy Hiapo* in my diary for a month."

Makalani laughed—at least she wasn't alone.

Sandy grew serious. "I heard what happened to his dad. What a grisly and freakish way to die."

"I know, right? Have you ever heard of such a thing?"

"You mean the old bullock pit, or getting hooked and stomped by your own bull?"

"Either. *Both.*"

"Don't worry. Nothing like that will happen to you. They'll probably have you shoveling horse manure, digging postholes, and rounding up cows. If you're lucky, you might get to wrestle a few calves."

"So, you think Larry Hiapo was in the wrong place at the wrong time?"

"Must have been. Either that or he made a series of bad mistakes. It can happen, especially when a cowboy is tired and overworked."

"Larry was semiretired."

"In that case, he might have been too old or too out of practice for the task. In any case, don't let the Hiapos push you into doing something that feels dangerous for you."

Makalani rolled her eyes.

"I'm serious. You haven't worked on a ranch since we were in high school. Even then, Dad never put you at risk."

"You mean aside from getting bucked off your horse?"

Sandy laughed. "Cowboys are tough. Don't worry. You'll fit in just fine."

CHAPTER FIFTEEN

Makalani followed the bright swath of light from her Explorer's high beams as she drove along Kohala Mountain Road to Hiapo Ranch. Although dry grass slopes descended to the ocean on the west and lush pastureland swept up the mountain to the east, all she could see in the moonlight were silhouettes and the occasional wind barriers of ironwood trees.

She slowed as she approached the mile marker for the ranch, which she would have passed if she hadn't set her GPS. The Hiapos' property didn't have any signage at all, only a woven-wire fence lining the highway and a locked metal gate. Since she habitually arrived early to any engagement, she drove onto the dirt road to wait.

4:50 a.m.

Louie said they served breakfast at five. Would he come unlock the gate, or had he not expected her to come since she hadn't actually replied? As she debated whether or not to text, she noticed the padlock hung loose through the rings.

"Leave it as you found it," Sandy had always told her when they were kids. So after driving through, she swung closed the gate and left the padlock hanging loose.

The road felt rougher and longer in the dark than it had when Brian had driven her here for his father-in-law's memorial and celebration of life. That morning, she had marveled at the expanse of rolling green hills, cattle in the distance, and horses grazing in nearby corrals.

With all that hidden from view, the sparsely illuminated farmhouse and tack room kept her focus ahead. As she drew closer, she saw movement in both.

A slim figure in a hooded sweatshirt, vest, baseball cap, and jeans walked out of the tack room, waved, and pointed toward a parking space off the driveway near a truck. Although well covered up in the cold, Makalani could tell it was Grace.

The young woman greeted her at the car door. "Kakahiaka nō. Mahalo for coming. We appreciate the kōkua. Come in and eat."

Makalani followed her up the lānai stairs. As with Tūtū's house in Anahola—and most construction in Hawai'i—the Hiapos had built their farmhouse on an elevated foundation. Although Makalani had admired the red house's white railings and trim, she had not ventured beyond its well-oiled deck. The modern ranch decor caught her by surprise, more magazine showplace than the rustic functionality she had expected to find.

Rumiko set a bowl of scrambled eggs on the bleached wood table beside the Portuguese sausage and rice. She wore a quilted kimono-style robe with her black hair secured in a bun. The wrinkles around her mouth cut deeply around her frown.

Grace nodded toward an antique sideboard. "Coffee and bowls are over there. Food's over here." She helped herself to both and left Makalani to help herself.

Aside from Grace, no one said a word. Only a fleeting glance from Grace's mother, setting down a pitcher of gravy, even acknowledged Makalani was there.

Okay . . . not uncomfortable at all.

She grabbed her coffee and bowl and sat beside Grace. As the athletic young woman drenched her food in thick gravy, Grace's father, Kenneth, picked through a small portion of eggs. At the end of the table, Kupunakāne, the elderly patriarch, took a second helping of rice. Before Makalani could settle on the proper amount, Louie came through the front door.

Louie acknowledged her with a nod, then filled his bowl to the brim. "We no goin' stop until lunch so, you know, don't be shy."

Kenneth put down his fork. "I'm sorry, but why is she here?"

Louie shoveled in a mouthful with a spoon. "She good wi' horses, and we need da help."

"Do we? Because I thought you and Malu had it all in hand."

Louie shrugged and nodded for Makalani to eat.

Rumiko and Carolyn sat beside Kenneth with their coffees while Kupunakāne eyed both of his grandsons and nibbled his rice.

Makalani slouched in her chair, wishing she hadn't come.

Kenneth continued to glare at his brother. "Isn't that what you said when I offered to help with the fence? 'No need, brah. Stay in your office and do what you do.' So why did you hire another hand without my consent?"

Louie stabbed his spoon into the loco moco like a flag. "Your consent? Who died and put you in charge?"

Rumiko gasped.

"Sorry, Mom, but Dad nevah say not'ing li'dat. He let Kenneth play wi' da books and left da paniolo work to me."

"Play?" Kenneth said.

"Enough," Rumiko said, sliding back her chair. "I will not have you disrespecting each other or your father."

Kenneth jerked his head at Makalani. "What about the new hire?"

"Eh, I nevah hire nobody," Louie said, gesturing with his spoon. "Makalani stay one ranger down at Puʻukoholā. She goin' work up hea on her days off fo' free."

Rumiko glanced at Kupunakāne to see if he would object, then settled on Makalani with a half-hearted smile. "Is this true?"

Makalani nodded even though she hadn't actually committed herself for that long.

Rumiko shrugged. "Okay, then."

"That's it?" Kenneth said.

Rumiko turned to her eldest son. "You want to turn down free help?"

"I didn't say that."

Louie snorted. "Pretty much did."

Kenneth glared at his brother. "Don't put words in my mouth. I want to know what happened to the ranch hand we actually pay."

"He's coming."

"When?"

"When I need 'im."

"That's not good enough."

"Is fo' me."

Receiving no support from either his grandfather or his mother, Kenneth shoved back his chair. "I'll be in the office, paying bills for the new fence you and your *friend* have yet to install."

Louie ignored him and ate.

Makalani nervously mashed her loco moco into mush. The tension between brothers reminded her of a particularly bad family breakfast the previous year. Her own 'ohana had been such a mess.

Why did I promise Rosie I would help hers?

CHAPTER SIXTEEN

Louie handed Makalani a rope halter and nodded as she switched the loop to her left hand. "You know how to tie um?"

"Sheet bend?"

"Pretty much."

He left the tack room door open. The hanging bulb helped illuminate the paddocks nearby. There were two: a large corral with a dozen horses and a smaller corral with only one. In the predawn twilight, the solo dark horse could barely be seen.

"You can ride Rocky Road today," Louie said, walking toward the larger corral. "He da brown gelding wit' da light and dark spots. When we get inside da pā, you'll be able to see."

"Rocky Road like the ice cream?"

Louie snorted. "Mo' like his trot is rockier dan riding on ʻaʻā lava. Aside from dat, he stay easy to ride."

Louie neglected to mention that Rocky Road did not like to be caught. With room to run, she couldn't get close. After the horse evaded every one of Makalani's advances, Louie told her to quit.

"Gotta make nice. Introduce yourself. Let him come to you."

He called to the horses, "Kakahiaka nō, my beauties. Who like work today?" Several horses wandered over for love and to check for a treat. He patted them all but gave extra attention to his father's horse.

"Eh, ʻOpihi. You like go nānā ʻāina wit' me?"

The mare nuzzled her nose deep into his hand.

As she nibbled her treats, he patted her neck and kissed the side of her face. "Nah. You relax. Stay hea and eat."

He looked at Makalani as he demonstrated on ʻOpihi what to do with the elusive Rocky Road. "Once he come to you, slip your arm over his shoulder, slide it down his neck, and geev um a hug. Wit' little bit pressure, he goin' turn his head into you." He released ʻOpihi, smacked her affectionately on the rump to send her away, and pretended she was still there. "Slip the halter up over his nose and do like you know."

"Got it."

"Aurite den."

He eyed the blue roan stallion in the smaller pā a few yards away as he came toward the fence and into the light. "How 'bout you, Auali'i? You goin' behave?" When the roan turned his back, Louie shook his head. "I get no patience fo' dealing wit' his stud antics today."

He reached into the small saddlebag at his hip and selected a few treats for Makalani. "Hold dis out to Rocky Road. He'll come ovah if he t'ink he can get easy food."

As Louie went to the next paddock to deal with his stud, Makalani lured the evasive horse to her and made nice with the treats. Grace watched Makalani tie on the halter, then nickered to the palomino she had ridden before. The mare rubbed Grace's hoodie off her head, exposing an uncombed mop of blond hair.

Grace hugged the palomino's neck. "Her name's Baby."

"She's gorgeous."

"Cow smart too. She has a Thoroughbred's speed and intelligence mixed with a quarter horse's endurance and strength. We work as a team. After Baby and I choose the cow to cut from the herd, I talk to her with the pressure from my legs and by shifting my weight with my lower back and hips. Then I drop my reins and hand to the saddle horn and hang on. It's all her after that. Baby keeps cows under her control."

They led their horses back to the shelter, where Louie selected Makalani's tack and supervised the way she saddled her horse.

He nodded with approval. "How you learn do all dis?"

"My best friend in high school came from a ranching family in Montana. You've met her before. Sandy Hall. She and her parents came to your ranch, maybe fourteen years ago, and bought one of your horses."

"Oh, yeah, I remembah dem. Haole family. Bought a chestnut quarter horse wit' a smooth gait."

Makalani remembered that horse well and the impression Sandy made the day she rode it to school. When the local kids saw her riding like a paniolo, they accepted her into the fold. "Sandy and her parents taught me to ride. I spent a lot of happy days helping out on her ranch in Kapa'a."

"On Kaua'i."

"Yeah."

"Good rain. Too many mountains. Little bit land fo' graze."

"That's one way to describe it."

"How you like da Big Island?"

She smirked. "It's big."

His beautiful eyes narrowed, but as he mounted Auali'i, Makalani noticed a slight grin. His amusement vanished as he maneuvered the impatient stud in tight figure eights.

Grace rode up on Baby, who stood hands taller than Rocky Road. "Saddle up or Uncle will leave you behind."

Rather than head straight up the mountain, the Hiapos headed across the rolling pastures on the mauka side of Kohala Mountain Road toward the sleepy town of Hāwī on the northern tip of the island. Makalani had driven the scenic Highway 250 a couple of times before and had noted the progressive dryness on the makai side down toward the sea. In the dim light before dawn, it all looked the same.

Louie led several paces ahead, wearing only a heavy work shirt to protect him from the cold. By contrast, Makalani had on the padded GORE-TEX jacket she wore on chilly Oregon hikes. Grace split the difference with her hoodie. All of them wore caps, jeans, and work boots, Louie's and Grace's with riding heels and spurs.

"Ease up on the reins," Grace said, circling Baby to walk alongside. "Rocky Road will pick his own way around the rocks and the pits. Just don't let him space out."

"Space out?"

"Yeah. If he's not cutting cattle, that horse can trip on his own feet."

"How will I tell?"

"Watch his ears. If they stop moving for too long and relax to the sides, pat his neck and tell him, 'Ala pā! Wake up!'"

Pick his own way, but don't let him fall asleep?

It seemed contradictory to Makalani, but she'd keep it in mind.

"Oh, and never trot or lope a horse unless you're with one of us. When you do, be sure to ride right behind. There are tons of hazards hidden in the 'āina—hog holes, lava tube skylights, and gulches you won't see until you ride up to the edge."

Makalani nodded. "I rescued a boy from a lava tube cave-in last week. I saw one of those skylights from the inside before I found another way out."

"Fo' real? I thought rangers only gave tours. I never knew they did hero stuff."

"Well, according to my supervisor, we don't."

They shared a laugh.

"Any more of those cattle pits around?" Makalani asked.

"What, like the one Grandad fell into?"

"Sorry. I shouldn't have brought it up."

"Nah, it's a fair question. Not that I know of, but a famous guy died in one on the other side of the island back in the 1800s. You know Douglas fir trees, right?"

"Sure."

"It was the botanist who discovered them."

"He fell into a pit?"

"Maybe. Or maybe he was pushed. People got suspicious when nobody found the gold."

"Gold?"

"I'll tell you the story. It's a good mo'olelo for a long ride like this."

Makalani patted Rocky Road's neck. "This isn't a bedtime story, so don't fall asleep."

Grace circled her long-legged Thoroughbred–quarter horse to match Rocky Road's slower pace.

"Okay, so this botanist, David Douglas from Scotland, traveled to San Francisco and the Pacific Northwest where he discovered the pine trees they named after him. Apparently, the guy introduced hundreds of plants and trees to Britain. Super famous and a notable mountaineer.

"Anyway, on one of his expeditions, he came to Hawai'i Island. He loved it so much, he came back the next year. Climbed all the way up Mauna Loa. Impressive, right? Then he tried to climb Mauna Kea and never made it down."

"What happened?"

"He stopped by a cabin to talk story with his friend. Some say, the friend was an escaped convict from Australia. He was also the one who found Douglas's body in the pit and carted him, his stuff, and his dog back to town. But Douglas was supposed to also have gold. So when the guy never turned it over to the authorities, some people suspected he had robbed Douglas and tossed him in the pit with a bull."

"A bull?"

"Yeah, just like Grandad. It hooked and stomped Douglas to death. Or at least, that's what the friend said when he brought the body into town."

"Was he tried?"

"Nah. Not even charged. Douglas could have been killed by the bull or robbed and murdered by somebody else. Or maybe he never had any gold. The only witness was the friend and supposed ex-convict, who said he found the body in a pit with a bull. But, you know, I doubt they could tell what had actually killed him back then."

Makalani followed Grace's gaze toward the area where her grandfather had been killed.

Had an autopsy been performed on Larry Hiapo?

Makalani wanted to ask but wasn't sure how. "It's hard to believe someone had died like that before."

"Right?" Grace shook off the sudden gloom. "A plaque marks the spot off Mana Road where Douglas died if you ever want to see. The Hawaiians named it Ka Lua Kauka, Doctor's Pit."

Louie turned in his saddle and called at his niece. "Enough talk story, especially 'bout dat."

"Sorry, Uncle."

He continued to glare until Grace bowed her head. The show of dominance felt unwarranted and unnecessarily harsh.

Louie nodded toward the ocean. "Take Makalani across da road and nānā ʻāina below. Check da water and fences. And watch how she rides. I no like her bad habits messing up my horse."

Bad habits? Guess he's not as pleased with my horsemanship as I thought.

He backed up the stud, as if demonstrating what a skilled paniolo and a well-trained horse were able to do. Then he maneuvered Auali'i in a tight circle and spurred him up the slope.

Containing the stud's energy or intentionally showing off?

It didn't matter. Despite her annoyance, Makalani could not look away.

CHAPTER SEVENTEEN

"Hele mai," Grace said, walking Baby into the rising sun's rays and effectively blocking Louie's departing silhouette. If she noticed Makalani's admiration, she didn't let on, only continued to circle in front of Rocky Road and headed downslope.

A fence ran mauka-makai—mountain to sea—on their right, separating the pasture they were in from another beyond. Black and Red Angus grazed throughout the rolling hills.

"Is that land a part of your ranch?"

Grace nodded. "We rotate the pipi every couple days so the grass can recover."

"*Pipi* means cattle?"

"Cattle or cow."

"And *pipi laho* means bull?"

"Now you're learning."

Makalani grinned. "I've helped out with horses, but never with cows. Driving cattle sounds fun."

As she sat taller in her saddle, Rocky Road picked up into a trot.

"Eh," Grace said. "You forget what I said?"

Makalani reined him back. "I didn't do anything."

"Yeah, you did. Louie trained all the lio to react to body tension and seat. When you got excited, he felt your energy and knew you wanted to go."

"How do I let him know I just want to walk?"

"Relax your lower back, hips, and legs. When you want to stop, sink back in the saddle like this."

Without using her reins, Grace stopped Baby with the change in her seat. When Makalani tried the same, Rocky Road stubbornly continued to walk.

Grace laughed. "Kupunakāne says we learn by doing. So you know, ma ka hana ka 'ike—keep practicing, yeah?"

"Is this what your uncle meant when he said I would ruin his horse?"

"Nah, it would take more than that to ruin Rocky Road. You just need to prove to this old guy that you're worthy to lead."

Makalani sighed. "I'm sensing a theme."

"With what?"

"Men."

Grace laughed. "That's why I chose Baby. When she acts up, I still feel like we're on the same side."

Makalani thought about Ranger Machado and Louie as Grace urged her mare ahead to unlock the roadside gate. Neither of her supervisors felt exactly on Makalani's side.

Is that what Louie is, a supervisor?

What else?

Before she could sort through the possibilities, Grace and Baby swung open the perimeter gate. The road was dead quiet.

"Is this where the car alarm spooked Vinnie's horse?"

"Rosie told you about that?"

"Yeah. She said you saved the day."

Grace smiled. "Glad to hear it. I can't always tell what she feels."

Makalani doubted Rosie would want her to know. "Where do you think it came from?"

"The car alarm? From down the road maybe. Hard to tell with the way sound bounces up here. Probably some rich haole with a fancy kine car. I mean look around. If someone came to steal something up here, they'd be after cattle, horses, or land."

"You have cattle rustlers?"

"Nah, just joking with you. Keep close to the fence, aurite? It's not electric so don't worry about that."

Once Rocky Road came through, Grace sidestepped Baby and pushed the gate shut. Even hanging over the side, she was able to indicate through the subtle pressure of her legs and by rolling her spurs where and how Baby should move. Vinnie had probably meant to emulate her in the arena the other day. Once they crossed the road, Grace repeated the process with the oceanside gate.

"Do you ever move cattle across this highway?" Makalani asked.

"All the time. We drive them upslope in early summer when the lowland grass dries out, then back down in the winter when it gets too cold in the mountains for the calves. We have one pā kuni on each side of Kohala Mountain Road."

"Pā kuni?"

"Branding corral. Our pipi are divided into two herds. One herd calves in the autumn, the other calves in the spring."

"Sounds like a lot of work for a small family ranch."

"It is. That's why we're so happy you're here."

"And by *we* you mean?"

"Everyone. Well, except maybe Dad."

Makalani scoffed. "Yeah, except him."

Grace laughed. "Hiapo men. What can you do?"

By the time Grace and Makalani had checked all the water tanks and mineral licks in the lowland plains, the morning sun was high in the air. The makai side of the ranch was a good thousand feet lower in elevation than where they began. It was also on the leeward side of the island where the mountains blocked the trade winds coming in from the east and northeast. Grace had long since stuffed her sweatshirt in a saddlebag. Makalani felt uncomfortably warm, but her jacket had been too bulky to fit. If she had understood the terrain they would ride, she would have left her GORE-TEX in the car.

Grace came over as Makalani struggled to take it off. "Give me the reins. And try not to flap your jacket or Rocky Road will spook."

Makalani had so much to learn, not only about horsemanship but about this family as well. "I'm sorry if I got you in trouble for telling that story about the botanist and the pit."

"Not your fault. Everything's been off since ʻOpihi came home alone."

Yeah, about that . . . If the Hiapo family wakes before dawn to eat breakfast together, wouldn't they sit down to a family dinner as well?

"I'm surprised no one missed your grandfather the night before."

"Usually we would have, but Grammie spent the night at her sister's house. When Grandad didn't come home for dinner, we assumed he had stayed out with his friends."

"Did he do that often?"

"Almost never. But with Grammie away, Dad figured Grandad should have a good time."

"Did your Uncle Louie agree?"

Grace scoffed. "What do you think?"

Instead of answering, Makalani rolled the jacket against her hips and tied the sleeves around her waist.

Grace handed her the reins. "You can say it. Everybody knows Dad and Uncle don't get along. They're too different, like scalloped potatoes and poi."

Makalani paused. "Your dad's the *potato*?"

"Only the fancy kine."

She laughed. "Okay. I can see that."

Kenneth's tailored palaka looked so much nicer than the standard work versions worn by Louie and the other paniolo men, but it was Louie and not Kenneth who had made the greater impression on her. Even a decade on the mainland had not changed Makalani's ideal image of a man—strong, rugged, and Hawaiian like her dad.

Pāpā would love this land.

Peaceful māmā cows and their keiki grazed or lay in the yellow-green grass. The ocean stretched before her toward all the other Hawaiian Islands, ending with Kauaʻi and tiny Niʻihau. Although it was painfully dry, Pāpā would appreciate the expanse. The sheer space of it all would give even the most stress-tensioned person ample room to breathe. For that kind of space on Kaua'i, she and Pāpā had paddled out to sea.

Grace circled Baby in front of Makalani. "Wait here, okay. I need to check on a cow."

As she loped across the plain in her faded T-shirt and jeans it was hard to imagine the cowgirl enjoying the company of her *fancy kine* dad. What would they do together? Shop for hats? It was hard to imagine Kenneth riding the range.

He's a Hiapo, she reminded herself, *born and raised on this ranch.*

Kenneth had paniolo blood from two sides of his family going back to the earliest days and, unlike his sister, Rosie, he still lived and worked on family land. No matter how different he might seem from Louie, Makalani had to assume Kenneth had paniolo skills and was equally committed to Hiapo Ranch.

Grace returned with a smile. "I saw a cow limping, but she just had a rock in her hoof. Eh, let's head back to the house. It's almost time for lunch."

As Grace took off at a lope, Makalani made sure her gelding followed directly behind.

CHAPTER EIGHTEEN

Skip Una sized up the man sitting across the picnic table. Although he had sounded younger than his ninety-one years when they spoke on the phone, Hoʻolohe Reed looked close to death. He must have had his son later in life, because Flint, although ragged, looked younger than Skip. What a loser. How could a man live half a century and have nothing to mark his existence—no money, no accomplishments, no family, just his geriatric dad and a forested plot of land in Waimea he had no resources to exploit?

Skip shivered despite the hot noon sun. Flint Reed's fate could easily have been his.

He sipped the rich local coffee and watched a toddler chase a chicken through the grass in the center of Parker Square. During his high school days, he and his friends would stake out this same picnic table in the sun, eschewing the shady porch seats where tourists and the old-timers like to sit. A trio of ancient paniolo would talk story beneath the Waimea General Store sign, leaning against the barn-red railings in their woven lauhala hats. Skip had yearned to grow old like that.

He still could.

Skip had finally found his golden opportunity to expand Una Ranch, not under the volcanic smog of erupting Kīlauea or the harsh saddle between Mauna Loa and Mauna Kea, and definitely not South Kona's arid desert with its grass-killing bugs. After the bountiful pastures of Oregon, only Waimea, home of the famous Parker Ranch, would do.

"When you get in?" Ho'olohe asked.

"Tuesday morning."

"So, when you spoke with that detective—"

Skip smiled. "I was already here."

Flint shifted in his seat. "You called the cops? Why?"

"To plant a few seeds."

"And grow what?"

"I'm not sure yet. Perhaps you can tell me. You've lived alongside Hiapo Ranch your whole lives. You and your father must have learned something useful about them." When Flint didn't answer, Skip offered a prompt. "What do you know about Roselani Hiapo?"

"Rosie? She teaches at HPA."

"My old stomping ground. Does she help out at the ranch?"

"Not anymore. Her kid rides, though." Flint chuckled. "Don't think she's too happy about that."

"Why not?"

"Rosie's kinda uppity, you know? Too smart to get dirty. It must piss her off that her son wants to hang out with cows."

"You don't like her much, do you?" When Flint's jaw tightened, Skip grinned. "Or maybe too much. A childhood crush?"

"Of course not. I'm older than Kenny. Rosie was just a kid."

"I thought she was only a year younger than Louie."

"Yeah, which is five years younger than me. Why would I care about her?"

The tension in Flint's face suggested he did. Either he had a thing for Rosie, or he felt insulted when he couldn't even befriend the youngest Hiapo kid.

"Well," Skip said. "*If* you cared, you might be able to convince Rosie to back the sale of Hiapo Ranch."

"I guess," Flint said. "I mean, she probably would if she had a say."

"You don't think she does?"

Flint shrugged. "The men run the ranch."

"What about Louie?"

"He's an asshole, just like his dad."

"Were they close?"

"Ha. Close enough to punch."

Skip leaned in. "Are you saying Larry beat his son?"

Flint smirked, emboldened by his sudden upper hand. "When Louie was younger. Then he got bigger and fought back. After that, who knows? It's a big property. We can't see much from our fence."

"Not anymore," Hoʻolohe said bitterly.

"What do you mean?" Skip asked.

"We used to own the southern pastures on both sides of Kohala Mountain Road. After Dad sold um to the neighbors, me and him would ride through a break in the fence and poach the cattle grazing on our old land. One night, we rode all the way to their house and saw Larry's father arguing with *his* father and grandfather. I admired him for standing up to them li'dat, but the food his mom and grandmom cleared away after dinner could have fed me and my dad for a week. Everyone calls Larry's father Kupunakāne now. To me, he will always be Luke. I thought he was different when I was young, but he's Hiapo through and through."

Skip sat back on his bench. Although he harbored his share of resentments, the Reeds had carried theirs for generations. They clearly blamed all their misfortune on the family next door. He filed this away. If Detective Kim refused to investigate Louie Hiapo and became suspicious of him, he could always point her toward Hoʻolohe and Flint.

"They sound like a family of bullies. Could one of Larry's sons have had something to do with his death?"

Flint twitched. "What, like murder?"

Skip shrugged. "Patricide happens."

"Why would you think that?"

"Not me. What matters is what the *police* are led to think."

"Why would you want the police to investigate Kenneth or Louie?"

Hoʻolohe's eyes narrowed with understanding. "To divide the family and make them want to sell."

Skip nodded. “Kenneth is already willing. You said Larry used to beat Louie, but now the son is stronger than him. That gives Louie motive and means.”

Flint shook his head. “Eh, I never liked the guy, but I can’t believe he would kill his own dad.”

“It doesn’t matter what you believe, only what the Hiapos are forced to defend.”

“I don’t get it?”

“Money,” Hoʻolohe said. “That’s what they care about, money and power.”

Skip nodded. “Unless the Hiapos have a big savings I haven’t been able to find, they would need to take out a second mortgage to pay for Louie’s defense. That is, assuming they don’t hang him out to dry. Either way, Kenneth would have a clearer path to sell me their ranch. And don’t forget, if the Hiapos sell, I’ll buy your property too.”

Flint squirmed on the bench.

Hoʻolohe smacked his arm. “What’s the matter with you?”

“Nothing. It’s just, how could someone kill a person with a bull, right? I mean, like, how?”

Skip eyed the grown man fidgeting and babbling like a busted kid. Louie might be squeaky clean, but Flint Reed had something to hide. “We can leave that part to the detectives. What I need is the why and the who. Your dad said you could help.”

“Yeah, but . . . I thought Larry *didn’t* want to sell. Wouldn’t that put him and Louie on the same side?”

“It would, if anyone knew. But I told the detective that Larry and I were about to close on a deal. I threw Louie under the bus because . . . well . . . can you picture Kenneth as a killer?”

“No.”

“Neither would the detective. Louie is the better suspect.”

“Definitely,” Hoʻolohe said. “Louie Hiapo is the best paniolo around. If anyone could figure out how to kill someone with a bull, it would be him.”

Flint grumbled. "I'm sure someone else could figure it out. I mean Louie's good, but he's not the only paniolo around." When his dad flashed him a stink eye, he threw up his hands. "What? I'm just saying he's not the best. If I had grown up with all those advantages, I'd be better than him."

Skip stifled a laugh. How Flint could believe he'd be better than Louie Hiapo at *anything* was a mystery to him. That said, he knew from experience how helpful the unsavory types could be—provided he never used the same person twice.

"Look, we all want the same thing here, Flint. You seem like a resourceful guy. How do *you* think we can convince the Hiapos to sell?"

Skip sipped his coffee as the gears turned in Flint's mind. Now that Larry was dead, Skip needed someone—anyone—to clear his path to buying Hiapo Ranch.

CHAPTER NINETEEN

Fragrant smoke billowed from the giant steel grill as chicken grease hit the coals. A middle-aged ranch hand Makalani had yet to meet plucked the charred thighs off the racks. His lean, strong arms glistened from the heat. A baseball cap protected his already sunbaked face. He reminded her of what Aunty Kaualana's skinny husband, Uncle Eric, would look like if he got off his ʻōkole and worked.

The ranch hand added grilled corn to the platter of huli huli chicken and set it on the buffet table beside the macaroni salad, cone sushi, and fruit.

Makalani chose a cone sushi from a platter and bit through the tofu pocket into the sweet vinegared rice. She could tell from the juiciness of the deep-fried inari age that the sushi was homemade. Although she could get the tofu pockets in grocery stores on the mainland, they came in disappointing rectangular shapes. Only people in Hawaiʻi cut the pockets diagonally to make them look like a cone.

Grace grabbed one too.

Makalani nodded toward the skinny man at the grill. "Is that your other ranch hand?"

"Who, Lono? Nah, he lives up the road on a small section of our ranch. He cooks in exchange for room and board. He also helps with the machinery and UTVs. Handy guy to have around. Keeps to himself. Doesn't take up much space. The pipi treat him like he's one of their own." She ate the cone sushi in two bites. "Eh, will you grab the paper plates from the kitchen? Grammie left them by the counter."

"Sure, be right back."

But when Makalani entered the main house, Kenneth's angry voice traveled down the hall.

"We cannot abandon our cow-calf operation on a whim."

Although quieter than his brother, Louie's voice sounded more in command. "Just because you nevah consider somet'ing no make it a whim."

Makalani paused. Grace had sent her for plates. Although she didn't want to intrude, if she went back empty-handed, she would have to explain. It seemed smarter to grab what she needed and keep her mouth shut. Her ears were another matter. The intensity in Louie's voice made him hard to ignore.

"Our beef need stay at home. Not ship all ovah dakine place, den come back to us at triple da price."

"That isn't our concern," Kenneth shouted.

"Yeah, it is. Da kuleana is ours and dat of every oddah kanaka rancher."

"Oh, and now you're speaking on behalf of the entire Hawai'i beef industry? And here I thought you were just a cowboy."

"See? Dass exactly what's wrong wit' you, brah. Paniolo were nevah *just* cowboy. You would know dat if you evah took your nose out o' da books. All you care 'bout is money. You no mahalo our paniolo traditions. You no mālama what happens to da Hawaiian people. You no respect or care 'bout not'ing except what dey taught you at school."

When Kenneth spoke again, his voice sounded smug. "Then why did Dad put me in charge?"

"He nevah did dat."

"Sure he did. I handle the business. You move the cows and clean up the shit."

Makalani froze in the kitchen, one hand on the plates.

"Are you fo' real, brah?" Louie said. "You don't know da first t'ing 'bout what I do. If not fo' me, you and Dad would have not'ing to sell."

"Dad's dead."

Louie scoffed. "How convenient fo' you."

"What's that supposed to mean?"

"I don't know, brah. Maybe because Dad was checking wit' da slaughterhouses befo' he died?"

"For what?"

"To see if dey could handle processing our herds when we switched our operation from cow-calf to Hawai'i-finished beef."

"Bullshit."

"No lie. And what's mo' . . . I bet you knew."

The silence that followed sucked in Makalani's whirling thoughts. Could Louie actually believe Kenneth was responsible for their father's death? Was Larry Hiapo planning to change the direction of the ranch as the younger brother claimed, or had he actually put the more-educated elder brother in charge? What, if anything, did this have to do with Larry Hiapo's gruesome death?

A door slammed into a wall. Boots stomped down the hallway. Kenneth yelled for his brother to come back and explain what he meant.

Makalani hurried toward the kitchen door and ducked around the corner as the brothers came into view.

Kenneth grabbed Louie's arm and spun him around. "Take it back."

Louie shoved him into the wall. "Wassa mattah, brah, you no like da truth?"

Kenneth held out his hands. "Truth about what? Are you seriously suggesting I had something to do with Dad's death?"

Louie pulled him in by his shirt. "Did you?"

"Of course not. Did you?" Kenneth practically spit.

Louie shoved him away. *"Me?"*

"You're the one throwing around accusations."

"So?"

"That's what guilty people do. It's called deflection. If you had taken a college course in psychology, you would have known to avoid it. Oh, I forgot. You never made it to college. You dropped out of school."

Makalani cringed at the low blow. Even between brothers, the dig seemed especially harsh.

Louie pounded his fist on the wall. "I took da GED."

"After the fact."

"What difference dat make on a ranch? School no can teach what I know and what I do."

"Which makes me wonder," Kenneth said. "Why didn't you go after that lost bull?"

Makalani held her breath, waiting for Louie's response. She had been wondering the same thing. By all accounts, Larry Hiapo had stepped back from paniolo work. Why would he come out of semiretirement to chase down a lost bull?

When Louie didn't answer, Kenneth threw up his hands and walked out of her line of sight. "I don't have time for this nonsense, I have a business to run."

His footsteps retreated up the hallway.

Has Kenneth taken over his father's office?

With Rosie in Waimea Town with Brian, where did her brothers sleep? It seemed to Makalani, the home court advantage went to anyone who occupied the big house.

She was so lost in her thoughts, she didn't notice the heavy tread of boots until Louie crashed into her side.

"Whatchu doin' hea?"

She held up the stack of paper plates. "Fetching this for Grace."

He had her off balance in more ways than one. The very same qualities that had impressed her about Louie made every nerve in her body scream to take flight. This was not the same cowboy who had helped her catch and manage her horse. That man had been formidable but fair, honest in his assessment of her abilities while encouraging her to improve. The angry man in front of her was nothing like that. His masculine brows had knit into a furious ridge, and his strong Hawaiian jaw was clenched hard enough to crack rock. He was larger and more muscular than her father, who was already taller and heavier than her.

Although she usually welcomed the natural order of things, where she didn't tower over men, at this moment, Louie's size and aggression made her feel weak.

I'm a ranger, not a child.

As Louie invaded her space, she planted her feet and remained perfectly still. If he had been a horse and not a man, she would have pushed him away and reminded him who was boss. In the Hiapo kitchen, all she could do was stand her ground and try not to blink as his hot breath hit her eyes.

His chest expanded as he inhaled, imposing his dominance and making her feel confined. With such close proximity, his whispering voice came out like a growl. "Dis not your place."

"You're right. I'll pack up and leave."

He grunted in exasperation. "I meant take da plates outside and get somet'ing to eat."

Makalani blinked in confusion. Louie turned his aggression on and off like flipping a switch.

He stepped aside to let her pass. "Aftah lunch, we get fences to build." The raging bull had vanished. The intriguing man had returned.

The heat of his breath still clung to her skin.

If I share something with him, will he open up to me?

Although Makalani knew she should go, she wanted to stay.

"My sister and I are very different."

When he didn't respond, she headed out of the kitchen in defeat.

"As different as Kenneth and me?"

She turned carefully, as if facing a wild animal on a trail. "More so. My sister, Pua, is carefree and fun. She's pretty and flirtatious, loves to party. She works as a hostess in a Waikīkī restaurant, but if she could live near the action and not have to work, she would. Everybody loves her even though she never helps out." Makalani sighed. "She's half my size yet so much brighter and bigger than me, like a star with her own gravitational pull." She shut her mouth, embarrassed by what had rolled out.

"Yeah," he said. "Your sistah sounds plenny different from you."

Although he had agreed, a part of her wished he had not.

I can be fun . . . sometimes.

But that wasn't it. Makalani had hoped he would argue that she was prettier than she believed.

It doesn't matter what he thinks.

Except, for some reason, it did.

"Your sister stay on O'ahu, living her own life. But Kenneth and me both live and work on da same ranch."

She nodded. "Yeah, that's harder, for sure."

His eyes pinched in annoyance. "So maybe you should keep your opinions to yourself." He stormed out of the kitchen, leaving her shocked and confused.

What in the absolute hell?

A second ago, they had seemed to connect. How could a person flip switches so fast?

Her father's stern voice filled the space where Louie had been. "When a man shows you who he is, Makalani, you bettah believe."

CHAPTER TWENTY

By the time Makalani returned, a small crowd had gathered for lunch.

Grace hurried over and took the plates while her grandmother, Rumiko, escorted her father-in-law to the front of the line. Although ninety-seven, Kupunakāne moved as spryly as her. Was ranching the secret to longevity, or did the Hiapos have good genes? Either way, Kupunakāne's son had been cheated out of decades of life.

When Rumiko motioned Kenneth and Grace forward, Makalani marveled at how different and alike a father and daughter could be. Although Grace looked haole and Kenneth Japanese, both had the thick Hiapo brows and broad face from their Hawaiian and Mexican genes. Kenneth was polished, his daughter was rough. If Makalani hadn't known they were related, she might have assumed Grace was a cowgirl on loan from the mainland or another Big Island ranch.

Makalani searched for Grace's uncle to compare and found him by a silver pickup truck in a heated conversation with a local man she hadn't met. Her fixation was broken by a gentle touch on her arm.

Rumiko looked up from Makalani's side. "Mahalo for getting the plates. I forget so many things these days." Despite her work shirt and jeans, she looked as fragile as a doll.

"I'm happy to help. And mahalo for the lunch."

Rumiko waved away the thanks. "Did you enjoy your morning ride with Louie and Grace?"

"I did. Your land is beautiful."

She offered a sad smile. "Larry called it his ʻāina nui, his abundant land." She nodded toward the picnic table where Kenneth was needlessly assisting his grandfather to sit. "Really, though, it belongs to him."

"Kenneth?"

She coughed out a laugh. "No, this ranch belongs to Kupunakāne no matter who does the work."

Makalani thought about her grandmother's homestead. Regardless of who helped out or even held the Hawaiian Homeland lease, as long as Tūtū was alive, the Anahola farm would always be hers. Makalani's grandparents had secured the original lease, cleared the jungle for the fruit and nut trees they wanted to plant, and walled in the mud loʻi by the river where their kalo would grow. Pahukulas had cared for their ʻāina through three generations and, God willing, would continue to care for it in the generations ahead. Is that what Rumiko meant about Kupunakāne, or did the Hiapo patriarch have something else in mind for his ranch?

Rumiko rubbed her cracked and wrinkled hands. The hapa-Japanese woman had to be seventy. From what Makalani could tell, the tiny woman still did a lion's share of the work. Why the bitter comment about Kupunakāne? Didn't Rumiko feel the ranch also belonged to her?

Meanwhile, Louie's posture had solidified into stubborn defiance as he listened to the newcomer by the silver truck. The man was shorter and leaner than Louie, with a horseshoe mustache and a scraggly goatee. His long black hair glistened as if rubbed with coconut oil to keep it contained. Whatever the topic, Rumiko's second son clearly did not agree.

Makalani nodded toward the men. "Who's that with Louie?"

Rumiko's mouth pinched with distaste. "Bad fish I can't seem to throw out."

Makalani blinked in surprise. The comment sounded particularly vehement coming from her. Although, compared to Louie's handsome vitality, the newcomer had a dark, almost slippery vibe—Scar to Simba or Vader to Obi-Wan. That said, if Makalani had seen the newcomer without Louie around, she might have admired his wilder appearance, the polar opposite of Louie's closely cropped hair and clean-shaven face. In fact, aside from their shared Hawaiian ancestry, the men looked and behaved nothing alike.

Bad Fish gestured emphatically, then clenched his hands into fists. His expression alternated between cajoling and disgust.

Who is he, and what does he want Louie to do?

Rumiko blushed with embarrassment. "Forgive me, my comment was unkind."

"No need to apologize."

The woman had lost her life partner only nine days ago, the same day Corey's father had almost lost him. One soul taken, another soul remained. Did God make these decisions, or was it bad luck or fate?

Rumiko sighed. "I fear we will need Malu's help even more now that Larry is gone."

"Is he the hired ranch hand Kenneth mentioned at breakfast?"

"Yes. They don't get along."

Makalani looked back at the men. The energy of the conversation had changed. Instead of defiant, Louie looked exasperated and tired.

Why had the Hiapos hired a man no one seemed to like?

"It doesn't matter," Rumiko said. "We all need to accept. Malu is family, like it or not."

"Family?"

Rumiko shrugged. "Soon to be, or is . . . I don't know. Close enough. The point is, his opinions will matter even more now that Larry isn't here to object. Guess I better get used to the smell of . . ."

"Bad fish?"

Rumiko's hand covered her smile but couldn't hide the amusement in her eyes. "I'll grow to love him in time or, at least, dislike him a little less. What choice do I have? Louie chose him."

Makalani's stomach clenched. "So, he's not just a ranch hand?"

"No, he's much more than that." She squeezed her eyes as if to dispel an ill thought. "One day, Malu could be running Hiapo Ranch."

Makalani studied the men more closely and noticed clues in their body language she had not noticed before—the mirroring of posture, the inclination of their heads. Although quarreling, they stood closer than angry men normally would. Louie and Malu were lovers. But what did that actually mean?

Aside from me being a fool?

As confusing as Louie was to her, Makalani couldn't deny the strong attraction she had felt. Just remembering his proud stature as he rode his blue roan stallion up the slope caused an unwelcome warmth to rise up her neck.

"Are you feeling okay, dear?"

Makalani had forgotten all about Rumiko.

"You're probably dehydrated from the ride. Drink extra water with lunch."

Makalani had forgotten about that as well.

"Mahalo, Aunty, I will."

Rumiko motioned her ahead. "You first. Take two scoops of rice. The carbohydrates will give you energy for whatever work Louie has planned."

"Will Malu be joining us?"

Rumiko shrugged. "He usually does. Excuse me a moment, I need something from the house."

As she left, Louie and Malu approached. Or was it the other way around and she had left *because* they approached? Perhaps Larry's widow had not accepted the inevitable quite yet.

Which inevitability, Malu as a son-in-law or Malu as the boss?

Makalani hung back from the buffet table and watched the others react. Kenneth stabbed his chicken thigh with his fork as they passed. *No surprise there.* His wife, Carolyn, flashed him a cautionary look. *Peacekeeper? Or the control behind the man?*

Grace popped her chin in salutation, her expression a mask. "Eh, Malu, about time you showed up."

"Howzit," he said, then inclined his head to Louie's grandfather in respect. "I like give everyone room fo' grieve."

Kupunakāne nodded and greeted Malu with a long stream of ʻōlelo Hawaiʻi. Malu replied in kind. Their fluent Hawaiian blended words together in a poetry of sound that Makalani couldn't translate, exactly, yet still understood. *Hanohano* meant honored, *kūpuna* meant elders, and *mahalo iā mākou* meant gratitude to us. Malu's response had ended with *iā ʻoe i ka mahalo*, which was a gracious way of giving thanks back to Kupunakāne. The respect and appreciation between these men was clear. Whether or not they were aligned in other ways, they were bonded by ʻōlelo Hawaiʻi that so few kānaka maoli spoke in their daily lives.

Louie's scowl softened into a hint of a smile.

Kenneth tore off the chicken thigh meat with his teeth.

Carolyn slipped her hand onto her husband's knee while their daughter, Grace, shoveled in another mouthful of food.

The huli huli cook beckoned Makalani forward with his tongs, then dumped a half chicken on her plate. "Come back if you like grind more."

"Mahalo, I'm good." Makalani had more pressing thoughts on her mind than food.

Larry's widow said the ranch belonged to Kupunakāne no matter who did the work. She had also said Malu, who was apparently Louie's lover, might one day run Hiapo Ranch. After the exchange in ʻōlelo Hawaiʻi she had witnessed between Malu and Kupunakāne, Rumiko's fear made more sense.

Makalani watched Kenneth brood over his food. Although he claimed his father had put him in charge, maybe it was his brother who would benefit from their father's death.

"Dat chicken not goin' eat itself." Louie stood behind her, waiting for his turn.

"Oh, sorry about that."

She moved out of the way, wondering if she been staring at Malu and, if so, what Louie must think. Makalani had never been good at hiding her feelings, as her family continually pointed out. This was especially true when she was attracted to a guy. Had Louie noticed her interest in him?

How obvious had I been?

She wasn't like her sister who flirted and dated with ease. If a man didn't show an interest in Pua, she wrote him off quick. When that rare occurrence happened, she usually assumed he was gay.

"Pua would have known," she mumbled.

"Whatchu say?"

"Huh?"

"Just now," Louie said, annoyance rising in his voice.

She was making an embarrassing situation even worse. She needed to control the narrative and pretend she had never felt anything for him other than respect.

"Deny, deny, deny," Pua would say. "No one knows anything for sure unless you confess."

Beyond the picnic tables, Malu had left Kupunakāne to fish for a soda from a bucket of ice.

"Is that your hired ranch hand?" she asked, as if she didn't already know.

Louie scoffed. "You could say dat. He one good paniolo—when he like show up."

Makalani was surprised. "He doesn't live here?"

Louie blew out a gust of frustration. "Beats me. His friend leases a small ranch on Mauna Kea. Sometimes, he stay ovah dea." He shook his head. "Whatevah. He's hea now, right? Not my business what he like do wit' his free time."

Not his business? Were they lovers or not?

Louie's relationship—if he even had one—didn't sound as solid as his mother believed. Either that, or his trouble with Malu was the source of her concern. Based on Louie's reaction, his lover had the power, or at least the freedom to do and go wherever he wished. It didn't make sense to Makalani since, in her eyes, Louie was the much better catch. Not only was he infinitely more handsome, he was an heir to a magnificent ranch. After the authority she had seen him exert over horses and people, it confounded her that he would let his lover's careless behavior slide.

Unless Malu wasn't careless at all.

Makalani had so many questions, but Louie had turned away to fill up his plate. How long had his lover been gone? Were they in a committed relationship, or was Louie about to cut him loose? What were Malu's ambitions and influence on this ranch?

"What?" Louie asked, when he caught her staring at him.

"Nothing. I'm just spacing out."

And wondering if Malu could somehow be responsible for your father's death.

CHAPTER TWENTY-ONE

Rona zipped up her new parka as she took a seat beside the open window at Detective Dan's desk. Although the man had enough meat on his ribs to not mind the cold, skinny-ass Rona was still shivering from the morning frost. The sun had warmed the streets by midday, but none of those sunbeams shone on her.

Dan tipped his chair back on two legs. "I don't know, Rona. This Skip Una sounds full of shit. The Hiapos have one of the first ranches on the island. I can't believe Larry would sell. Even if he wanted to, his old man is still alive and would never consent."

"How old is old?"

"Hmm . . . gotta be close to ninety-eight by now."

Rona shrugged. "Doesn't sound like much of an obstacle."

Dan scoffed. "Only because you've never met Luke."

"Luke, Larry, and Louie? The family has a thing about *l*'s."

"Yeah. They broke the pattern with Kenneth, then picked it up again. Actually, I could see *him* wanting to sell. He's the polar opposite of Louie, more of a city boy, like you."

The unfavorable comparison made Dan's preference between brothers clear. Was that why he found it so hard to believe a *true paniolo* like their father would want to sell his family's ranch to Skip?

"Maybe Larry wanted out," she said.

"I doubt that very much."

"We could interview the family."

"And stir up bad feelings? For what, because some rancher from Oregon called on the phone?"

"He says he's from the Big Island. His name is Skip Una. You said you know everyone."

"In Waimea maybe. Hawai'i Island is *big*. Skip Una doesn't ring a bell. Besides, our cases are backed up. We can't afford to waste any more time on a ranching accident."

"What if I check with the banks to see if the Hiapo family have any outstanding loans or if their mortgage is upside down. Larry might have had reasons to sell that his elder son knew about and his younger son did not."

Dan tipped his teetering chair forward with a thud. "No you won't, because this case is closed. Turn in the paperwork. We're moving on to the next."

"But—"

"But nothing. You've been here all of one month, Detective Kim. Waimea isn't like Honolulu. Our community was built around and thrives because of the ranching industry. Have you not noticed the shopping centers and schools bearing the Parker Ranch name? And they're just the biggest. We also have Ponoholo Ranch, Hiapo Ranch, Kahua Ranch—which, in case you didn't know, is owned by our state senator. Are you starting to realize what you obviously do *not* understand?"

Rona nodded.

"The Hiapos trace their roots to the early Mexican vaqueros and the Hawaiian paniolo they taught. They acquired one of the first parcels of ranch land. Luke's father added even more. The man died in a riding accident on one of their pastures and left the ranch to Luke when he was only seventeen. Like I said, there is no way that old man would have allowed his son to sell."

Rona shrugged. "Unless he's too feeble to have a say."

"Don't even go there. In this community, we show our kūpuna respect."

Rona grimaced but refused to feel shame. She understood respect and filial piety as much as, if not more than, he did. As with many

Korean and other Asian families, her grandmother still lived with her parents as she and Harabeoji had when Rona was a child. Although Rona's grandfather had passed on many years earlier, Halmeoni would stay with Rona's parents for as long as she lived.

"I would never call Luke Hiapo feeble to his 'ohana. I only said it to you because I think we need to consider all angles of this case."

Dan shoved back his chair. "We have. File the papers, and tell Animal Control to release the damn bull."

"It's only been under observation for eight days. What if we want to order more tests or have it checked out by a vet?"

"For what, lethargy? The initial toxicology came back clean, and the rancher says the bull spends all his time lounging under a tree. If he were any calmer, he'd be asleep." He grabbed his sunglasses off his desk. "I have meetings in Kona. Take care of this today."

He walked out of the office, leaving Rona steaming at his desk. She unzipped her parka, and cranked open the window as far as it would go. She had four hours to find a justifiable reason for keeping that bull where it was.

CHAPTER TWENTY-TWO

Makalani wolfed down her chicken, keeping her eyes fixated on the plate so Malu wouldn't catch her staring at him. She had lost her appetite, but Tūtū had raised her to never waste food. Besides, the sooner she finished, the sooner she could distance herself from people and think.

Tūtū's calming voice entered her mind as it often did during times of stress. "E hoʻolohi, Makalani. You have to slow down."

As always, her grandmother was right—not only about eating, but about how she should proceed. Makalani needed to take her time and consider all possibilities. Any hint of suspicion that Larry Hiapo had been murdered would rip this ʻohana apart, which was the exact opposite of what her cousin Brian had convinced Rosie she could do.

"Remember how Makalani helped her ʻohana sort through their problems?" he had said. "Maybe she can do the same for yours."

Now Rosie expected her to look out for Vinnie, check into her father's death, *and* mend the rift between her brothers so her family could heal.

Am I the family therapist now? Auwē! As if a law enforcement ranger wasn't enough.

Makalani choked on the corn. Did she actually believe Louie's paniolo boyfriend could have somehow killed his father with a bull? The idea was ludicrous. Yet, he might have a motive if Larry Hiapo had been standing in Louie's way. Kenneth claimed their father wanted him in control. Rumiko insinuated that Malu might one day run the ranch.

How could that happen unless Louie was in charge and made his lover his second in command?

She swallowed the last bite of corn and dumped her plate in the trash. According to Rumiko, the only person in this ʻohana with the power to decide was disappearing across the field.

Makalani found Kupunakāne on the concrete lānai of a small corrugated steel barn. Rust had tinged parts of the metal walls and roof to a reddish-brown hue. The rest was aged with various shades of gray. A tiny, weathered house stood close by, its blistered turquoise skin scaling like eczema to reveal previous coats of green, yellow, and peach. It sat on a plantation-era foundation, the kind with wood posts set on manini tofu blocks. *Manini* meant poured in ʻōlelo Hawaiʻi. *Tofu* described how the poured concrete blocks looked. Makalani had helped rebuild houses with foundations like this and brought them up to code. The tiny house and barn appeared even older than the elderly man kneeling on the hard lānai floor with a cattleman's knife poised over the cured hide.

Makalani held out a napkin-wrapped treat. "Aloha mai, Kupunakāne. They brought out brownies after you left. I thought you might like one for dessert."

He gave her a well-practiced stink eye and returned to his work. "Mo' like Grace sent you to fatten me up."

Makalani smiled at his mistaken assumption. "Or maybe your moʻopuna wants you to take a well-earned break."

He shrugged. "Whatevah. Put um on da bench. I no goin' eat not'ing until I stay done wit' my work."

He held the hide in place and continued his spiral cut from the edge. The previously cut strip trailed up and down the deck. A drying rack stood in the sun beside an empty, shallow steel tub. Kupunakāne's project had already required many laborious steps.

He noticed her watching and leaned into the cut. "My son start dis kaula 'ili befo' he die. I t'ink, maybe if I finish it fo' him, his 'uhane ho'opilikia will leave our ranch and go to pō where it belongs."

The old man thinks his son's spirit is haunting the ranch?

"What about Larry's spirit feels disturbed?"

"Hard to explain. But, you know, a faddah can tell."

He shook off the sudden bout of grief and dug his blade deeper into the hide. Makalani could tell by the tension in his forearm how difficult it must be. At least twenty feet of the three-inch strip trailed around the lānai.

"Did you cut all of this yourself?"

"Yeah. Larry soaked um in lime and scraped off da hair. Den he soaked um two mo' days in da sun and stretched um on dat frame ovah dea. He followed da old traditions I taught."

"How about your grandsons?"

"Ha. One say he too busy to learn, da oddah no care."

Makalani could easily guess which brother was who, although neither seemed to match their grandfather's ideal.

"What will you do with the rawhide after it's cut?"

"Braid it into kaula 'ili. You know what dat is? Dakine lasso paniolo use to rope pipi. *Kaula* means strap or rope. *'Ili* means leather. *Paniolo* means cowboy. *Pipi* means cattle or cow. If you goin' kōkua—help out on dis ranch—you goin' need learn wala'au kanaka."

"What's wala'au kanaka?"

"Paniolo talk. Been li'dat from befo' time when da Mexican vaqueros try teach da Hawaiians and oddah locals how fo' do cowboy work."

Makalani thought about the terms she had heard Louie and Grace use.

"What does nana 'āina mean?"

He frowned at her pronunciation. "Not *nana* like a type of kalo you grow to make poi, *nānā* like notice or inspect. When paniolo nānā 'āina, we examine da health of da land, da grass, and da water. We check da fences and make sure da māmā and keiki cows stay hauʻoli—happy—and olakino maikaʻi—in good health."

Makalani remembered the mineral licks, water troughs, and limping cow Grace had checked. Louie had probably done the same on the upland pastures.

Kupunakāne wiped his brow and cut another curved section of rawhide. "We also look out fo' wild pigs we can hunt. Puaʻa cause big damage to grazing land. At least we no get wild sheep ovah hea, not like da ranchers on Mauna Kea. Some of dem poor buggahs get hundreds of hipa ʻāhiu eating up da grass."

"Louie said Malu has a friend with a Mauna Kea ranch."

Kupunakāne nodded. "Hard worker. Rough land. Get oddah business on da side. No can survive by ranching alone. He make little bit money by hosting hunters on his land. He and Malu do lots of good work."

"Good work with ranching?"

"Yeah, dat too."

Makalani wanted to ask more, but Kupunakāne waved the subject away. If she didn't hold his attention, he might do the same to her. "We don't have sheep on my home island, but the puaʻa cause problems for us as well."

"No hea mai ʻoe?" he asked. *Where are you from?*

"Anahola, Kauaʻi."

"Ah," he said. "Beautiful ovah dea."

She smiled, grateful for the first compliment she had heard about her island since she arrived. "It's beautiful here too."

"Yeah it is. My great-grandmother, Lalama, and her husband, Pauʻole, were awarded part of dis ahupuaʻa—land division from mountain to sea—during da Great Māhele and da Kuleana Act of 1850. You know 'bout dis?"

Makalani sighed. She was well familiar with the great land division in which King Kamehameha III ended the Hawaiian feudal system by dividing the land equally between the Hawaiian nobility, the konohiki headmen, and the maka'āinana who worked the land. Although the king's intention had been to protect all his people, most of the commoners, like Makalani's ancestors, didn't understand why or how they needed to apply. After two years had passed, maka'āinana—commoners—like the Pahukulas lost their title rights. If not for this, her 'ohana might own millions of dollars' worth of land.

"It's a sore topic in my family" was all she could say.

"Ah, your ancestors nevah apply?"

"They did not."

"E kala mai ia'u." *I'm sorry.*

"Mahalo. It was a long time ago, but Pāpā and Tūtū still put up a fight."

He nodded in approval. "More kānaka should. Unfortunately, my son did not agree. He say, 'Too late for them already. Why fight for something you can nevah get back?'" Kupunakāne sighed. "Easy to say when your 'ohana own da 'āina and da grass your cattle eat."

Kupunakāne cut another long strip of hide.

"You know, my mother's faddah was plenny kine rich. He owned hotels in Hawai'i, oddah places too. When my mother got married, my grandfaddah gave um fifty head as a wedding gift and enough money to buy da lower portion of our neighbor's ranch. You know most Hawai'i ranchers lease, right? Even da big ones like Parker Ranch dat own plenny kine land still lease little bit hea and dea. But dey can handle if da government take um back."

Makalani nodded. "Tūtū leases her homestead from DHHL."

"Den you know. Department of Hawaiian Home Lands get one hundred thousand acres on Mauna Kea, but dey only awarded t'ree leases. *Three.* Dass it. No water, no power, no not'ing. Just lava fields and whatevah tough grass can grow in between. Dass what our government do fo' Hawaiians around hea. Ranchers who have cared fo' da same land ovah generations, are now on a month-to-month lease. 'A'ole pololei! Dis not right. We need mo' young Hawaiians like Malu to speak up and resist."

Makalani perked up. The connection between Kupunakāne and Malu went deeper than their fluency and use of the Hawaiian language. They also appeared to be politically aligned.

"I'm guessing Malu and Larry did not see eye to eye."

"Eye to eye?" Kupunakāne laughed. "If Larry had his way, he would have kicked dat māhū to da street."

The old man used the word *māhū* without any rancor or distaste. A third gender had been acknowledged in Hawaiian culture since precolonial days. Back then, moe aikāne—sleep friends—were valued and treasured, even among royalty. That acceptance changed when the missionaries arrived and spread their moral ideals. Sodomy laws were enacted that would take over a hundred years to retract. Makalani was glad that modern Hawaiian attitudes were more aligned with their precolonial past.

"Was Larry aware of their . . . friendship?"

Kupunakāne squinted at her. "You always dis polite?"

"I do my best."

He laughed. "My son nevah mind how Louie was, only who he chose. Larry hated Malu from da first time he get up in his face."

"About how the ranch should be run?"

"Dat, and da future of Hawaiʻi. Malu get strong opinions but, you know . . . i ulu nō ka lālā i ke kumu . . . branches grow from da trunk. We only hea because of our ancestors. Malu knows dis. He should have treated his boyfriend's faddah wit' mo' respect."

Kupunakāne rubbed spit in his hands and continued cutting the hide.

"You don't share Malu's opinions?"

"Of course I do. Dass not da point. Would you talk to your boyfriend's faddah li'dat?"

Makalani shook her head. "Not unless he was abusive to me or to someone powerless." She didn't add that she had never had an official boyfriend on whose father she could test her resolve.

"Powerless. Malu? Not a chance. Larry was plenny kine stubborn, and he could put up a fight. But whatchu mean by abusive, like punching and stuff?"

"That, or using language that is insulting or harsh."

"Sheesh, sounds like every argument dey evah had. But Larry nevah got physical wit' Malu."

"How about with Louie?"

"*Louie?* He breaks studs into cow horses. Larry taught him to be strong. Boys need discipline, especially on a ranch, and dat boy gave back whatevah his makua kāne dish out."

Makalani studied the Hiapos' patriarch as he returned to his work.

Had Kupunakāne just told her his son beat his kid? If so, it must have been a long time in the past because Louie was considerably stronger and bigger than any of the Hiapo men, including his father, based on the family photographs Makalani had seen in the main house. Why wouldn't Kupunakāne consider that abuse?

Unless he had been raised the same way.

From the shoving match Makalani had witnessed between brothers, she had a fair idea of what Kupunakāne meant by strong.

She stared at the old man hunched over the hide, arm trembling as he struggled to finish the work his son had begun. She remembered the grief choking his voice as he spoke during the memorial in front of Larry's favorite wiliwili tree. Makalani knew that love did not discount the possibility of abuse, and yet, she could not bring herself to believe this of him. When Kupunakāne exhaled a gust of frustration, she knew why.

So like Pāpā.

It was so obvious, she was surprised she hadn't recognized it before. Their devotion to family, dedication to work, passion for justice. In truth, the same could be said of Tūtū and her. No wonder she felt a kinship for this kupuna. He embodied everything she missed about home. If she had been his moʻopuna—his granddaughter—she would have stuck by his side and learned everything she could. How foolish his grandchildren were to let the opportunity slip by.

Kupunakāne wiped off his blade. "I bettah stop. My bad feelings goin' ruin dis work."

Makalani smiled. "Hoʻopilikia ka manaʻo maikaʻi ʻole i ka hana." *Negative thoughts ruin the work.*

His eyes widened in surprise to hear her recite the Hawaiian proverb. "How you know dis ʻōlelo noʻeau?"

"My tūtū teaches me."

"You fortunate to have her."

"And your ʻohana is fortunate to have you."

He shrugged. "I hope my family feel dis way. Pōmaikaʻi mākou—we are blessed. Dass why my grandparents name my faddah Lucky, so dey nevah fo'get and so he continue da good luck."

"What did your parents name you?"

"Luke."

"Lucky, Luke, Larry . . . Why did your son break the tradition with Kenneth?"

"Auwē. Larry stay mad at me back den. He like go college on Oʻahu, but I needed help on da ranch. My faddah die young, only forty-seven li'dat." Kupunakāne scoffed. "Guess he wasn't as lucky as everybody hope. Anyways, when Larry's wife get hāpai, I say, 'Dass it, you gotta stay, work here, and care fo' da child.' Anger rose in him like I nevah see."

Kupunakāne sighed. "I like t'ink he name his first child Kenneth out of aloha for my wife, Kanani, because she wen' college like he wanted to do. But, in my heart, I know he did it to hurt me." Kupunakāne sheathed his knife and set it reverently on the hide. "Larry named his second son Louie aftah we made peace. Even so, everybody knows da kids got da wrong names."

Makalani lowered her eyes, affording him privacy and concealing her thoughts. Could the rift between brothers have begun with their names? It wouldn't be the first time a break in tradition had upset the hierarchy of birth. Kenneth could have felt shoved out of his place. Louie could have felt mandated to lead. Or perhaps their names dictated who they would become: a college graduate like Kanani and a paniolo like Luke.

Makalani pictured slender Kenneth in his tailored palaka shirt. Had his younger brother's size and aptitude with horses and cattle made Kenneth not want to compete as a paniolo? In any event, it must have been hard on the eldest to not have been given his younger brother's name.

"Who came between your great-grandmother and Lucky? Did that child's name begin with an *l*?"

"Nah. Lalama named her son Hiapo, which means first. Hawaiians nevah use last names back den. So when Kamehameha IV signed da surname law, dey registered Hiapo as his last name. Since da law say he needed a haole first name, he called himself Guy."

Kupunakāne arched his stiff back. "Enough talk. Grace is right, dis old man need eat. Hand ovah dat brownie, yeah?"

Makalani helped him to stand and brought him to the bench. "Mahalo for sharing your history with me."

"Noʻu ka hauʻoli." *The pleasure is mine.*

He patted her arm. "Come by if you like hear more. I enjoy talk story wit' you."

"Mahalo, Tūtū," she said, using the affectionate grandparent word young people use for their elders, instead of the more formal Grandfather everyone in his family used for him. If he had been of a younger generation, she would have called him Uncle instead.

He smiled as if he liked it, but shook his head all the same. "I been Kupunakāne long time already. Dass good enough fo' me."

The rumbling of a four-person UTV interrupted them as it drove across the dirt and braked beyond the drying rack, kicking up a cloud of dust.

"ʻĀwīwī, Makalani," Grace shouted. "We gotta go."

CHAPTER TWENTY-THREE

Makalani held the grab bar as Grace sped across the plains, dodging mounds and dips as if loping on her horse. She slowed to the speed of a trot as the obstacles increased, then crept at a pace Baby would have walked.

"No horses?" Makalani asked.

"Nah, we're carting too many tools. Dad wants this fence up before branding day."

"When's that?"

"This weekend. When do you go back to the heiau?"

"Sunday through Wednesday."

"Does Uncle Louie know that?"

"Yeah."

"Okay, since today's Thursday, we'll probably have it on Saturday, while you're still here."

Kenneth dictates the deadline. Louie decides on the day. Makalani still couldn't tell which brother was actually in charge.

"Who runs the ranch now that your grandfather is gone?"

"In some ways Dad. Other ways Uncle Louie. I don't know, I just do what I'm told."

"Sounds confusing."

"Yeah, well. It is what it is."

"Was it like that when your grandfather was alive?"

Grace's face crinkled through various emotions, and then she opened her hands on the steering wheel as if to say, "Who knew?"

She grabbed the wheel tight when the UTV jogged to the side. "FYI, if you ever drive one of these things, be sure to keep your thumbs on the outside of the steering wheel with your fingers. Uncle Louie knows this braddah who hit a bad bump and caught his thumbs in the puka. Ripped um right off."

Makalani gave her a doubtful look.

"Okay, maybe not fall-on-the-ground ripped off, but dangling from his hands. Even after the surgeries, he still can't grip anything. Really messed up his life."

Grace shivered, as if imagining what it would mean not to rope, ride, and work on the ranch. The thought made Makalani cringe as well. She didn't know who she would be if she couldn't pull her own weight.

Grace drove up to a cattle gate and jumped to the ground. "Come help. You should learn how this works."

Although Makalani had seen her share of electric fences, she let the young paniolo lead. She knew, from experience, how hard it was to earn your spot as a woman in a predominantly male occupation. Grace would have gone the extra mile to keep up with the men. It wouldn't surprise Makalani if the young woman took more risks than she should.

Grace unhooked the latch and swung open the gate. "The fence is still hot so, you know, don't touch the wires. Close and latch it when I get to the other side."

Makalani did as instructed and hopped back into her seat. "Have you always wanted to do this?"

Grace shifted the gear into drive. "Ever since I could walk. They put me on a horse and, that was it."

Makalani grinned as she imagined toddler Grace with her tiny legs sticking out the sides of a saddle. "Who taught you to ride?"

"Everybody! Well, you know, except Mom. She hates horses and cows. Wouldn't be here if she hadn't met Dad."

"She handles the books, though, right? That's an important position on this ranch."

"I guess. Grandad hated that stuff. He was happy to turn it over to her."

"Her *and* your dad, I bet. He must have trusted them both."

"Well, sure. Dad went to college for ranch management—animal science, agriculture, business, all of that. Pushed hard for me to do the same but, you know, I'd rather be a cowboy like Uncle Louie."

"What about Malu?"

Grace frowned. "What do you mean?"

"He's a tough paniolo like your uncle, don't you also want to be like him?"

"I guess. I mean Malu's a good cowboy and all, but he's not a Hiapo—yet."

There was an edge in her tone. Was Grace hoping the men would break up?

"You don't get along?"

"We did. These days, I don't know."

"What's changed?"

Grace shook her head, clearly not wanting to say more.

Makalani was confused. The only people on the ranch who seemed to want Malu around were Kupunakāne and Louie, and Makalani wasn't convinced Louie still did. So, if Malu's relationships with the family were so tenuous, why was Rumiko worried he might one day run the ranch?

Makalani switched tracks. "Your great-grandfather's amazing."

"Right? He's OG."

Makalani laughed to hear the gang term applied to Kupunakāne.

"No lie," Grace said. "He knows all the old paniolo ways. Used to compete in rodeos like me."

"I didn't know you competed."

"Oh yeah, double mugging and poʻo wai u events."

"What are those?"

"Double mugging is where me or my partner ropes a calf from horseback while the other one flips it and ties up the calf's legs. Poʻo wai u is an old paniolo roping technique where cowboys would wedge their kaula ʻili in the fork of a tree to secure wild cattle back in da day. Kupunakāne passed it down to Grandad, Uncle Louie, and me."

"Not your father?"

"Nah. He can rope, but he didn't see the point of learning poʻo wai u since our cattle are tame. But it comes in handy when you're alone and a stubborn pipi hides in the forest or when a bull gets testy and puts up a fight. Grandad understood, which is why what happened to him doesn't make any sense."

"With the bull?"

"Yeah. I mean, what was he trying to do? There weren't any trees nearby to tie him up, and he didn't have another cowboy there to rope the bull's legs. Was he hoping that laho would climb up the side of the pit and just follow him home?"

"They don't do that?"

"Well, yeah, they can if they're calm. But the ground around the pit was churned up as if Grandad was riding fast. The bull had to be agitated, right? Why didn't Grandad leave him alone and come get one of us?" She looked at Makalani with heartbreak in her eyes. "Maybe he thought we didn't care enough to help."

Grace gunned the UTV when she reached a well-worn path through the land, charging down a dip and chugging up the other side. Although her clenched jaw signaled an end to this topic, Makalani's mind had only begun.

Rosie and I aren't the only ones suspicious about Larry Hiapo's death.

If Grace was right about her grandfather, why would he believe no one cared enough to help?

Unless he was too proud to ask?

If Larry's family was making him feel old and useless or pressuring him to step down, he might have wanted to prove himself with the bull. For people who knew him, it would have been an easy thing to predict. Grace said a calm bull could be led by a rope. Could someone on the ranch have manipulated Larry into risking his life? Aside from Grace's mother, every paniolo at Hiapo Ranch had the skills needed to bring back a bull, including Kupunakāne, Rumiko, and Grace. Who among them would benefit from Larry Hiapo's death? Louie, Kenneth, and Malu were at the top of her list.

Grace gassed the UTV along the edge of a gulch, fighting with the steering wheel to keep it on track.

"You ever tip this thing over?"

Grace laughed. "Once or twice."

Makalani reached for the safety belt.

"No worry, beef curry. I've never tipped one here, only in the real rough country."

Great, Makalani thought, letting the belt slide back in the seat. She wouldn't earn any ranching cred with Grace if she wimped out over a bump.

"Where's that?"

"At a ranch on the slopes of Mauna Kea where Malu sometimes stays. His friend's land is too rough to drive fast like this. I tried once and almost rolled down a ditch."

"You work there?"

"When they need extra help. That's how it is in the ranching community, everybody helps everybody out."

"Even your dad?"

Grace flashed a sly grin. "Oh yeah, he can get dirty when he wants." The grin vanished as she focused ahead. "Dad's not as clean as he looks." The edge in her tone sounded like disdain.

But for what? Was Kenneth hiding a devious nature beneath his polished attire?

In the argument between brothers Makalani had overheard, Kenneth had claimed their father had put him in charge. But Louie had said their dad was leaning toward Hawai'i grass-finished beef, the direction Louie—not Kenneth—wanted to go. Was Kenneth lying? Because it seemed to Makalani that Larry Hiapo could have been standing in his elder son's way. If that were true, Kenneth, and not Louie, would benefit from their father's death.

Auwē, am I really going there?

Although bizarre and tragic, Larry Hiapo's death was easily explained. What else would happen to a man trapped in a pit with an angry bull? Of course he was stomped and gored. An animal can't be controlled by remote like a drone. It reacts however it will, no matter how domesticated it might seem.

Unless someone was there.

To do what, egg it along?

Makalani grabbed the bar as Grace hit a bump. The plastic flap of the zipped-open window bounced against the door. The distraction stopped her inner conversation from spinning out of control. Although Rosie had begged her to investigate, fabricating a murder would only prolong her grief. If Larry's death had truly been an accident, the best course of action would be to look out for Vinnie and help Rosie's family work out their differences as best as she could. Even that might be meddling too much.

"You have a good heart," her mother had said before Makalani went to the mainland for school. "But you sometimes cause trouble when you butt in to help."

"Sometimes?"

Māmā had laughed. "Maybe let people make their own mistakes. You have enough on your plate dealing with your own."

That advice had helped Makalani make friends in college and later in ranger training and at work, but it took constant effort to keep herself on track. When an obsession grabbed hold, not butting in was like asking Grace not to ride.

Makalani looked back at the tough, determined young woman beside her, working her ass off to prove her worth. With so much in common, Makalani should strive to forge a friendship with Grace instead of snooping in directions that would tear her world apart.

And yet, even Grace had said what happened to her grandfather didn't make any sense.

CHAPTER TWENTY-FOUR

Rona shut her eyes, weary from staring at the screen. She had spent the last hour checking if any of the Hiapos had criminal records—which they didn't—then searched the Hiapo name in every Hawai'i news outlet, hoping to find a clue. Twenty-three articles mentioned the ranch. Two news outlets had done profile features about the patriarch, Luke Hiapo. But Luke's deceased son, Larry, was barely mentioned anywhere until the news outlets began running reports on his shockingly gruesome death. In spite of the click-worthy headlines, his obituary was brief.

Why such disregard for the man who had recently run Hiapo Ranch?

In contrast, Larry's youngest son, Louie, was featured in a four-page spread about horse training and breeding in the *West Hawaii Today*. Although his father and grandfather were mentioned, the article was entirely about him. It made sense to Rona. After all, training and breeding horses sounded a lot sexier than raising cows. The rodeo painting above the office coffee station implied her coworkers might feel the same.

Was that attention a source of pride or resentment for the Hiapo 'ohana? Rona was especially interested in how Louie's elder brother might feel.

Kenneth had the least mentions of all. Even their sister, Rosie—who taught high school chemistry—had received more press than him. In fact, aside from Kupunakāne, the most news mentions went to Kenneth's daughter, Grace, who had won or placed in every Parker Ranch July 4 rodeo or junior rodeo for the last ten years.

Rona smirked. What would the Big Island Boys make of that?

Although the varying levels of media attention didn't have a direct bearing on her case, she wondered if Larry and his eldest son, Kenneth, might have felt slighted by their family and media.

Had Larry been obstructing his son's vision or success?

"If so, which son?" Rona muttered.

According to what Skip Una had told Rona on the phone, Louie, who allegedly did not want to sell Hiapo Ranch, might have the most to gain from his father's death.

Rona shook her head in frustration. "No convictions, no arrests, not even social media chatter about Louie getting out of line." She glared at the three empty desks in the room. If her colleagues knew any stories about Louie Hiapo's past juvenal delinquency or violent tendencies, they had kept it from her.

Unless Skip had been lying. He had sounded pretty slick over the phone.

"I'm running out of time. There's got to be something I can do."

She brought up the skimpy pathology report on the bull. Dan's requests had been minimal, but as long as the case was still open, Rona was justified in asking for more.

She punched in the number.

"Hello, this is Detective Rona Kim from the Waimea office. May I speak with Sharon Yee?"

"That's me."

"Hi, Sharon. Your laboratory did an initial toxicology report on a bull for us six days ago. Larry Hiapo case."

"Oh, yeah. I remember. It was an unusual request."

"How so?"

"Well, we don't usually get livestock requests from detectives. It happens more frequently from farmers and ranchers. You know, checking on the health of their animals, especially if one of them gets sick. Sometimes, we're asked to run tests on steroid toxicity in cattle."

"Did you run that on our bull?"

"Sure did."

"And what did you find?"

"Nothing. Urine was clean. No evidence of any anabolic steroids. Pretty sure it was in the report." Her bubbly voice took the sting out of her words.

"It was. I'm just crossing all my t's."

"Got it." The woman slurped through what sounded like a straw, followed by gentle thumping, and a burp. "Sorry about that. Mocha frapps get me every time."

Rona smiled. It must be nice to feel comfortable enough at work to do something as natural as burp. Even with the Big Island Boys out of the office, Rona still found it impossible to relax.

Another slurp. "So, what else do you want to know?"

"If the bull had been dosed with an unusually high level of testosterone, would you have seen it in the results?"

"Definitely."

"What else did you test for?"

"The typical livestock show drugs. None present. Even checked for Bovine Spongiform Encephalopathy."

"Mad Cow Disease?"

"Yep, negative on that too."

"Do you have any more samples?"

"We have blood, but the urine is only good for up to twenty-four hours. Is there something else you'd like me to check?"

The office door opened with a burst of laughter from the other two detectives as they returned from their late lunch. Dan was still in Kona. Rona only had two hours left to submit the paperwork that would close Larry Hiapo's case, not long enough to receive lab results, but more than enough time to order new tests.

Rona pressed her mouth closer to the phone, not wanting anyone to hear. "I'd like you to check for any prescription or illicit drugs."

"The livestock show drug panel covered a lot of that."

She turned away from the men. "Not livestock drugs. Human."

Sharon chuckled. "You think your bull might have been popping the rancher's meds?"

"Something like that. I'm especially concerned about amphetamines, cocaine, hallucinogens, or anything else that could induce violence."

"Oh, damn. A bull on LSD would be bad."

"Real bad."

It was a long shot, but Rona couldn't think of anything else that might force Dan to keep this case open.

The pathologist tapped on the computer as she spoke. "This is kind of fun. The only toxicology request I've ever had for an animal using human drugs was for a pet. Poor thing was found dead beside the deceased owner. The detective wanted to know if they might have died of the same thing."

"Had they?"

"Yep. The woman had ingested half a bottle of oxycodone. Her poodle ate the rest. It was a sad and messy situation."

Rona let that slide. No amount of mess could compare to the gore of Larry Hiapo's death.

She glanced at the men still chatting in the center of the room. "Will you email the results directly to me?" Rona definitely did not want Dan to know. "I'll start a new thread we can use."

"Sure thing. I assume you want this quick?"

"Yes, please."

"Say no more. Lucky for you, this is a slow and boring day."

CHAPTER TWENTY-FIVE

Makalani pounded the metal T-post into the ground beside the wire Malu had already laid. She slid the post driver sleeve off the top and moved seven paces ahead. Grace did the same from the other end. By the time they met in the middle, each of them would have driven fifty or so posts into the hard ground.

"Done," Grace yelled, raising her steel post driver overhead.

Although Makalani was stronger, the young paniolo had years of practice. She also had the benefit of the UTV transporting her metal posts. Grace had dumped Makalani's posts, every forty feet in groups of four, which meant Makalani had to carry the remainders to the next spot before she pounded them into the earth. She hadn't labored this hard since she helped harvest and replant the kalo in Tūtū's lo'i, then carried tubs of corms and stalks from the river up to the house. The physical exertion felt wonderful, but she would feel it tonight.

Louie whistled from upslope and waved for them to come.

Grace hopped into the UTV. "Break time's over."

Makalani did the same. "When did it begin?"

"The moment he saw us standing still."

By the time they reached Louie, he had already looped and crimped the insulators and steel wire strainers to the paddock's center post. He had used another post to brace it against the wire tension they planned to apply. Since the electric fence Kenneth wanted them to install would divide an already enclosed twenty-acre paddock, it didn't require the added strength of woven or high-tensile wire. A three-wire fence of medium weight with metal T-posts would suffice. When the center wire was hot, the cattle wouldn't cross. If it short circuited or was knocked down in a storm, the cattle would still be contained within the larger paddock.

As Makalani and Grace jumped out of their four-person vehicle, Malu drove up the slope in a single-seat quad, leaving a second line of wire unrolling in his wake.

Louie pointed to the cargo bed of his side-by-side UTV. "Grab another spool for Malu, den drive back and start clipping on da last two wires."

"On it," Grace said.

She and Makalani hefted the heavy spool and carried it to Malu at the back of his single-seater. "This is Makalani. She's Brian Pahukula's cousin from Kaua'i. You remember him, right? He's married to Rosie."

Malu's tied-up hair bounced with his nod. He sized up Makalani. Seemingly unimpressed, he removed the nearly empty spool from the unroller's spindle and dumped it at the base of the wood post.

Grace spoke through the effort as she and Makalani loaded the new spool. "Makalani's a ranger down at Pu'ukoholā Heiau."

Malu cut the end of his wire. "No, she's not. I know all dem. Nevah met her."

Makalani stuffed down her rising anger. She had been dismissed before, but never as summarily as this. Malu hadn't even given her a chance. She would not allow someone she had just met to put her down without a fight.

"I started two weeks ago. Transferred out of Oregon from Crater Lake National Park."

He fed his end of the wire into the strainer and began the wrap. He glanced at Makalani, then shoved the ratchet into the spindle and cranked it back and forth to tighten the wire. "Mainland ranger, huh? Whatchu doin' hea?"

Makalani brushed the dust from her gloves as she brushed off his tone. "I wanted to come home. Puʻukoholā was the first opening that came up."

He ratcheted the spindle to maximum tension and tossed the tool into the basket on his front rack. The clanging metal made both Grace and Makalani jump.

"What the hell, Malu?" Grace said.

He popped his head angrily at Makalani. "Dis malihini need show some respect."

Foreigner?

Grace seemed equally indignant but for a different reason. "She doesn't even know you, Malu."

He stepped up to Grace, chest puffed beneath his Hawaiian Sovereignty tank, hands clenched below the tribal designs of his full arm and shoulder kākau. The symbolic geometric patterns of his tattoo continued across his shoulder blade and up the right side and back of his neck. Malu had his Native Hawaiian indignation on full display.

He slapped his chest. "Not for me. Respect for da sacred place where she work."

Makalani stepped forward to draw Malu's anger back onto her and stop the rising tide of his tirade before it grew too big to defuse. "Number one, I'm not a malihini, I'm kanaka maoli like you. Number two, I have great respect for the heiau where I work. Number three, I'm happy to hear you know everyone there. Pretty soon, I will too."

Malu studied her for a moment, then let out a grunt that could have signified his approval, disbelief, or utter disdain. At this point, Makalani didn't care. The man might be important to Louie and, to varying degrees, other family members on the ranch, but her only interest in him was whether he had contributed to or orchestrated Larry Hiapo's death. At the moment, he was top on her list.

"Kulikuli," Louie shouted. "Mo' work, less talk." He grabbed a box from his cargo bed. "I goin' put in a second solar charger on da main fence so none o' dis short out. You t'ree finish up so we can move in da herd."

Malu shifted his stink eye from Makalani to Louie. "Whatevah you say, *boss*."

He sneer-grinned at Makalani, hopped on his quad, and tore up the grass as he turned it around. Clumps of grassy soil kicked into the air as he sped down the slope.

Louie muttered a curse and stomped away with the solar charger box.

Makalani turned to Grace. "What's with them?"

Grace started up the engine. "No clue, but they've been at it since before Grandad passed away."

Makalani raised her voice as Grace sped after Malu to the starting point of the new fence. "How long have they been together?"

"Five years."

"Whoa."

"I know. Might as well get married already."

"Why haven't they?"

"Uncle Louie won't say."

"You've asked?"

"Teased more like. Not anymore, though. Uncle can get scary."

"I noticed."

"Right?" She laughed. "He's pretty intense."

Malu drove past them the other way, unspooling the final wire onto the ground. Grace flashed him a shaka sign he didn't return.

Makalani frowned. "Your uncle isn't the only one who's intense."

"You noticed that too? You watching us, or what?"

Makalani was worried until she saw the corner of Grace's mouth raise in a smirk. The last thing she wanted was for Grace or any of the Hiapo 'ohana to feel studied or judged. "Kinda hard to miss."

"Yeah, Malu rubs everyone the wrong way."

"Even you."

She shrugged. "He's a good cowboy. Kupunakāne likes him because he speaks almost fluent ʻōlelo Hawaiʻi. No one in our family except Grandad ever took the time to learn."

Grace pulled up to the end and tossed a bag of wire clips to Makalani, parked the UTV a dozen yards up the fence line, and jogged back while pulling on her gloves. "I'll stretch the wires, you clip them in place."

They worked with efficiency, switching up jobs, and moved their vehicle as they progressed. All the while, Makalani pondered what Grace had said about how only Kupunakāne, her grandad, and Malu spoke ʻōlelo Hawaiʻi. It was a shame that what could have bonded Malu and Louie's father had not.

Kupunakāne had said Larry hated Malu from the start. But was it really political differences that divided them, or had Larry seen something in Malu he didn't trust? Either way, Malu must have known his lover's father didn't want him around. Now Larry was gone and Malu remained. And according to Rumiko, Malu's opinions would matter even more now that Larry wasn't alive to object.

"You said Malu is a good cowboy. Did he grow up on a ranch?"

"Yeah. Hawaiian Home Lands took back his family's lease when he graduated high school. Messed them up big-time. His parents and younger brother moved in with his uncle's family on Maui. Malu refused to go. Said DHHL owed him land and he would stay and fight until they gave it back."

"Do you think they will?"

"Nah, Malu's family were on a month-to-month. Never even had a ninety-nine-year lease. They just kept ranching and caring for the ʻāina like they had in the past. Invested everything they had to rebuild the walls, fences, and pipes. Then one day, the government took it all away."

"Wow."

"Right?"

"And now he works here?"

"Yup." Grace frowned. "Like it was his own."

Did Grace share Rumiko's concern that Malu would somehow take over Hiapo Ranch? If so, Larry might have felt the man's ill intent and taken some sort of action to thwart Malu's plans.

Like what?

When they reached the end of the fence, Makalani pulled her wire and passed it to Malu, who crimped it around the wire strainer Louie had attached to the post. Malu made sure to ratchet it tight. Despite her suspicions, Makalani couldn't deny the care with which he worked.

Louie returned from installing the extra solar charger. "All pau?"

"Yeah," Malu said, tossing the ratchet into his quad's bin with a clang.

"Aurite den," Louie said. "You and me head back to da house. Grace and Makalani can bring in da herd."

"No mo' work?" Malu asked hopefully.

Louie glared back. "We got t'ings to discuss."

As he drove away, Grace mouthed "someone's in trouble" to Makalani behind Malu's back.

Malu caught her smiling. "You get somet'ing you like share?"

Grace feigned innocence. "Not me."

"Good. 'Cause I no like hear not'ing from you."

He fired up his engine and tore across the field.

The women watched for a moment, glanced at each other, then laughed.

Grace imitated Malu's pissed-off expression. "Good. 'Cause I no like hear not'ing from you."

Makalani snorted, then double-checked that the man had truly gone.

Grace hopped onto her seat. "Come on, cowgirl, I'll show you how it's done."

The lush upland vale they had been fencing sat in a shallow well between a small puʻu on one side and a larger promontory on the other. Dense forest covered the latter and continued up a ridge into the mountains beyond. Somewhere behind this barrier was the route the memorial procession had taken to reach Larry Hiapo's tree. As Grace drove toward the paddock's perimeter fence, a herd of mother cows and their calves looked up from the other side. The grass had browned in places where cattle had grazed the most. The difference in pasture color between the paddock they crossed and the one up ahead explained why the herd was grazing near the fence.

Grace opened the gate. "Hūi, pipi, pipi!" She repeated her call until all the Black Angus cows and their mixed Angus-Charolais calves ambled into the newly fenced enclosure. When the slowest of the lot finally passed through, Grace hopped back into the UTV.

"That's it?" Makalani said incredulously.

Grace drove to the other side and closed the gate. "What did you expect?"

Makalani hopped into her seat. "I don't know, rounding them up?"

"What, like *Yellowstone*?"

"Well, yeah."

Grace chuckled. "Sometimes it takes a little more work, like if they're in a big pasture with lots of tasty grass. But these cattle have been eyeballing the green grass over here for days. If this fence wasn't electric, they might already have crossed."

"It has that much current?"

"Knock you flat on your 'ōkole. Trust me, I tried."

CHAPTER TWENTY-SIX

Flint drummed the steering wheel as he drove to the end of the road. The neighborhood properties grew bleaker with every turn. No trimmed hibiscus or lawns. No kids' bicycles or slides. Just old cars and trucks beached on dry grass, the wreckage behind them often barely fit to call a house.

His scalp itched from sweat as he coasted toward the mobile home perched on blocks. A shirtless man half Flint's age was pulling painter's plastic off the front wheel of a bright-aqua coupe. Filipino tribal tattoos swirled on his glistening brown back and up the side of his neck, even more noticeable with his long hair tied in a sloppy knot on his crown.

Skip had called Flint resourceful, and this was the best idea Flint had. Even so, he would have turned around if he hadn't already been seen.

"Ho, Flint, your phone broke, or what?" the man asked, wrapping up the protective plastic as Flint got out of his truck.

"Phone's fine, Jay. Just wanted to drop by."

"Way ovah hea?"

Flint attempted a grin. "The other place stinks."

Jay laughed. "Right? Rule numbah one, no shit where you eat."

"Yeah, about that. I need your help."

"Sorry brah, dass not part of our deal. We do us. You do you. Everybody's solid."

Flint startled as the screen door of the house squeaked open and slammed shut. A second man with swirling designs shaved into his crew cut stepped onto the elevated deck in bare feet, a tank top, and shorts. He crossed to the end of the lānai and leaned on the wood railing over where Jay stood. Similar tribal designs ran up his arms.

"What's Flint doing hea?" he asked Jay.

"I don't know, Goyo. I still try figure dat out."

Flint tensed as both of the gangsters focused on him. He needed their help, but he didn't want them to know why. If they knew he might be coming into money, they would pressure him for a cut.

"It's no big deal," Flint said. "I could just use some help getting my neighbors off my back."

Jay grabbed a buffing towel and twisted it into a rope. "Are they getting nosy? Because if they are . . ." He snapped the towel and let the threat hang.

Flint couldn't tell if it was aimed at the Hiapos or him. "Nothing like that, I just don't want them around. They stole land from my family a long time ago. My dad's getting old. He wants his revenge."

Goyo laughed. "Like our families back home in Manila, yeah Jay? Da old buggahs always hold da grudge."

Jay nodded, his eyes still on Flint. "Dat rancher died. Dass not enough payback fo' your dad?"

Flint chewed on his lip. All the way down the coast, he had struggled with how much to share. Too little and the gang wouldn't help. Too much, and they might turn on him. He had to give them the perfect amount.

"This guy on the mainland made a lowball offer on our neighbors' ranch. If they take it, the grandfather—the man my dad hates—will die without his land. We think the grandfather will go along if his grandkids push him to accept."

"How old are da grandkids?"

"Like me. The eldest grandson already wants to sell. We just need his younger brother and sister to agree."

Goyo laughed. "Alla dis is so one old guy can stick it to one oddah old guy?"

Flint chuckled nervously. "Pretty much. Dad wants Luke Hiapo to die without his land."

"So what you like from us?" Jay asked. "Pressure da younger braddah and sistah?"

Flint sized up the men before him. Even armed with guns or knives they might not be tough enough to pressure Louie Hiapo to pour a cup of coffee let alone sell his family's ranch. Besides, hadn't Skip already set up Louie as a murder suspect? Maybe Flint could leave the intimidating paniolo to him and have these guys focus on the weaker link.

"Just the sister. Her name is Rosie Pahukula. She's a chemistry teacher at Hawai'i Prep."

Jay nodded. "She live on your neighbors' ranch?"

"No. Rosie lives in Waimea with her husband." Flint's voice tightened whenever he thought of the outsider who had swept his dream girl out of his life. Nothing would make him happier than to see that man hurt. "Brian Pahukula teaches there too. I can get you details if you want to influence Rosie through him."

Goyo cocked his head. "Pahukula? That last name sounds familiar. He stay from da Big Island?"

"Kaua'i I think."

Goyo shook his head. "Huh. It'll come to me."

"Rosie also has a son."

"How old?" Jay asked.

"Eight." Flint knew Vinnie's birthday as well, if they wanted to know. He had kept track of every major event in Rosie Hiapo's life.

"He visits da ranch?"

"Yeah, he rides several times a week. His grandfather gave him a horse before he died. He already thinks he's a big shot paniolo like him and the other Hiapo men."

"How 'bout da mother?" Jay asked. "She like ride too?"

"Not much anymore." Flint gazed at the clouds, as if picturing Rosie there. "She rode like a goddess once upon a time."

Silence, and then laughter brought Flint back to earth.

Goyo thumped the corner post of the lānai. "Our boy's still hot fo' dis girl."

Jay nodded in agreement. "His father's not da only one who wants his revenge. Isn't dat right, Flint? Is dat why you like us take dis Pahukula guy out?"

Flint hid his embarrassment behind a grin. "Call it a bonus."

Jay grew serious. "Fo' us or fo' you?"

Flint dug his nails into his palms. He should have kept his mouth shut. Although he would love to cause Brian Pahukula as much pain as the man had caused him, he barely made enough money for him and his dad to survive. He didn't have extra funds to fulfill idle fantasies, no matter how sweet.

"I was just kidding. You can leave Pahukula alone."

"Uh-huh," Jay said. "Dass what I thought. So, before we *somehow* convince dis sistah to support selling her family's ranch, I need to know what's in it fo' us?"

That was the part Flint hadn't entirely worked out. If Skip bought the Hiapo Ranch, he would also buy theirs. Jay and Goyo would want their own vengeance if Flint and his dad didn't give them a cut.

"If all goes well, we might be able to pay."

Jay frowned. "If? Might? Sorry, brah. Too sketchy fo' us."

"Look, the guy who wants to buy is loaded. He wants it taken care of."

"By you or by us? Because whatever deal you worked out wit' dis mainlander, we goin' want half."

"Half?" Flint said.

Goyo laughed at his distress. "Good point. Half's not enough."

"No, half's good," Flint said before Jay upped their cut.

When the gangsters nodded, he realized what he had done. Half of his deal was a quarter of the money he and Dad would get for the ranch. It was way too much, but what choice did he have?

Before Flint could change his mind, Jay nodded and said, "Deal."

CHAPTER TWENTY-SEVEN

Makalani closed the final gate beside the ranch compound and hopped into the moving UTV as Grace drove back to the shed. Both of them were hot, tired, and ready to pack up their gear for the day when Rosie and Brian walked over from their car.

Makalani waved. "Eh, cuz. What're you guys doing here?"

"Checking on you," Brian said.

Rosie flashed him a scolding look, then smiled at Makalani. "To see how you liked your first day on the ranch."

Makalani shrugged. "It was great."

"Yeah," Grace said. "We put her to work."

Brian nodded. "That explains it then."

"What?" Makalani asked.

"The satisfied look on your face."

Her cousin was right, this day had felt more productive and fulfilling than any since coming to Hawai'i Island.

"You guys staying for dinner?" Makalani asked.

"Nope," he said. "We're taking you out."

She patted the dust from her clothes and grimaced. "Don't know about that. I'm kinda gross."

"There's a shower at the bunkhouse," Grace said.

"I wasn't planning to stay the night."

Grace shrugged. "Pack a bag tomorrow, you might change your mind."

"What happens tomorrow?"

"Not sure yet. But if Louie hears you aren't tired, he'll work you harder for sure. Besides, you're going to want to wake up here for lā kuni pipi on Saturday morning."

"Branding day?"

"Very good. Breakfast is at three thirty. We go out in the dark." Grace turned to Rosie. "Is Vinnie coming?"

Rosie sighed. "Unfortunately, yes."

"No worries, Aunty. I'll keep him right by my side."

Rosie arched a brow. "Forgive me if I'm not relieved." When Grace left, she side-eyed Makalani. "Have you seen that woman ride?"

"She's amazing."

"And reckless, just like Louie."

Makalani bit her lips. Although uncle and niece rode and drove hard, neither had done anything to make Makalani feel unsafe—except for that one moment when Grace could have tipped the UTV.

"You don't agree?" Rosie said.

"Huh? No. I was just thinking I should go home, shower, and change."

"Don't be silly," Brian said. "This is Waimea, ranching capital of Hawai'i. The restaurants are used to a little dust."

"Fair enough, but I still have to help Grace."

"I got this," she yelled from inside the shed. "Go, have fun. Order something fancy for me."

Makalani shrugged and spanked the remaining dust from her pants. "Okay, lead the way."

Twenty minutes later, she pulled her SUV into the space beside their car and joined them inside The Fish & The Hog.

Brian opened the menu. "We order family style. You okay with that?"

Makalani sat back. "Always."

Family style entailed fried brussels sprouts, macaroni and cheese with smoked brisket and bacon, poke nachos, a full rack of baby back ribs, and slaw.

"This all?" she teased when it arrived, eager to dig in.

"Well, you know," Brian said, "we gotta save room for dessert."

"Where's Vinnie?"

Rosie spooned slaw onto her plate. "He's eating at a friend's, which gives us the perfect opportunity to check in with you."

Brian dropped an enormous serving of mac and brisket onto her plate, then did the same for his own. She took a bite and nearly swooned.

"Good, right?"

She nodded.

He wiggled his brows. "So, how'd it go with Louie?"

"Um, what do you mean?" If Brian had noted her momentary infatuation, she'd pack it in and quit.

"He's the foreman, right? Aren't you working under him?"

Under?

She rolled the water glass against her cheek to reduce the sudden heat. "Nope. I mean kind of. It's hard to say who is actually in charge."

"You mean my brothers, right?" Rosie said. "Kenneth and Louie have been at it since we were kids, always vying for control, even over me. That's one reason I left the ranch. Bad enough to have my parents hovering over the only girl in our family without my older brothers telling me what to do."

"What was the other reason?"

Rosie glanced at Brian and received an encouraging nod. "The neighbor boy was . . . I don't know . . . stalking me? Can you say that about a kid? He was five years older, always watching, always trying to make friends with my brothers and me. He made me feel . . ." She shook her head. "I stopped speaking to him, but he wouldn't leave me alone. Whenever I saddled up, he would ride his horse along the highway fence as if waiting for me to cross. After I caught him with binoculars, I always felt watched."

"Did he become friends with your brothers?"

"No way. He couldn't ride for shit, but always acted like he could."

"Did you tell anyone what he was doing?"

"I tried. There wasn't anything definitive I could say. Hiapo men aren't big on 'feelings,' but if he ever tried to touch me, they promised to bust up his face."

"What about your mom?"

"She told me to stay clear of him in town and that I was safe on the ranch."

"But you didn't feel safe."

"No, only in school. That's why I became a teacher. School was my refuge and my ticket away from the ranch."

Makalani couldn't imagine a scenario where her parents wouldn't have supported her and intervened. "I'm sorry no one believed you."

Rosie looked up from her plate. "Do you?"

"Of course. Girls should be taught to trust their intuition, not suppress those feelings until it's too late."

"Boys, too," Brian said. "Bad stuff going on in this world. But you know what? We don't need to think about all of that right now. Let's enjoy this meal. Appreciating the moment is important too."

"Right as always, my love," Rosie said, then dished out helpings of the brussels sprouts. Once the bad feelings had dissipated, she brought up her brothers again. "They're too different, you know? They almost never agree."

Makalani nodded. "And yet both of them want to be in charge."

"Exactly. So who's taking control of the ranch?"

Makalani shrugged. "Kenneth is in the office, Louie's out in the field, but Rumiko says Kupunakāne is ultimately in charge."

"Huh. That doesn't sound clear."

"Let her eat," Brian said. "They probably worked her to death. Besides, how would she know? She's only worked there one day."

Rosie left it alone until after the plates had been taken and they ordered dessert. "Are my brothers working together, at least, or are they locked in a power struggle?" She took in Makalani's expression and sighed. "This is exactly why I had hoped Dad would leave directions in his will. If they don't work things out, they're going to bankrupt the ranch. I may not be involved in the day-to-day, but I still have equal share in the land. Or at least, I hope I do."

Brian covered her hand. "Maybe Larry didn't have the title. If not, your grandfather would still have control."

Makalani nodded. "That's the impression I got from your mom."

"She said that? So what, I might not inherit anything?"

Brian squeezed her hand, then thanked the server for the banana cream pie and passed dessert forks all around. "Who else would he leave it to?"

"Kenneth or Louie. Both of them and not me. Bequeath it to Kamehameha Schools or Hawai'i Land Trust. Who knows what's going through that old man's mind?" Rosie stabbed at the pie. "He and Dad didn't always get along."

Makalani had gotten that impression too.

"Dad seemed preoccupied before he died. Whenever we visited, he kept to himself and didn't engage—not only with us but with anyone—as if his mind was spinning with thoughts he didn't want to share."

"You think Larry and Luke were fighting again?" Brian asked.

"Could be. I don't remember the last time I saw them sitting or laughing together."

Makalani nibbled at the pie. Was Kupunakāne's determination to finish his son's kaula 'ili motivated by devotion or guilt? And what about the ranch? Kupunakāne was clearly frustrated with his heirs and their lack of interest in perpetuating the old paniolo ways. Did he have a more deserving beneficiary for his legacy than them?

"What about Malu?" Makalani asked. "Your mom seemed to think he could end up running the ranch."

Brian frowned. "He and Louie aren't married."

"Close enough," Rosie said. "I've seen Kupunakāne chatting with him a lot."

"Kenneth wouldn't allow it."

"Kenneth might not have a say." Rosie put down her fork. "Dad should have put someone in charge when he retired."

"Semiretired," Brian said, and took another bite.

"See what I mean?" she said to Makalani. "Dad wouldn't give up control. All the Hiapo men are stubborn, even my son."

Brian flashed Makalani a look that said he would have thrown in the Hiapo women as well. From what Makalani could tell about Rosie, Grace, and Rumiko, she was inclined to agree.

"Kenneth has a degree in ranch management," Rosie said. "He understands the future of ranching. He should be in charge."

"Did your father value that education?" Makalani asked.

"Absolutely. He wanted it for himself, but Kupunakāne wouldn't let him go. That's why it's so important for Vinnie to do well in school. He needs a college education to succeed in life."

Although Makalani valued her higher education, she didn't necessarily agree. Tūtū and Pāpā never attended college, and they lived full and happy lives. Then again, Rosie might have a different way of measuring success. She pushed the pie toward Brian, far more interested in what Rosie had to say.

"What was it like growing up with your dad?"

Rosie's frustration drained, leaving pain and melancholy in its place. "He was a complicated man: caring of animals and the land, demanding of his sons, protective of me. Loving, fierce, unforgiving."

"Violent," Brian whispered.

Rosie nodded. "Sometimes."

"With you?" Makalani asked.

"No. Mostly with Louie, although he teased Kenneth mercilessly for being weak. Dad and Louie butted heads about everything except horses and cows. The beatings ended once Louie got big enough to fight back."

"When was that?"

"About fourteen."

Makalani nodded, sad to be right. "No one reported him or stepped in to help?"

"By that time, Louie had begun training wild and problematic horses. Any breaks or bruises were attributed to that."

"What about your family?"

"Mom and Kenneth tried. But when Dad turned on them, Louie made them stop, said he could take whatever Dad dished out. The implication being that Mom and Kenneth could not. I don't think Kenneth ever forgave Louie for that."

Makalani understood. As the elder brother, Kenneth would have felt responsible to keep his siblings safe. Not only had he not been strong enough to do so, his younger brother had thrown it back in his face. How much of Kenneth's personality stemmed from proving his worth to his brother and to himself?

"And Kupunakāne?" she asked.

Rosie slumped in her chair. "I think he approved. Cowboy life is grueling and dangerous. Paniolo need to be tough. I suspect he raised Dad the same way."

As Makalani watched her cousin's wife shrink into herself, she thought about Grace. Rosie's niece was tough. Had one or more of her relatives had a hand in forging that steel?

"Wait," Makalani said. "Are you afraid one of *them* might be arranging accidents for Vinnie to toughen him up?"

Rosie met Makalani's gaze with apprehension in her eyes. "He wants to be paniolo. I never did, so I don't know what that means to a family like mine. I don't know how deep the roots of family abuse might go. It might have begun and ended with Dad, or it might have started generations ago and still be going on."

Makalani recalled the memorial ceremony. Although beautiful, it hadn't felt right. "Is this why none of you spoke at your dad's service?"

"You noticed that, huh?"

"Yeah."

"I wonder if anyone else did. Mom asked if we wanted to contribute but, you know, what were we going to say? Dad was her husband. It seemed best to leave it to her."

Which explains why Rumiko's remarks were so brief.

As things fell into place, Makalani wondered again who might want Larry Hiapo dead—the son he beat yet admired, the son he valued yet belittled, or the wife who had finally decided enough was enough? Rumiko was an expert paniolo. Could she have found a way to kill her husband with a bull?

CHAPTER TWENTY-EIGHT

Flint leaned forward from the back seat of Jay's aqua Hyundai and pointed through the windshield at Rosie coming out of The Fish & The Hog. "That's her. That's Rosie."

"And dass her husband?" Jay asked.

"Yeah. Brian Pahukula."

Goyo drummed his fingers on the dashboard. "I swear I know dat name. Why can't I remember?"

Jay snorted. "Because you been lacing your weed."

"Only couple times."

"Couple times too many. I told you, leave our product alone."

"Still . . . Pahukula rings a bell." He shook his finger at Jay. "And no say in my head." He slapped the dashboard. "I remember now. I heard dat name when I was talking story wit' Gabe."

"Your cousin on Kaua'i?"

"Yeah. I just can't remember what he said. Somet'ing to do with a paka lōlō bust and his sistah working out a deal wit' some ranger. Whatevah, it will come."

Jay shook his head at his partner and popped his chin at the trio heading for their cars. "Who dat walking wit' Rosie and her husband?"

Flint shrugged. "I don't know, maybe a new paniolo from the ranch?"

"Why would you think that?"

"Her boots and clothes look like she's been working outside, and there's a bandanna hanging out of her jeans pocket like the yokes paniolo wear around their necks."

"I thought you said Rosie didn't hang at the ranch?"

"No. I said she doesn't ride much anymore."

Jay looked back at the women. "She stay pretty friendly wit' dat wahine. Would she pressure her 'ohana to sell if we do somet'ing to her?"

Flint gritted his teeth. In all the years he had known Rosie growing up, she had never once hugged him as she was hugging the Hawaiian woman goodbye. "Maybe. But I don't know who she is."

"Me and Goyo will check it out tomorrow, go by da ranch, see if dat wahine friend stay work ovah dea."

"No killing," Flint said.

Jay turned in his seat and fixed him with an icy glare.

Flint slumped in the back seat and stared at his knees. These guys were dangerous and reckless, having broken away from their primary gang. He didn't want their anger focused on him.

Jay slapped Goyo's arm and pointed to Brian Pahukula. "In da meantime, call your cousin Gabe and see if knows dat guy's family. Maybe we can use it against him to pressure his wife."

CHAPTER TWENTY-NINE

Makalani's video call window opened with Māmā's smiling face. "There's our girl. We called at seven but you didn't answer."

Makalani sat up taller in her bed. "Sorry about that. Brian and Rosie took me out to dinner."

Pāpā appeared over Māmā's shoulder, his big face filling the screen. "Brian Pahukula? Good man. Glad he's looking out."

Makalani rolled her eyes. "I can look out for myself."

"We know you can," Māmā said. "But it never hurts to have an extra pair of eyes on the job."

Makalani's parents had become overly protective in the last eight months. She couldn't blame them. Having your daughter nearly killed in front of you had that effect. Although she enjoyed the Thursday night video calls, the daily texts she had received when she returned to Oregon had grown tiresome fast. They hadn't kept tabs on her like that even during her first year in college. After ten years living on her own, it had been hard to adjust to their constant inquiries and concerns. The incessant texting had stopped once she moved back to Hawai'i. She expected the video calls to ease up as well when her parents realized how boringly safe her life on the Big Island had become.

"What you do on your day off?" Pāpā asked. "I hear da shore fishing stay plenny good at Spencer Beach near where you work, or A-Bay little mo' south."

Makalani smiled. Pāpā loved to fish. "I'll take you there when you visit."

"Sounds good. But you need somet'ing to do now. You know how you get when you not working or helping out."

"Actually, I'm working on a ranch."

"No kidding? Dass awesome."

"Doing what, exactly?" Māmā said with less enthusiasm.

Here we go.

Makalani needed to lay this out carefully, or she'd open a fresh can of worms.

"Today was my first day. I rode out with Rosie's paniolo niece to check on the cattle and the land, then we helped Rosie's brother and friend build an electric fence."

"Dass my girl," Pāpā said.

"Not so fast, Kawika," Māmā said. "Remember what happened the last time she rode out on a horse?"

"Nothing happened," Makalani said.

"Maybe not that day, but it led to a lot."

Pāpā rubbed Māmā's shoulders. "Easy, Julia."

She brushed off his hands. "I'm not a horse to be calmed. I'm her mother, and I want to hear more."

A man's voice called from off screen. "Is dat Makalani?" Her former football star cousin squeezed her parents out of the shot. "Howzit, cuz?"

"Eh, Solomon. You look good."

He really did. His eyes looked brighter, his skin had cleared, and the flabby shell of a man had filled out with new energy and purpose. Instead of lounging around the homestead, he did his share of the work—fishing, hunting, butchering, farming, and building whatever improvements Tūtū wanted him to make. His bum knee still gave him trouble, but his new outlook and determination had lessened the pain, or at least stopped the pain from minimizing his life.

Solomon posed in his new aloha shirt. "I got a date."

"Whaaat?"

"No lie, cuz. I met her at AMP Country Line Dancing Night."

"You *line dance*?"

"She works at da thrift shop ovah dea. Lives on a homestead like us."

"Okay, you're blowing my mind right now." Not only was her cousin socializing outside a bar, he was hanging out at the Anahola Marketplace, developed on DHHL property to generate mercantile opportunities for Native Hawaiians? "Who *are* you?"

"I know, right? Life is good, one day at a time."

"Is dat Makalani?" Solomon's mother yelled before bumping him out of frame with her sizable girth. Aunty Kaulana was the youngest and largest of Tūtū's children. Fear of losing her only son had scared her into new behaviors as well. Pāpā said she was harvesting kalo out of the lo'i with Tūtū and pounding her own poi!

"Look what I get," Aunty Kaulana said, holding out a pan of freshly steamed kūlolo. She was also an impeccable cook.

"You trying to torture me?" Makalani said, drooling over the kalo–coconut milk squares. The last time she ate kūlolo, her aunty had steamed it in Pāpā's imu with the pig.

Aunty Kaulana squinted at the screen. "What you eat ovah dea? You look skinny as an eel."

Makalani laughed. Only Aunty Kaulana would call a woman Makalani's size skinny. "I just went out for ribs and brisket mac-n-cheese." When Aunty made a face, she added, "And they fed me breakfast and lunch on the ranch."

Māmā pushed Aunty out of the way. "About that . . . Why are you working on a ranch?"

"It belongs to Rosie's family. They needed extra help after her father died."

"When was that?"

"Last week."

Māmā tensed. "Before or after you rappelled into a caved-in lava tube?"

"Um, the same day?"

"And you didn't think to mention this during last Thursday night's call?"

"I didn't know until Sunday, when Brian invited me to the memorial."

Māmā relaxed. "Okay, fair enough. How did he die?"

Makalani stared back blankly as she searched for the blandest response. "Ranching accident."

Māmā's eyes narrowed as if she detected a lie. "What kind of ranching accident?"

"Um . . . with a bull?"

"Spit it out, Makalani, the whole gory truth."

If Māmā knew exactly how gory Larry's death had been, she'd come to Hawai'i Island the next morning and drag Makalani off the ranch. If she believed Makalani was leaving out crucial information, she'd still hop on a plane. The only way to keep Māmā on Kaua'i was to stick to the facts and tone down the truth.

"He was trampled while retrieving a lost bull."

Pāpā squeezed into the frame. "Seriously? How dat happen, I thought bulls were domesticated li'dat?"

"They are. This one got scared because it had fallen into a pit."

Māmā nudged to the center of the screen. "Let me get this straight. Rosie's father died in a ranching accident, and then she asked you, who knows nothing about ranching, to step in and help?"

Makalani took a breath and relaxed her twitching mouth. "It wasn't like that. Her 'ohana is having a hard time. Brian thought I could help."

"Oh, because of how you helped your own family back in February?" Māmā said with a bite. "The kind of help that nearly got you killed?"

"No. I mean, yes—the family part, not almost getting killed."

Māmā scoffed. "Well thank goodness for that." She glared directly into the camera so Makalani would feel it in her bones. Then she shook off her displeasure as a dog dries its wet coat. "Okay. If this is what you want to do . . ." She leaned back in. "But I trust you won't be herding any bulls."

Makalani held up her hands. "No ma'am, not that I know of. The only cattle I've seen are māmā cows and their calves." She clamped her mouth shut before she added anything else, like how she planned to see the killer bull up close for herself.

"Okay, then." Māmā nodded, as if granting her twenty-eight-year-old law enforcement ranger daughter permission to live her own life. "I suppose the physical exertion will eat up that troublesome extra energy you have."

Makalani fought the grin rising on her face, then gave up fighting when Tūtū burst into the room. The family matriarch had more energy than women half her age. Even at eighty-five, she nearly matched Makalani in height and weight, only losing an inch of her majestic six feet to the gravity of age. When she shouldered in front of Māmā, she completely eclipsed her from view.

"How come nobody wen get me fo' dis call?" Tūtū leaned in so close she filled the entire screen with her face. "Pehea ʻoe e ka moʻopuna?" *How are you, granddaughter?*

"Maikaʻi wau, e Tūtū, a ʻo ʻoe?" *I'm fine, Tūtū, and you?*

"Maikaʻi wau, mahalo. Howzit goin' at da heiau?"

"A little boring, but good. I haven't studied like this since I was at school."

"Dey not teaching you how Kamehameha conquered Kauaʻi, are dey? Because you know dass not correct. King Kaumualiʻi chose da white stone, not da black. He put his aloha fo' his people above his own sovereignty."

Here we go.

"I know, Tūtū."

"His mahiole aliʻi hulu manu—his royal feathered helmet—was not as tall as Kamehameha's, and yet, he was da only aliʻi nui in all of Hawaiʻi to retain his autonomy. In dis way, he protected his people and perpetuated da peace Kauaʻi and Niʻihau had enjoyed fo' so many generations."

Makalani nodded dutifully. Everything Tūtū said matched what Ranger Akaka had taught while still placing an emphasis on Kauaʻi's importance and Tūtū's own island pride. The subtle differences between Tūtū's and Ranger Akaka's perspectives didn't seem worth the disagreements that would undoubtedly arise. Better to shift to more stable ground.

"Yesterday morning at Puʻukoholā, the ranger who is teaching me about the heiau was crafting a royal feathered cape."

Tūtū's eyes widened. "He one kahuna hulu nui?"

"Yeah. His work is meticulous."

"Was he making a replica?"

"No. He said the cape was for a *living* ali'i."

"Ahh . . . dis serious work he do. And dis man teach you about Kamehameha's heiau?"

"He does."

"Hmm. Maybe okay den. But if anyone evah try tell you Kamehameha conquered Kaua'i, you send um to me."

Makalani laughed. "Okay, Tūtū. I will."

"You get work tomorrow?"

"I'm off this weekend, but I'm working on a cattle ranch."

"Whose?"

"Hiapo."

"Oh, dey one o' da oldest paniolo families in Waimea."

Makalani nodded. "Back to the earliest Mexican vaqueros."

"Dey lease?"

"Fee simple." Owning land, with full rights and permanent tenure, was a huge deal in Hawai'i, where more than half the land was owned by the state or federal government, or by a large private entity. It wasn't uncommon to pay an exorbitant amount for a condo or house you might be forced to surrender at the end of the land's lease.

Tūtū looked impressed. "Akamai."

"Yeah, very smart. Their ancestors applied for the initial ranch land during the Kuleana Act. One of the descendants bought neighboring property to expand."

"Ho, smart and rich."

Makalani laughed. "Not rich anymore, but doing okay."

Tūtū shook her head. "Rich in land matters way mo' dan rich in money, mo'opuna. I bet whoevah sold dem dat extra property wished dey had not."

CHAPTER THIRTY

Makalani arrived at the ranch late enough to miss the family breakfast drama and early enough to watch the mountains gain definition against the emerging peach-and-lavender sky. She had packed an overnight bag as Grace had suggested, in case she decided to spend the night, and munched the rest of her fried egg sandwich in peace. Whatever the day had in store, she wanted her mental slate clean. Or as clean as it could be with Tūtū's words creeping along the edge.

I bet whoevah sold dem dat extra property wished dey had not.

Kupunakāne had said his maternal grandfather had given his parents money to buy the lower portion of their neighbor's land. Makalani had driven past a wooden gate that might lead to the property the neighbor's family had retained. If so, the land they had sold was closest to Waimea Town. Did the heirs regret that decision? It must be worth a fortune today.

A beam of light shone from the Hiapos' main house as the front door opened and bounced against the wall. A large figure walked out and down the front steps. As he headed down the dirt driveway, the door swung closed. No longer backlit, the first light of dawn illuminated Louie's surprise when he spotted Makalani standing beside her car.

"What you doing out hea?" Louie said.

She held up her final bite of egg sandwich and popped it into her mouth. "I brought my own breakfast and an overnight bag."

He grunted with approval. "Akamai. Tomorrow is lā kuni pipi. We always start early on branding days."

"That's what Grace said."

He pointed to the Kona side of the lot. "Bunkhouse is behind da trees, above da utility shed. Take your pick of rooms."

She grabbed her backpack. "What's on the agenda for today?"

"I go pick up da bull while you guys start on da chores."

"The bull that killed your dad?"

"Dass da one. KPD finished their investigation, said we could take um back."

"What will you do with him?"

"Get um back in shape so he can cover plenny kine cows."

Makalani followed him toward the utility shed, where the UTVs and mechanical equipment were kept. "You taking anyone with you?"

"Nah. I need Grace and Malu to work da herds and pastures."

"What about me?"

"Huh. I guess dat would work. Might come in handy to have an extra set of hands. Drop off your pack and meet me at da trailer."

"Roger that."

She headed for the bunkhouse at a brisk yet not overly excited pace. If Louie thought she was too eager, he might not want her around. The man was bristly even at dawn, but she was dying to know more about what happened to his father and see the killer bull for herself.

She returned as he was sliding open the rear gate of a sixteen-foot aluminum stock trailer. Another considerably larger and taller trailer with slatted walls was parked alongside.

Makalani joined him and looked inside. "What kind of flooring is that?"

"Recycled rubber. It stay sealed against moisture, hoses down easy, and makes it mo' comfortable fo' da pipi to stand. We put dis one in last year. Still looking good."

"How can I help?"

He nodded toward a four-by-six rubber mat in the back of his F-150 truck. "One of da panels needs to be replaced. You said you did construction, so I assume you can cut um to size?"

"Sure."

He handed her a retractable utility knife. "Let me know if you need anyt'ing else. I goin' check da lights, tires, and everyt'ing li'dat. Should be good, but I always double check. It's a short trip. I called Animal Control yesterday. Dey goin' make sure our bull is properly fed and watered before we arrive."

As Louie took care of his tasks, Makalani pocketed the knife, grabbed a crowbar, and hefted the heavy rubber mat into the trailer. She spotted the damaged section right away where the center had been gouged out by hooves. She pried up the edge, pulled it off the wood floor, and slid it toward the gate.

"You okay in dea?" Louie shouted.

"Yeah."

She slid the new piece into the gap and kicked it flush against the wall. When the lip overhung, she creased it enough to mark, sliced the length of the mat, and stomped it into place. She picked up the crowbar and extra rubber as Louie rounded the corner.

He looked at her in surprise. "You done already?"

She stepped out of the way so he could inspect her work. The rubber mat fit seamlessly in place. He gave a slight nod, but she could tell he was impressed. Without waiting for direction, she stored the crowbar, knife, and rubber strip in the truck's tool bin while Louie tossed a length of rope and two flag sticks into the bed. When he strapped a long cattle prod against the interior wall, she gave him a questioning look.

He shrugged. "Nevah know what will happen wit' a bull."

Considering this animal's history, she definitely agreed.

Sorry, Māmā. Guess I'll be herding bulls after all.

She hopped into the cab of the truck opposite Louie and watched as he skillfully maneuvered the trailer out of its spot and down the dirt driveway to the road. Every action was meticulous and efficient, with little fanfare directed at himself—a professional in his element, a paniolo at work.

"Where's the holding pen?"

"At a ranch in Upland Kona. Since Animal Control no get livestock calls too often, dey rent a corral from dem. Driving slow fo' da trailer, it probably take us ninety minutes or more."

Makalani looked out her window at the passing ocean view.

Plenty of time to encourage him to talk.

After a few minutes of companionable silence, she broached her first question. "What happened the morning you arrived on the scene?"

"Da scene? You mean finding my dead faddah in a pit wit' a bull?"

Good going, Makalani. Way to ease in.

He grunted with amusement. "No worry, I know what you meant. And, yeah . . . it was definitely a scene."

"It must have been horrible."

"And strange."

"How so?"

"Da bull stay lying dea, all content, you know? Like he woke from a nap. He hardly noticed my dad a few feet away. Just twitched his ears at da flies."

"Animals usually don't like to be near death."

"Right? But he was so chill. Charolais bulls are big suckahs. Dis one's creamy-white coat was brown from dirt and dried blood on his face, forelegs, and chest. He didn't even move when I climbed down to check on Dad." He scoffed. "Guess he wore himself out."

Makalani let the horrifying image pass.

"Who was with you?"

"Grace found him, den waited for Kenneth, me, and Malu to come. I wen' down. Kenneth called da ranch on da walkie-talkie and told Mom. She called 911. An HFD chopper arrived first and had me secure da bull while dey checked da vitals fo' demselves. I put a rope around da bull's neck and tossed it up to Grace, who tied it onto da UTV, but dakine didn't even stand up. Nobody did not'ing else until HPD arrived."

Makalani noticed the slight difference between Louie's and Brian's stories. Her cousin had said the bull was up and snorting when firefighters arrived and that Malu helped rope the bull. Louie said the bull hadn't even stood up. Had the retelling changed as it passed from Louie to Rosie to Brian to her, or had Louie intentionally toned down Malu's participation and the bull's more aggressive response?

"How long did it take for the police to arrive?"

"I don't know, maybe an hour? Dat pit stay pretty close to da easement road leading to our neighbor's place, so it wasn't too hard fo' dem to find."

"Why the chopper?"

"Mom made it sound like he was in a lava tube."

Makalani chuckled under her breath.

"Why you laugh?"

She shook her head. "As life would have it, I was in a lava tube the day your dad was killed."

"Fo' real? How come?"

"A kid was off-roading with this dad. He jumped his ATV into a dip and fell through the ceiling of an undiscovered tube. The dad found me at the heiau's resource management station. I went up to help, climbed into the cave, and found an alternate exit to extract the kid."

"He survived?"

"Yes."

Louie shook his head in thought. "Two unlikely accidents. A boy lived. An old man died. Ke Akua was busy that day."

"God?"

"He had to decide who to take, right? Bettah to leave da kid."

Makalani studied him in silence. Was he justifying ill deeds, or finding consolation in religious theology? Either way, the choice of young over old had not occurred to her. Larry was only sixty-seven when he was killed. He had decades of good life ahead.

Or decades of interference. How did Louie actually feel about his father's death?

"What happened when the police arrived?"

"Dey took control and asked a bunch of questions. Why was Dad out there alone? Did we have oddah pits like dis on our land? How come a killah bull no act aggressive now?"

"Why *was* your dad out there?"

"He stay one rancher. Dass what paniolo do."

"Yeah, but why not you, Grace, or Malu?"

"Shoots, you as bad as my braddah. Why *not* Dad? He stay semiretired, not dead." Louie shook his head when he realized what he had said.

"I know what you meant."

"T'anks, eh? Sometimes I forget he's not hea. Anyways, after we took out da bull, da cops examined and photographed da scene."

"How did you get him out?"

"We brought up planks, made a ramp, and pulled dis trailer up to the top. Malu and I climbed down into da pit and encouraged him up da ramp."

"Encouraged?"

"Yeah." Louie chuckled. "Like what you and me goin' be doing."

Makalani kept her expression neutral despite her racing pulse. "Did the bull cooperate?"

He grinned. "He did then."

Implication: He might not today.

"Well, the bull must have passed inspection if they're releasing him to you, right? Did pathology run tests or just observe?"

"Both. Dey didn't find any kine drugs or disease dat would make him aggressive. And from what da rancher observed dis past week, our bull seems pretty chill."

"Puzzling."

"Yes and no. Bulls are lazy creatures. Dis one just got scared."

Makalani nodded, unconvinced. "Guess we better not *scare* him today."

Louie laughed. "Yeah. And don't piss him off."

CHAPTER THIRTY-ONE

Rona clicked from one case file to the other, maximizing the gruesome photos they contained: dead man on the left, bloody bull on the right. Although Dan had forced her to close the Hiapo case the previous day, the agent of Larry's death refused to let her go.

Agent, not killer.

The word had popped into her mind on the long drive to work. The more she thought it over, the more convinced she became. If the bull was as complacent as Animal Control claimed, then someone or some*thing* had enraged it enough to kill.

She checked her inbox again for test results from Sharon Yee. When she didn't find any, she returned to the new case she was expected to solve.

Unlike Larry Hiapo's freakish "accident," Paul Campbell had obviously been murdered. Thirteen stab wounds riddled his bare chest. That's how many Rona had counted as he lay, robe open, on his living room rug.

Her cursor drifted to the file nested behind. Before she could focus on the new case, she needed to tie up the loose ends.

The massive white bull stared at Rona with calm, black eyes, unconcerned with the blood staining his face, chest, and legs. His short, thick horns curved forward and down above large ears that opened like twin satellite dishes as if to hear what his audience might say.

She zoomed in on the blood. The deepest saturation extended from the top of the bull's head down the ridge between his eyes, then lessened as it spread around the sides of his face. The blood on his blunted white horns had turned a dark rusty brown. The saturation was consistent with the bull impaling and bludgeoning the victim with his horns and his head.

Although cattle had strong jaws from chewing continuously throughout the day, they didn't use them to fight. So why was there grime around this animal's mouth and pink nose?

She clicked to Larry's autopsy photos, but couldn't find teeth marks among the wounds. They could have been gouged out by the horns and hooves, but she doubted the grime on the animal's mouth had come from this fight.

She checked the other photos of the bull. Blood caked his forelegs up to his knees and stained the loose skin dangling below his wide chest. More blood splattered along his muscular body as if flung from his horns.

With or without Larry Hiapo attached?

She clicked to Larry's autopsy photo. The hoof-shaped gouges, bruising, and crushed bones were consistent with deadly foreleg stomps. The man's upper right arm was so mangled it was hardly attached. If he had suffered other injuries to the arm, the evidence of it was gone.

She clicked back to the bull and magnified the scrapes running down his lower front legs. She couldn't discern their severity amid all the blood. Nor could she tell how much had come from the victim and how much had come from the scrapes. Neither she nor Dan had examined the animal up close at the scene. In fact, no one had been close enough, except Louie Hiapo and his crew—the same Louie Hiapo who Skip Una claimed had fought with his father about selling the ranch.

What if Louie or the others had removed a damning piece of evidence or injected the bull with a tranquilizer or some other drug that would keep him calm for the week? Did such a drug even exist? Rona had no idea.

Yet another reason they shouldn't have closed that case.

And why had Dan allowed Louie and his crew to load the animal into their own trailer? Granted, they later hitched it to an Animal Control truck. But the fact remained that a crucial piece of evidence, if not the actual killer, had not been independently secured.

Had Dan made a grave error in allowing the Hiapo cowboys to load the killer bull? Had he given up on a possible homicide because the chain of custody issues would have ruined the case? If so, why had Dan—a seasoned investigator and a rancher's son—not considered this before?

Rona scrolled to the earlier crime scene photos, aligning their chronology with her memory of the day.

She and Dan had arrived at the scene shortly after the fire department's paramedic and rescue team. Louie, Kenneth, Kenneth's daughter, Grace, and a ranch hand named Malu Au were also at the scene. Before HFD arrived, Louie had gone into the pit to check his father's vitals and loop a rope around the bull's neck—which meant Louie, and perhaps one or more of the others, had unsupervised access to the victim, the alleged killer, and the scene. All of them had assured Rona and Dan that only Louie had gone into the pit and had not otherwise disturbed the scene the photographer had shot. Although this seemed accurate to Rona at the time, Dan later established how little she knew about cattle or ranching.

She sipped her third cup of black coffee and stared at the screen. What if Louie had done something no one else could have seen while down in the pit or loading the bull into the trailer? Once again, she worried that Dan had made a critical mistake. That said, she could have spoken up at any time—having agency over her life included not passing the buck. If she had found something incriminating, she should have kept open the case no matter how much Dan had pushed back. Since she hadn't, perhaps it deserved to be closed.

Dan entered the office while finishing a croissant. "You're here early."

Rona maximized the window of the new homicide case. "Just arrived."

Dan glanced at the wet coffee cup rings on her desk and raised a skeptical brow. "Any word on the victim's wife?"

"Nothing yet. You think she's still on the island?"

"Her name didn't trigger any flight alerts."

"Maui is close. Could she have sailed?"

Dan scoffed. "You know less about boats than you know about bulls. Only a serious sailor would cross Alenuihāhā Channel at night. We're talking thirty miles of rough seas."

Rona bristled at the dig, but after everything she hadn't said on the Hiapo case, she didn't want to make the same meek mistakes. "We should still check if the wife knows how to sail."

"I already did. Not the adventurous type. Penny Campbell has a gym membership and that's about it."

Penny and Paul Campbell. They sounded too cute for words. If she *had* killed her husband, Rona wondered what put her over the edge.

The homicide call had come in last night as Rona had arrived at her apartment, only to turn around and drive up the coast to a ritzy resort neighborhood at Waikui Beach. Frustrated by the Hiapo case and the lost dinner she had expected to enjoy, she donned her gloves and shoe covers and entered the small yet opulent condo. After Detective Lau found naked photos of college-age women in the victim's marital bed, they put out an APB on the wife.

Rona opened the folder with the photos they had taken from the condo. Penny Campbell smiled back in various shots, her long auburn hair swept up in a bun at an elegant event, hanging free at the beach, tied in a ponytail at a coffee shop. She didn't look the type to camp out on the lam.

"If she's still on this island, where did she sleep?"

Dan frowned. "You think she had a lover?"

Rona shrugged. "He did. Why not her?"

"Seems awfully unfair to murder your husband if you're getting some on the side."

"Unless her fling was retaliation for his. She might have snapped when he wanted a divorce."

"Fair enough. I'll check for a prenup and compare it to the life insurance. We'll see which favored Penny the most."

Rona fanned the other images on the desk. "I'll hunt down the women in these photos. There might be a jealous murderer in the bunch."

When Dan left Rona's desk, she clicked on the photos of the bull and zoomed in on the image with Louie, Malu, and Grace in the shot. Jealousy didn't only happen between lovers. The same was true about rivalry or power. Had one of these cowboys benefited from Larry Hiapo's death? If so, could they also have tampered with that bull?

CHAPTER THIRTY-TWO

Louie turned off Hawai'i Belt Road onto a private paved lane that wound up the slope through farmland and wild grasses. After a while, they came to a wooden swing gate that led to a ranch. Mixed-breed cows grazed in small herds across the fields. A small fenced pasture stood off to the side away from the house, shed, and horse corral. In the center of the pasture, an enormous creamy-white bull lounged beneath a tree.

A man in a two-toned cap and a navy polo shirt stepped out of the white Animal Control SUV. He ambled over as Louie parked his truck.

"Good morning," he said. "You from Hiapo Ranch?"

Louie shook his hand. "Kakahiaka nō. I'm Louie Hiapo. Dis Makalani Pahukula. We good to take home our bull?"

"If you can get him to move. Laziest damn animal I ever observed."

Louie walked over to the fence, took in the bull and the size of the pasture, which looked about twenty yards across. "No chute?"

"Nope."

"Dis goin' be tough."

"I'm not a cowboy."

"Dass okay, neither is she." He laughed at the man's surprise. "Jus' kidding. We got dis."

Makalani side-eyed Louie, then stared at the massive, lounging bull. No way would a couple of flag sticks be enough to move that beast out of his nice comfy pasture and into a hot aluminum box.

"You wait here," he said to Makalani. "I'll turn around and line the trailer up wit' da gate."

Makalani joined the Animal Control officer at his car as Louie maneuvered the trailer in a multipoint turn. "Do you hold livestock often?"

"Almost never."

"Did the bull behave strangely while he was here?"

"Not that I or the rancher could tell."

Louie parked the truck and waved Makalani over to help.

"What's the plan?" she asked.

He handed her the sticks and the prod. "Don't use any of dis unless I say. No sudden moves. Not'ing aggressive."

Her heart beat faster. "I'm going in there with you?"

Louie cocked his head. "What good are your extra pair of hands out hea?"

Makalani fake-smiled. She did offer to help. "How much does he weigh?"

"Why? We not goin' carry um."

"I know. I'm just curious. Maybe a ton?"

"Nah, dis a big buggah. Mo' like twenty-five hundred pounds."

He slipped into the corral and tied one end of his rope to the side of the gate. Then he beckoned her to follow as he walked into the pasture, uncoiling the rope. He gave the bull a wide berth and circled behind the tree.

"Wait hea, yeah?"

"Where you going?"

He smirked. "To make dakine chute."

After tying the other end of the rope to the other side of the open gate, he returned to Makalani, pleased with his work. The ropes provided a visual channel to where he wanted the bull to go.

He took the prod and extra stick. "I'll go left. You go right. Da idea is to gently encourage da bull to get up and move. Do what I do and pay attention to what I say. If t'ings go bad, don't run. Just come back and hide behind da tree." When she nodded, he added, "We got dis."

Sure we do. I mean, what could go wrong?

The bull turned his head as she circled behind the tree, round black eyes watching every move she made.

Louie spoke softly from the other side of the makeshift chute. "Slowly extend da flag stick over da rope toward da tree." He did the same on his side to model what she should do.

The bull's ears twitched as strips of yellow and red vinyl fluttered in from the sides.

Louie angled his flags toward the ground. Makalani did the same. Together, they stretched their sticks closer and gently fluttered the flags behind the bull's back. The massive creature rose with a huff, turning his white head between the flags, Louie, and her.

Louie stepped forward along the rope and spoke in soothing tones. "Eh, pipi laho. Hele mai." When the bull didn't move, Louie tapped him lightly on the rump. "Come on, you big buggah, time fo' go home."

The bull moved away from the annoyance toward Makalani.

"Show um your flags."

The bull stopped, but continued to glare.

Makalani whispered, "What do I do now?"

"Look down, but stand tall. You need convey control wit'out acting like a threat."

She focused her gaze on the bull's knees and hoped her flags would turn him away. The shins—or whatever ranchers called the lower legs—were healing from deep scrapes. Had they come from stomping Larry Hiapo to death?

"Aurite den," Louie said. "Geev um a gentle tap on da rump."

"Gentle *tap?*" She swallowed the nervous giggles that crept up her throat. What on earth would she tell her family during next Thursday's call?

It was nothing, Māmā. I just smacked a bull on the butt, and he did what I said.

Unless he didn't.

She imitated Louie's call with a trembling voice. "Eh, pipi laho, time to go home."

He shifted away from her when the flags touched his back.

"Okay," Louie said. "Now we keep da annoyance behind so he like walk down dis chute."

"By chute, you mean this flimsy rope you strung on the sides?"

"Dass da one. If he try brush it on my side, I goin' jolt him like it's an electric fence."

"And if he tests my side?"

"Smack um wit' da stick."

She clenched her lips tight and cursed Louie in her mind.

The lazy animal didn't move. "What now?" she asked.

"We wait."

"Seriously?"

"You get somewhere else to go?"

"No, but . . ." She was about to reply with a snappy retort when she realized he was equally trapped. With no horses, paniolo, or proper cattle chutes to force the bull into the trailer, all they could do was wait for the bull to grow irritated by their presence and move on his own. Which gave her another organic opportunity to pry.

She took a steadying breath and began chatting as if they weren't separated by a killer bull. "So, uh . . . you and your family must be relieved."

"By what?"

"Well, if they're releasing the bull, it means the investigation is over and KPD ruled your father's death an accident."

"What else would it be?"

Yeah, Makalani, what else?

Did she really want to bring up the possibility of murder, now?

If not now, then when?

"Well, on the way here, you called the accident unlikely. I thought you might have considered foul play."

He nodded toward the stubborn bull. "Using dat?"

"Maybe. I mean, what if the animal had been intentionally trapped. Could your dad have been lured into the pit?"

Louie tensed. "Is dis dakine work you did up in Oregon? Because I doubt it's what you do at Puʻukoholā."

"You're right. The heiau is pretty quiet, but I *am* a law enforcement officer, so—"

"So dis how you t'ink."

"Occupational hazard." She paused. "What did you mean by *unlikely*?"

"Jeez, Makalani, I meant what were da odds?" He huffed at the dirt, looking more like an angry bull than the lazy creature between them who stubbornly refused to budge. "Besides, who would hate my dad enough to do what you suggest?"

She watched as he drew lines in the dirt with his boot. Was he considering his own feelings about his dad? According to Rosie and Kupunakāne, they had a complicated and violent relationship. How many times had Louie wished his father were dead?

"A person wouldn't need to hate," she said quietly. "They might only want him out of the way."

"To do what?"

She shrugged. "You'd know better than me."

Louie waved his flag behind the bull and received a stink eye in return. Makalani did the same, waiting for Louie as he waited for the bull.

Louie nodded at the animal. "Dad could be stubborn li'dis. Always in control. Dass who he was. Said he wanted to retire, but we knew he nevah would."

"You and Kenneth?"

"And everybody else. Dad got in everyone's business, like he nevah trusted us to do a good job. But if dass how he felt, why he put us in charge?"

"Who *is* in charge? It's hard for me to tell."

Louie snorted. "Join da club."

The bull ambled forward.

Louie waved the flag to move him past a tempting patch of grass. Although Makalani did the same, the animal turned and snorted at her.

"Eh, pipi," Louie said.

The Charolais turned, back and forth, deciding who annoyed him the most.

"Back off, Makalani. Bettah to let dis laho focus on me."

As she complied, Louie backed up slightly and positioned the cattle prod over his side of the rope while his other hand still waved the flag stick on the tree-side of the bull. What occurred next happened so quickly, she couldn't tell if the bull freaked out before or after he was shocked.

The animal bellowed and torqued to the side, swinging his horns inside the narrow rope chute.

Makalani stumbled back.

Louie planted his flag stick in the ground and poised the cattle prod in case the bull needed another shock.

"Be still, Makalani. Keep your eyes down."

She didn't need the instruction because her body had frozen in place.

Louie spoke in Hawaiian, as if hearing ʻōlelo might calm the bull down. Instead, he whipped his mighty head toward Louie and lowered his horns.

Without thinking, Makalani called to the beast and drew the attention back to her. "Noho mālie, pipi laho. Be still. We mean you no harm. Please, let us take you back home."

This time, when the bull glared at her, she kept her gaze soft and hummed the "Pūpū Hinuhinu" lullaby Māmā used to sing. When the animal calmed, she extended her flags back into the chute. Still humming the tune about pretty, shiny shells, she nudged the flags closer to the bull's side. He turned away from her and the flags and ambled farther down the chute.

Surprised it had worked, Louie did the same with his flags. When the bull reached the trailer, he smacked the flags on the rump, and the bull jumped inside.

Makalani sagged with relief until Louie ducked under the rope. He followed the bull into the trailer and swung the center gate shut to confine the animal in front. She was still gaping at him when he jumped off the back, slid the rear gate closed, and locked it into place.

He chained the gate tight for good measure, then looked at her in surprise. "What? Sometimes da slide lock bumps out."

She stared back, unable to express the terror that had hit her when he jumped into the trailer behind the bull. He could have been kicked, trampled, or gored right in front of her eyes. What had he been thinking to take such a risk? Were all the Hiapo men this arrogant, or just his father and him?

Louie untied the ends of the rope and began coiling it in. "What made you sing 'Pūpū Hinuhinu'?"

"Seriously? What made you follow an agitated bull into an aluminum box?"

He chuckled. "You calmed him pretty good by den. Besides, I can't have over a ton of weight swinging da trailer side to side while I drive. It stay dangerous to give a laho dat size too much space to move." He tossed the coiled rope into the truck's bed with the flag sticks and prod. "Hinuhinu covers plenny kine cows. I no can afford to have him injured on da way home."

"Wait, his name is actually Shiny?"

Louie winked. "It is now."

CHAPTER THIRTY-THREE

The whole family had gathered at the bull pasture by the time Makalani and Louie returned and he backed the trailer up to the gate. He hopped out of the cab and joined his brother at the fence.

Kenneth eyed him with concern. "You sure about this?"

Louie squinted at the other bulls in the distance. "If dey get problems wit' him, bettah to work it out now."

"What if he has issues with them?"

"Same t'ing. We gotta know what we dealing wit', yeah? No can have fighting bulls when we turn um out wit' da cows."

"Any ideas why this one wandered off on his own?"

Louie shrugged. "Coulda been bored. Or maybe da younger bulls chase um off. Hinuhinu been top dog long time already."

Grace laughed. "Hinuhinu?"

"Eh, blame Makalani. She named him."

"I did not," Makalani said. "I just sang him a song."

Louie remained serious. "You sang him a lullaby dat calmed his ass down." He looked at Grace, Malu, and everyone else leaning against the fence. "Can you believe da holding place nevah get one chute?"

"How you get um in?" Kupunakāne asked.

"Wit' guide ropes and flags."

Malu harrumphed. "You should have taken me."

"Dass what I thought—especially when I had to jolt um away from da rope. Da buggah geared up fo' one fight." He nodded at Makalani. "But she drew um back to her." He laughed. "Crazy ranger, I thought you was dead. And den you start humming 'Pūpū Hinuhinu'?" He chuckled. "Damn if it didn't work."

Everyone cracked up, even Grace's shy mom. Everyone, except for Kenneth.

"She could have been killed."

"I jus' said dat."

"How would we have explained that to the police, to the national parks service, to our buyers? Do you have any idea what trouble this could have caused?"

Grace gaped at her father. "You mean other than Makalani being dead?"

"That would have been tragic, of course, but Louie is the foreman. The responsibility is his."

Louie glared down at his brother. "Foreman, huh? Dass what you t'ink I am?"

Kenneth, inches shorter and at least seventy pounds lighter, stood his ground. "You don't have the judgment or the education to be anything else."

Makalani held her breath as the tension between brothers grew tight enough to snap. Rumiko stared at her hands. Kupunakāne gazed into the field. Kenneth's wife, Carolyn, glanced at their daughter, who seemed fixated on her boot. Malu, on the other hand, glowered at Kenneth with eyes full of hate.

Makalani's hand slid to her belt where a telescopic baton would have been. During her career as a law enforcement ranger, she had seen fights that had begun exactly like this. As she considered how to forestall the inevitable, Hinuhinu kicked the trailer's aluminum wall.

Kenneth jumped back.

Louie turned toward the threat.

Malu shook off his anger and went for the rear gate. "If we goin' do dis, we bettah do it now."

Louie grabbed a hook from the truck and fed it through a slot near the top of the trailer's exterior wall. "Let me know when you're clear, and I'll slide open da small gate."

Malu kept to the side as he opened the trailer's rear gate in case the bull had somehow escaped its confinement at the front. He climbed over the fence and yelled, "Clear."

Louie used the hook to unlatch the smaller sliding portion of the center gate and pulled it open. The trailer shook and clanked as Hinuhinu turned around in his confinement, squeezed out of the smaller opening, then jumped off the back and onto the grass. Once freed, the creamy-white beast took in his audience.

Rumiko sniffed back her tears. "So he's the one."

Grace came in for a hug.

Her grandmother put up a hand. "I'm okay." She looked at each of her sons in a way that was both accusatory and resigned. When they each dropped their gaze, she turned her back and left.

Kupunakāne stayed focused on the bull. "Look at um. He no cause trouble. He jus' happy to be home."

As Makalani watched Hinuhinu amble across the grass, she had to agree. The bull who had nearly attacked her and Louie seemed as amiable as a pet.

A very large pet.

With horns.

"It's noon already," Louie said. "Anybody fix lunch?"

Kenneth turned his back to follow Rumiko toward the house. "Mom and Carolyn put out a spread. Don't forget to thank them for their work."

"I always do. Mahalo, Carolyn, Mom," he yelled after them.

Neither turned around.

Grace scoffed at her uncle in disgust.

"What?" he said. "I t'ank um every time."

"With what, your mind?"

When Grace followed her mom, Louie turned to his grandfather for help.

"No look at me," Kupunakāne said. "You dug your own pit. Stay stuck or climb out, no mattah to me." He looked at Makalani. "'Pūpū Hinuhinu.' Ha! Dass good one. I gotta try dat."

Makalani's phone vibrated in her pocket as everyone walked away. She checked the caller and smiled. "Wassup, Sandy?"

"Eh, Makalani. How you like your new paniolo life?"

"Eventful."

"Oh, yeah?"

"Louie and I just transported a bull. Moved him into a trailer with a guide-rope chute and stick flags. It got a little dicey but, you know, I just sang him a lullaby and smacked him on the butt."

Sandy laughed. "Good to know you're still a little nuts."

Only Sandy or Māmā would describe Makalani in that way. To everyone else, including Pāpā, Makalani was the most serious and responsible person they knew. She missed the playful times she still spent with her mother and the youthful antics she had enjoyed with her only true childhood friend.

"It's a good story," Makalani said, "but I'm heading up for lunch."

"I won't keep you too long. Just wanted to let you know I've been hearing some buzz about Hiapo Ranch."

"Really? Concerning Larry Hiapo's death?"

"Nope. How they might want to sell."

Makalani stopped walking. "What did you hear?"

"A rancher from Oregon named Skip Una made an offer. I only heard about it because my dad is friends with Skip and sold him calves to grass-finish in Oregon in the past."

"Tight community."

"It is, which is why I thought you should know. According to Dad, Larry Hiapo refused to sell."

Makalani stopped walking. "And now he's dead."

"Uh-huh."

"And the sale?"

"Guess that's dead too."

CHAPTER THIRTY-FOUR

Flint Reed stared through the binoculars as Jay and Goyo climbed onto the back of his father's ancient blue truck. The extra height of the truck's short-bed cargo box gave them just enough elevation to see over the woven-wire fence and across the Hiapos' Kona-side pasture downslope of the gulch. Flint had been watching Hiapo Ranch for the last half hour since Louie had come home and backed his trailer to the Hāwī-side pasture beyond the horse training arena.

Jay and Goyo had arrived only moments ago, driving up the easement road in Jay's conspicuous aqua car. The color was so bright, Flint wished they had parked behind the trees. Then again, it's not as if any of the Hiapos would be looking their way. No one in that family gave two shits about the Reeds.

"What they doing?" Jay said.

"Unloading a bull."

Goyo grabbed the binoculars from Flint. "Ho, big suckah. Dey brought him home in dat metal trailer? Why he no run around his pasture now dat he free?"

Flint took back the binoculars. "Bulls don't run unless they're spooked, angry, or after a cow in heat."

Goyo laughed. "Eh, sound like solid reasons to me."

Flint ignored him and focused on the family members watching the bull. Kenneth was standing with his wife and mother. Kupunakāne was there too. The grandfather was older than Flint's dad, yet looked annoyingly strong. The others seemed angry or upset, especially Larry's widow, who was heading up to the house. It had to be hard knowing her husband's killer had returned.

Flint muttered, "Why didn't they sell it or slaughter it for beef?"

"Enough about da bull." Jay grabbed the binoculars and took in the scene. "Almost everybody went up to da house. I don't see da sistah or her husband wit' dem. But dat big wahine from last night stay watching at da fence next to a kāne even bigger dan her."

"That would be Louie Hiapo."

"Da braddah who no like sell da ranch?"

"Yeah. The other brother, Kenneth, is the skinnier guy leaving now."

Even without the binoculars, Flint could tell it was Kenneth from his stuck-up posture and the way he marched up the hill. So much arrogance for such a puny man. Even as a teenager, the eldest brother had always acted superior to everyone else, especially the poor neighbor boy whose family got screwed over by his. Kenneth never spared a moment in his privileged life to even say hello to Flint, let alone invite him to their ranch.

Jay chuckled. "He looks plenny pissed off."

"Always is." Flint's resentment was as hot now as it was then.

Jay lowered the binoculars. "Okay, den. No sistah, no husband, no kid. I say we follow da big wahine and see where she go."

Flint shrugged. "I still don't know who she is, but if Rosie and Brian took her out to dinner, she must matter to them." He looked at Goyo. "Did you ask your friend about Brian Pahukula?"

"Who, Gabe? He's my cousin. We talk story little bit last night. He and his sistah had to move their paka lōlō farm to another location last winter because of Kaua'i Vice. Big-time hassle. He blamed everyt'ing on some teenage girl."

"What's that got to do with Brian?"

"She's connected to da Pahukula 'ohana."

"Connected how?"

"Cousin or somet'ing, I don't know. But Gabe said her family showed up at da farm. Told um Vice was on da way."

"I don't see how that helps us?"

"One of dem was a ranger."

"So?"

"Gabe said da ranger was a big Hawaiian woman." Goyo nodded toward Hiapo Ranch. "Maybe like the one ovah dea."

Flint snatched the binoculars from Jay and focused in on the woman standing at the fence. She was hapa-Hawaiian like Brian with similar features and build. They could be related. If so, Rosie might be upset if her husband's relative got hurt doing paniolo work—upset enough to pressure her family to sell Hiapo Ranch.

Flint adjusted the focus. "Louie is parking the trailer. The woman is following the others up to the house. I can see smoke from the grill. They're breaking for lunch." Flint's phone rang from a now-familiar contact, one he didn't want to speak with in front of these men. He jumped off the back of the truck. "Hello?"

"Eh, Flint. It's Skip Una. How are things going on your end?" The guy was so loud.

Flint walked away from the gangsters like he was chatting with a friend. "Good. How about you?"

"*Me?* I'm waiting to close a deal, which I cannot do until the Hiapos fall into line."

"Right. Of course. I'm working on that."

"By doing what?"

Jay and Goyo watched him from the truck.

"Um, can I call you later? This isn't the best time."

"Oh, sure," he said, sarcastically. "It's not as if I don't have other things to do—eat papaya, work on my tan, rethink my generous offer on your ranch."

"No, don't do that. Look . . . I think I found a way to convince Rosie to sell."

"How?"

"Her husband's cousin is working on Hiapo Ranch. She and Rosie seem close. If she got hurt doing cowboy work, Rosie might want to sell."

"Because of her husband's *cousin*?" Skip said skeptically.

"Yeah, and because of her son. With no ranch to run to, Rosie can guide him to something else. Anyway, I'm working on it."

"Not fast enough. But here's some motivation for you. I'm going to lower the asking price on your ranch ten thousand dollars for every day I have to wait."

"Until what?"

"Until I'm in escrow for Hiapo Ranch."

Flint glanced at the men sitting in the truck's bed, legs extended as if preparing for a nap. "It's gonna take time."

"Time is money. The longer you take, the less you're going to get." Skip ended the call.

Flint stuffed the phone in his pocket and stomped back to the truck. "What are you guys doing?"

Jay opened his eyes. "Getting comfortable while you get us some grindz."

"What?"

"It's lunchtime. You said it yourself."

Flint bit back a retort. If these a-holes expected lunch, they'd have to settle for peanut butter bread.

"And somet'ing to drink," Goyo added.

Flint held up a hand in acknowledgment as he walked up the easement road, then flipped them the bird when he turned behind the line of trees. Although galling to wait on them like a butler, he now needed them even more. Ten thousand bucks gone every day? That was seventy grand a week. Skip had only offered four hundred for their property. They'd be down to almost nothing if it took a month before the Hiapos agreed to sell Skip their ranch.

"Dad's gonna lose it."

As if summoned, Hoʻolohe opened the front door of the house. He still wore his ratty plaid pajamas even though it was midday. "Where's my truck?"

"I parked it down our road."

"Why?"

"Because the fence needs mending and my tools are in the back."

"What tools?"

"Fence-mending tools."

"Since when you mend fences?"

"Since you got too old to do anything except eat and complain."

The old man grumbled and stomped back into the house. Flint heard him shout through the screen door, "You're late fixing lunch."

Flint hated living at home, or rather, living at home with him. It would be another thing if he had this property to himself. With a little seed money, he could turn it into a self-sustaining farm—a dozen cows for milk and beef, chickens for poultry and eggs, vegetable garden and fruit trees to balance what he ate. Sounded pretty chill. And he could kick Jay and Goyo off his land for good.

Who was he kidding? That would involve too much hard work. Better to sell the land to Skip Una and keep all the money for himself. If only his dad would cooperate and die.

CHAPTER THIRTY-FIVE

After a filling lunch of barbecued Korean short ribs, sesame cucumber salad, and rice, Makalani and Grace squeezed into the back seat of Louie's truck. Malu sat in front. They were headed to his friend's cattle ranch on the slopes of Mauna Kea, four thousand feet up. The morning's conflict had cleared like the clouds, leaving everyone in a more amiable mood. The men laughed as they spoke, but between the Hawaiian reggae playing, the truck's engine, and tires on the road, Makalani couldn't hear what was said. Instead, she considered Sandy's news.

Skip Una wants to buy Hiapo Ranch. Larry Hiapo refused to sell. But what if Louie and/or Malu knew about the offer but didn't know Larry had refused. Could one or both of them have thought Larry was going to pressure Kupunakāne to accept?

Makalani studied the men laughing in the front seats. Neither of them would have let Hiapo Ranch be sold without a fight. The question was, how far would they have been willing to go?

She leaned toward Grace. "Do you guys help out often at Malu's friend's place?" Since she couldn't ask about Skip Una, this seemed like the next best thing to know. On her first day at the ranch, Louie had seemed awfully testy about where Malu spent his time.

Grace nodded. "Kam only ranches part time so the work piles up. His family helps some but, you know, they're not paniolo."

"What's his main occupation?"

"Infrastructure maintenance—fixing roads, repairing broken water mains, stuff li'dat."

"It must be hard to work two strenuous jobs."

"Man's gotta eat." Grace looked out the window. "This is hard country to ranch."

From what Makalani could see, she was inclined to agree. This was her first time on Saddle Road, originally built by the federal government as an access road to the US Army's Pōhakuloa Training Area. Since Hawai'i's government lacked the funds to bring it up to state highway standards, the two-lane road between active Mauna Loa and extinct Mauna Kea was a roller coaster of blind turns, rolling hills, and abrupt stops for single-lane bridges. Although fun to traverse, Makalani couldn't imagine driving this route as often as Malu apparently did, nor trying to raise cattle on the dry and bumpy terrain.

Where did Malu lay his head at night, and why didn't he live, full time, with Louie at Hiapo Ranch?

Makalani could never have lived on this barren volcanic tundra where hardly anything other than cactus, fountain grass, and prickly gorse bushes broke through the black 'a'ā lava chunks. It was so dry. The trade winds that carried the evaporated ocean water up the mountains dumped all their rain onto the wet windward side. Only scant inches of water remained for the inner-island valley and the leeward plains down to the West Coast. "The Saddle" between the volcanoes was especially stark.

"Did a paniolo give this area its name?" Makalani asked Grace.

"Not sure. The old lava flows that overlapped between Mauna Kea and Mauna Loa must have reminded *someone* of a saddle. Could have been a paniolo I guess, but I never heard that said." She pointed down the road. "Kam's ranch is down there."

"Down where?" Makalani didn't see anything *anywhere* that resembled a ranch. That opinion did not change as they drove up the rocky dirt path.

They parked beside four sturdy horses in a three-rail corral across from a tractor and a beat-up UTV in the midst of repair. A mutt barked at them as they hopped out of the cab. When it saw Malu, it wagged its tail and came over to be petted.

A burly Hawaiian man in a sweatshirt and cap looked up from the engine. "Eh, Malu, Louie. Howzit, Grace." He popped his chin in salutation and quickly finished his task. He lowered the hood and met them at the gate. "T'anks fo' coming, yeah?"

"Always, brah," Malu said. "Kam, dis Makalani, a cousin of Louie's brother-in-law and one ranger at Pu'ukoholā Heiau. She's been helping at da ranch, so we brought her wit' us to help you."

"A ranger, huh? Okay den. Mahalo no kou hele 'ana mai." After thanking her for coming, he recited a Hawaiian proverb, "Kōkua aku kōkua mai, pēlā ka nohona 'ohana." Then he walked away without waiting to see if Makalani understood.

As luck would have it, she had heard Tūtū recite this proverb before when reminding Makalani to treat others like family by helping and accepting help in return. Accepting help was the part Makalani needed reminding of the most.

She took in the aged leather tack and rusted metal gear hanging in the pitted-wood and corrugated steel shed. An isolated rancher could never have done all the necessary work. Kam must have embraced this 'ōlelo no'eau in order to survive.

Would I have learned to accept help if I had grown up in this unforgiving place?

"We're going to be out a long time," Kam said. "Lua's in da back if you like use."

Makalani followed Grace through Kam's rustic home. Hunting trophies and photos of early paniolo days hung on the walls. Eating utensils and condiments sat in trays on the picnic table between the kitchenette and the couch. A guitar perched against a well-loved chair. Bottles of Johnnie Walker and a generic rum sat on a ring-stained table with a selection of glasses as if always expecting friends.

Grace opened the back screen door and led Makalani to a makeshift bathroom off a low, narrow deck. The guerrilla-style construction made use of every possible scrap as if mindful of cost, resources, and space. Once done, Makalani walked farther down the deck as Grace took her turn.

Doors to a couple of bunk rooms stood open, presumably to air them out from a strong scent of ammonia coming from inside. Makalani guessed Kam had recently cleaned or had a pack of very annoyed cats. The larger room at the end was closed and hidden by drapes.

A propane tank stood a few yards away. Giant water drums sat in the dirt along the deck. Clear plastic bins held recyclable bottles—one for plastic and another for glass. A third bin contained and assortment of random cleaning supplies, rubber tubes, gloves, filters, and masks.

"Let's go," Grace said, wiping her wet hands on her jeans.

This time they walked outside the house past the horse corral and tack room to a dirt road leading off to the side. Kam and Louie drove slowly in a flatbed utility vehicle with tools strapped to the sides.

Malu waited in the front seat of a passenger UTV with the plastic window flaps unzipped. "Put on your gloves. We get hard work ahead."

Malu wasn't kidding. After the first hour of cutting through spiny branches and pulling gorse roots out of the hardened earth, sweat was pouring into all their eyes. The sturdy clothes they needed to protect themselves from cuts and the high-altitude chill also trapped in the heat. No one dared wipe their faces with gorse bristles on their gloves. After the second hour, even Makalani was ready to call it a day.

"What happens to all of this?" Makalani asked Kam.

"I get a small grant from the government to control the gorse. I truck it to them to burn or whatever they do. I give some to my friend who has a small mill. Gorse is high in protein. Cattle won't graze it, but they'll eat it when milled into feed. Horses like it, especially the yellow flowers that bloom early in the year."

"Why not let it grow?"

"It takes over the land. Plus, it's a major fire hazard. When Mauna Loa erupted in 2022 and the lava came down that slope, the gorse lit up like the sun. I stay lucky the fire and lava never crossed over here."

They stacked most of the gorse bundles onto the bed of Kam's flatbed UTV and strapped the rest to the back of Malu's four-seater. When they returned to the ranch, they transferred all of it to Louie's giant truck.

"Thanks for doing this," Kam said. "I'll hose it down after so you don't take any seeds home." He looked at Grace. "Can you go with Louie to help him unload?"

"Sure."

"Good. Then me, Malu, and Makalani can move up the herd."

Makalani turned to Kam. "I can unload if you need Grace here."

"Nah," he said. "Let the young one do the hardest work. You ride with Malu. I'll go on horseback."

Kam headed for his tack room. Grace hopped in the truck with Louie. Malu trudged back to the UTV. Makalani glanced between them, wishing she could join someone else. As Louie's truck turned onto Saddle Road and passed a bright-aqua car that hadn't been there before, Makalani considered running down to see if the occupants needed help. They were in the middle of nowhere. They might have broken down.

"You coming or what?" Malu said, obviously annoyed. He knew she was stalling, but with Grace and Louie underway, neither of them had a choice.

Makalani jumped in the passenger seat, where they sat in silence until Kam trotted past them and onto the trail. Although they had driven across the rough terrain earlier, Makalani noticed more in the front seat than she had before while riding in the back. This time, she saw the chunks of aged lava that caused their vehicle to lurch and rock down the narrow suggestion of a path. As the steering wheel jolted violently to the sides, Makalani understood why Grace had cautioned her to keep her thumbs out of the wheel's center holes. If Malu had not cupped his thumbs with his fingers, the forceful torques could have torn them right off.

The side door popped open as they hit the next rock, causing the zipped-down plastic windows to flap out of place. She clutched the center seat belt neither of them had used and reached for the handle. If she hadn't anchored herself, the next jolt would have thrown her into the shallow gully off the edge of the trail. Malu continued his pace as Makalani struggled with the window flaps and door. Once she remembered the order of operations, she untangled the flaps and latched the door shut.

"Is the trail like this all over his ranch?"

Malu nodded. "Sometimes worse."

"How did Kam put it in?"

"He didn't. Parker Ranch leased um befo'. Da trail was still hea when DHHL leased da property to Kam."

With the gorse on one side and the gully on the other, Makalani couldn't imagine where Kam's cattle could graze. All she saw was more rough, uninhabitable terrain.

Malu stopped abruptly as Kam pointed to the east.

"Can you see um?" Malu said.

"See what?"

"Must be eighty or ninety wild sheep."

Makalani squinted at the shrubs and boulders to see if any of them moved. "Where?"

"Down by Saddle Road."

She peered into the ridges and gully until the slow-moving figures appeared. Once she knew what to look for, she saw them up and down the rocks, not just to the east but up Mauna Kea's lower slope.

"They're everywhere."

"Yeah. Eating Kam's grass. Even da hunting parties he hosts no can keep da numbahs in check."

As they drove around a bend, cattle finally appeared, ambling up the wider, and marginally grassier, lava-strewn path. Unlike the plump Angus-Charolais herds on Hiapo Ranch, this handful of cows looked as lean and rugged as the land. The largest among them trailed behind, glaring at the vehicle that disrupted her peace.

Kam motioned Malu to continue while he steered his horse into a side gully to round up a stray cow. Malu and Makalani gathered more cattle as they drove higher up the slope. With scant grass left on the lower trails and the rest growing in rocky gullies better suited for wild goats, Makalani understood why they needed to drive the herd upslope.

"How far does Kam's ranch go?"

"Seven thousand feet. Hard on da horses, even harder on UTVs."

"You help him a lot. Is that why you live here?"

"Who say I live hea?"

"Oh, I guess I misunderstood."

"Misunderstood who, Louie? He stay talk stink about me?"

"No. I mean . . . I don't think so. I've had a fire hose of new information, I probably just heard something wrong."

"Damn straight." He yanked the steering wheel as the tires veered off a rock. "Bet it was Kenneth. Dat stuck-up buggah is as bad as his dad."

"Larry was Louie's dad too."

"You t'ink I don't know dat?" He yanked the steering wheel the other direction, dangerously close to an edge. "I no like speak ill of da dead but, you know, good riddance to him."

Makalani saw her opportunity but wasn't sure how far she could pry or what she could say that wouldn't push him figuratively—and literally—over the edge. Malu fought with the vehicle like he was fighting with a man.

"It must have been hard to work with your . . ." She stopped, not knowing how to describe Louie in relationship to Malu, or whether she was even supposed to know about them as a couple.

"My what, lover's faddah . . . is dat what you meant?"

Makalani shrugged, feeling safer if she stayed mute.

"Larry was an asshole to everyone he met. Small mind. Smaller heart. Only cared about two things in life: his animals and his land."

Makalani added this perspective to the already varying portrayal she had heard from Kupunakāne, Rumiko, Louie, Rosie, and Grace. Everyone seemed to have a different impression of the man who may or may not have had control over Hiapo Ranch.

Malu veered onto a small plateau where a couple of cows and their calves had wandered to graze. He drove between them and the edge of another ditch, beeped his horn, and zigzagged until the stragglers joined the herd walking up the main path.

"Stingy fake," he said, spewing his complaints about Larry with every torque of the wheel. "Nevah help nobody. Nevah deserve what he get. Nevah care about our people or how he mess up da ranch."

He accelerated over a bump and caught a rock with the front tire. The UTV lurched to the right, jostling Makalani into him. When he jerked the wheel left, she slammed into the side door. The sudden changes of direction and weight tipped the vehicle onto two tires. Makalani grabbed on to the rails and stared into a twenty-foot ravine.

"Move ovah to me," Malu yelled as he struggled with the wheel.

Makalani fought against gravity and wedged her feet against the UTV's frame, when a tire hit a rock and the door bounced open again.

Malu drove on the berm like a daredevil on a ledge, trying not to tumble the vehicle by turning too suddenly away from the threat. As the vehicle's balance tipped toward the safety of the path, Makalani looked over her shoulder at Malu. Instead of relief, she saw a calculating gaze.

"You nevah shoulda come to our ranch," he yelled.

It happened so quickly she couldn't be sure. But in that fleeting moment, as the UTV's suspended tires began to lower, Malu's calculation darkened into a more sinister intent.

He won't do it. Not with Kam close enough to see.

Unless his friend wouldn't care. Why had Kam really sent Louie and Grace off the ranch?

Don't do it, Malu. Please.

But the steering wheel either jolted out of Malu's hands or he yanked it intentionally, and Makalani fell out the open door.

CHAPTER THIRTY-SIX

Makalani grabbed for the UTV's frame as she toppled out the door and caught the window's zipped-down flap instead. Gripping with one hand, she slammed against the slope while the jostling vehicle dragged and spun her against the rocks.

The plastic ripped.

She fell backward into the ravine, swimming her arms in the air in a futile attempt to return to the ledge. Brush caught her jacket and hair. Although the shrubs spared her skull as she flipped, the branches and rocks scraped her forearms and face. The rest of her tumble was lost in a barrage of impacts and pain.

A final grunt burst from her mouth as she slammed to a stop.

She remained still, unsure of the damage her body had sustained. Instead, she cataloged the aches, beginning with her head. Aside from the sting and wetness on her face, she didn't feel any throbbing that would suggest her head had been hit. Her mind felt clear, so she was probably not concussed. Her shoulders and arms felt bruised and scraped. The left socket was sore but not dislocated, likely from getting wrenched while grabbing shrubs to stop her slide. Her shins and knees throbbed, and her entire back ached.

But can I move?

When she managed to wiggle her ankle, she exhaled with relief.

"I'm coming, Makalani," a man yelled from above.

She opened her eyes and saw Kam climbing down the rocks.

"Don't move yet, okay?"

She closed her eyes against the cascading particles and dirt, content to wait for Kam as she sorted her memory into logical sense.

The vehicle had tipped on two wheels. A bump opened her door. The left tires were falling safely toward the trail. So how did she fall out?

Kam squatted beside her. "You okay?"

"More or less."

"What happened?"

She looked up the rocks and saw Malu at the top staring down. From the bottom of the ravine, he looked impossibly tall.

What did you do, Malu?

She remembered the cold calculation in his eyes and the moment a decision had appeared to have been made.

"What did Malu say?" she asked.

Kam glanced up the ravine. "Your door opened and you fell out."

"Is that all?"

"Yeah. Why, was there more?"

She looked into Kam's compassionate eyes and reminded herself that this was Malu's close—perhaps *closest*—friend. No matter what she said, Kam would never believe Malu had yanked the steering wheel to throw her out the door. She wasn't entirely sure she believed it herself.

"I'm just trying to piece together what happened."

"Time for that after we get you patched up. You think you can move?"

When she nodded, he helped her to sit. When that went okay, he helped her to stand. She placed a hand on his shoulder for balance as he checked her for injuries.

"Your clothes stay ripped on your back, arms, and legs. Lots of cuts. Nothing too bloody, so that's good. You standing okay. How your ribs feel?"

She straightened up and took a deep breath. The aches felt more like bruising than breaks.

Kam sighed with relief. "You one tough wahine. I expected much worse."

She looked up the twenty-foot ridge. "Guess I was lucky."

"That's for sure. You could have been killed."

He took the cloth yoke off his neck and wiped the blood from her face. "Head wounds bleed like a stuck pua'a. Hard to tell how deep this cut is until I wash it up back at the ranch."

Above her, Malu stood as still and impenetrable as stone. Although she desperately wanted to leave, she didn't want to ride beside him. How could she ask Kam to drive without appearing to distrust his best friend?

"Is the UTV damaged?" she asked hopefully.

"From what?"

"We hit a lot of rocks. It tipped on two wheels as we drove along the edge."

Kam's face pinched with alarm. He had clearly not seen this happen or heard the report. "I'll drive and tie my horse to the rail. This happened on my land. I need make sure you're okay."

She nodded. "Whatever you think is best."

When they reached the top, Malu had already moved to the back seat. Kam helped her into the front, then made sure her door was securely closed and latched. Despite his driving skill and familiarity with the road, the ride down the trail was as rough as the way up. Had Malu been doing his best to drive on a difficult path? What about the decision she had seen—or thought she had seen—in his eyes? With all the jostling and jeopardy, she couldn't know what had passed through his mind. Even during the calmest moments, she had a poor track record of reading people's thoughts. It was far more likely that she had projected her fears onto his face.

We see what we believe, and we doubt those we already mistrust.

She had watched this happen to her family not too long ago when preconceptions and suspicions nearly tore her 'ohana apart. Was she guilty of the same thing, or had Malu intentionally knocked her down the ravine?

CHAPTER THIRTY-SEVEN

By the end of the day, Detective Rona Kim was beat. She had been working her butt off to solve Paul Campbell's murder even while images of Larry Hiapo's gruesome death kept flashing in her mind. It took every bit of discipline not to recheck her inbox or scroll through the photos of the killer white bull she had uploaded to her phone. The more tempted she had felt, the more determined she had been to focus on her work. If she solved Campbell's murder quickly, she could indulge her growing obsession with Larry Hiapo and maybe find cause to reopen the case.

She had identified all five of the young women in Paul Campbell's photographs and interviewed four. So far, all the women admitted to having affairs. Three had returned to their mainland colleges. The fourth was a waitress at the Kona bar where all of them had met Paul. The fifth coed shifted nervously on her couch.

Rona noted her dilated pupils and the scabs on her emaciated arms. This and the neglected state of her tiny apartment pointed to drug abuse. Jen Farber was high, most likely on meth, which did not seem in keeping with the murder victim's type.

"When did you last see Paul Campbell?" Rona asked.

"I don't know, last year, maybe longer. It was just a couple times, maybe six, something like that."

"Two or six?"

"I don't know, maybe more? It lasted a month or so while I was in school."

"Are you still enrolled?"

"No, I, um, dropped out after that. Had other things to do."

"Like what?"

"I don't know—life, work, something other than studying and tests. Why does this matter? I hardly knew the guy."

Rona handed Jen the seminaked photo of her on Paul Campbell's bed. "You remember this?"

Jen's expression flipped through shock, puzzlement, and agitation until finally settling on fear. "Where did you get this?"

"In Paul's condo, along with compromising photos of four other young women."

"He brought them home? What an asshole, he told me I was the only one. He made all these promises to take me to Honolulu, set me up nice, said he needed time to prepare before he left his wife." Jen gestured erratically as she spoke. The woman was tweaking for sure.

"What are you on?"

"I'm not on anything. I just haven't slept in a while, that's all, too much coffee and Coke. Pepsi, I mean, not the other kind. I'm not a drug addict or anything like that, I just . . ." She grabbed her chest, panting and shaking her head.

"Easy, Jen, I can help. How long ago did you use?"

When she didn't answer, Rona called it in. The woman's pulse was racing and sweat dripped from her face.

"Help's on the way, Jen. Let's slow your breathing, four counts in, four counts out. Can you do that for me?"

When Jen nodded, Rona hurried to the kitchenette and returned with a glass of cool water and a damp towel for her neck. She turned up the fan and helped Jen drink.

"I need to know what you took and where you got it before the paramedics arrive." When Jen shook her head, Rona cradled the woman's face. "We need to know what's inside you so we can make the pain stop. That's what you want, right, Jen? To make the pain stop? Now tell me what you took so we don't make this worse."

Jen's eyes darted down to the side. Buried between the cushions of the couch, Rona found a baggie of white powder.

"Meth?" Rona asked, guessing the Big Island's main illegal drug.

Jen jerked a nod before throwing back her head as her rigid muscles shook.

Fists pounded on the door. The paramedics yelled from outside.

Rona raced to the door and directed them to the couch. "This is Jen Farber, twenty-five, on meth, grabbed her heart ten minutes ago, showed signs of sweating and accelerated pulse. I'm Detective Rona Kim. I arrived ten minutes before that. Her eyes were dilated at that time. She seemed jittery but otherwise stable."

As one paramedic attended to Jen, the other quizzed Rona and prepped a syringe. "Any opioids?"

"I don't know."

"Alcohol or other drugs?"

"None that I've seen."

He injected the naloxone, helped his partner lift Jen onto the gurney, and left as quickly as they had arrived.

Rona called Dan.

"Did you find her?" he asked.

"I'm in her apartment. The paramedics just rolled her out."

"Was she attacked?"

"Overdose. Apparently meth."

"Huh. Think it's related?"

"Not sure. She claimed Paul promised to leave his wife and bring her to Honolulu. She seemed bitter and upset."

"Upset enough to stab him thirteen times?"

"If she had known about the other women, I'd say yes, but she seemed genuinely shocked. She blew up at me when I told her about the other photos we found. If I had to guess, I'd say she turned to drugs after he dumped her. I seriously doubt he would have been attracted to her in this present state."

"Drug addicts lie."

"True. But she's twenty pounds skinnier than she was in the photo and looks like a wreck. Paul wouldn't have pursued the woman I met today."

"That may be true, but meth can definitely incite rage. Did you say she let you into her apartment after you identified yourself?"

"Yep. And I'm still here."

"Good. Let me know what you find."

Rona stared at her phone. Dan was 100 percent behind her handling of this case. Why couldn't he have done the same with their investigation into Larry Hiapo's death?

CHAPTER THIRTY-EIGHT

Exhausted from her tumble down the ravine and drowsy from the pain relievers Kam insisted she take, Makalani passed out as soon as Louie drove his truck off the ranch. She didn't begin to stir until a sudden jolt made her groan.

Grace shook her again. "We're home, Makalani. Time to get out."

"Huh?" she said, struggling to wake.

"We're back at Hiapo Ranch."

"Right, um . . . I stashed my stuff on, uh, one of the beds. I'll grab it and drive home."

"What? No way. You can't drive in this state. You might be concussed. Someone needs to watch over you in case you hit your head."

"I'm not concussed."

"And forget about that drafty bunkhouse. You're staying with me."

Makalani swayed on her feet, trying to figure out where she was in relation to her car and her gear.

Grace put an arm around her waist and walked her toward the main house. "We're going to soak out your pain with a nice hot bath. It'll be good for your wounds too. Old rodeo trick. Trust me, it works. And don't worry about your stuff. I'll fetch it before you get out."

Makalani nodded, too tired to object.

Grace bypassed the dining area where everyone had gathered and headed for the stairs. "Be down soon."

Her father intercepted them. "Hold up, young lady. What happened to her?"

"Took a little tumble."

"Out of what, a helicopter?"

Makalani snorted. Not good. Giddiness had set in.

"I'll be right down, Dad. Just let me set her up."

Kenneth stepped in her way. "What's going on?"

Grace shuffled Makalani around him and onto the steps. "Nothing. She just needs a bath and a good night's rest."

"Did you take her to emergency?"

"We offered."

"And?"

Grace guided Makalani to the second-floor landing and glared down at her dad. "She said nothing was broken or needed stitches. She's a ranger, Dad. She oughta know."

Whatever Kenneth said after that was lost as Grace led Makalani around the corner to the bathroom down the hall. The tub looked inviting. The place she had rented in Waimea only had a shower. She had to admit, a hot soak sounded great.

Grace opened a cupboard behind her. "Here's a towel and a washcloth. Scrub your wounds good, but don't hurt the flesh." She turned on the water and brought out a box of first aid supplies. "I'll be back with your gear before you come out."

"You sure your dad's okay with this?"

"All good. Enjoy your soak. I'll bring your dinner up here."

Grace closed the door, leaving Makalani alone. The vanity lights over the mirror invited her to look. No wonder Kenneth was alarmed. If one of Makalani's junior rangers had come in looking like this, she would have driven them straight to the ER.

She peeled off her bloodstained clothes and laid them on the toilet's immaculate white lid. Then she stared into the vertical mirror behind the door and saw her bruised body for the first time. The colors of her scraped and ripening skin made her wince.

She peeled off the bandages Kam had applied to her forehead, shins, and arms. Nothing too deep. No stitches required. She sank into the tub. The heat stung, then enveloped her in a comforting hug.

Her phone vibrated on the bath mat where it had fallen from her jeans. She closed her eyes and waited for the intrusion to stop. When it stubbornly refused, she finger-dragged the mat closer and answered the call.

"Hey, Māmā."

"Why didn't you answer with video?"

"I'm in the tub."

"You said you didn't have one."

"I don't. I'm at Hiapo Ranch."

"Oh, really?" she said, as if Makalani was telling her about a hot date.

"It's nothing like that. I just needed a soak."

"What did you do now?"

"Nothing. Why do you always assume I've done something wrong?"

"Not wrong. Careless or dangerous. Which is it this time?"

Makalani bent her knees more and sank deeper into the heat. Although modern and new, Grace's tub was still standard size.

"I helped the Hiapos clear gorse bushes from their friend's ranch."

"And?"

"Nothing."

Māmā scoffed. "There's always something with you. Why do you think I called. I can feel it all the way from Anahola."

If her mother's sixth sense had kicked in, she would drag the truth out of Makalani tonight or show up on her doorstep the next day. Even the farthest islands were less than an hour apart.

"Okay, the door of a UTV opened on a rough trail, and I fell into a ditch."

"A ditch. And suffered what injuries?"

"A couple of scrapes. Honestly, it's no big deal."

"Honestly."

"Will you stop repeating what I say?"

"Will you start telling me the truth?"

So much for a relaxing bath.

Makalani sat up. "Fine. I fell into a small ravine. No broken bones. No stitches required."

"Who was driving?"

"Malu, a paniolo at Hiapo Ranch."

"Not one of the family?"

"The boyfriend of one of the sons."

"Uh-huh."

"Uh-huh what?"

"I'm filling in the spaces of your strategically sterile story."

Makalani activated the video.

Māmā gasped, then nodded as she assessed the forehead cut and the bruise on Makalani's right cheek. "Okay, not too bad. But what's the deal with this Malu?"

"It's more than him. I'm afraid Rosie's father may have been killed."

"As in murdered?"

"Yeah."

"Spill it, and don't you dare leave anything out."

Makalani spoke fast, not knowing when Grace might return. Although impossible to include everything, she laid out the grisly scene, the trouble between Rosie's brothers, their mother's fears about Malu, and their grandfather's apparent control of the ranch. After describing Malu in greater detail, including his quarrels with Louie and his dislike for her, she explained what she believed had happened at Kam's ranch.

"So you think Malu did it on purpose?"

"I don't know. The more time goes by, the less certain I feel."

Māmā nodded. "Confirmation bias."

Makalani laughed. "Look at you sounding all official."

Māmā smiled. "I try to keep up."

When Makalani entered law enforcement training, Māmā began reading articles and binging old episodes of *NCIS* despite Makalani's assurances that her ranger job was nothing like DiNozzo's and Gibbs's. After this year's events, that argument was becoming harder to defend.

"Tell me the truth, Makalani. Are you in danger?"

"I didn't think so."

"And now?"

"I'm not sure."

"You won't leave this alone." Māmā said this as a fact. "Even though you could get even more seriously hurt, and it could rip Rosie's family apart."

"They're already floundering."

"Not because of you."

She's right.

And yet . . .

"I promised Rosie I would do this. If one of them is a murderer, she and the others need to know."

"And if they're not and they learn what you're doing, your suspicions could poison this family forever."

Makalani sighed. *Like polluted water flowing downstream.*

Grace knocked on the door. "I brought dinner."

"I have to go, Māmā. Call you later."

"Tread carefully, Makalani."

"I will."

She wrapped herself in a towel and hastily began applying ointment and bandages on her cuts.

Grace knocked again and opened the door enough to present Makalani's pajama pants and shirt. "Hope you don't mind, I pulled these out of your pack. Help yourself to the lotion. My room is next door."

Bandaged and refreshed, Makalani found two sandwiches and apple slices waiting for her on the bed.

"Mom fixed curry for dinner, but that was too messy for up here."

"This is perfect, thanks."

"Eat up. You can sleep on the left."

Makalani wolfed down the first ham and cheese sandwich. "How did you score a queen-size bed?"

"This was Uncle Louie's room before he built his own place up the hill."

"The yellow one-story behind Kupunakāne's barn?"

"That's the one. He moved in when I was born. Ten years later, Dad and Grandad remodeled this house."

"Kupunakāne never lived here?"

"Nah. He and my great-grandmother always lived in the old house. He helped build this one for Grandad when he got married. Mom moved into Dad's room with him, I got Uncle Louie's, and they keep Rosie's room for her and her family in case they want to stay overnight."

Makalani bit into the second sandwich as she considered the origins of the house. Although Kupunakāne retained ownership of the ranch, he had set up his son like the patriarch in the big house. Had he done it from guilt for not sending him to college, or was this part of their agreement when he forced Larry to stay? "Can I ask you something kinda sensitive?"

"Like what?"

Makalani stared at her plate. Once she spoke the words, she wouldn't be able to take them back.

Grace glanced at the door, as if checking it was shut. "Say it, Makalani. Ask whatever you want."

In for a penny . . .

"Have you had any doubts about the way your grandfather died?"

Grace nodded slowly. "Yeah. I just didn't want to bring it up."

"Because it might upset your grandmother?"

"That too. But mostly, I mean, how will my ʻohana survive if someone we trust was involved?"

Makalani sighed.

This is so much more than a pound.

"What about his death seems most suspicious to you?"

Grace coughed out a laugh. "Besides everything? I guess what troubles me most is why that bull was even there."

"In the pit or the pasture?"

"Both. Malu was supposed to have moved the bulls to the Hāwī side of the ranch. That's to the north, not the Kona side on the south. That Charolais bull should not have been anywhere near that pit. And if Grandad had asked Malu or Louie where to look, they should have steered him toward the pastures on the other side."

"Your uncle would have known?"

"Uncle Louie knows *everything* that happens on Hiapo Ranch."

"Did he know there was an offer to buy it?"

"What? No way."

"It came from Skip Una, who I believe finishes your cattle up in Oregon. And if your uncle knows everything, I'm assuming Malu does too?"

Grace nodded. "He would have known. Malu is, or at least *was*, fiercely protective of Uncle Louie, especially where Grandad was concerned."

CHAPTER THIRTY-NINE

Makalani woke to the scent of frying SPAM and feet thumping around the room.

"Ala pā! Wake up, sleepyhead," Grace said, pulling on a hoodie. "How does your body feel, good enough to ride?"

Makalani stifled a groan as she stretched in the bed. A long, hot shower would ease the stiffness, although, based on the sounds and smells, she doubted there would be time. It was pitch dark, and everyone in Waimea seemed to be awake and in this house.

"What time is it?"

"Three thirty. I let you sleep in."

Branding day.

Makalani swung her bruised legs out of bed. "Be down in a sec."

Ten minutes later, Makalani entered the dining room, crowded with family and friends. She recognized a few from the memorial. Most she hadn't met. All were dressed for hard work, cool temperatures, and sweat. A half dozen kids between five and seventeen stuffed toasted sweetbread, gravy-drenched eggs, and SPAM into their mouths. Makalani's heart swelled. All these families had woken up in the middle of the night to help the Hiapos bring in the cows.

Grace stood in the corner, chatting with volunteers. When she caught Makalani watching, she popped her chin in acknowledgment but stayed where she was. Clearly, this was not the time to make sure everything between them was okay. After sharing her initial fears on the bed, Grace had clammed up and suggested they sleep.

Makalani thought back to Rosie's suspicions. *At least we're not crazy. Someone else on this ranch suspects Larry Hiapo might have been killed.*

Brian nudged her shoulder in greeting. "Morning, cuz." Then he pulled her into an overly exuberant hug. He released her just as quick when he noticed her flinch. "You okay? What's with the cut and bruise on your face?"

She rubbed her aching sides. "Tumbled down a ravine."

"Why'd you do that?"

Ha! Why indeed.

She rolled her eyes. "I'll let you know when I figure it out."

Brian leaned in. "Seriously, everything okay here?"

Before she could answer, Vinnie rushed over with a mounded bowl of loco moco and a toasted wedge of Hawaiian sweetbread perched on top. "You're coming today, right? Uncle Louie says paniolo gotta eat."

Makalani accepted the gift before Vinnie ran off.

Rosie came over. "He's been talking about you since that day you calmed Uila in the corral."

"Louie saved him."

"Only because Vinnie was still dangling from his horse." She touched Makalani's arm. "Will you look out for him today?"

"Of course, I promised I would. You're not going?"

"Haven't since I was a kid." Rosie's pained expression reminded Makalani of why. "Brian and I will be waiting at the pā kuni, the branding corral. You'll hear lots of wala'au kanaka today."

Paniolo talk.

Kupunakāne had told her the same thing.

"I'll keep Vinnie safe."

"Mahalo." She grimaced at the loco moco. "The gravy's already congealing. You better hurry up and eat."

Makalani dug into her breakfast, standing since there weren't any seats, while Louie rose from the table and acknowledged the guests.

"Kakahiaka nō. Mahalo i kou hele 'ana mai." *Good morning. Thank you for coming.* "Everybody get enough kaukau?"

The crowd responded with varying affirmations.

"Maika'i. Because you goin' need every one o' dem calories you ate." He paused for the laughter. "Okay, so . . . we get enough horses fo' me, Grace, Malu, Makalani, Vinnie, and four oddah people." He turned toward twin brothers in their forties, one heavier, the other grayer, who had ridden up to Larry's memorial tree. "Phil and Pete, you guys brought your own, yeah?" He looked at the teenage girl and her younger brother standing beside Phil. "You bring horses fo' Sue and Darius?"

"Yep."

"How 'bout you, Pete? You bring a lio fo' Ana?"

"Our trailer didn't have room. Can she borrow one of yours?"

"Sure t'ing. Dat brings us down to t'ree." He looked at Phil's wife. "You riding, Lani?"

She pinned her squirming five-year-old against her hip. "Jaime and me will help at the corral."

"Me, too," Rumiko said.

Louie looked surprised. "You not goin' ride, Mom?"

She smiled sadly. "Not this time. I'll help Carolyn and Lono prepare the lunch."

Kenneth's wife nodded while Lono, the Hiapos' handyman-cook, held up his thumb.

"Brian and I will help too, Mom," Rosie said.

"Mahalo, sweetheart."

Louie turned to his grandfather. "How 'bout you, old man?"

"You kidding? I goin' back to sleep."

Everyone laughed.

"I'll ride," Kenneth said.

From the stunned expressions, this was clearly an unusual event. As the brothers stared at one another, Makalani—and seemingly everyone else—waited expectantly for Louie's response. Would Kenneth take orders from his cowboy brother? Or would he try to exert his power in Louie's domain? Makalani, for one, was curious to see.

Louie turned back to their friends. "Dat leaves two lio. Who else like come gather cattle wit' us? Tai, how 'bout you and Fetu?"

A stocky Samoan woman in her early fifties nodded beside a heavy-set, thirty-ish man. "Our trailer busted so, yeah. Fa'afetai—thank you—from me and my son."

"Aurite den. Use da facilities if you need um, and meet us outside."

When Makalani realized Malu and Grace had already left, she stacked her empty bowl and hurried out the door. All was dark except for the lights bleeding from the tack room onto the hitching rails. Malu was saddling the chestnut gelding on the right, so Makalani joined Grace as she cinched the dappled gray on the left. It was too early in the morning to deal with Malu's moods or address what may or may not have happened the previous day, not to mention what Grace had said about him not moving the bulls. Makalani didn't want to be anywhere near the man on a day as chaotic and potentially dangerous as this.

Grace nodded toward Rocky Road. "Cinch the kaula 'ōpu and you're ready to go."

"I could have saddled him," Makalani said.

"I know. But we both know it would have hurt your ribs. Take it easy until you're sure you're okay. There's no shame if you have to come back to the house."

Saddles creaked. Tails swished. Horses blew through their noses. When everyone had mounted their lio, they gathered around Louie for the prayer. He removed his leather hat and laid it on his saddle horn. All went quiet except for the occasional stomp and the jingle of spurs.

Louie offered the pule in 'ōlelo Hawai'i, filling the chilly darkness with his deep, quiet voice. He repeated the prayer again in English so everyone would understand how grateful he was for their friendship and for the Hiapos' bountiful land. He ended by asking God to keep everyone safe as they worked.

"'Āmene," he said. *Amen.*

"'Āmene," they replied.

Louie ran a hand through his cropped hair and put on his hat. Then he led the paniolo and their helpers onto the range.

When Malu joined him, Makalani couldn't help but admire the dashing couple they made against the indigo sky. Louie's breadth and height in his work shirt, Malu's lean angles his hoodie couldn't hide, the silhouette of Louie's cowboy hat and Malu's hair flowing out of his cap—both of them sat tall and at ease in their saddles as they rode side by side.

Kenneth came next, urging his lio to walk faster and keep up with the men. Although he sat tall in the saddle, his effort to catch them denied him the leadership he craved.

Tai and her son, Fetu, twice her width, hung back with the twin fathers, Phil and Pete. Stout pair of Samoans on the left, two lean hapa-haole on the right, together they bookended the three chatty teens. As the darkness receded, Makalani could see the warm breath puffing from their mouths.

Vinnie pressed Uila forward but couldn't fit in the tight group. It might have been a cousin thing, but Makalani suspected it was the difference in age. An eight-year-old, even one with his own horse, would seem like a little kid to them.

"Chillax, Vinnie," Grace said quietly, holding her long-legged Thoroughbred–quarter horse in check. "The back of a roundup is the best place to be."

"Really?"

"Of course." She glanced at Makalani and shook her head *no*. "Who you do you think gathers all the strays?"

"Malu and Louie."

Grace chuckled. "Yeah, but who else?"

"Everyone in the front."

"Nah, they're too busy moving the herd. Besides, none of them are full-time paniolo like me. Do you really think Uncle Louie would put me back just to babysit you? No way."

She flashed an annoyed look at Makalani and mouthed, "He actually did!"

Vinnie was too busy sulking to catch the exchange. He kicked Uila into a trot.

"Eh. You know bettah than that. This ground has rocks hiding beneath the grass. Give Uila more rein, and let her pick her own way. Horses have a better sense about where to go than kids."

"I'm almost nine."

"You're eight and a half."

"Well, I ride better than Darius and he's fourteen."

"And I ride better than all of you, and I'm telling you to walk your damn horse."

"Ha! I made you swear. You owe me five bucks."

"What kind of math are they teaching at HPA? Five bucks? In your dreams baby boy."

Makalani grinned. So far, this cattle drive was not at all as she imagined it would be.

Vinnie's straw cowboy hat jiggled on his head as he teased, "When I tell Mom, she's gonna tell Uncle Kenneth to make you pay up."

Grace snorted. "If you want to be a paniolo, you better pay more attention to who is actually in charge."

And there it was again, the question of the day.

Makalani eased Rocky Road closer to Grace. "Does your dad usually ride on branding days?"

"Nah. He stopped coming a couple years back after Grandad semi-retired. Said he had too much work in the office to spend a day on the range."

"How many has he missed?"

"Well . . . we divide our heifers into two breeding groups, which means we wean, brand, and process one batch in the spring and the other in the fall. A month or so after that, we bring in the weaned calves and ship them to Oregon to be grass-finished at Una Ranch. In between, we bring in any straggler calves to be weaned and processed because, you know, if a cow is in heat out of sync with the others, sometimes a bull will jump a fence. And sometimes, we need more riders when we move cattle across the highway. So, I guess maybe Dad has missed six or eight?"

No wonder everyone was surprised.

When Kenneth finally reached Louie and Malu, he rode several yards to the side.

Two against one. Do Louie and Malu always act as a team?

Makalani sat taller in her saddle to stretch. Although stiff, she felt surprisingly good.

"I'm sorry you got hurt," Grace said. "I should have been looking out." Then she loped after their young cousin who had strayed farther from the group.

Is Grace riding in the back to watch over Vinnie or me?

The sun had risen over the mountains by the time the roundup party had reached the upper pastures of Hiapo Ranch. Makalani passed the time chatting with Vinnie about school, family, and his aspirations to become a famous cowboy like Ikua Purdy, the National Rodeo Hall of Fame paniolo who set the steer-roping record in 1908. Purdy, along with Eben Low and Archie Ka'au'a, had competed in that year's Frontier Days Rodeo in Cheyenne, Wyoming, winning the hearts and esteem of the national cowboy elite.

"Kupunakāne says Purdy came from old paniolo stock just like me," Vinnie bragged, omitting Purdy's more illustrious ancestors like John Palmer Parker and King Kamehameha the Great. "He says I can be a good paniolo like Uncle Louie, Grandmom, and Grace."

"What about your Uncle Kenneth?"

Vinnie shrugged.

The only Hiapo who seemed to have believed in and praised Kenneth was dead.

CHAPTER FORTY

Riders called from inside the forest, encouraging the stray cows and their calves to "hele, hele" out of the trees. The cattle had either chosen to sleep undercover or had hidden when they heard the horses approach. Makalani couldn't blame them for not wanting to leave. The uppermost pasture offered a rich buffet of thick grass and tasty greens.

Makalani and Vinnie rode along the northern tree line and gently pressured a cow and her calf toward the center of the meadow. Pete, Phil, and their kids did the same from the south. Kenneth and Grace kept cattle from drifting up toward the ravine. Everything was peaceful until a red cow burst through the trees.

In the seconds it took Makalani to spot the distressed animal, Grace had already pivoted her leggy palomino and raced over to help. Her bouncing blond bob swung in concert with the mare's flaxen mane. As they maneuvered in unison, the golden morning light cast them both in a celestial glow.

"Eh, pipi," Grace called, over and over, as she cut off the calf's options and drove him to the herd. She nodded approvingly when Makalani rode up and closed in the cow. "Look at you, acting all paniolo li'dat."

Makalani laughed. It was something Pupule, her cousin Solomon's jovial buddy, would have said back on Kaua'i. She tipped her cap with her best "rangerly" expression. "No problem, ma'am. Just doing my job."

As the māmā cow's lowing calf found her in the herd, another red calf plowed out of the trees with Malu close behind. When the calf dodged to the side, Malu cut him off. The calf blared in protest as he tried to evade.

Kenneth yelled, "Stop scaring the cows."

Malu ignored him, passed the calf off to Pete, and returned to the trees. When the keiki cow gave Pete the slip, Kenneth cut him off, sidestepping his gelding as the animal's direction changed. The calf worked himself into a frenzy of movement and noise, triggering a mooing response from the rest of the herd. When Malu returned with the māmā, he shook his head at Kenneth as if to say, *Now who's scaring the cows?*

As Kenneth glared back, the frantic calf broke free. Malu waited for him to reach his māmā, then guided both toward the now agitated cattle. Tai and Fetu emerged with a calmer pair of Black Angus from the northern side and added them to the herd.

Kenneth transferred his annoyance with Malu to them. "Where's Louie?"

Fetu grinned. "Coaxing one big suckah dat no like come out."

"Why do we even have cattle up this high?"

"Why wouldn't we?" Malu said. "It's only October. Da weather's still mild."

"I was talking about the new fence," Kenneth explained. "Why didn't you guys clear the upper pasture before you put it in?"

"What fo'? These cows no boddah us."

An animal bellowed from the trees. Leaves trembled. The ground shook. Then a horned rusty-brown Hereford cow plowed through the branches and onto the grass.

Pete's horse startled and flipped around to run from the threat.

Kenneth held his lio in check.

Grace loped into the white-faced cow's path and steered it away from the group. When she stopped, Baby dug her rear hooves into the earth. Although not as large as the bull Makalani had helped usher into

Louie's trailer, a horned cow could do significant damage if provoked. The cow's tipped horns were still a good six inches long.

When she swung her horns in a new direction, Grace was already there. Horse and rider moved as one, shifting, stopping, cutting off the cow. Makalani couldn't tell if Grace was guiding Baby or going along for the ride.

Louie jogged his horse to Grace's side, helping to calm the cow with his low voice. "Hele ma kai, pipi 'ula. Hele, hele. Come on, red cow, time to go home."

The cow's pink nostrils flared. She snorted at Grace and Louie, then trotted a few yards down the slope, where she stopped and gave Louie the meanest stink eye Makalani had ever seen.

Grace laughed at her uncle. "Ooh, you in trouble now."

"Not me," Louie said. "You da one got her all fired up."

Having delivered her message, the cow turned her white face and sashayed down the hill.

Louie sat forward. "No get grouchy wit' me, Big Red. If you no get hāpai next season, I goin' sell your fat ass."

The departing cow mooed.

Malu cracked his short rawhide uepa behind the lowing herd, startling the cattle and the riders into moving. "Hele, hele, pipi. You heard da boss. It's time to move."

As the riders walked their horses alongside the herd, Kenneth remained frozen in place, back stiff in the saddle, seething that Malu had taken control. Worse than that, Malu had called Louie *the boss.* Worse still, everyone had obeyed.

"Did you see how Grace handled her horse?" Ana said to her friends as they rode by Kenneth.

"I saw horns. Was that a bull?" Darius asked.

"Cows can have horns too," Sue told her brother, then turned to her friend and shivered. "But, OMG, did you hear Louie's voice as he calmed down that cow?"

Ana nodded and pretended to swoon.

Vinnie muttered about the *dumb teenagers* while Makalani kept her eyes on Kenneth, expecting him to explode as the girls fawned over Louie and Grace. Instead, he urged his horse into a jog and moved down the hill.

Taking a cue from his uncle, Vinnie also jogged ahead, but stopped in front of the teens to show off his own paniolo skills. He reined Uila in tight figure eights, displaying how well and how quickly she could bend right and left. When the teenagers didn't respond, he jogged into their view and did it again.

Grace whistled for his attention, then beckoned him to join her and Makalani at the rear of the herd.

"Nice horsemanship," Makalani said, hoping to take the sting out of the teenagers' disregard.

Vinnie shrugged one of his shoulders, then slumped.

Grace rode beside him. "Do you want to be a paniolo for yourself or for them? Because stinking of cows and horses will not get you girls."

Vinnie grinned. "You and Makalani are girls."

"Cheeky buggah. We are women. And your cousins." She flicked his leg with her reins.

As the herd were funneled through the next gate into a lower pasture, Louie rode back to Vinnie and nodded at a straying calf. "Gather dat keiki ovah dea."

"By myself?"

"You need someone else to handle one calf?"

"No way." Vinnie took off as if asked to round up a steer.

Grace rolled her eyes. "Where do you want us?"

He looked across the plains to the south beyond another electric fence. "You, me, Malu, and Makalani goin' gather da rest of da pipi on da Kona pasture."

The pasture that should not have had any bulls the morning Larry Hiapo had died.

Louie and Malu took off along a stretch of well-trodden grass. Grace gave Makalani a meaningful look, as if confirming her thought, then caught up with the men. Makalani grimaced as Rocky Road did the same. Every bruised muscle and bone from her tumble down the ravine screamed against the assault of his choppy gait. Even Rocky Road's lope sent concussive shocks up her spine.

Louie motioned Grace and Malu downslope toward a cluster of cows, then he beckoned Makalani to him. "Cattle like to graze in da shade on da border of our ranch, so you and me goin' rustle um out of da trees. I'll start on da mauka end, you start makai. We'll meet in da middle and bring whatevah cows we gather to join Malu and Grace."

He nickered to Auali'i and the blue roan stud jogged up the slope. Not a breath of air passed between his seat and the saddle as they skimmed over the land.

Makalani patted Rocky Road's neck. "See how it's done?"

The horse blew out his nose.

"Yeah, I know. We'll never be that cool. But, hey . . . let's give it a try."

Whether inspired by her pep talk or their example, Rocky Road jogged a teensy bit more smoothly across the slanting plain toward the makai end of the trees. When the 'a'ā lava chunks increased, he slowed to a walk and picked his way on the squishy grass in between. Fragrant eucalyptus mingled with the fertile scent of wet earth. The effect was so heady, Makalani wished she could lay on the rough ground, massage her sore back on the rocks, and breathe in the eucalyptus all day. She had nearly forgotten the task Louie had given her when she spotted the gulch emerging from the grove.

The gulch angled toward the ocean along the Kona border of the ranch, where a woven-wire fence ran down to Highway 250, Kohala Mountain Road. Unlike the electric fences that divided the fields, this was sturdier perimeter fence like the ones Makalani and Grace had passed through to the lower pastures on her first day.

Louie whistled from upslope.

She had a task to do, but the crunch of gravel pulled her attention back to the south where an old blue truck rumbled up an access road on the other side of the fence. Dust kicked up from the tires, obscuring the driver as the truck came farther up the hill. It wasn't Louie's or Malu's or any of the other trucks she had seen during the memorial or her days on the ranch. But if it wasn't connected to Hiapo Ranch, why was there a second woven-wire fence on the *other* side of that road?

Everyone has them.

Really? Exactly like those?

Makalani peered at the twin fences as the truck disappeared behind the grove. Where did the road lead? And who owned that land?

Louie whistled even louder.

No way would he believe she hadn't heard that.

With a last look to make sure the access road actually began at the highway, she noticed another dip in the land near the base of the gulch. The dip had defined corners and steeply cut sides. Nature would not have formed such a geometric shape. Although eroded by weather and time, the rectangular pit had to be the man-made—the bullock pit in which Larry Hiapo had been killed.

If I walk down the gulch, will I find bloodstained earth?

CHAPTER FORTY-ONE

It was nine thirty on a Saturday morning, and Detective Rona Kim was freezing her butt off at a bull breeding ranch. It would warm up as the day progressed, but this was the only time Freddy Liu had to spare.

She found the burly Hawaiian man in front of a giant steel contraption out of which popped a black bull's head. The sides of the narrow steel box seemed to clamp the animal in place while rubber tubes coming out the top and down the sides—like the human battery pods from *The Matrix*—did God only knew what.

Freddy checked the information on the machine's screen, saw Rona, and popped up his chin. "Howzit. You Detective Kim?"

"I am. What are you doing with that bull?"

Freddy laughed. "Today? Just vaccinations and weight. Although the Silencer can inseminate as well."

"The Silencer?"

"Yeah. It's my new toy. It's a hydraulic squeeze chute for holding cattle in place. I'm just joking about the toy. It's actually a state-of-the-art multipurpose machine."

The bull didn't look all that happy about the new toy to her. "Are you going to let him out?"

"Of course."

"I mean, like, *now*?"

He chuckled. "Tell you what. Why don't you stand behind that gate while I let him go."

The gate was made of heavy steel bars, otherwise she would have opted to wait in her car.

Once she was secure in her side pen, Freddy stood out of the bull's path and released him from the chute. As soon as the sides of the metal box opened, the animal bolted out of his confinement, then proceeded at a more dignified pace. Apparently, he had done this many times before. Once he headed out to pasture, Freddy closed the paddock gate.

Rona came out of her pen, feeling a tad foolish for her concern.

Freddy laughed again. "No worries. Everybody's nervous around bulls."

"How dangerous are they?"

"Well, I've raised them for a decade. My dad was a rancher twice as long before that. I can tell you this, no matter how well you think you know them, you don't *ever* trust a bull."

Rona followed him to the paddock fence where the newly released animal wandered over to a tree. Two other bulls shared the pasture.

"They're okay together?"

"These three are. It took a while for them to work out their trash talk from other sides of an electric fence. After they snorted, stomped, and flung dirt at one another, they settled down and got used to each other's scent. The electric shocks discouraged any types of attack. They can share a pasture now as long as no females are around."

Rona pointed to a pasture with what appeared to be a dozen or so bulls. "What about them?"

"Those are steers."

"Castrated?"

"Yup. No balls, no aggression."

"But don't you earn your income from stud service?"

"Yeah. But life's too short to deal with an aggressive bull. Besides, not all of my calves grow into quality studs. I have plenty more bulls in other pastures, some on their own, and others with their friends. That said, fights break out on occasion. Sometimes it's bad."

Rona took out her phone and brought up an app. "Do you mind if I record our conversation? There's just so much I don't know."

"Go for it."

"Thanks." She hit record. "Have any of your bulls ever injured a person?"

Freddy nodded. "Several times. One charged my dad when I was a kid. Nearly killed him."

"What did your dad do with the bull?"

"Cut off his balls and turned him into a steer."

"Is that what you do?"

"Sometimes. Or I sell him to a slaughterhouse. I had one bull piss me off so bad, I just shot him on the spot."

Rona thought about the killer bull being returned to Hiapo Ranch. "So, if you had a bull that hurt or killed someone, you'd either castrate, kill, or sell him?"

"Yeah. Bulls, steers, and cull cows bring in the same price per pound."

"What's a cull cow?"

"One that's too old to breed."

"Got it. And you wouldn't keep an aggressive bull."

"Not intact."

"What if he seemed completely docile?"

"I'm confused. You said this bull killed somebody, but he's docile?"

"Apparently so. He never caused any trouble before or since. By all accounts, he's a very calm bull."

Freddy shrugged. "Well, like I said before—"

Rona finished, "Never trust a bull."

"That's right. Unless . . ."

"What?"

"Was he cornered?"

Rona shrugged. "He was trapped in one of those old pits used to catch wild cattle back in the day. The rancher either climbed down the sides or fell in with the bull."

Freddy nodded. "Then he might have felt cornered, especially if he was already upset. Cattle are flight animals, even bulls. Their instinct is to flee. If they can't, and they feel threatened, even a heifer will put up a fight."

Rona paused to consider. "Are you saying this might have been a situational attack?"

Freddy laughed. "Well, I never heard it put that way before but, yeah . . . and a lot of bad luck."

Like poor Larry Hiapo. An experienced rancher like him would have known a cornered bull would attack, which meant he would not have intentionally entered that pit. Had he fallen or been pushed?

Rona pictured the surrounding land as she remembered it. The ground had been churned up by at least one horse. Louie Hiapo, Malu Au, and Grace Hiapo had all ridden up on horseback before she and Dan had arrived. Had they churned up the earth then, or had one or all of them done it before?

That still didn't explain the copacetic bull.

"What about drugs or disease?" Rona asked. "Can you think of anything that would make a normally calm bull aggravated for a short period of time?"

"No, more the other way around. We would use sedatives to relax an animal for a procedure. Aside from that, just vaccines and medications. Believe me, it's not helpful to agitate a bull."

"Unless you wanted him to attack."

"Like in a rodeo? Sure, but that's a whole other thing. I don't know of any medications a rancher would use that would produce violent side effects like that."

"What about human drugs?"

Freddy shook his head. "We don't use human drugs on livestock."

"Not intentionally, you mean."

"What are you suggesting?"

Rona shrugged. "Thank you for your time. I'll get out of your hair."

She headed for her car before he could ask anything else. Although she had hoped for something more conclusive, the trip wasn't entirely a bust. The breeder and the first toxicology report had both ruled out any typical livestock medications a cattle rancher might use. That left her with the possibility of illicit human drugs, something with a short half-life that would move out of a bull's system fairly quick.

She sat in her car and focused her rearview mirror toward her own eyes. "Are you trying to get yourself fired? Because that's what's going to happen if you bring this drug theory to Dan."

CHAPTER FORTY-TWO

Makalani studied the pit where Larry Hiapo had died while higher up the slope, cows lowed by the grove. Could Hinuhinu have wandered away from the shade and into the gulch? If so, how could he have fallen into the pit?

Makalani had seen how cattle avoid treacherous terrain during her adventures on Kam's Mauna Kea ranch. She had also witnessed the lazy nature of bulls when she and Louie went to fetch Hinuhinu and found him lounging beneath a tree. She stared at the steep, rocky gulch.

With lush grassland all around, why would a grazing animal go down there?

Louie yelled from upslope. "Hūi, Makalani. All da pipi up hea."

With a final look at the pit, gulch, and mysterious road, she reluctantly guided Rocky Road back up the hill.

Louie was circling his cows when she arrived. "Stay in da back and push um along."

"What if they don't want to go?"

"Smack um on da ass."

She laughed. "Right, because that worked so well with the bull."

As it turned out, once Louie led the way, the cows followed happily behind. When they joined up with the others, the combined herds added up to 180 head.

Kenneth surprised everyone by taking the lead. "Puka nānā! Let's go, pipi, look for the gate."

He jogged his horse ahead and stopped suddenly at the gate, leaned over his saddle, and struggled with the latch. Makalani stood in her stirrups to see, but the cattle had hurried after him, blocking the view.

She yelled to the closest riders, "Is he okay?"

No one responded or rode up to help. Unlike Vinnie, Kenneth was a proven paniolo. Either he wasn't in danger or, having started the task, the wannabe leader was expected to finish it alone.

A dirt cloud kicked up as the herd trotted over hardened ground and picked up their speed. Kenneth would be trampled if they plowed into a closed gate. Grace must have thought the same because she leaped ahead along the high side of the herd. This time, everyone reacted. Makalani chased after Grace. Louie whistled and shouted commands. Phil, Tai, and Fetu rode between the cattle trying to slow down their pace. The kids tried to help, but confused their cow horses with their haphazard cues.

The only paniolo not in motion was Malu, who watched the spectacle from a hill.

Makalani glared at him as she passed.

Why don't you move? Why won't you help?

As she neared the front of the accelerating herd, she braced herself for Kenneth's cries and the squeals of panicked cows as they crashed into the electrified fence. Grace was in that cloud of dust with her dad, but all Makalani could hear was the noise of the slowing, widening herd.

Makalani charged onto a mound above the dust and saw Kenneth's horse running free in the pasture beyond. Cattle were moving through the now-open gate, but the man who had supposedly opened it was nowhere to be seen. All the paniolo were still on this side of the electrified fence, with Grace and Louie funneling cows through the gate. Everyone else, including Malu, was managing the herd and rounding up the strays.

Where's Kenneth?

Then she spotted him hanging on the gate—hat gone, shirt ripped, blood on his chest. He had swung into the far pasture and was trapped for the moment but otherwise safe. Makalani relaxed until three cows in a row bumped against him as they passed. Grace and Louie were too occupied with cattle to see when Kenneth lost his grip and slid to the ground.

"Go!"

Rocky Road flew down the mound, showing his cow sense as he threaded through the herd. Once through the gate, Makalani pulled him to a stop and jumped to the ground. Although cows brushed against him, Rocky Road stayed in place as she lifted Kenneth in a fireman's carry and raced him into the pasture away from the herd.

He thumped on her hip. "Put me down. This is embarrassing. Did you hear me? I'm fine."

When she laid him on the grass, he kicked her away. "You had no right to do that."

"You could have been trampled."

"And you think this is better?" He dabbed the blood on his chest. "You don't have a clue."

She whistled for Rocky Road and was surprised and impressed when he came. "I may not have a clue, but I have antiseptic and bandages for that wound." She pulled a first aid kit from her saddlebag. "Were you clipped by a horn?"

Kenneth shook his head. "Wires or nails on the fence. Is this really necessary?"

"Only if you want to avoid an infection."

He unbuttoned what was left of his shirt. "Fine. But do it quick before Grace or Louie come through the gate."

She didn't have the heart to tell him they were watching from across the fence. Meanwhile the cattle were sprawling across the new field. Since Kenneth hadn't given anyone time to ride through the gate in advance of the cows, the herd would have to be gathered again—which explained Louie's scowling expression as he approached. Kenneth shoved Makalani away and finished taping the bandage himself.

Louie glared down from his stallion. "What the hell, Kenneth. You try show off fo' da crew, or what?"

"Just doing my job."

"No, brah. You made everybody else's job harder to do."

"The latch slipped. It happens. Don't make a big deal."

"Me? You da one getting nursed for a scratch."

Kenneth sprang to his feet and headed for the gate. "This wasn't my idea. Your new ranch hand overreacted."

Louie yelled after him, "Saved your ass mo' like."

Makalani stuffed the first aid kit back into her saddlebag. "Your brother could have been trampled."

"T'rough no fault of mine."

"Is that all that matters to you, who's to blame?"

Louie gestured to the sprawling cattle. "Dass my concern. And yours." He thumbed behind him. "And theirs."

The riders had assembled behind Louie, awaiting instructions on what they should do next. They had lowered their sweaty yokes to reveal dirty stripes across their foreheads and, if they weren't wearing sunglasses, their tired, squinting eyes. Saddles creaked as they watched Kenneth close and latch the gate—all except for Grace, who had ridden into the new pasture and was leading back her father's horse.

Louie turned to the volunteers. "Gather da pipi. We need make up da time." Then he rode in front his brother, who was heading toward his horse. "You wanted to prove you were paniolo? Well, guess what? All you proved is dat you belong behind a desk."

"You and your boyfriend cut me out."

"Cut you out? You're a man not a cow."

"That's right. And I'm in charge of this ranch."

"You're in charge of an office."

"Only because Dad died before he and Kupunakāne could make me CEO."

Auali'i stomped at the ground, clearly sensing his rider's annoyance. "No way." Louie sidestepped his stallion to keep him contained.

Kenneth backed away from the horse. "I have rough drafts in Dad's handwriting. He had more confidence in me than in you."

Although Louie looked surprised, Malu, hanging back within hearing distance, did not. When he caught Makalani watching him, he grinned and pushed his horse into a ground-covering jog.

CHAPTER FORTY-THREE

The regathered cattle ambled behind Louie, who called, "Hele, hele," over his shoulder as if encouraging his kids. The other riders called variations of the same, filling the quiet pasture with a gentle chorus of paniolo talk and moos.

After the frantic events of the morning, Makalani appreciated the peace. Even Vinnie seemed content to follow the plodding herd.

Grace rode several yards away, lost in her thoughts, sitting tall in her saddle, a paniolo who had earned her place with dedication and grit. Makalani could relate. The young woman was not that dissimilar from her.

Grace had known what she wanted even as child and would have traded her playtime, parties, and the precious downtime kids and teenagers adored to do grueling chores and the endless tasks on the ranch. Learning to ride and train horses must have been way more fun than anything she could have done with kids her own age.

And learning to mālama the land and the cattle would have felt more important than school.

Who would have taught her those skills and values? Kupunakāne would already have been in his eighties. Larry would have been busy running the ranch. Kenneth would have pressured her to focus on school, fighting against what she wanted every step of the way. Only Louie would have had the knowledge, passion, and need to train a future paniolo who could help him with the work. No wonder Grace admired and emulated her uncle. He was probably the most important person in her life.

As Malu headed toward the rear of the herd, Makalani wondered if he felt the same. How deep did *his* admiration go, and what would he do to protect Louie from a threat? Malu had grinned when Kenneth told Louie about their father's intent. Had he learned about it from Kupunakāne and removed Larry before the documents could be signed?

As she considered the possibility, Malu rode back to Grace. "Louie said to give you a break. Go where you like. I goin' babysit fo' you."

Grace flashed an apologetic look at Makalani and jogged away.

Vinnie saw Malu and drifted back to chat.

Malu shook his head and nodded toward the cows. "Back to work, keiki. A paniolo sticks wit' his herd."

"Okay, Malu. I'll keep them in line."

Puffed with importance, Vinnie urged Uila into a trot and rode back and forth behind the ambling cows.

Makalani sneaked a look at Malu and caught the smile in his eyes.

How could a man inspire a child whose grandfather he may have killed?

Makalani wasn't sure about anything related to this man, including what had happened before she tumbled down the ravine. Malu hadn't acknowledged the incident or asked how she was. She couldn't tell if he had written it off as one of the many hazards in paniolo life or if he was annoyed that his attempt to scare her into leaving had failed.

When the herd stopped moving to funnel through the next gate, Makalani broke the ice. "They're all in a line, like ducklings following their mom."

Malu grunted in agreement. "Dis how it supposed to be, mellow li'dat."

"Then why do you need all the help?"

"In case something goes wrong, or da pipi scatter and dey too paʻakikī to come."

Makalani nodded, familiar with stubborn creatures of the two- and four-legged kind.

"But you know," Malu said, "it's not always about needing help. Branding days stay mo' about building community and sharing our paniolo traditions. Dass why we invite our children to participate, so we can teach them how to work wit' purpose and intent. You obviously know dis. You coulda worked just as hard on da mainland. Why else you come home if not to care fo' Hawaiʻi?"

Makalani stared at him in surprise, not only for the questions he raised but because, aside from his conversation with Kupunakāne, this was the longest she had ever heard him speak.

"What?" he said. "Am I wrong?"

"No, it's just . . ."

"You nevah expect to hear it from me."

She shrugged, embarrassed to have been called out. In truth, she had judged Malu harshly from the moment she had seen him arguing with Louie by the truck. His actions since had lowered her opinion of him even more.

My opinion? He threw me down a ravine!

Did he, though?

Makalani still wasn't sure.

He's an asshole.

Well, yeah . . . that much is definitely true.

"Whatevahs," Malu said, disrupting her inner argument. "Dese days, all I hear is 'Kānaka come home. Kānaka come home.' You know what, though? It not enough fo' kānaka to come home. You need do something once you hea."

Makalani's sore muscles clenched for a fight. She helped people every day. No way would she let this stuck-up local give her heat. "I do plenty."

"Oh, yeah? Have you marched against da military base in Pōhakuloa? You even know what goes on at da PTA? I no talk about Parent Teacher Association li'dat. Da Pōhakuloa Training Area stay right across da road from Kam's ranch. Fo' ovah seventy-five years, da military has defiled our wao akua—da godly realm between da three volcanoes, Mauna Kea, Mauna Loa, and Hualālai. Dey bomb it in war games, pollute da energy wit' violence, and leave uranium to poison da ʻāina. Do you stand against dem? What about da TMT on Mauna Kea? What you do in Oregon to stop da Thirty Meter Telescope from getting built? Nothing, dass what."

Malu was on a roll. If he could stir up this much righteous animosity for a person he barely knew, what kind of vitriol had he aimed at Louie's dad?

"While you pretend to help, kānaka like me stand on da line. We get arrested, sue, object, make our voices heard. Even when nobody else pays attention, we stand up and fight."

Sweat poured down his face. He had worked himself into such a frenzy his poor horse kept trying to bolt only to have Malu sink into his saddle and pull in the reins. "But you do plenny, right?"

"That's not fair," Makalani said.

"Fair? You know what's not fair? Everybody say dis mattah, dat mattah, all dakine mattah—but nobody shows up. Nobody takes a stand. Nobody does da hard work. Everybody waits fo' somebody else to do what needs to be done."

Makalani stared at the violence in his eyes. "Is that what you do, Malu, what needs to be done?"

"Damn straight."

"What about Louie's dad? Did he stand up? Did he stand up against you?"

Malu spat on the ground. "No talk to me 'bout dat man."

"Why not?"

"Because you nevah earned da right."

He urged his horse toward the gate as the last cow and paniolo passed through. Makalani trotted behind, determined to make him talk, yet acutely aware she had already pushed him too far. To her surprise, he waited at the gate.

"Larry and me nevah get along."

She had heard the same from Kupunakāne but wondered what reasons Malu would give. "Larry didn't approve of your relationship?"

Malu scoffed. "I didn't approve of *him*. He used to beat on Louie when he was little, you know 'bout dat? Nasty sumbitch. Knocked all dat shit off by da time I came around. Good t'ing fo' him because I woulda dropped him on da spot." Malu's eyes turned deadly cold. "Dat man deserved everyt'ing he get."

CHAPTER FORTY-FOUR

The delay caused by the gate incident and having to regather the cows made for a quick and late lunch back at the ranch. No one spoke, not even the kids. Kenneth took his poke bowl into his office and never came out. Once the humans were full and the horses refreshed, Louie led the roundup crew toward the small grassy paddock above Kohala Mountain Road where the cattle they had gathered grazed along the fence.

"Listen up," Louie said. "We goin' lead dis herd across da highway." He pointed to Fetu. "Go help Malu wit' da gates. When da pipi enter da makai pasture, you and him keep um moving downhill. Me, Grace, Tai, and Makalani goin' hold back any traffic and make sure da herd crosses safely. Pete, Phil, and da kids goin' keep da cattle calm on da mauka side and moving toward us. Da māmā cows done dis plenny times already, so dey know what to do. Just make sure no pipi keiki get left behind."

"We got this, Uncle," Vinnie called from the back.

Louie pointed at him. "I know you do."

It was the first smile Makalani had seen from Louie all day.

This is what he loves, moving cattle and sharing his knowledge with the kids.

"Okay den," Louie said. "Mākaukau?" *Are you ready?*

The crew responded with, "'Ae!"

As per Louie's instructions, Makalani blocked off the Hāwī-bound lane while Grace did the same on the Kona-bound side. Although the family in the first car Grace stopped watched the cattle crossing with interest, the two men in the aqua Hyundai behind Makalani seemed more interested in her.

Probably willing me to move faster with their stares.

The driver stuck his head out the window. "Eh, how long dis goin' take?"

"Mahalo for your patience. We're about a quarter way through the herd."

He nodded, jiggling his loose topknot, then looked at the line of cars behind him. As he did, Makalani could see the Filipino tribal art tattooed up the side of his neck. Meanwhile, his friend's stare bored a hole into her head. What was his problem? She considered riding over to ask when her young cousin rode out of the mauka pasture gate.

"Vinnie. I thought you were bringing up the rear."

"The other kids are doing that with their dads. Can I help you instead?"

So far, Makalani hadn't seen anything to confirm Rosie's suspicion that someone was targeting her son. That said, this was the exact location where a car alarm had spooked Uila and nearly caused her to bolt. But she and Grace had stopped traffic, so Vinnie should be safe.

"I don't mind, as long as your uncle agrees."

"Uncle Louie," Vinnie called. "Okay if I help out here?"

Louie frowned to see him, then shrugged his assent.

Makalani glanced back at the Hyundai. The men were deep in conversation, having lost interest in her.

"Maka'ala Makalani," Louie shouted. "Pay attention. You're losing a calf."

She whipped her head toward the escapee. Rocky Road reacted immediately when he felt the shift of her weight. Since the cow horse had more experience than her, she kept her reins loose, grabbed the saddle horn, and let him do the work. By keeping her eyes on the calf, the shifts in her body communicated where she wanted to go. Rocky Road did the rest.

The calf bleated in alarm and veered back toward the gate.

Rocky Road and Makalani changed direction to cut him off again. After a full morning in the saddle, she was finally feeling at one with her mount. Instead of dictating her will, she had opened a two-way conversation with the horse, something Sandy had described in their youth but Makalani had never quite felt. The more she relaxed, the more she worked in tandem with Rocky Road to get the job done.

I gotta call Sandy and tell her about this!

When she finally returned the keiki to his māmā, all eyes were on her.

Grace made a shaka sign with her hand and yelled over the cattle. "Hūi, Ranger Pahukula. Dass how it's done." Then she and Tai went back to minding the cattle on their side of the road.

Vinnie rode over, beaming ear to ear. "You looked like a real paniolo. When did you learn to do all of that?"

"Ha. I think it's more like when did I learn to let Rocky Road do what he's been trained to do."

Makalani felt good about herself, until she caught the passenger in the aqua Hyundai staring intently at her.

What's this guy's problem?

There was work to be done and another hundred head to help cross, but as Louie had said, the māmā cows had done this many times before. They knew the routine. Most of their calves followed close at their heels. The easy crossing wasn't demanding enough to distract Makalani from the bad feeling she couldn't shake off. She glanced at the men and saw them staring to the right.

They're watching Vinnie.

If they had stayed focused on her, she would have let them slide. Watching her eight-year-old cousin? No way.

She walked Rocky Road to the passenger side of the car, noting how the swirling designs shaved into the man's crew cut matched the tattoos on his arms. Both he and the driver looked to be Filipino in their mid-to-late twenties.

"Eh, guys. Everything okay?"

The passenger grinned. "We good, ranger. How 'bout you?"

"Excuse me?"

He popped his chin toward Grace. "Dass what she called you, right, Ranger Pahukula? Funny, I nevah knew rangers worked on ranches."

"We don't usually, unless it's federal land."

"Dis land belongs to da government?" he asked, surprised and mildly alarmed.

"No," she admitted, although she enjoyed watching him squirm. "You seem very interested in me."

"Oh, I thought I might know you is all. Pahukula must be a popular name. Your family from around here?"

"No."

"Huh. Kaua'i maybe?"

Makalani tensed.

The driver leaned over. "Don't mind dis guy. It's good to see a ranger working wit' her kid." He raised his brows as if waiting for validation. When she didn't offer any, he glanced at Vinnie and grinned flirtatiously at her. "Nah, you look too young to be his mom."

Alarms fired in her head.

She leaned forward in her saddle, scanning the interior of their car for weapons or suspicious items as she patted Rocky Road's neck.

"You okay, Makalani?" Vinnie asked, riding over toward her.

"Stay with the cows, Vin. I'll be right there."

She sat up tall and glowered down at the men. "I've never seen auto paint this color or hairstyles quite like yours. It sticks in the mind. Come to think of it, I have seen this car before."

"Doubt it."

"No, really. You were parked on Saddle Road yesterday. I was going to check on you because I thought you had broken down."

The driver shook his head. "Not us, ranger. Musta been some oddah aqua car. Da color stay mo' popular dan you t'ink."

Makalani fake-smiled. "I'll be on the lookout, then, in case I see more."

She rode over to Vinnie. "Hey, buddy. Why don't you guard the gate in case a calf tries to bolt up the road." She didn't want her cousin anywhere near those lying men.

"Sure," he said brightly.

"Thanks. I'll work over here."

When Louie flashed her a look of concern, she nodded with more confidence than she felt and focused on the cows.

What did the passenger know about her or her family? Why had the driver been fishing to see if Vinnie was her son? And why had they been parked at the entrance to Kam's Mauna Kea ranch?

She checked her phone contacts for a number she had never expected to call again.

"Hello, you've reached Detective Shaw at Kaua'i Services Bureau. Please leave your name and message after the beep." Considering the source, his message was expectedly stiff.

"Detective Shaw, this is Ranger Makalani Pahukula. I'm working on the Big Island now and wondered if you could run a license plate through your system for me." She recited the make, model, and license number while it was fresh in her mind. "I'm sure you remember all that my family went through. I would appreciate this favor and hope to hear from you soon."

All that my family went through.

She could have said, *all the misery you caused my 'ohana*, but chose to remind him more subtly of his debt.

CHAPTER FORTY-FIVE

Skip tossed his coffee cup into the trash. Another day had passed with no word from Kenneth or Flint. His aspirations to own Hiapo Ranch were vanishing like Waimea mist. Although Flint's lack of progress had saved Skip ten thousand bucks, he would gladly double his offer to buy the Reed property if they could only convince the Hiapos to sell.

Not that I'd tell Flint. Men like him respond better to the stick.

Skip had already offered four hundred grand for the Reeds' woodsy lot and crap house. If that wasn't sufficiently motivating, maybe reminding him of his ten-grand-a-day loss would get Flint off his butt.

He made the call. "Flint, it's Skip Una. Have an update for me?"

"It's only been a day."

"I know. You've saved me ten grand. I guess I should be pleased."

"Don't do this, man. We need that money. I mean, this is going to add up."

"Only if you drag your feet."

"I'm trying."

"What about the husband's cousin, the Pahukula family? Any progress there?"

"The big Hawaiian woman? Yeah. Pretty sure she came in from Kaua'i. We're checking it out."

"We who?"

"Me, alright? But I need time."

"You have all the time you can afford."

Skip ended the call mid-whine and looked up Kenneth's number. Five days had passed since they had spoken on the phone. Maybe the eldest son was ready to sell. If so, Skip could offer to pitch the deal to his siblings, his grandfather, and anyone else who might have a say.

"This is Kenneth Hiapo. Leave a message at the beep."

"Hey, Kenneth, it's Skip Una. Hoping we could grab a coffee and discuss your ranch. I'm here in Waimea and might be able to sweeten the deal."

No stick for Kenneth. He's a carrot guy, for sure.

Skip called the final number on his mental list.

"Aloha, this is Detective Rona Kim, how may I help you?" She rattled off her salutation with such minimal engagement it took him a moment to realize it was actually her.

"Detective! This is Skip Una from Oregon. We spoke on Tuesday about the Larry Hiapo case."

"Yes, Mr. Una, I remember. What can I do for you today?"

"I'm here in Waimea. I was just wondering how it's going."

"It's not. Larry Hiapo died from a tragic accident."

"Well, uh, that must be a tremendous relief for the family."

"You know them, right?" She sounded doubtful. "You should call and ask."

"I will, of course. I just wanted to give them time."

"It's been ten days, Mr. Una. I think they've waited long enough to hear from a friend."

Why is this woman busting my chops?

"Good point," he said. "I'll call today."

"Especially if you're still hoping to buy Hiapo Ranch. Are you?"

"Sure. If they still want to sell."

"Had you spoken to anyone besides Larry?"

"His son, Kenneth."

Detective Kim paused. "That's interesting."

"Why?"

"Well, when we spoke before, you said that Louie, not Kenneth, knew about your offer on Hiapo Ranch."

"You sure?"

"It's right here in my notes. You claimed Larry said Louie was, and I quote, 'mad as hell about the sale.'"

"Right. I forgot about that. I must have spoken with Kenneth later and had him on my mind."

"Later, since his father died?"

"Yeah, I guess."

"But at the beginning of *this* call, you told me you wanted to give the Hiapos time to grieve? Which is it, Mr. Una?"

Skip was sweating. *What did I say?* "Oh, I see what happened. I meant I hadn't spoken with anyone since you finalized the accidental death." He waited through her silence, hoping what he claimed made sense.

"So, to your knowledge, Mr. Una, which of the sons knew about the potential sale *before* Larry Hiapo died?"

"Louie, I guess. Maybe Kenneth. Why do you ask?"

"Did Kenneth feel the same way as his brother?"

"Oh, no. He was on board to sell."

"What about the wife and grandfather?"

Skip wiped the sweat into his hair. If he had known she would interrogate him, he never would have called. "I'm confused. I thought you said the case was closed."

"It is. How about the sister? Did Rosie Hiapo oppose the sale?"

"She's a teacher. Why would she care?"

"How about Luke Hiapo? I'm sure he would care. Do you know if *he* supported the sale?"

Skip squirmed in his seat. "Larry never brought up his father, so I really couldn't say."

"And yet, Larry *did* bring up his younger son."

Since she hadn't phrased it as a question, he prudently kept his mouth shut. She must still be investigating. And if the case *was* still open, and she *was* investigating the Hiapos, his original plan to sap their finances in a legal defense might still force the family to sell.

Stick for Flint, carrot for Kenneth, guard rails for the detective to keep her on the right track.

"Now that you mention it," Skip said. "I got the impression that Louie was a third wheel. Larry and Kenneth seemed far more business savvy than him."

She absorbed the information in silence, then abruptly switched course. "Hey, you're a rancher. Have you ever had cattle ingest illegal drugs?"

So much for staying on the right track.

"What kind of drugs?"

"Anything that would affect animal behavior in unexpected ways."

Ah . . . she's thinking about that bull.

"Never on my ranch. But then my ranch hands follow medication instructions carefully, so that's probably why."

"And they probably don't leave recreational drugs laying around."

"Of course not."

She left airtime for him to fill. "Anything else you'd like to share?"

"Nope. Just calling to check in."

"Okay then, Mr. Una. Enjoy your stay in Waimea."

He stared at his phone as she ended the call.

My stay?

After all that, she still treated him like a tourist, as if he wasn't born and raised on this island, as if he didn't belong. It was like living at boarding school all over again.

She wouldn't treat me that way if I owned Hiapo Ranch.

None of the locals would.

Now more than ever, he needed that land.

CHAPTER FORTY-SIX

Makalani waited with Louie for Grace to shut and lock the gate. The cattle and riders had crossed the road into the ranch's lower, drier fields. Traffic had continued. The aqua car was gone. The memory of those creepy men remained.

Louie sent Grace ahead to help Malu, then turned to her. "Keep an eye on Vinnie, okay? Kid's feeling pretty full of himself 'bout now. Don't let 'im do not'ing stupid."

"Roger that." Makalani flipped her fingers in a casual salute. Another mandate to look after her cousin *and* be far away from Malu? Sounded perfect to her. There was only so much of the man's bad temper she could take. But when Malu eventually rode back to Louie, Makalani sensed his agitation and rode closer so she could hear.

"Bulls knocked down a fence and mingled in wit' da cows," Malu said. "None of da pipi wahine are in heat so, you know, no need worry 'bout dat. But da pipi laho stay giving everybody hard time."

Louie nodded. "Someone could get hurt."

"Yeah," Malu said. "Whatchu like do?"

"Auwē. We stay running behind time because of Kenneth, and we still have mo' dan two hundred pipi down hea. I say gather up da bulls wit' da māmā and keiki cows. We can separate um at da pā kuni."

Makalani returned to Vinnie. With bulls roaming in this paddock, she wanted to stay close.

"Eh, Vinnie. How often do cattle knock down the electric fences?"

"I don't know. Is that what some cows did?"

"The bulls."

"Rad. Where are they now? I want to see."

"Hold on, cowboy. Your Uncle Louie told us to bring up the rear." She didn't add that he also wanted Vinnie kept safe and out of trouble. She gave him a wink. "No worry beef curry, we'll see them at the corral."

"Then we better hurry," Vinnie said, and jogged off to gather a slowpoke calf.

Makalani looked toward the upland slopes. If there were bulls down here and on the Hāwī side of the ranch, why was Hinuhinu in the pit on the Kona side the day Larry Hiapo died?

"I got him," Vinnie yelled as he herded in the calf.

Makalani joined her cousin, determined to focus on the day's task, which wasn't hard because the constant rumble of hooves and moos drowned out all thoughts of Larry Hiapo's death. Makalani raised her Hawaiian tribal-print yoke over her nose. The thick clouds of dust made the air hard to breathe. Even when the herd slowed to near standing, their shuffling stirred up the dirt.

She sat tall in her saddle and surveyed the valley of cattle below. Because of the slope, she also had an unobstructed view of the multisize processing pens where the calves would be weaned from their māmās, inoculated, and castrated if they were male. But since the calves were glued to their māmās' sides, they first needed to be separated and contained in the various corrals. Before that, the roundup and branding crews would need to cut out the bulls.

Paniolo voices traveled upslope, cutting through the lowing cattle noise.

"Puka nānā," Malu, Grace, and Tai yelled to the cows walking in front. *Look to the gate!*

Paniolo farther back yelled, "Pipi pā," so the cattle would cling to the fence.

Much to Makalani's amazement, the domesticated cows did as they were told. Their calves—and the nine bulls mixed in with the crowd—followed them along.

Makalani laughed.

So this is how four kids and eight adults bring in four hundred head.

As Makalani descended, she could see trucks and UTVs parked along a dirt road beside assorted sizes of adjacent corrals. Beyond the metal pens was a roomy paddock enclosed by an old pā pōhaku dry-stack rock wall. A dozen people milled around in preparation, their tiny bodies looking inadequate to handle the incoming herd. Makalani recognized Lono, the Hiapos' resident grill cook and maintenance guy, by his bright-yellow cap. Fetu's brawny wife, Alofa, was there as well in her magenta T-shirt. As the slow wave of cattle approached, Louie, Malu, and Grace funneled them through a small transitional pen with a chute. Lono and Alofa stood on a platform, opening and closing gates to direct the bulls through the chute and turn the māmā and keiki cows toward the giant receiving corral in the back.

Vinnie rode closer to Makalani as the visibility decreased. His eyes crinkled with delight above the army camouflage bandanna covering his face.

Kids at Disneyland aren't as excited as him.

Makalani stood in her stirrups to watch the paniolo at work. She had underestimated the magnitude of the job, not to mention the volume of dust and noise.

Voices shouted at the bulls. "Hele, pipi laho. Hele, hele. Get out!"

Whether they obeyed the commands or simply wanted to escape, the bulls shoved one another through the exit into the roomy pasture enclosed by the old pōhaku wall. Meanwhile, the māmā cows and their keiki mooed as they ambled into their pen.

The dust settled as the remaining cattle crept toward the pā.

Makalani lowered her yoke and turned to her cousin.

But Vinnie was gone.

He wasn't zigzagging behind the slowpokes or walking his horse alongside to keep the ambling cattle contained. He wasn't hounding the three teenagers or their dads. He wasn't up front near the gates with Tai. He wasn't inside the pens with Louie, Malu, or Grace. It was as if Vinnie had vanished in a cloud of dust while an illusionist had distracted her attention with the bulls.

Would he have ridden ahead to Rosie?

No way.

Although many kids might have wanted to share their excitement with their moms, Vinnie cared more about proving himself to his mentors. He would not have abandoned his station.

Unless he found something more impressive he could do.

Makalani spun Rocky Road and spotted Vinnie riding toward the north. It was a picturesque sight—a small boy on a long-legged horse, Pacific Ocean below on the left, fields sloping up to the road on the right. She might have recorded a video for his parents if not for the rocky hazards ahead. On Makalani's first day, Grace had warned her to *never* trot, jog, or lope a horse on Hiapo land unless following behind an experienced rider. Vinnie wasn't in that category, and neither was she.

Makalani searched for someone more experienced than her, but all the riders were too far away. She spun her horse back toward Vinnie's departing figure.

Sorry, boy. We don't have a choice.

She squeezed hard with her legs, and Rocky Road bolted ahead. Although she could be thrown and crushed during this suicidal ride, Rosie had entrusted her son into Makalani's care. There was no room for failure. Makalani would bring Vinnie home safe.

Please, please don't step in a hole.

Or trip on a rock.

Or fall into a ditch.

She remembered what Grace had told her and loosened the reins, allowing the well-trained lio to choose his own path. She was the newcomer. This was his land.

Fear eased its grip when Vinnie slowed down. Rocky Road would catch up with Uila soon. The north-side fence would keep them contained.

So help me, Vinnie, I'm gonna walk you back in disgrace.

He's just a kid.

Who could have been killed!

She shut out her thoughts. She hadn't saved him yet.

As she drew closer, she could see the stray calf Vinnie had been chasing. She mooed frantically as Vinnie stopped Uila and jumped to the ground. He tried to grab her, but the calf slipped out of his arms. As he teetered for balance, Makalani knew what would happen next.

She yanked Rocky Road to a stop and jumped to the ground. She did it quickly, but not quick enough—Vinnie fell into the electrified fence.

CHAPTER FORTY-SEVEN

Vinnie jumped away from the fence as the pulse of current jolted his upper back. He stumbled on the rocks and fell to his knees. Aside from his shocked expression, he appeared to be unharmed.

Makalani rushed to his side. "Hey, buddy, are you okay?"

He gaped at her in surprise, then his eyes widened with alarm. "Don't tell my mom."

She laughed and helped him to his feet.

Electric fences delivered a pulsating charge designed to teach animals to stay away, not to cause harm. Since they didn't have a continuous current, the pulsating charge didn't grab and hold the way an electrical outlet, damaged appliances, or downed power lines would do. Higher voltage got the animal's attention. Lower amperage kept them safe. Neither were powerful enough to knock a boy to the ground. Vinnie had fallen because he tripped over a rock.

"Did anyone else see?" Vinnie said, looking across the field.

"Is that all you care about?"

"At the moment, yeah. Louie will send me home if he finds out about the fence. Grace will tease me forever. And Malu . . ." He hung his head in shame.

"What about Malu?"

"He'll treat me like a kid."

"You are a kid."

"You know what I mean."

Makalani frowned. "Actually, I don't. Malu isn't family, and he's not in charge of the ranch. Why are you giving his opinion so much weight?"

Vinnie shook his head. "You wouldn't understand." He retrieved his hat and stared at the bleating calf. "She misses her māmā. We better take her back."

Makalani unstrapped several coils of Vinnie's kaula 'ili and slipped the looped end around calf's neck. "This is so she doesn't run away. From what I've seen, if we call and lead, she'll follow us to the pens, especially since she hasn't found her māmā on her own."

Vinnie mounted Uila and slumped. "Everyone will see us coming and know you brought me back."

"Not if we ride side by side." She glanced at the lariat still strapped to his saddle. "After all, you're the one with the calf."

It took three times longer to walk their horses instead of jogging over the pitted ground. By the time they neared the processing area, half of the four hundred head had been sorted out of the holding corral and into other pens. The swirling dust and sound obscured the activity and overloaded Makalani's brain.

Vinnie's worried mom intercepted them at the gate. "Where have you been? No one could find you. I've been worried sick."

"Sorry, Mom. The calf strayed on the wrong side of a gulch."

"Why didn't you tell someone?"

Vinnie's eyes pleaded with Makalani to help.

She turned to Rosie. "Everyone was busy bringing in the herd so . . . Vinnie and I brought her back."

Rosie held Makalani's gaze, then settled on her son. "Take the calf to Grandma, she'll tell you what to do."

Grateful to have escaped Rosie's wrath, Makalani and Vinnie found Rumiko in the sorting pen, looping ropes around the necks of the incoming calves. The keiki cows had already passed back through the same chute as before and been guided to the left by Alofa's swinging gate. At the same time, Lono had swung his gate to send their māmā cows to the holding pen on the right where the bulls, who had been released into a pasture, had originally been led. While this took place, voices yelled commands in wala'au kanaka to direct the cattle and identify the calves as female or male.

The separated cow-calf pairs were then passed into side-by-side paddocks where they could drink water and find one another along a shared metal fence. The process worked like a railroad switch for cattle, except trickier since the māmā cows and their keiki bunched together and changed directions at will—which was why Fetu and Phil, who were both big men, helped to sort the cattle and guard the pen gates on foot.

Vinnie rode up to the fence where Rumiko worked. "Grandma, we found a stray."

"Bring her in." Rumiko opened the side gate. "Untie your saddle strings and wrap the end of your kaula 'ili around your saddle horn. You remember what that's called?"

"'Ōkumu!"

"That's right."

As Vinnie did as she instructed, Rumiko removed the lasso from the calf's neck and draped the loop on the ground. When the calf walked through it, she snared her hind legs, and laid her on her side.

"Drag her in, Vinnie." Then she smacked Uila on the rump.

Having "roped" one kid's calf, Rumiko did the same for Phil's young teenage son. Meanwhile, Tai and Pete leaned over in their saddles to snare their own calves out of the group. The assembly line continued as new calves were filtered into the pen and dragged off by their heels.

"How can I help?" Makalani asked from the other side of the fence.

Rumiko pointed toward the large, circular pen where Vinnie had gone. "Go to the pā kuni and check in with them."

The activity in the branding corral made the sorting pen look calm.

Vinnie and Darius had dragged their calves into their own areas, where Grace helped Sue and Ana pin the animals on their sides by tucking in their forelegs and kneeling on their ribs. When Tai dragged in her calf, Brian snagged the foreleg en route. By the time Pete brought in his calf, Ana had released Grace's and hurried over to help her dad.

And if calves got wiggly, the youngest kids, Jaime and Lagi, piled on top. If not for the efficiency and precision of the work, Makalani would have mistaken it for a loud and dusty game.

Kupunakāne joined her as she dismounted and tied Rocky Road's lead to the fence. "I saw you come in wit' Vinnie. Watched you go aftah him too. T'anks fo' looking out. But, you know, you and your horses coulda got seriously hurt."

"I know. I'm so sorry I put your horse in danger. E kala mai iaʻu. I didn't know what else to do."

Kupunakāne clasped her face, touching her forehead and nose with his own. "Mahalo. Aloha wau iā ʻoe."

Makalani had asked his forgiveness, and Kupunakāne had responded with *Thank you, I love you*, just as Tūtū would have done. The sincere exchange cleared the air between them and settled her heart.

"Dat keiki burns to prove himself," Kupunakāne said, watching Vinnie. "Grace was da same way. Kenneth and Louie too. A paniolo can get in plenny kine trouble li'dat." He leaned on the fence and watched the kids and grown-ups work. "But dass how we grow."

Makalani leaned on the fence beside him. "They're all moving so seamlessly, I don't want to stop their momentum by asking what I should do."

"You good fo' now. Stay hea wit' me." He pointed to his younger grandson. "Watch and learn."

Louie pulled a red plastic tag out of a pouch and loaded it into a handheld tool of some kind. After glancing at the calf's belly, he used the tool to punch the tag into her right ear, stashed the punch gun under his armpit, and retrieved a clipping tool from his pocket and cut the other ear. Having finished with one calf, he moved to the next.

"You saw what he did?" Kupunakāne said. "We ear-tag every calf on our ranch to establish ownership and identity—left ear fo' kāne, right ear fo' wahine—and include da year and month of dis herd's birth. Blue, yellow, or red tells us if da calf is Angus-, Hereford-, or Charolais-mixed breed. Every ranch get their own system, but dis what Hiapo Ranch always do."

"Why did Louie clip the other ear?"

"Dass fo' ownership. In befo' time, cattle rustlers would cut da brand mark off da ear. When we clip um already with our mark, dey no can steal wit'out harming da cow."

"Do people still rustle?"

"Not so much. When I stay young, it happened plenny mo'. One time, my faddah and me caught our neighbor and his son butchering one of our cows. When we chase um back to their ranch and see how poor dey live, my faddah let um keep da beef. But he threatened to call da cops if dey evah do it again."

"Did they?"

"Hard to know. Pāpā died a month latah while jogging his horse across dat same field. His lio stepped in a trench and crushed him when he fell. Larry died nearby. I think maybe dat ʻāina is cursed."

Or something else.

It seemed highly unlikely to Makalani that two members of the Hiapo ʻohana had died in ranching *accidents* on the same field.

"Wouldn't your father have known about the trench?"

"Maybe. Maybe not. It stormed plenny hard dat month. Heavy rains change da land." Kupunakāne sighed. "He should have walked his horse."

"Was your ranch fenced as it is now?"

"Yeah."

"How did your neighbors get on and off your land?"

Kupunakāne shrugged. "If kānaka need eat, dey goin' find a way, right?"

"Can I ask you something else? We herded bulls in the lower pastures just now. Earlier, Grace told me there were other bulls pastured above the highway that had been moved to the Hāwī side of the ranch. Do you know why your son went searching for Hinuhinu on the Kona side by that pit?"

"Yeah. Malu told him he left one behind."

"Does that happen often?"

"Not usually but, you know, it can happen li'dat."

He nodded toward Louie as he clipped another calf's ear. "We used to cut um wit' a knife in da shape of an H. Larry had clippahs made to do dat in one punch. Akamai, right? My smart son always came up wit' good ideas li'dat."

Good ideas like making Kenneth the CEO of the ranch?

"What were some of his other good ideas?"

"Oh, you know, all da latest industry trends. Larry kept up to date and applied whatevah we could afford. Research ovah tradition, just like his son."

"He must have valued Kenneth's opinions."

"Yeah, even when he was wrong. Look at him ovah dea, working hard to make up fo' his bad judgment today."

Inside the pā kuni, Kenneth helped Rumiko and Rosie inoculate calves. After Malu branded the rump, the fully processed calves were set free and chased into the next pen. The keiki found their māmā cows and mooed at one another through the common fence.

Their distress tugged at Makalani's heart. "What happens to them now?"

"We move um to different pastures so dey learn how to graze on their own. Den we ship um out."

"By boat?"

"Plane stay quicker and less stressful on da calves. In befo' time, da paniolo had to *swim* da cattle to da boats. Dass how my grandfaddah's step-faddah die. His name was Pauʻole. He raised Hiapo like his own son aftah his vaquero birth faddah returned to Alta California. Pauʻole was one of da first paniolo da Mexican cowboys trained. He taught Hiapo so good dat he won da Children's Parker Ranch Race and was hired by dem when he stay only fourteen."

"Impressive."

"Right? Da next year, Hiapo stay watch Pau'ole and another Parker Ranch paniolo swim cattle into da surf and lash um to whaleboats, face up, by their horns. When sailors on da big ship hauled in da whaleboats, sharks would try kill and eat da cattle on da way. Sailors try fight um off wit' harpoons and guns but, you know, sometimes manō win."

"And Pau'ole?"

"A longhorn broke free and hooked um wit' his horns. Manō smelled blood in da water. Hiapo watched his stepdad die from da shore of Kawaihae Bay."

Makalani's eyes widened. That would have happened just up the coast from Pu'ukoholā Heiau where she worked. Although horrified by what the boy had witnessed, knowing sharks swam in those waters made her yearn to visit that bay. Perhaps her great-grandmother would visit in her deified 'aumakua, shark god, form. It would bolster Makalani's confidence to know Manō Nui Punahele had followed her here.

Kupunakāne's laughter drew Makalani's attention back to the corral, where a calf kept slipping out of Ana's grasp. Grace jumped in to help the teenager and wrestled the calf to the ground. By the time they subdued the wriggling animal, both of them were laughing and covered in dust. Paniolo life might be dangerous, but it was also good fun.

"The calves look so healthy. Why not raise them here?"

"Growing cows eat plenny kine grass. We would need cut our herds in half to support dem on our land, den wait two or t'ree years befo' dey big enough to sell."

"Would you earn back the loss?"

"Kenneth says no. Louie t'inks we might. But he also believes Hawai'i's food security and self-sufficiency mattahs more."

"What about Larry?"

"He only cared about da ranch. He sided wit' Kenneth. Had papers drawn to put him in charge."

Makalani looked away to hide her surprise.

So Kenneth was telling the truth about the deeds.

"Did Larry check the slaughterhouses?"

"What, to see if dey can handle? He did. 'Can, no can'—all depends if dey get backed up. Why you so interested in all dis?"

Eavesdropping on Kenneth and Louie.

"I, um . . . must have heard somebody talking. It didn't make sense to me until now."

Kupunakāne shrugged. "Larry said our ranch no can afford to change."

"And you?"

"I side wit' Louie—I say Hawai'i no can afford rely on da mainland fo' our food."

CHAPTER FORTY-EIGHT

Rona rolled her shopping cart down the produce aisle in disgust. Seven bucks for a papaya. Eight for a mango. Why so expensive for fruit she could pick from a tree? Even knowing the answer, it still didn't make sense. Locally grown produce was often shipped to mainland distribution facilities, then shipped back to Hawai'i to sell. She bought two apples instead. On Monday, she'd stop at the fruit stand on her way back from work and keep the money in the community where it belonged.

She ignored her pinging phone as she rolled her shopping cart toward the meats. Although more expensive than mainland choices, now that she worked in Hawai'i's ranching capital, she felt duty bound to buy local grass-fed beef. This time, her phone rang.

"Hello?"

"Hi, Detective. This is Sharon Yee from pathology."

"Oh, hi."

"I emailed you the test results, but since it's Saturday night and I knew you were waiting for this, I thought I should call."

"I appreciate that. What did you find?"

"The blood tests showed positive for methamphetamine."

"Really. How much?"

"Minimal. But keep in mind the half-life for meth is ten hours in blood and twenty-five hours in urine."

"So if we still had a viable urine sample to test?"

"There would have been more."

Rona did the math. Even if pathology had done their mandatory testing the moment the bull's samples had arrived, twenty-seven to thirty hours would have passed since Larry Hiapo's death. And who knew how long before that the bull might have been dosed. Could this lapse in time explain how a savage killer had turned into Ferdinand the Bull?

She thanked Sharon for calling and opened the email with the test results she had sent. There it was—positive for methamphetamine—in bold print. Rona lowered her phone. If she or Dan had asked for a full drug panel instead of settling for the typical livestock tests, their investigation would have taken a very different turn.

"Do you need help?" the butcher asked, stocking the meats.

She looked up in confusion.

He nodded to the rib eyes. "You've been staring at them for a while."

"Oh. I guess I was wondering if the local grass-fed beef is worth double the price."

"Hawai'i beef is ono. You never try?"

She shrugged. "Groceries are expensive enough."

He continued stacking his meats. "Treat yourself to a rib eye. You'll never go back."

Feeling too embarrassed not to take it, she grabbed a steak and called it a night. She could finish her grocery shopping the next day. Tonight, she needed her computer and the internet more.

But when she reached her car, she opened her phone. Skip Una was in the same time zone now, not too late to call. And aside from the bull breeder, he was the only rancher she knew who was willing to talk.

He answered on the first ring. "Detective Kim. This is a surprise."

"I hope I'm not interrupting your dinner."

"Nope. My belly's on Oregon time. Still too early for me to eat. What can I do for you?"

"When we spoke this afternoon, I asked about side effects from livestock medications. But have you had any experiences on your ranch with cattle ingesting illicit human drugs?"

"Like what?"

"Methamphetamine."

Silence.

"Mr. Una?"

"Sorry, I was trying to imagine what a drug like that would do to a bull."

"And?"

"I've seen all manner of livestock attack when provoked or challenged. But a bull on meth? I can't even imagine the destruction he might cause."

Rona didn't need to imagine. The images of Larry Hiapo's destroyed body replayed in her mind every night as she tried to fall asleep.

"Is that what you think caused the bull to kill Larry Hiapo?"

"I'm investigating all possibilities."

"Does that mean you reopened the case?"

"You sound oddly hopeful, Mr. Una. Is there anything else about this family or their ranch that you think I should know?"

Skip paused. "Only that it always seemed a bit unlikely to me that Larry would just happen to be killed in a pit by a bull."

Without expressing her agreement, Rona ended the call. As she started the ignition and drove back to her Kona apartment, four questions repeated in her mind:

How long before Larry's death could the bull have been dosed?

How had the drug been delivered?

Who had done it?

And why?

CHAPTER FORTY-NINE

Makalani trailed the roundup crew up the slope to Kohala Mountain Road. With the newly weaned calves branded, inoculated, and settled in their new pens, everyone was heading back to the ranch house for a celebratory feast. Lono, Rumiko, Carolyn, and Rosie had left earlier to prepare. The rest of the branding helpers returned in the vehicles they had brought.

Grace rode beside her. "How you holding up after your accident yesterday?"

"Tired and a little sore."

"I figured. That's why I didn't pull you into the branding pen to help. If this had been any other day, I would have told you to go home and rest."

"I'm glad I didn't. It was amazing . . . and eventful."

"Right? I don't know what Dad was thinking when he rushed to open that gate. Even if nothing had gone wrong, no one was in place to manage the herd. Thanks for patching him up and for chasing Vinnie when he went after that calf."

"You heard about that?"

"Oh, yeah. Louie did too. That boy's gonna catch hell at dinner."

For now, Vinnie rode happily beside the teenagers, exchanging their favorite parts of the day. When they reached the road, he followed them single-file while Phil and Pete waited on horseback to stop cars if they appeared. At the moment, the only vehicles in sight belonged to the family and helpers that had already crossed through the larger driveway gates and were heading up toward the house. Only Kenneth's black Yukon remained, partially blocking the road as he locked the makai gate. When he drove across, Makalani saw a car parked beyond him along the trees on the wrong side of the road—the same aqua car she had seen earlier that day.

With the same creepy men sitting inside.

She looked for Louie to tell him, but he and most of the riders had crossed into the mauka pastures. Darius and Vinnie were next through the gate.

"Everything okay?" Grace said from behind.

"The aqua car is back."

"Where?"

"Parked to your right on the shoulder along the—"

A high-pitched squeal cut her off as Vinnie's horse reared at the gate.

For a moment, the boy froze in picture-perfect form, like a painting his parents would have proudly hung on their wall—a young paniolo on his spirited horse. Then Uila shuffled on her hindlegs and raised even higher while pawing at the air. Vinnie let go of the reins to hug the horse's neck, but his arms were too short to reach with the swell of the Western saddle blocking his chest.

"No," Grace yelled, and kicked Baby ahead as Vinnie slipped off his saddle and fell over the side.

Makalani jumped off her mount, but neither she nor Grace could prevent Vinnie from landing, shoulder first, on the road.

Darius screamed from the pasture.

Phil and Pete shouted for him to stay where he was.

Uila finally came down and backed away from the boy's scream, stepping side to side at all the shouts. Her hooves flicked and stomped dangerously close to where Vinnie lay howling in the road.

Vinnie's shoulder had hit first, but his arm was also askew. Makalani tucked her body over him like a protective dome. Uila turned away and spun in the road. When Makalani looked, she caught the aqua car's passenger hanging out the window with something in his hand.

Vinnie whimpered in pain.

Louie lifted Makalani from under her arms. "Let me in. Go call 911."

As she placed the call, she watched the aqua car pull a U-turn and drive south. Hours had passed since the cattle crossing. Why had they been there?

Waiting for Vinnie.

"What is your emergency?" the dispatcher asked.

And for a split-second, Makalani couldn't settle on which one.

"My cousin fell off a horse on Kohala Mountain Road. His shoulder may be broken and definitely his arm."

But as she shared the rest of the details, she also thought about the creepy men. That same aqua car had been parked in front of Kam's Mauna Kea ranch the day before when she had come with Grace, Louie, and Malu to help. Did they have a grudge against one of them or against the family as a whole?

She hurried back to Louie and Vinnie. "Ambulance is coming."

"Good. I called Rosie. She coming too."

Makalani smiled encouragingly at Vinnie. "Helps on the way."

She waved to Tai, who had collected Rocky Road. "There's a jacket in my left saddlebag and a first aid kit in the right. Can you toss them to me?"

The Samoan woman nodded and tossed over her own hoodie as well. Makalani used her jacket to elevate Vinnie's legs and covered him in the softer sweatshirt to keep him warm. She cracked three instant cold packs and molded them around his shoulder and arm.

"I tried to stay on," Vinnie whispered.

"I saw. You looked like a paniolo."

"Yeah?"

Before Makalani could assure him, Kenneth's Yukon sped onto the road and screeched to a stop. Rosie, Brian, and Kenneth jumped out of the SUV. Rosie reached them first.

"Oh my god, is he okay?" She bent beside him and kissed his head. "Vinnie, baby, where does it hurt?" She took in the ice packs and the startling angle of his arm. "What happened to him?"

"He fell off his horse," Louie said.

Grace dismounted from Baby. "Uila reared at the gate."

Rosie glared at Makalani. "You were supposed to look out for him." She whirled on Louie. "And you were supposed to have trained that damn horse."

Brian knelt on the road and hugged her from behind. "*Shh*, Rosie. Focus on Vinnie, yeah? How you doing, son? Can you hear the sirens? The ambulance will be here soon."

"It wasn't their fault," Vinnie said through his tears. "I just couldn't hold on."

"Of course not," Brian said. "Don't worry about it. Every paniolo falls now and then." He looked to Rosie for confirmation, but she refused to respond and kept petting Vinnie's hair.

Kenneth marched up to his brother. "What made Uila rear?"

"Coulda been anyt'ing. You know how it is wit' horses. She might have got bit or kicked, scraped something on the fence, saw her shadow and freaked." He raised his voice over the siren as the ambulance drew near. "What difference does it make?"

"We're having too many accidents," Kenneth shouted back. "This is a sign. I'm telling you, we should sell while we can."

Rosie's head popped up from Vinnie. "Sell what, the ranch? Is there an offer?"

"It doesn't mattah," Louie said. "We nevah goin' sell."

CHAPTER FIFTY

Makalani huddled in the corner of the hospital waiting area with Louie, Kenneth, and Grace while Rosie and Brian remained with Vinnie and the doctors in the ER. Over an hour had passed. They were antsy for news.

"I hate hospitals," Grace said.

Her father cracked a smile. "Really? I would have thought you'd feel right at home. The last time you were here, they kept you a week."

"What was that for?" Makalani asked.

Grace cringed. "An ornery stallion flipped backward with me in the saddle."

"Seriously? How are you even alive?"

"I shook off a stirrup. Instead of crushing my whole body, he landed on my leg, snapped it in two places and messed up my knee."

Louie nodded with approval. "Akamai, yeah? Pushed off the saddle like she was taught."

Kenneth huffed. "And before that, she was bucked off a problematic mustang *you* had been hired to retrain."

"Eh, she learned one valuable lesson dat day."

"Yeah, what was that?"

Grace laughed. "To always listen to Uncle Louie when he says a horse isn't ready to ride."

Kenneth shook his head in disgust.

Louie shrugged. "Vinnie da same way."

"Which is exactly why we're here and why Rosie doesn't want him at the ranch."

"She can't keep him away. Dat boy get paniolo in his blood. Already he bettah dan most."

"Apparently not."

"How would you know? You evah spend time teaching him?"

"That's your job."

"Dass right, and Vinnie rides bettah dan you."

"And yet, he's in surgery."

"And Dad's dead."

Kenneth flinched. So did Makalani and Grace.

Louie quieted down. "What I mean is, paniolo work stay dangerous. I thought you figured dat ought by now, especially aftah what happened wit' da gate."

"It got stuck."

"See?" Louie said. "Shit happens, even to old guys like us. Vinnie rides good. Sooner or latah, every paniolo gets bucked, reared, or flipped off his horse."

"You think that's what happened to Grandad?" Grace asked.

"Maybe. He coulda roped Hinuhinu and da bull pulled 'im in. Or maybe 'Opihi came to one full stop and tossed Dad over her head. So many t'ings coulda happened dat day."

"Or any day," Kenneth said. "Look where we are. Vinnie could have broken his back or his neck. Next time, he or one of us might. Our 'ohana has had a string of bad luck for generations. Why not sell the ranch while we're still in relatively good health?"

"You seriously goin' bring dat up hea?"

"Why not? You know Rosie would agree. The ranching industry is changing. Prices for everything have increased. The money Skip Una is offering could take care of Kupunakāne, Mom, you, me, Grace, Rosie, everybody. We could retire or build something new on our own."

Louie shook his head. "I don't understand you, brah. Dis one family business. It's who we are. People would kill to have dakine life we get, and you like t'row um away?"

Kenneth shrugged, as if in apology or possibly regret.

Grace leaned in to her father. "Skip Una has his own ranch in Oregon. Why does he want ours?"

"He wants to come home."

Kenneth slumped in his chair. Louie and Grace did the same.

Makalani understood the pull to return. Every Hawai'i-born kanaka she knew of felt those yearnings now and again. They had grown stronger in her the longer she stayed away. After her epic visit home in the winter for Tūtū's birthday lū'au, she had only lasted a week in Oregon before she had given her notice at Crater Lake National Park. But as important as Skip Una's offer was to this family, Makalani believed something more urgent was at play. After waiting patiently for the Hiapos to deal with their emotions, her opportunity to discuss it had finally arrived.

"Remember that aqua Hyundai we stopped on the Kona side while we moved the herd across the road?"

Louie nodded. "The one wit' dose Filipino men who kept talking story wit' you?"

"They weren't talking story. They were grilling me about my name and asking if Vinnie was my son."

"Why dey care 'bout Vinnie?"

"I don't know, but they were watching him closely."

"What Filipino men?" Kenneth asked.

"The driver and passenger in the car. At first, I thought they were just impatient for the cattle to pass. Then I remembered seeing that same aqua Hyundai before."

"Really?" Grace asked. "When?"

"Yesterday at Kam's ranch. It was parked on Saddle Road when you and Louie drove the gorse to the mill."

Louie frowned. "I nevah noticed. You sure it stay da same car?"

"With that glaring aqua paint? Yeah. I'm sure."

Grace leaned in. "You think it followed us to Mauna Kea from here, or the other way around?"

Makalani shrugged. "Either way, it's too much of a coincidence to ignore."

"What about Malu?" Kenneth said. "Kam's his friend. He went with you to Mauna Kea and was moving the cattle here today. Maybe these men are friends of his."

Louie shook his head. "Dey nevah say not'ing to Malu at da crossing. Dey only spoke to her."

Grace turned to Makalani. "Could they be following you?"

"It's possible. After you shouted 'Hūi, Ranger Pahukula,' the passenger said he recognized my family name. He also questioned why a ranger was working on the ranch. Both he and the driver seemed surprised and alarmed. But if they didn't know who I was until that moment, they couldn't have been waiting for me at the cattle crossing or yesterday at Kam's ranch."

Kenneth turned on his brother. "Kam is Malu's good friend. This is your lover's doing. I knew he was bad news the moment you brought him into our lives."

"No lie, brah. You nevah like Malu because he's a man."

"You think I care that you're gay? I don't trust Malu because he's shady and no good for our ranch. And what's more, Dad felt the same way."

And now Dad is dead, Makalani thought, filling in what neither man had said. "Is there anyone who might hold a grudge against your family?"

Kenneth jutted his chin. "What, other than Malu?"

Louie stood up. "That's it. Let's take it outside."

Grace intervened. "Chillax, yeah? It was a fair question. Our family has been ranching forever. We must have made a few enemies over the years."

Louie glared down at his brother.

Grace moved between them. "All of us have strong personalities, me included."

Makalani rose to join them so she could keep her voice low. "What about your grandfather? Did he have a strong personality too?"

Louie turned his anger on her. "Don't go dea, Makalani."

"I'm not prying, Louie. I'm just wondering if anyone might hold a grudge specifically against him."

Kenneth stood to be included. "What are you suggesting?"

Makalani faltered.

We're in a hospital for Vinnie, is this really the time?

Grace touched her arm. "Go ahead. It needs to be said."

E ʻoluʻolu, e ke Akua. Please, God, let me find the right words.

Makalani began with Kenneth. "While waiting for the ambulance to arrive, you said there have been too many accidents. Before that, Rosie told me Vinnie had suffered a string of unusual accidents as well. But what if these incidents are not accidental?"

Louie gaped. "You t'ink someone killed our dad?"

"That's impossible," Kenneth said.

"Is it?" Makalani asked.

"Not entirely," Grace said. "I mean, you can't control a bull like a video game, but someone could have pulled Hinuhinu into that pit and pushed Grandad in too."

"Whoa, you mean like da guys in dat aqua car?" Louie shook his head. "I nevah get a close look, but dey no seem like paniolo to me."

"They didn't to me, either," Makalani agreed. "But that doesn't mean they couldn't be involved. After we moved all the cattle into the makai pastures, I called in a favor and ran the plates."

Kenneth gasped. "You called HPD about us?"

"No. A detective on Kauaʻi. And I didn't mention your names."

"So who owns da car?" Louie asked.

"I haven't heard yet, but I'll let you know when I do."

Rosie and Brian came out of the ER.

Kenneth hurried to them first. "How's Vinnie?"

Rosie shook her head to keep from crying.

Brian filled them in. "They were able to set his arm—closed fracture, no break in the skin—but the shoulder is going to need surgery. It's dislocated with multiple breaks. The surgeon wants to operate tonight to prevent any bone fragments from harming the surrounding tissue. They're prepping him now. You might as well go home. This will last into the night."

"We'll stay," Kenneth said.

"What's the point?" Brian said. "Once he's out of surgery, they'll want him to rest."

Rosie sniffed back her tears. "Brian's right. I love that you're all here, but there's nothing you can do."

Makalani left the waiting area first to give the Hiapos time for their goodbyes, then found a secluded place in the lobby to make a call.

Māmā answered with video after only two rings. "It's about time. I've been worried sick." She was sitting at the dining table with the kitchen to her back. "How are you feeling?"

"I'm okay. I'm sorry I couldn't call earlier, but branding day was a lot."

Pāpā leaned into view. "Wass dis 'bout you falling down a ravine?"

"No way, Kawika," Aunty Kaulana said, grabbing the phone. She smiled into the camera, then jostled the view as she carried it away. The screen went black and then jostled again as her son, Solomon, perched the phone on the table. This took several tries, giving Aunty Kaulana and Uncle Eric time to pull up chairs behind Makalani's parents and Tūtū, who were sitting on a bench.

"Enough wit' da phone," Pāpā said. "Tell us what's going on."

Māmā bumped against his shoulder. "I already told you about the ravine." She looked at Makalani. "Tell us about today. Were you able to ride? Did anything else happen? Are you okay?"

"Take a breath, Julia," Pāpā said, then glared at Makalani. "Well, hurry up."

Solomon leaned in from behind his parents. "Did you brand any cows?"

Aunty Kaulana shushed him. "Let da girl speak."

Makalani laughed. Her family's exuberance was a balm to her soul. She turned, looking for a place to sit and relax while she waited for her ride back to the ranch.

"Wait," Māmā said. "Are you in a hospital?"

Makalani hadn't meant to tell them, but she was surrounded by telltale signs. "Brian's son broke his shoulder falling off his horse."

"Auwē, dat sounds painful," Pāpā said.

Māmā raised a finger. "Did that man who knocked you out of the UTV have anything to do with this?"

Leave it to Māmā to dive straight to the point.

"It wasn't him."

Tūtū leaned forward. "I ka ʻōlelo no ke ola, i ka ʻōlelo no ka make—in language there is life, in language there is death. Consider da impact of your words befo' you speak."

As always, her wise grandmother was right. Her family already looked worried, and she had barely said a thing. She should have waited until the morning. It was selfish to call now.

"Don't do dat," Tūtū said, as if reading Makalani's mind. "We stay wait fo' your call all day long. You no can tell your makuahine about murder last night and t'ink she goin' keep it to herself. You owe us an explanation, but . . . me ka mālama . . . tell us with care."

So Makalani filled them in about the day's events and how she had seen the passenger of the aqua car hanging out his window with something in his hand right after Vinnie's horse had reared.

"You think it was a gun?" Pāpā said.

"Could be airsoft, or a slingshot. I didn't hear any sound."

Even carefree Uncle Eric looked concerned. "Dese guys were Filipino like Solomon's paka lōlō dealer friends?"

Solomon gaped at his dad. "Dey not my friends."

"Whatevah," Pāpā said. "I like hear what else my daughter got to say." He looked back at Makalani. "You seen dese men t'ree times, and now Vinnie is hurt. Have you told da family your suspicions?"

Makalani nodded. "I did."

"And?"

"They're concerned."

"Did you bring up the father's death?" Māmā asked.

"I wasn't going to, but Grace—his paniolo granddaughter—was also suspicious about how he died. She encouraged me to speak up."

"And?" Pāpā said again.

"Hard to say. Rosie and Brian came out with an update about Vinnie's surgery. We were all more concerned about him. Then Rosie asked us to go home."

"Well," Māmā said. "If Grace wanted you to share, then it's probably good that you did."

"Of course it is," Tūtū said. "No can change da truth by hiding." She leaned in toward the phone, filling the screen with her face. "If someone is hurting da Hiapo ʻohana, it stay your kuleana—your responsibility—as their paniolo and as a law enforcement ranger to help."

CHAPTER FIFTY-ONE

Makalani closed the textbook and stretched her back in the chair, mindful of the columns of boxes and last month's Hawaiian village display. Her heart ached with worry about Vinnie. Her body ached from riding and her tumble down the ravine. And despite her efforts to focus on the history of Puʻukoholā Heiau, her mind was exhausted and spinning out of control. Brian had been texting continuous updates about Vinnie—when he came out of surgery, when he was awake and eating, when he'd be discharged, and that, although the surgery had gone well, they wouldn't have a prognosis for over a week. Makalani wanted to tell him and Rosie about the creepy men who may have caused Vinnie's accident, but she didn't want to add to their fears. She also kept replaying what Malu had said to Louie at the branding day dinner party after they returned from the hospital.

Rumiko had insisted on feeding everyone and thanking them properly for all their hard work. Fetu was playing the ʻukulele, Phil and Pete were playing their guitars. Everyone else was singing along. Despite the grueling day and Vinnie's accident, Makalani knew the pāʻina would go well into the night. Unfortunately, she had to get up early Sunday morning for her actual job. But when she headed upstairs to gather her belongings from Grace's room, she overheard Malu trying to convince Louie to attend a rally the following night.

"I no get room in my life fo' dis," Louie had said.

Malu had been angry. "You say dat every time."

"Den why you hound me 'bout every rally you plan? Kahaluʻu Beach Park is an hour away. I no get da luxury fo' two late nights in a row."

"Please, Louie. We need ranch owners like you to speak out and inspire da kānaka to fight on their own behalf."

"I'm not a ranch owner."

"Not yet. But you know Kupunakāne goin' put you in charge now dat Larry stay gone. Why else I do what I do?"

Why else I do what I do?

Makalani had stared at the ceiling, unable to sleep.

What did you mean, Malu? What did you mean?

His words refused to wash away even as the evening rainstorm pounded her roof. And when she rolled out of bed in the morning, she found them stuck in her sleep-deprived mind like sticks in the mud.

Why did you say that? What did you mean?

The conundrum followed her to work. In Pidgin English, locals frequently used the present tense even when they referred to something in past. When Malu had said, "Why else I do what I do?" was he reminding Louie of something he was doing now or something he had done before?

Like kill Larry Hiapo so Kupunakāne could put Louie in charge.

The treachery was echoed in the story she was reading, about how Kamehameha's trusted military adviser and uncle murdered Kamehameha's rival cousin in Kawaihae Bay—the same bay where Hiapo's stepfather was killed swimming a steer to a boat. Makalani dropped her head into her palms as past and present muddled into a convoluted mess.

"Need a break from reading?" Ranger Akaka asked from the doorway.

"Yes!"

He laughed. "Come on. We can talk while we walk."

She glanced down the hall for her supervisor. "Won't Ranger Machado mind?"

Ranger Akaka smiled. "He's on Maui today."

The warmth of the midday sun eased the tension from Makalani's shoulders as they walked along the visitors' path. The stone heiau stood on the mauka side of the flat, barren land, muddy now because of the previous night's rain. The lava platform was huge, over two hundred feet wide and twenty feet high. She had never seen one this large or with multiple tiers.

"How did they actually use it?"

"Good question. The kahuna or ali'i—King Kamehameha I was both—would perform religious ceremonies or hold political meetings on this space. The attendees would sit on the lower two levels according to their standing in the community. Structures were sometimes built on the top level to offer shade for chiefs and advisers. Pu'ukoholā's size reflects its importance."

He gestured toward the ocean. "When the visiting chiefs and their entourages would sail their outriggers into this bay, one of Kamehameha's top warriors would throw a spear at the chief. If he caught the spear it meant he had enough mana—divine power and authority—to proceed."

Makalani thought about the treacherous bit of history she had been reading that morning. "Was that how Kamehameha's uncle killed his rival cousin?"

"No. Instead of throwing the spear, Ke'eaumoku opened his arms for a hug. Although the rival cousin knew Kamehameha would kill him as a sacrifice for the heiau, he had come to save his people from war."

"Then why murder him?"

"Kamehameha wanted to talk with his cousin first. Ke'eaumoku feared the rival would deter the king from his destiny, so he and his men slaughtered all but one. But the treachery happened on both sides. Although the cousin had come willingly, he had mutilated his body to taint the sacrifice. One version of this story says the rival chief had even decided to live and planned to assassinate Kamehameha when they met."

"So Ke'eaumoku acted without Kamehameha's knowledge?"

"There are many versions of this story, but the one I believe makes Ke'eaumoku seem like the General Patton of the Pacific and a mafia hitman rolled into one."

Makalani stared down at the beach, envisioning the multilayered treachery at play. In many ways, it reminded her of the Hiapo family today.

Could Malu have killed Louie's father to protect Louie from a perceived treachery in the way Ke'eaumoku had believed he was protecting his king?

"This is a touchy bit of history," Ranger Akaka said. "Many existing families are descended from both sides. But, you know, back then, so many of the ali'i and ali'i nui were related. Not only was Ke'eaumoku the uncle to Kamehameha, he was the father of Kamehameha's favorite wife, Ka'ahumanu."

"My tūtū was named for her."

"Really? Are you related?"

Makalani understood his surprise. Hawaiians didn't name their children after ali'i nui unless they came from the same 'ohana.

"Queen Ka'ahumanu was my grandmother's great-great-grandaunt."

His eyes widened. "Oh. Then you are also distantly related to Ke'eaumoku *and* Kamehameha. That makes the history of Pu'ukoholā Heiau even more relevant to you."

Makalani grinned. What would Malu think about that after calling her a malihini and treating her like a visitor who didn't belong? Although uncharitable, it would feel good to rub it in his face.

No, Makalani. You have more important concerns.

"Do you know about a rally happening tonight in Kona?"

"What's it for?" Ranger Akaka asked.

"Not sure. Something to empower kānaka maoli I think."

"We have a lot of Native Hawaiian *and* Hawaiian sovereignty activist groups. Do you know who's in charge?"

"Malu . . ." She shrugged. "I don't know his last name."

"Well, his first name means shelter or protection. Even so, be careful of people claiming to be more than they are."

CHAPTER FIFTY-TWO

Ranger Akaka's warning stuck with Makalani as she drove down the coast to Kahalu'u Beach Park. The setting sun streaked the sky with pink, lavender, and peach. It would have felt tranquil if not for the bold and conflicting colors of the flapping Hawaiian flags stuck in the ground. Someone had lined them from the entrance of the park all the way to the grassy area across from the beach. The clash of colors agitated Makalani's already unsettled mind.

The official flag of Hawai'i was designed by King Kamehameha I to pay homage to his relationships with America and Britain's Royal Navy. The red, white, and blue stripes with the Union Jack in the upper left corner clashed with the green, red, and yellow flags many Hawaiians preferred. Some of the kānaka maoli flags had the green shield with yellow canoe paddles in the center. Others had it placed high on the left. She also saw many of the red, white, and blue Hawai'i flags attached to the sticks upside down in the universal signal of distress.

Makalani parked on the ocean side of the beach road and remained in her seat with the windows rolled down. Across the way, she spotted Malu's silver pickup truck with a rally banner hanging along the side. A matching banner hung in the trees behind him where a dozen or so locals had gathered on the grass to hear him speak. Most nodded in agreement. Others gave him a hard time. A Hawaiian man in his forties seemed particularly incensed.

"You so full of it, Malu. Stay easy to say, 'Follow da old ways,' when you live on one fancy kine ranch. Try feed my 'ohana before you tell me how to live."

"So what, Keoni?" Malu said. "It's not enough dey take our land and sovereignty, you goin' let our traditions die, too?"

"I nevah say dat. But I'm going to take whatevah cheap deals I can find."

Others shouted their own opinions, for or against, then added their own grievances and solutions to the mix. Makalani hadn't arrived early enough to hear what Malu had proposed, but his rally had devolved into separate community disputes.

As Keoni walked away, Malu chased after him with fire in his eyes. "Eh, why you stay come to my rallies if you no like what I say?"

Keoni turned and got in his face. "Free country, brah."

Malu shoved his chest. "No. That's my point. It isn't our country at all."

Keoni shoved him back. "Old news, brah. Stirring up all dakine emotions won't pay da rent."

"Stay mo' dan about money."

Keoni laughed. "Only a braddah with money would evah say dat."

As Malu lunged to keep Keoni from leaving, a young woman ran crying into Malu's arms. He tried to shake her free, but she clung.

"Please, baby, you can't leave me like this. I need you."

Malu pried off her fingers. "I no get time fo' you, Patty. Maybe latah, but not now."

She threw back her head like a petulant child, shaking her tangled black hair from its bun. "I hitched a ride. How will I get home?"

"Auwē! Wait in my truck or walk."

She nodded frantically. "Sure, Malu, sure."

She cowered away from him as she turned, hugging her bare arms despite the Kona heat. Scratch marks marred her dry legs. She was skinny like Malu but not in an athletic or fashionable way, more like a person who lacked nutrients in their diet or depleted them with drugs.

Was she his girlfriend? Hard to believe. Even putting aside gender, Patty was nothing like Louie.

Unless that's the point.

By the time Malu had freed himself from Patty, Keoni was gone and the gatherers had dispersed, many to a picnic happening on the beach. Had they even known about the rally, or just dropped in to see? If the latter, the turnout was even more dismal than Makalani had thought.

As Malu gathered up the banner and stick flags, she noticed a missed call from Sandy. Two days ago, she had told Makalani that Skip Una had been negotiating with Larry Hiapo to buy Hiapo Ranch. What new information would her friend have today?

"Eh, Sandy. You called?"

"Sure did. Thought you'd like to know that ranch sale is still in play. Dad says Skip has been talking to one of Larry Hiapo's sons. He flew to the Big Island last week."

"Is he still here?"

"Not sure. Dad only heard through the grapevine today."

"Why is Skip Una such a hot topic?"

"A few years back, Dad and a couple rancher friends had floated the idea of acquiring Una Ranch. They've kept tabs on Skip ever since."

"Is Una planning to sell?"

"Nah. Word is he's going to pass his ranch to his son."

"Interesting. Thanks for letting me know."

"No prob. How's paniolo life suiting you? Any more bull encounters?"

Makalani laughed. "Not directly. Although I did go on a roundup and helped bring in four hundred head."

"Whoa. Well done, tita. Did you brand any?"

"Not this time. They had a full crew helping out. I watched from the fence and got a play-by-play from the Hiapo patriarch who is ninety-seven years old."

"I've heard about Luke Hiapo. Dad says he still rides."

"Not only that, he still cuts and braids rawhide. This was my second conversation with him. He speaks fluent ʻōlelo Hawaiʻi and preserves the old ways."

"Like your tūtū."

"Yeah. I really miss her."

"You should come home for a visit."

Makalani considered it. With her four-day-on, three-day-off ranger schedule, she definitely could, but that would mean bailing on Hiapo Ranch after she had only begun. "Maybe next month."

"Nice. Let me know in advance and I'll rearrange my schedule to be free at least one day while you're here. Or you could join me on another rescue."

"What about your grumpy lieutenant?"

Sandy chuckled. "After the help you provided last time, I think he could be convinced."

A wave of homesickness hit Makalani. As active and interesting as her days off had become, she yearned to spend time with her ʻohana and friends back home.

She spotted Malu returning with the flags.

"I gotta go. Talk soon, okay?"

He headed for his truck, where he had told Patty to wait inside. Instead, she leaned against the back. Standing beside him with her scraggly black hair, Patty could have passed for his younger sister. But would a sister have called him *baby*? Probably not. When she pushed her hair aside, it was clear they looked nothing alike.

Makalani struggled to hear their argument through her open window. Patty appeared to be pleading for something. A fix? A ride? What did Patty want that Malu couldn't or wouldn't provide?

If he's dealing drugs, he might know she won't pay.

With that thought in mind, the unfolding drama made more sense—Patty calling him *baby*, begging him for help, Malu's stony expression as he, once again, shook his head no.

What about Louie? Maybe the trouble between them is actually about this.

When Patty pleaded again, Malu gave up and motioned her into the truck. Everything seemed to have resolved until a guy on a dirt bike honked from the beach road.

Patty leaped out of her seat.

This time, Malu pleaded with *her*. When she refused, he became more insistent and shook her by the arms.

She recoiled and struggled to escape.

Malu gripped tighter and yelled loud enough for Makalani to hear. "You can't go wit' him!"

Fearing for Patty's safety, Makalani jumped out of her car.

Patty broke free and ran across the grass.

Rain began to fall.

Malu yelled for her to come back, telling her not to do it. "You goin' regret dis, Patty. I promise you. Come back!"

Although trembling with frustration, Malu didn't pursue. He just stood in the sudden downpour as Patty hopped onto the dirt bike and rode away with the man.

CHAPTER FIFTY-THREE

The next day, Makalani applied every trick in the book to focus on her studying. The morning lecture on canoe carving helped, but although she was interested, thoughts about Malu, Patty, and the aqua Hyundai festered in her mind. It was noon and she still hadn't heard from Detective Shaw on Kauaʻi about who owned that car.

Maybe the haole detective doesn't feel the same kuleana I would have felt to make things right.

As she considered how best to follow up, his message arrived with no salutation or information other than a name.

Jay Alegado.

It meant nothing to her. She considered calling him back, but didn't want to beg. Either the detective felt responsible for his treatment of her family, or he did not. If the roles had been reversed, she would have done everything in her power to help.

As the canoe carver continued his lecture, Makalani's thoughts returned to Malu and the unknown woman at the beach.

Wayward younger sister? Disgruntled secret girlfriend? Strung-out addict in need of a fix? Who are you to him, Patty, and why were you there?

When the presentation ended, Makalani took her sack lunch to a shady tree and searched the contacts in her phone to make another unlikely call. Ever since Uncle Eric had asked if the Filipino men in the aqua car were like Solomon's friends back home, she had been thinking about Kalei. Makalani had added the paka lōlō dealer's phone number to her contacts last winter in case she reneged on her agreement to stop selling to kids. So far, Kalei had honored their deal. Whether or not she still felt grateful to Makalani remained to be seen.

The phone rang.

A harsh female voice answered, "Yeah?"

"Kalei?"

"Yeah."

"This is Makalani Pahukula." No response. "Becky's cousin." Nothing. "The *ranger*?"

"I know who you are, just not what you want."

"I have a question about the drug scene on Hawai'i Island."

Kalei snorted. "Den why call me?"

"I'm not familiar with how things work over here. You seemed pretty connected. I was hoping you'd know."

"Really. So you not calling because you t'ink I owe you somet'ing li'dat?"

"Well . . ." Makalani said. "You kinda do."

Silence.

Scowling Woman, as Makalani had dubbed Kalei before learning her name, was not the type to be easily cowed. She and her brother had lived off the grid in the Keālia Forest Reserve with their gang, scraping a living from the marijuana they illegally grew. Makalani didn't know where they had landed since then. Kalei and her brother, both Filipino, had a passing resemblance to the men in the aqua car.

Could they be related? Is that how the guy with the swirly shaved head knew my name?

Once Makalani broke the ice with Kalei, she'd ask about those men.

"Whatchu like know?" Kalei sounded suspicious yet resigned.

"What are the most popular illegal drugs over here?"

"If you no count paka lōlō, fentanyl stay growing, but meth is still king. Why you ask?"

"Who's dealing it?"

Kalei laughed. "Hawai'i stay called da Big Island fo' one reason."

"On the west side then, Kona, Waimea, Kawaihae."

"What, so you can bust um?"

"Nothing like that. One of them might be hassling my 'ohana."

"Ho, dat again? Maybe your family attracts trouble. Evah thought about dat?"

More than I'll admit to you.

Kalei chuckled at her silence. "Okay den, Miss Ranger, most o' da meth is trafficked by Mexican cartels and sold by local Filipino gangs."

"Anyone you know?"

"Maybe. But I stay look out fo' *my* 'ohana too."

"Fair enough. Could there be any dealers not associated with that gang?"

"Maybe, but dey bettah be tough."

Makalani replayed the highlights of Malu's temper—with Louie at the truck, with her and Grace at the fence, with Patty at the park. Additional arguments flooded in the gaps along with images of Malu's snarling face. The only smile she had seen from him had been for Kupunakāne.

And Vinnie.

Malu had been surprisingly encouraging to him.

"How tough?" Makalani asked.

"Meth dealers I know on da Big Island like machetes and knives. One guy against dem? I don't know, maybe if he stay John Wick."

Malu as Keanu Reeves?

"No way, not even close."

"Den he goin' need plenny kine friends, right? And if he's not selling meth fo' da cartel, he goin' need a lab to make his own stuff. Da fumes pilau, yeah? Bettah if nobody is around to smell da stink."

Makalani had smelled a strong scent of ammonia and fuel at Kam's isolated Mauna Kea ranch that she had attributed to cats and Kam's diesel UTVs. Could she have been smelling the chemicals used to make the drug? The bins of plastic bottles that made sense for recycling could also be used with the rubber tubes to make "shake and bake" meth.

Would Kam risk blowing up his home and ranch?

He might if his need and reward outweighed the risk.

"Kalei, can you check if anyone has been encroaching on that Filipino gang's turf?"

"And dass it?"

Makalani considered the men in the aqua Hyundai. They were obviously Filipino from their looks, tribal tattoos, and the name Detective Shaw had texted. If Jay Alegado was Kalei's relative and a member of the Filipino gang dealing meth for the cartels, Kalei would lie to Makalani and tell them about her. Better not to ask for anything more. "Whatever you can get would be great."

Kalei ended the call.

Makalani had two more full days of work. If Kalei came back with Malu or Kam's name, what excuse could she use to return to the Mauna Kea Ranch? With the barren landscape, Kam would spot her the moment she drove up his gravelly dirt driveway; and if the gate was locked, her SUV would stick out parked on the shoulder of desolate Saddle Road.

Forget about that.

Makalani couldn't count on Kalei. Even if she discovered something, she might keep Makalani waiting only to say no one was encroaching on cartel meth, or if they were, that it wasn't Malu and Kam. Makalani needed something she could do *now*.

"Eh," Ranger Akaka said, driving up in a pickup truck, rear bed empty except for the tools strapped to the sides. "You done with your lunch?"

She looked at her uneaten sandwich. "Working on it."

"Hop in. You can finish while we ride."

Ten minutes later, they had descended into the shallow wash of a gulch along an estuary where visitors were usually allowed to roam. Rangers had cordoned it off with yellow tape after the previous night's storm had flooded the upland gulch and carried branches and shrubs down the slope. Although the water levels had lowered, the flood had left a mess on the land and destabilized the bank.

Ranger Akaka shook his head. "None of this would have happened in ancient times before modern thinkers decided to build the Port of Kawaihae."

"What was there before?"

"Only a beach, not even a pier."

"Is that why the early paniolo had to swim their cattle to the boats?"

"That's right. But when they excavated the coral and built the peninsula, they changed the natural flow of the land. Now the narrower channel causes the estuary to back up, erode the shore, and clog the passage under the bridge. If we don't clean up this mess, the next flash flood could undermine Kawaihae Road."

"When do we start?"

He grinned. "You wanted to get out of the office, right?"

Makalani brightened. "You mean no more studying?"

"Don't get too excited. You still have to get through the materials, but you can take a break and work here in the afternoons. Since low tide happens at the end of your shift, you'll be able to walk across the water onto the remnants of Hale o Kapuni Heiau. Just follow the branches caught in the rocks. The height of your boots will keep your pants dry. Make sure to wait until we're closed; we don't allow our visitors in these waters."

"Because the temple is sacred?"

"That too, but mostly because of the sharks. This heiau was built by a chief to honor his family's 'aumakua. He used to sit up on that cliff and watch the sharks come and eat the offerings he left. If you're lucky, manō might come and visit you."

"Our family 'aumakua is also a shark."

"Then you are welcome to make offerings if you wish."

"Mahalo. I hope Manō Nui Punahele will bless me with a visit. It's been a long time since I've seen my great-great-grandmother in her silvery-green form."

"I hope she does too." He stepped out of the truck. "Okay, have fun."

"You're not going to help?"

"Nope." He gestured to the mess along the bank. "All of this is for you."

Makalani pulled on her gloves as Ranger Akaka walked away. Although excited at the prospect of visiting with her family's ʻaumakua, she looked forward to her afternoon work.

As expected, the hard labor of chopping, stacking, and clearing the debris kept her mind off Malu, Kam, and Kalei. Ranger Akaka popped in to check on her progress but otherwise left her alone, so her phone alarm surprised her when it signaled the end of her day.

She packed the tools in the truck and headed for the beach. As promised, the tide had receded. With no offerings other than her aloha, Makalani aligned herself with the row of caught branches and stepped onto the path of submerged rocks. She paused to marvel at the sensation. Although she could see the remains of the ancient lava wall beneath her boots, it was hidden from the shore. To anyone watching, she would appear to be walking on water. A foot to the side and she would sink thigh deep into the calm, sandy-bottom bay—just deep enough for hungry or curious sharks.

Makalani walked out to the wider platform of the submerged heiau and held out her arms. "Aloha, Manō Nui Punahele. I am Makalani Pahukula, daughter of Kawika, granddaughter of Kaʻahumanu. You blessed me with a visit when I was sixteen years old in the waters of Anahola Bay. I know it's presumptuous to ask, but would you please visit me here in Kawaihae. I will bring you offerings tomorrow at this same time. Please feel free to invite your friends if you wish. All manō are welcome at Hale o Kapuni Heiau."

She bowed her head over her clasped hands and added a silent prayer. *Please come, I miss you so much.*

CHAPTER FIFTY-FOUR

Three days had passed since Rona watched Jen Farber go into convulsions and called the EMTs. Her subsequent search of Jen's Kona apartment revealed evidence of a lovesick woman trying desperately to deaden her pain. Jen confirmed this in the hospital the following day when she admitted to using meth after Paul Campbell broke off their affair. Neither Jen—nor the journal entries Rona had found and read in her apartment—demonstrated any anger, resentment, or a desire for revenge. Jen Farber wasn't a murderer. She was heartbroken and simply wanted to forget.

Rona stared at the tarp-covered body under the tree at Kahalu'u Beach Park an hour south of Waimea but only ten minutes from Kona where Rona now lived. Another overdose. What inner demons had driven *this* woman to homelessness and drugs?

Detective Daniel "Call me Dan" Lau waved her over to the cave-like shrub where the woman had presumably camped. Numbered red tags marked every item they had found.

"Find something new?" she asked.

Dan pointed to the torn corner of a green, red, and yellow paper. "These colors remind you of anything?"

She nodded. "The kānaka maoli flag. You think it ripped from a Hawaiian Sovereignty Movement flyer?"

"Could be. Or for any group that supports or promotes Native Hawaiians. I looked around, but none of the papers near her shelter match."

"I'll check the trash cans."

"I already did. Garbage pickup came this morning. Based on the degree of rigor mortis, body temp, and paleness of her skin, she probably died during the night. Whatever had been dumped in the cans would be gone."

Rona considered what they knew. No identification. No signs of sexual assault. No signs of a struggle. Clear signs of overdose, but no evidence as to what type of drug. A nest in the shrubs made from a beach towel and sweats suggested at least one night spent at Kahaluʻu Beach Park.

"How do you want to play this?" she asked.

"The autopsy will tell us more, but this looks like a self-induced overdose to me. Let's stay focused on the Paul Campbell murder and get that one solved before anything else comes up."

"Like another locked room mystery with a killer bull in a pit?"

Dan chuckled. "I doubt you'll see any more cases like that."

Rona smirked. If Dan learned about her visit to the bull breeder or the other toxicology test she had ordered, he'd file a complaint and get her sent back to Honolulu before the end of the month. Honestly, she wouldn't blame him if he did. No one in her department knew she was still pursuing that case. And although she'd learned more than she had ever wanted about cattle husbandry, her obsession with the killer bull was leading her to meth—the same drug that had nearly claimed Jen Farber's life. The same drug that had possibly caused this new woman to OD. If the cases were related, she couldn't see how.

She watched Dan walk away. "And neither would he."

As Dan greeted the men from the body removal service, Rona noticed a tall Hawaiian woman watching from the road. She had risen from the driver's seat of an SUV and paused in the wedge of her opened door. Instead of wearing beach attire, she wore a national park ranger's uniform, which struck Rona as odd since Volcanoes National Park was two hours away.

CHAPTER FIFTY-FIVE

Makalani studied the petite Korean detective, standing in front of the police tape as her partner—a stocky, middle-aged hapa-Hawaiian plain-clothes detective—spoke with the body removal services men who had just arrived. The female detective had been staring off in Makalani's direction, as if puzzling through a problem. Once she locked eyes with Makalani, she wouldn't let go.

What do I do now?

Makalani had driven down the coast as soon as she learned from Ranger Akaka that a dead body had been found at Kahalu'u Beach Park. She worried it might be Patty, the woman she had seen arguing with Malu. If so, the detectives would want to know.

Unless they're the types who don't welcome unsolicited help.

Makalani had run into more than her fair share of those. She was also self-aware enough to know she had a bad habit of inserting her *help* with things people didn't want fixed.

They're detectives, not family, she assured herself. *They'll want this case solved.*

She could almost hear Pāpā's amused voice. "Oh, you mean like wit' Detective Shaw?"

Her most recent encounter with Hawai'i law enforcement had not gone as planned. For some reason, she was the only person who had not predicted those results.

Am I really that naive?

Her meddling had caused a lot of trouble for her ʻohana back home, and she didn't want to make a similar mistake here. Besides, she wasn't in Oregon where her federal law enforcement position held sway. Here, she was barely more than a tour guide at a national historic site. Why would these Big Island detectives care what she had to say? Or worse, what if they became suspicious of her?

Too late.

The detective was walking her way.

Makalani closed her door and met her on the grass. "Looks like a rough day for someone."

The detective shrugged. "Not anymore."

"Dead?"

She glanced at Makalani's uniform. "Ranger, huh? You're a long way from Volcanoes. You just get off work?"

"I'm a new transfer to Puʻukoholā."

"Transfer from where?"

Makalani smiled, glad for the opening to establish her creds. "I was a law enforcement ranger at Crater Lake National Park in Oregon. I wanted to move home, and this was the first job that opened."

As the detective mulled over this information, a curious range of expressions flickered across her face before settling into the all-too-familiar law enforcement mask. "Welcome to the Big Island. What brings you to Kahaluʻu Beach Park?"

Makalani gestured to the surrounding beauty. She wasn't ready to mention Malu's rally or his quarrel with Patty until she knew for certain who was getting zipped into the bag. The last thing she wanted was to leave a trail for the detective to her extended family on Hiapo Ranch.

"I found this beach my first week on the island. Good place to swim. I drive down from work every now and again."

The detective furrowed her brows. "You don't look ready to swim."

Makalani gritted her teeth. This was exactly how her last interaction with Hawaiʻi detectives had begun, cordial inquiries followed by the third degree. She needed to turn the tables before the focus cemented on her.

She nodded toward the body being loaded onto the gurney. "Overdose?"

"What makes you think that?"

Makalani shrugged. "The last time I was here, I saw a woman who looked pretty strung out."

"When was that?"

"Over the weekend. Were you able to ID the body?" The detective cocked her head, as if Makalani should know better than to ask. "I just wondered if it was the same woman—twenties, maybe younger; local; long, black hair. She was very thin with scratches on her legs."

The detective studied Makalani as if deciding whether or not to believe the description she had given, her credentials, or both. After a moment, she seemed to relax. "Not the same person. Our vic was blond and definitely a teen. I'm Detective Kim. What's your name?"

"Pahukula." Makalani sealed her mouth as Detective Kim waited for more.

The woman chuckled at the tactic she had undoubtedly used many times herself, then held out her hand. "Rona."

Makalani shook it. "Makalani. Nice to meet you."

"I transferred from Honolulu last month."

"Oh, yeah? How you like Hawai'i Island?"

Rona glanced back toward her partner. "Not sure yet."

Makalani smiled. "Boys' club, huh?"

Rona grinned back. "Little bit."

Makalani nodded toward the men loading the body bag into the van. "Overdose or homicide?"

"Probably OD. Have you seen anyone dealing?"

"No." Makalani hadn't witnessed Malu doing anything illegal. Until she knew for certain, she'd keep her suspicions to herself.

Rona's partner beckoned her to meet him at their vehicle. "I've got to go. It was nice to meet you, Makalani."

"You too."

As she watched the detective leave, Makalani considered calling her back. This was her first nonranger, nonranch interaction on the island. If they sat down over coffee, they might become friends. Makalani's career path and experiences would probably be more similar to Rona's than to the rangers at Puʻukoholā.

Makalani jogged after her. "Rona, wait up."

The detective turned in surprise.

"You wanna grab coffee sometime?"

After a flash of suspicion, Rona nodded and grinned.

That wasn't too hard.

They exchanged numbers and went their own ways.

With no reason to inspect the cordoned-off area, Makalani found a curving tree trunk where the grass met the beach on which she could sit and enjoy the setting sun. She had grown up near Anahola Beach on the east side of Kauaʻi and would paddle downriver to the bay and greet the rising sun. Now, on the west side of Hawaiʻi Island, she could end her day by gazing across the same ocean amid an orange-streaked, indigo sky.

As dusk settled in and the detectives had left, the knots in her shoulders began to ease. Although ranch work expelled her excess energy, it also introduced complicated social interactions that added to her stress. If she didn't find a way to cope, the stomach pains would begin.

Not if I focus on Larry Hiapo's death.

Staying in ranger mode kept her social anxiety at bay. She should call home. Her family saw things about her she buried or ignored. Two nights had passed since their video chat.

I'll grab some takeout and give them a call.

She was headed back to her vehicle, feeling calmer than she had in a week, when she spotted the silhouette of a person standing in front of the police tape where the overdose victim had been. With their back bowed forward and their long hair draped around their face, she couldn't be sure of the gender or age. Nor could she tell if the person was praying or searching for something on the ground.

Curious stranger, or sorrowful friend?

When they straightened up and arched their face to the darkening sky, she saw the outline of a long mustache and goatee. The man—not a teen—turned toward the ocean and headed for a familiar silver truck.

CHAPTER FIFTY-SIX

Makalani slipped into the shadows as Malu opened his door. The overhead light made his scowl more extreme. Had he sold drugs to the teenager? Or had he come looking for Patty and then saw the police tape stretched around the trees where the victim had been found? If he knew who camped there, Makalani could tell Rona.

Right, because Malu will be so eager to share.

The man already hated her and may have intentionally jolted her out of that UTV either as a warning or to scare her away from the ranch. What would he do if he thought she had followed him here?

She ducked out of sight and waited for him to leave, then hurried to her SUV and followed him out of the park. Although her dusty black Explorer was common enough, she trailed him at a distance so he wouldn't recognize her behind the wheel. When he headed up the coast, she expected him to continue up Highway 19 to Hiapo Ranch or turn onto the 190 in the direction of Kam's Mauna Kea ranch. Instead, he turned left into a warren of streets and parked in the lot of a small church.

Makalani parked across the way, utterly mystified as to why Malu would go there. Try as she might, she couldn't picture him praying or singing in the pews.

"No be judgy li'dat," Aunty Kaulana would have said. "Most Hawaiians get religion. Why not him?"

Makalani's stomach cramped.

Because I've already made up my mind that he's bad.

The realization made her ill. What if everything she had thought about Malu was wrong? He could have met the overdose victim in church and come to share the sorrowful news. Or he might be upset about her death and have come for the solace the pastor or congregation could provide.

Or he could have sold her the drugs and felt a burning need to repent.

As Makalani wrestled with these ideas, Malu got out of his truck, but instead of walking up the church's front steps, he disappeared around back. When she reached the lot, she found steps to a dimly lit entrance beneath the church. She followed them down and put her ear to the door.

"Eh, lady. You going in, or what?" A tough-looking teenage boy was waiting at the top of the steps.

She gave him room to pass. "What's happening inside?"

"If you don't know, maybe this isn't your place."

As he squeezed by and opened the door, Makalani saw a circle of chairs in the center of a small room. Tables had been pushed against walls adorned with Hawaiian posters, prints, and crafts. As the early arrivers took their seats, Malu wrote Hawaiian virtues on an easel whiteboard.

Makalani let the door close and backed up the steps. Two girls came down the stairs behind her, one hapa-haole, one more Hawaiian, both looking aged beyond their years. They eyed Makalani's ranger uniform with suspicion.

"You goin' shut us down?" the hapa-haole girl asked.

"No. Why would I?"

She brushed passed Makalani and opened the door. "Because that's what cops do."

Malu called from inside. "Dana, everyt'ing okay?"

Makalani tried to back into the shadows, but the second girl blocked her escape as she followed her friend down the stairs.

Malu saw her and frowned. "Go inside, Leimomi. I'll handle dis."

He jutted his chin for Makalani to go up the stairs, then he stormed past her and kept going around the back of the church. Once they were away from the lights, he stopped so suddenly, she bumped into his back. He pushed her away as he turned.

"What you doin' hea?"

"I, uh . . . saw your truck."

"Uh-huh. From where?"

"The street."

"In Kailua—because dis stay *so* close to da heiau where you work."

He knew she was lying. She might as well come clean.

"I saw your truck at Kahaluʻu Beach Park. I heard about an overdose victim and went there to check."

"Why you do dat?"

"Why did you?"

"I know da kids who hang out around dea. I check on um every couple days to make sure dey okay."

Makalani hid her surprise. Checking on the welfare of kids didn't gel with the man who had stood aside and done nothing while Kenneth was nearly trampled to death. "Do you know who was camping under that shrub?" Even without lamp light, she could see the sorrow on his face.

"ʻEhu wahine?"

Dark skin and hair. He thinks it's Patty.

Makalani shook her head. "Blond."

He sighed. "Musta been Gigi den. Dey find any pipes?"

"Why do you ask? You sell her the drugs?"

"What? No! Damn, tita, is dat what you t'ink? I run a recovery group for teen addicts."

"You *what*?"

"Why you act all surprised? Dat stay so hard to believe?"

Yes, she wanted to yell, but felt too guilty to speak. She had judged Malu from the moment she had first spotted him arguing with Louie at the ranch—his horseshoe mustache and scraggly goatee, his long, greasy black hair, the scowl on his angular face. She had been so enamored by Louie's heroic looks that when she saw them arguing, she cast Malu as the darkness to his light. Rumiko's obvious distaste for her son's lover had compounded the bad first impression. Malu's nasty attitude toward Makalani while they worked on the fence had sealed it in stone. From then on, she had become suspicious of everything he did.

For good reason.

Helping kids didn't make him a saint. The ripening bruises on her body attested to that.

"What about Kam's ranch?"

"What about it?"

"When we nearly tipped over in the UTV, you told me to slide closer to you."

"Yeah?"

"You looked me in the eyes, Malu. Then you jerked the steering wheel, hard."

He started to object, then exhaled whatever fight he had left. The regret in his eyes confirmed her suspicions.

"You did it on purpose. Why?"

"I been wit' Louie fo' half a decade. You work at da ranch fo' t'ree days and already dey treat you mo' like family dan me. I nevah meant fo' you to get hurt, I just . . ."

"You wanted me gone."

"Yeah, pretty much."

"You could have killed me."

"I know. I only meant to scare you off. You already get a good job at da heiau, you no need work at da ranch."

"Rosie asked me to help."

"I know, it's just . . ." He dropped his head in disgust. "Nevah mind my excuses. I know bettah dan dis." He raised his head and looked her in the eyes. "E kala mai ia'u." *I'm sorry, please forgive me.*

He had admitted his transgression and apologized from the heart. Now, in essence, he was asking her to forgive him for the harm he had caused. In order to restore harmony between them, she not only needed to forgive, she needed to let go of her anger and hurt.

But not yet.

"You could have killed me."

"Yes."

"Are you sure you didn't mean to?"

He shrugged as he considered. "When your door opened ovah dat ravine and I saw you hanging on li'dat? I don't know, I acted in da moment. I truly believe I only meant to scare you enough to leave."

Makalani studied his face and body language for signs of deceit. His confession felt sincere. She had to give him a chance.

"I believe you."

"Mahalo. E kala mai ia'u."

Auwē. He said it again.

Tūtū had led their 'ohana through this cathartic practice of ho'oponopono—the Hawaiian practice of conflict resolution and forgiveness—earlier in the year. Although Makalani knew what she needed to say, telling him she loved him in English was too much. She needed the nuanced meanings 'ōlelo Hawai'i could provide.

"Mahalo for your apology, Malu. Aloha wau iā 'oe."

Surprise mixed with his relief. But for what? That she had forgiven him, or that she had known the appropriate response? Either way, she needed to ask forgiveness for the transgressions she had done to him. "E kala mai ia'u."

"For what?"

"For judging you harshly and not giving you a chance."

"Ha! I did da same t'ing to you." He swallowed hard and responded as he should. "Mahalo. Aloha wau iā 'oe." He shook his head. "Please believe me, dis was nevah about you. Me and Louie been having hard time befo' you arrive. His faddah's death made it worse. I hated dat man. No can pretend oddahwise jus' because he stay dead."

Makalani nodded. Malu had shared his hatred while gathering cattle on the range. This, combined with his disregard for Kenneth's safety when the cattle had charged him at the gate, had shown her a motive and temperament for murder.

Malu frowned as a new thought appeared. "Wait . . . you nevah t'ink I had somet'ing to do wit' his death?"

Makalani sighed. "Yeah, I actually did."

When he dropped his head into his hand, she apologized again.

He waved her away. "No need. You get every reason to talk stink about me."

She offered a slight smile. "I kept most of *those* thoughts to myself."

He scoffed. "Well, t'anks fo' dat. But if you t'ought I killed Larry, maybe Louie and everybody else t'inks da same."

"I doubt it. If Kenneth or Rumiko had suspected you, I think they would have gone straight to the police. As for Louie, his frustration feels more like hurt."

"You see plenny fo' someone new to da ranch."

Makalani shrugged. "Easy to guess. Losing a parent is hard. Especially when they die suddenly in such a horrible way."

Malu nodded. "I regret what I said before—no one deserves to die li'dat, not even him."

"How do you think it happened?"

"I get no idea. As much as I hated dat man, he stay one primo paniolo, like Kupunakāne and Louie. He shoulda handled it or come back fo' help. Da question I ask is why a Hiapo bull stay in dat pit in da first place, and why it stay agitated enough to kill."

"Yeah, about that. Grace said you were supposed to move the bulls to the Hāwī-side pastures."

"I did. I brought um down from da mountain and across. But one of my kids got picked up by da cops dat morning. I stay so worried 'bout him, I nevah counted da bulls. Nevah realize one wen' missing until da next day. Larry gave me such shit about it, I gave um back twice as bad. Called him one useless old man. Told him to leave da paniolo work to us."

"So that's why he was out alone on the Kona side of the ranch, to prove himself?"

"Yeah. I nevah thought he'd get in trouble. I mean, dat pasture stay so close to da house. He shoulda swallowed his pride and come to get us when he found dat bull in da pit. But how could he, right? Aftah everyt'ing I say?"

Makalani kept silent and simply received. A big part of ho'oponopono was providing a safe space to speak.

"You know," Malu said. "I bitch to Louie all da time 'bout his 'ohana, but I nevah admit how bad I treat dem. No wonder dey all hate me."

"Not all. Grace knows your worth. Vinnie idolizes you. And you seem very close with Kupunakāne."

Malu smiled. "Dat old man carries da heritage of our people in his soul. When he dies, so much goin' be lost. I do what I can to pass on his wisdom and knowledge but, most o' da time, I get deaf ear."

Makalani thought about the hecklers and general apathy Malu received during his rally at the beach. "What about these kids? How does Hawaiian heritage keep them off drugs?"

"Pride. Dey fail all da time—at home, at school, wit' friends. Even when dey seem successful li'dat, deep down, dey feel rotten like overripe fruit. Learning about our Hawaiian heritage connects dem to somet'ing bigger and mo' special dan what dey believe about demselves. We need elders like Kupunakāne to remind dem who dey are." He heaved a great sigh. "Dis is why I do what I do."

Why I do what I do.

That's what he meant!

Malu hadn't been referring to anything nefarious when she overheard him with Louie at the branding day dinner. He had been talking about his mission to help kānaka maoli, especially the young, connect with their heritage and heal.

Makalani nodded with understanding. "My grandmother does that for my 'ohana. She keeps us grounded in our language and traditions.

Growing up on a homestead taught me to respect and care for the land. I feel this kuleana wherever I live."

"And I called you a foreigner. One mo' way I misjudge you."

Makalani had stopped counting all the ways she had misjudged him. In his own way, Malu wanted to help. Maybe he would be willing to help Detective Kim, after all.

"What was Gigi's last name?"

"You goin' tell da cops?"

"Yeah. Her family deserves to know."

CHAPTER FIFTY-SEVEN

The next day working at Pu'ukoholā passed quickly—studying in the morning, lunch under the tree, clearing debris brought down by the flood. The south bank of the estuary was almost ready for visitors to roam and relax after touring the grounds in the sun. Makalani could easily imagine the ancient Hawaiians living, eating, and resting under these trees. Those ancient residents would have fished off Pelekane Beach, where visitors could have beached their outriggers on their way to meet with King Kamehameha I. Working alone on this 'āina connected her to the history she was studying and, by virtue of her distant relationship to Queen Ka'ahumanu, her family's history as well. Eventually, she found herself smiling and humming a tune. She was actually looking forward to the books she would read the next morning at work and hopefully finish over her three-day break.

Who in their right mind would think of paniolo work as a break?

Her phone alarm chimed, signaling the end of her shift. Since her usual closing duties were being handled by another ranger, she retrieved her backpack and headed for the heiau submerged beyond the shore. Once there, she pulled out the bag of raw meat she had packed.

Maybe this time, Manō Nui Punahele will come.

The water came slightly higher up her boots than before as she picked her way over the remains of the lava rock wall to where Hale o Kapuni Heiau was believed to be submerged. Once again, she announced her presence and gave blessings to the shark 'aumākua of the long-ago chief. She did this in English and then switched to ʻōlelo Hawaiʻi as she called to her own deified great-great-grandmother with the phrases and chant Tūtū had suggested she use. She pulled chunks of raw meat from the bag and tossed them in a straight line to the open ocean so Manō Nui Punahele would have a path to find her.

On her fifth recitation of the "Oli Aloha" welcoming chant, she spotted a grayish-green fin and the telltale silver markings cascading from the shark's head.

"I've missed you," she whispered.

When her great-great-grandmother had visited in Anahola Bay, she had brushed her smooth skin against Makalani's thigh.

If I swim with you now, will you do it again?

Makalani bent forward and extended her hand, then pulled it back when the shark opened her jaws as she passed.

She smells the meat.

Although Tūtū claimed Manō Nui Punahele favored Makalani, her ancestor was still a shark.

"Mahalo for coming. When you last visited me, our ʻohana in Anahola was suffering. This time, on Hawaiʻi Island, the father of your great-great-grandson's wife has been killed. It doesn't feel like an accident to me. I'm afraid someone intentionally caused this harm."

Manō Nui Punahele circled in the water.

Makalani took it as a response.

"I know there's nothing you can do for them from here, but my mind is clouded by suspicion. Is there anything you can do that will help me find clarity to see?"

Manō Nui Punahele raised her nose from the water. Was she smelling for meat or confirming she could help? Either way, Makalani felt acknowledged and heard.

"Mahalo nui no kāu kōkua ʻana. I appreciate your help so much. Thank you for coming here and looking out for me. Kaʻahumanu, who is your favorite and my grandmother, sends her love."

The shark circled once again, then swam out to sea beneath a glorious indigo and orange-streaked sky. Makalani watched until the fin disappeared. Her mind felt calm and clear. With a heart full of gratitude, she returned to the beach.

Her phone rang as she climbed into the NHS truck. Her adrenaline spiked when she saw the name on the screen. A day and a half had passed without hearing from Kalei.

"Hello?"

"Okay, Miss Ranger, I got you a name."

CHAPTER FIFTY-EIGHT

Makalani barely had time to process the name Kalei had given before another call chimed on her phone.

"Eh, Brian. Wassup?"

"It's bad, Makalani. So bad. I don't know what to do."

"Whoa, whoa, Brian. Slow down, take a breath. Tell me what's going on."

"Vinnie lost consciousness. We're back at the ER."

"Have the doctors seen him yet?"

"Yeah. They found a lump on the back of his head. He's getting a CAT scan now."

"A lump? Oh, Brian, I'm so sorry. He landed on his shoulder and arm. I didn't think to check his head."

"Neither did the doctors. Either everyone missed the lump, or it rose after the initial exam."

"What now?"

"We're waiting for the results."

Makalani closed her eyes, trying to remember at what point Vinnie might have bounced his head against the road. If he hit the base of his skull near the spinal cord . . .

Dear God, how can I even ask?

"Did you hear me, Makalani?"

"What? No, sorry. Say that again."

"Family's on their way."

"Same hospital?"

"Yeah."

"Be there in twenty."

She sped out of the wash, kicking up dirt and bouncing dried branches out of the bed of her truck. She would call Ranger Akaka once she pulled onto Kawaihae Road. If Supervisory Ranger Machado took issue with her for taking the truck and not signing out, she'd happily pay the price.

Eighteen minutes later, she hurried into the hospital waiting room and found Brian pacing circles around Rosie. "Any news?"

"Not yet," he said. "Vinnie's still getting scanned."

"How are you holding up, Rosie?"

Her mouth quivered. "This is my worst nightmare coming to life."

Makalani felt horrible. "I should have checked his head."

"It wouldn't have mattered. The doctor said it probably swelled overnight. But if it keeps swelling . . ."

Brian stopped pacing to give her a hug. "Only good thoughts, right?"

Rosie nodded and sniffed back her tears. Then she ran to her mother as Rumiko rounded the corner with Kupunakāne and Grace.

Rumiko held Rosie tight. "It's okay, baby, I'm here."

Kupunakāne went to Brian. "Where Vinnie at?"

"CAT scan for his head."

"Still? I fell off lio, plenny kine time. I nevah had one of dose."

"Me neither," Grace said.

Brian sighed. "They're concerned about swelling in or around his brain."

"He should have been wearing a helmet," Rosie said through her tears.

Kupunakāne frowned. "No paniolo goin' do dat."

"Vinnie's not a paniolo. He's eight."

"Dass old, already. I stay six when my faddah put me to work."

Rosie glared. "Times are different now. We have child labor laws to prevent that kind of abuse."

Kupunakāne shook his head. "I nevah understand you, Rosie. You rode bettah dan Kenneth. How you give up everyt'ing so easy?"

"Nothing was ever easy for me, or for my brothers, not with you and Dad pushing all the time."

Rumiko stroked Rosie's hair. "*Shh*, daughter. The time for that has passed."

"Has it, Mom? Because my son is getting his head scanned for brain damage because Dad and Kupunakāne went against my wishes and bought him a horse."

"Any lio coulda reared," Kupunakāne said.

"Exactly. Why is this so hard for all of you to understand?" Rosie's anger included her mother and Grace. "Vinnie is smart. He could excel in anything if he's given a chance to explore, which he won't if he's tethered to the ranch." She returned to her grandfather. "Kenneth said Skip Una made an offer. I think we should sell."

"No."

"No? That's it. No discussion?"

"About what? How much Hiapo blood stay soaked into our ʻāina? How my kupuna wahine nui—my great-grandmother—stay buried in da upper pasture near my keiki kāne, my wahine, my mākua, my kūpuna? Where you goin' bury *me* if we sell Hiapo Ranch, a graveyard in town?"

"This isn't about you. It's about Vinnie. I keep telling you, someone is targeting my son."

As Kupunakāne started to argue, Grace held up her hand. "I believe you."

"You do?"

"Makalani saw these shady Filipino guys watching Vinnie from a car when we crossed the highway with the cattle and again before his horse reared."

Rosie turned to Makalani. "You think they made it happen?"

"I do. The passenger had something in his hand when he pulled his arm back into the car. I think he shot Uila with a pellet or a rock."

"Why didn't you tell me?"

"We were dealing with an emergency. I was going to tell you later but . . . there's been so much going on."

"More important than my son?"

"Of course not. But it may tie into other accidents on your ranch." She turned to Kupunakāne. "Your father died a month after the two of you caught your neighbor and his son stealing a butchered cow. Is the neighbor's son still alive?"

"Yeah, living in dat same beat-up house. He one old man now. His wife die plenny years back. His son lives wit' him, nevah moved out."

"How old is the son?"

"Fifty, maybe. Little bit older dan Kenneth."

"Does he ever come on your land?"

Kupunakāne shrugged. "His ʻohana stop poaching aftah my faddah die. But when a calf goes missing, I wonder if it could be dem."

"Has anyone checked?"

"Nah. Bettah dey steal little bit dan starve on da oddah side of our fence."

"Did your son agree?"

"No way. He said our neighbor's ʻohana stay rotten to da roots."

"And now Larry's dead."

"Where you going wit' dis?"

Makalani turned to Grace. "Were the bulls Malu moved grazing along the border of your neighbor's property when Hinuhinu went missing?"

"Not right along the border. There's a eucalyptus forest in between them and the upslope pasture and the gulch down below. The access road beyond the Kona fence is an easement we gave our neighbors so they can drive to their house and the property they kept."

"Do they raise cattle up there?"

"They can't."

Kupunakāne cut in before Grace could answer. "Da forest took ovah. Dey nevah put in da work like our ancestors did. *Our* cattle can graze to the top of da ridge. My son probably looked fo' Hinuhinu up dea too. Why you ask all dese questions?"

Makalani remembered what Tūtū had said about how land wealth meant far more than money: "I bet whoevah sold dem dat extra property wished dey had not."

Makalani shrugged. "Family feuds often begin about land."

The Hiapos considered this in silence.

Kupunakāne finally shook his head. "Even if our neighbors somehow killed my faddah and my son, Grace said da men you t'ink shot Vinnie's horse were Filipino. Our neighbors are hapa-haole. It couldn't be dem."

"Unless they're working for your neighbors."

"Dey no get money to pay."

"What about Skip Una? He has money. Is it possible your neighbors are working with him?"

"To do what?"

"Help him buy your ranch."

Rumiko frowned. "Why would they want that?"

"To cause you trouble and pain. Look at the turmoil Skip's offer has caused already. What would happen to your family if you actually sold the ranch?" She turned to Rosie. "And then there's what you told me about the son. He might still be obsessed."

Rosie stiffened, but Rumiko spoke up again. "He was always watching and bothering you as a child."

Kupunakāne tensed. "Why you nevah say?"

"I did," Rosie said. "But you brushed me off. Dad, Kenneth, and Louie did too. All of you made me feel like I didn't matter, like I was making it up." She turned to her mother. "So did you."

"I know," Rumiko said. "I'm so sorry I didn't stand up for you then. But why does this matter now?"

Everything Makalani had puzzled over for the last week came together in one clear thought. She looked at everyone, one by one. "What if the son is getting revenge for losing his family's land?"

Kupunakāne bristled. "Eh, my grandparents paid dem plenny money fo' dat property."

"Yes. And their 'ohana has suffered ever since."

Brian hugged his wife, who was visibly upset. "I don't know, Makalani. From what Rosie has told me, this sounds way too ambitious for a lazy guy like Flint."

Makalani's head snapped up at the name. "Flint *Reed?*"

"You know him?"

Two hours earlier, Kalei had given Makalani Flint Reed's name.

CHAPTER FIFTY-NINE

Rona slurped the last of the saimin broth directly from the bowl and laid her chopsticks across the top. She slid it to the far side of the two-person table and wiped the soup splatter before picking her laptop up off the floor. She would clean and stow everything properly before she tucked in for the night. Living in the Kailua-Kona studio was like living on a boat; tiny and efficient, just like her.

She typed her password into the investigative case management program she used. Of the three cases she had so far, the two open ones both involved meth. She opened the email reply from a vice detective in the Kailua-Kona branch where she had expected to work. In it, he listed the known meth dealers on the island. The highest activity on the Big Island's west side came from a Filipino gang known to work with a Mexican cartel. Vice had been trying to nail them for years. Jennifer Farber—in rehab after her overdose—and Gigi Smith, who had died at the beach, had probably purchased their meth from them.

Rona tapped her fingers on the table as she stared at the list. She was on homicide, not vice. Did she really need to know who sold them the drugs, or was she spinning off course as she had with the bull? Unless Gigi had been murdered, her death, although tragic, didn't qualify as a case. And if Jennifer Farber hadn't murdered Paul Campbell, neither did she.

Rona's phone vibrated on the table with a now-familiar name.

"Hi, Makalani."

"Eh, Rona. Sorry to call so late."

"No prob. Thanks for texting me Gigi's name."

"You're welcome. Were you able to track down her family?"

"Working on it. With a common surname like Smith, it might take a little time."

"Yeah, especially if she moved here from the mainland."

"Right? So, are you calling to set up that coffee date?"

The ranger chuckled. "Actually, I'm calling with another name."

"Gigi's drug dealer?"

"Hmm, I hadn't thought of that, but . . . maybe. This one's more of a favor to me."

"What's up?"

"I've been helping out on my cousin-in-law's ranch. It's been a rough month for her 'ohana. First, her father died. Now her eight-year-old son is in the hospital."

"What happened?"

"He was reared off his horse. But here's the thing . . . I don't think it was an accident. I think the horse was shot by a pellet or a rock."

Rona didn't see the connection between a potential drug dealer and a boy falling off his horse, but Makalani was a new friend and she wanted to help. "What do you want me to do with this name?"

"I'd like you to run it and see if anything comes up. He might be connected to men in an aqua Hyundai who had been studying Vinnie as we helped move a herd of cattle across the highway. They recognized my family name and were fishing to see if Vinnie might be my son."

"You think they hurt him to get at you?"

"I don't know, but my intuition tells me these are not good men."

Rona nodded, certain she would have felt the same way.

She logged in to a database. "What's the guy's name?"

"Flint Reed. He and his father live on Kohala Mountain Road in Waimea, on the Kona side of Hiapo Ranch."

Rona stopped typing. "What's your cousin-in-law's name?"

"Rosie Pahukula. She married my cousin Brian. I only mentioned her family's ranch because it's one of the oldest and largest on the island. It shows up on Google Maps."

Rona's new friend was related to the Hiapos and worked on their ranch? Maybe she knew how Larry Hiapo had been trapped in that pit. Although the bull breeder she had spoken with had explained how bulls would attack if they had no route of escape, the scenario still didn't ring true. If the pit presented a danger to cattle, wouldn't the older generations of Hiapo ranchers have filled it in? And if Larry Hiapo was such a skilled paniolo, wouldn't he have tried a safer way to extract the animal without putting himself at risk?

And now Rona's new friend was offering a name. Could Flint Reed be involved in Larry Hiapo's death?

Although Rona wanted to question Makalani, she didn't want to say anything that might get back to the family. They believed Larry's death was an accident. Even the suggestion of murder would cause them distress, not to mention the damage it would do to her career if her partner learned she was still investigating the case. But if she ran a name for a fellow law enforcement officer and *happened* onto a lead, she could take that information to her partner and let him decide whether or not to reopen the case.

Rona typed in Flint Reed's name and willed her screen to light up with a list of violent priors or—better yet—an arrest for a suspicious accident that took place on a ranch. When it came back with nothing, she sighed loudly enough for Makalani to hear.

"Nothing, huh?"

"Afraid not." Although Makalani's lead hadn't helped her closed case, perhaps Rona could do more to help her. "What about the men in the car?"

"A contact of mine ran the plate. The owner is Jay Alegado."

Once Rona typed in the name, her database coughed out a list of arrests.

"Jay Alegado, twenty-nine, arrested for drug possession, harassment, illegal discharge of a weapon, petty assault during a brawl, and misdemeanor theft. He's also believed to be a member of a Filipino gang that's currently under suspicion of dealing meth for a Mexican cartel."

"Do you have a photo?"

"Looking at it now."

"Does he have a topknot with swirling tribal tattoos up his neck?"

"Yep."

"Do you have photos for the other members of this gang?"

Rona brought up a series of mug shots and surveillance photos. "What are we looking for?"

"Black crew cut with shaved tribal designs. Matching tattoos on his arms, muscular body, mean-looking black eyes."

"Found him," Rona said. "He's in a surveillance photo with Alegado. Name's Goyo Mendozas. He's served time for first-degree assault."

"Weapon?"

"Machete."

Makalani went silent.

"You still there?"

"Yeah. I'm just picturing how much worse this could have been."

"You mean if it was them?"

"You think I'm imagining it?"

"The threat? No. This particular crime?" Rona shrugged, then remembered that Makalani couldn't see. "Is there any evidence of trespass?"

"The horse reared at the ranch gate on Kohala Mountain Road. I saw the aqua car parked on the shoulder and the passenger hanging out the window with something in his hand. They drove away while I was calling 911."

"Suspicious timing."

"Right?"

"And their connection to Flint Reed?"

"I don't know of any, but I have a hunch one exists."

Rona respected hunches. Why else would she still be investigating Larry Hiapo's death? "What's the deal between neighbors?"

"Generational feud."

"And the Hiapos suspect Flint?"

"They don't suspect anyone. A paka lōlō dealer on Kaua'i dropped his name when I asked her who was dealing meth on the Big Island."

Alarms fired in Rona's mind. Her new friend's investigation overlapped both of hers. "Makalani, what made you ask about meth?"

"It's a long story about someone I misjudged."

"So, nothing to do with the bull?"

"The one that killed Larry? You know about that?"

"I investigated that case."

"And you didn't find it suspicious?"

Rona laughed. "I was the only one who did. My partner insisted we close it, but I haven't let it go."

"Me, neither." Makalani chuckled. "We have more in common than I thought."

Rona agreed. "What else did this paka lōlō dealer say?"

"She told me meth on the Big Island is run primarily by a Filipino gang and the cartels. She also said anyone who went against them would have to be tough. When I asked for details, she clammed up. Said she had to protect her 'ohana, but she's Filipino, so she might have meant her community instead."

"And your contact thinks Flint Reed is that tough?"

"She didn't say one way or the other, she just called me back and gave up his name. But the Hiapos make Flint sound like a middle-aged lazy bum."

"Huh. Think your contact could be setting you up?"

"For what?"

"Taking out the competition. Could be this guy, Flint Reed, has started cooking and dealing on his own. And if he's connected with Alegado and Mendozas, the Filipino gang could have given your contact Flint's name to lead you to them."

"Oh my god," Makalani said. "You think they're using me to close down a rogue lab?"

"Beats me. I'm just trying to connect the dots." Although Rona kept her voice calm, inside, she wanted to shout. *Finally,* someone believed Larry Hiapo might have been murdered besides her.

"Rona?"

"Still here. Look, I'm going to share something that needs to stay between us."

"Of course."

"I'm still investigating Larry Hiapo's death, and I have reasons to believe that bull may have been drugged."

"By *meth*?"

"Sounds crazy, I know. But the more I learn, the less accidental it sounds."

"Yeah. Whenever I ask about Larry's death, the family tells me stories of past accidents on the ranch to explain how dangerous paniolo life can be. On branding day, Kupunakāne—Larry's father—told me *his* father died while riding his horse across the field that borders the neighbor's land. The horse stepped in a trench no one knew had been there."

"How could they not know?"

"Right? When I asked the same question, Kupunakāne said heavy rains can change the land. But he also said he and his father, Lucky, had caught Flint's father and his dad poaching beef off one of their cows weeks before. Flint's father is still alive and living next door with Flint."

Rona rubbed her eyes as she mentally sorted through Makalani's information. "Was anyone suspicious of Lucky's death?"

"No. Just me."

"Same here. What are you going to do now?"

"Vinnie's back in the hospital for a CAT scan after he passed out at home. They found a lump on his head we all missed. I'm going to stay at the hospital to hear what the doctors have to say."

"And after that?"

"Not sure, either home or to the ranch. I'd sleep better if I made sure that aqua car wasn't around."

"Be careful. If someone is targeting the Hiapos, they might not be done."

CHAPTER SIXTY

Makalani mulled over the new name Rona had given her as she drove toward the ranch. The passenger in the aqua Hyundai with the tribal swirls shaved into his hair sounded more dangerous than the driver. Goyo Mendozas had served time for first-degree assault. Jay Alegado had only been arrested for misdemeanor crimes. But as Kalei had said, anyone who interfered with the Filipino gang selling cartel meth had to be tough. If Mendozas and Alegado had been members of the Filipino meth gang, maybe Rona was right and the gang had given up Flint Reed's name hoping it would lead Makalani to their lab.

Are drug dealers using me to exact their revenge?

Makalani pulled onto the shoulder of Kohala Mountain Road. If Flint was helping Alegado and Mendozas steal customers from the cartel, Makalani should be armed. Unfortunately, her ranger position at Puʻukoholā did not include law enforcement, which meant she kept her firearm locked in her apartment fifteen minutes back the way she had come. All she had on her was an everyday carry knife and the tools strapped to the bed of the heiau's truck. Not much defense against a machete or a gun.

I'm already here. I'm not going back.

Although the aqua car wasn't in sight along the road, that didn't mean it wasn't nearby. She looked up the easement access to Flint Reed's property illuminated by the moon. The road technically belonged to her extended family on whose ranch she worked.

Am I sure about that?

The answer was no. If Louie's ancestors had given the Reeds an exclusive easement, she would be breaking the law. Even if the Hiapos had retained land usage rights, it didn't mean those rights extended to her. She could probably talk herself out of legal trouble given her occupation, extended family relationship, and volunteer paniolo work, but Supervisory Ranger Machado would use this as an excuse to fire her from Puʻukoholā.

So what? Family comes first. I can always find another job.

She wasn't leaving until she checked out Flint Reed's property, which included an unimpaired view of the gulch and the Hiapo Ranch pastures beyond. The easement ran so close to the edge, she could have shot an arrow into the cattle pit where Larry Hiapo had died.

Could Flint or the Filipino gangsters have shot the bull with a drug to make it attack?

Or could they have shot Larry Hiapo to make him fall off his horse?

From the photo she had seen, Larry's body looked too mangled to tell.

She left the pickup on the shoulder and walked up the gravelly road. With the full moon high in a cloudless sky, she could see across the Hiapo Ranch pastures all the way to their compound, where porch lights had been left on for the main house and Louie's cabin up the slope. Kupunakāne's shack was dark. Either he, Rumiko, and Grace had not returned from the hospital, or they had driven home right behind Makalani, and he had gone directly to bed.

When I finish snooping here, I'll make sure Alegado and Mendozas aren't lurking over there.

She jogged silently on the grass growing alongside the fence. When she came to the first eucalyptus tree, she stopped. This was the border of the Reeds' property. One more step and she'd be breaking the law.

She turned on her phone's flashlight and peered into the grove. It was denser than she had realized, more like a forest with a thick canopy that blocked the moon's light. The fence she had been following collapsed from decay a few yards ahead. Whether by neglect or intention, the Reeds had clear yet hidden access to the gulch. If the forest grew denser upslope, the Hiapo cattle would have been contained without needing a fence.

She switched off her light and returned to the road. Up ahead, moonlight shone on a vintage blue truck parked in front of a dilapidated one-story house. Even from a distance, Makalani could tell it was the same blue truck she had seen rumbling up the access road before. A soft glow from the far side of the building suggested lights might be on in the back.

I can't do this. I'm a federal officer with no justifiable reason to be on the Reeds' land.

But as she turned to leave, a car door clicked shut. A small car, the size of Alegado's Hyundai, was nestled against the trees. The moonlight illuminated a patch of aqua paint.

A fourth sighting of the same aqua car? That's justifiable enough for me.

A light flickered through the forest as the driver headed toward the gulch. Rather than following, she hurried back to the fence. The trees blocked her view. Eucalyptus oil pierced her sinuses as her boot sank into the soggy bed of fallen leaves. The canopy blocked most of the moon's light. She allowed her vision to adjust. When her other senses awakened, she picked her way silently into the forest. Not so with her quarry. She could have tracked the bearer of that flickering light by their tromping steps alone—which grew louder as the land began to slope toward the gulch.

They're headed toward Hiapo Ranch.

The light bobbed lower, then dimmed as moonlight shone between the thinning trees. When she came to the break in the forest, she saw that the grove continued on the Hiapo side of the gulch. When she had seen the eucalyptus trees on branding day from the Hiapos' land, she hadn't known it was a forest this wide or that the gulch continued within it, becoming shallower farther up the slope. No fence in sight. It would be easy for a person to cross from the Reeds' property to the

Hiapos' at any point in this gentler gully and emerge from the forest or descend into the steepening gulch and come out by the pit.

As she scanned the area for her quarry, a brighter light appeared in the gully. A door had opened from a shack, illuminating two men. One stood in the doorway, lit from behind. The other held his phone like a flashlight as he carried a large crate. Even at a distance, his distinctive topknot gave him away.

The man in the doorway held a large plastic jug. He walked out and took off his mask, not bothering to close the door or dim the light from the shack. It was Goyo Mendozas. He was surrounded on three sides by forest on an outcropping well below the level of the land. The jags in the gully even hid the shack from the mouth of the gulch lower on the slope. No one could see him except from above, where Makalani now stood.

Mendozas paused to greet Alegado, then carried his jug down a path behind a rock ledge. Alegado set his crate on the ground beside piles of discarded plastic containers and trash. A sulfuric stench wafted on the breeze. Makalani had smelled it before in Oregon when she and her fellow park rangers had joined the local LEOs on a meth lab bust.

Rona was right. The Filipino gang wants me to shut down this lab.

If they only wanted to eliminate their competition, they could have told Kalei to give up Alegado and Mendozas. Why offer up Flint Reed unless they wanted Makalani to come here? The location was perfect. The gully and forest contained the fumes. The breeze from the mountain dissipated the particles and blew any hint of toxicity toward the sea.

Makalani looked to the spot where Mendozas had vanished and began to understand how Larry Hiapo had died.

CHAPTER SIXTY-ONE

Makalani crept closer to the rock ledge behind which Goyo Mendozas had taken his plastic jug. Given the sulfuric stench that still lingered in the air, she had a strong hunch of what came next. But a hunch was not enough; Makalani had to *know*. When Jay Alegado returned to the forest with his now-empty crate, she dashed to the path. It cut through rock formations as it wound down. If Mendozas returned, she'd be trapped.

She picked up her pace, landing on solid rocks or clumps of wild grass and avoiding the eroded lava that would crunch beneath her boots. Pāpā had taught her many tricks while they hunted wild pua'a on Tūtū's homestead or in the Keālia Forest Reserve. Makalani later honed those skills during her Oregon wilderness hikes. No way would Mendozas hear her approach.

The path opened near the base of the gully where a shallow creek still flowed after Sunday night's storm. Mendozas squatted alongside and dragged his jug through the water. The moonlight reflected on the plastic as he raised it to drain. If he had used that container to shake and bake meth, he was poisoning the water with a high concentration of a dangerous drug. And if he had washed a crateful of those jugs on the day Hinuhinu had wandered up the gully to drink, the bull could have ingested a significant amount.

Oh, Hinuhinu. It wasn't your fault.

A cartel meth lab in rural Oregon had dumped their toxins in a similar way and poisoned the land along the border of a neighboring farm. When one of the farmer's rams drank from a puddle, the drug remnants in the water drove it mad. It injured two other sheep and the farmer before it was contained. The farmer had complained many times about the neighboring cartel, but without evidence, the officials were never able to check. This time, the farmer demanded they run tests. They arrived the next morning to draw blood. When no drugs or toxins were found, they told the farmer there was nothing they could do and suggested he keep his sheep farther from the fence.

Why hadn't I remembered this? Rona was right. The Hiapos' bull had been poisoned by meth.

The effects of methamphetamine exposure to animals included accelerated heart rate, increased blood pressure, agitation, and disorientation. Photos of Hinuhinu showed mud on and around his pink mouth. Although Makalani hadn't asked anyone about it, she didn't think it was blood. Cattle only had a lower set of teeth, which they mashed against their upper gums to shred the grass as they ate. Even when fighting, bulls didn't bite.

But if he drank from a puddle . . .

Hinuhinu had probably freaked out and run out of the gulch, scraping his legs against the rocks, and fallen into the pit. Cattle were flight animals. A trapped bull would have fought. Larry would have known this, but he might have assumed the bull would calm down once he roped and led him up one of the more eroded slopes. He couldn't have known the animal was poisoned with a violence-inducing drug.

Leave. Now!

Makalani's boots crunched more loudly on the way up, but it couldn't be helped. She had to get out of the bottleneck before Alegado returned with his next load of supplies. If he cut off her escape, she'd have to fight her way out before Mendozas came up the path; her gut told her he was the more dangerous of the two. This time, her gut failed.

She had almost reached the top when Alegado came around the rock formation and pointed a pistol at her face.

"Dass far enough," he said quietly, then whisper-shouted to his friend. "Goyo, hurry up. Your ranger friend came to say hi."

Rocks crunched behind her as Mendozas ran up the trail. He stopped when he saw her, tossed the plastic jug, and flicked open a knife.

Makalani turned sideways to keep an eye on them both, rocking between her slightly higher and lower feet. If she overpowered one, the other would get her for sure.

"Where's Flint?" she said, buying time as she planned. If she could lure Alegado closer, she could yank him into Mendozas and hopefully escape.

Alegado stepped forward. "Dat who you're aftah?"

"I'm not *after* anyone. Just taking a walk in the moonlight. You guys doing the same?"

Mendozas chuckled. "Yeah, we should party. Wit' all dese trees and rocks, nobody goin' hear us if we make a little noise."

Makalani suppressed a shudder. Even cadaver dogs might not find her here. "Nah. I'll take a rain check. It's getting kinda late."

Alegado double gripped his pistol and aimed at her leg. "I think you should stay."

Mendozas grabbed her wrist and yanked her past him down the path. She stumbled to her knees. He kicked her in the back. Face planted in the dirt, she felt around her for a rock. No way would she give up without a fight. But when she found what she needed and turned to attack, she saw that Mendozas had unwittingly blocked Alegado's line of fire.

The Hawaiians say, "Learn bravery, but also learn to run."

Makalani bolted down the path to the gully, sliding on the gravelly dirt as she ran. Behind her, the men cursed and yelled in pursuit. Makalani had spent years hiking through rugged, high-altitude terrain. If she could make it to the floor of the gully, she could follow it out the mouth to the pit. But when she jumped to the bank of the creek, she saw her mistake.

A bullet ricocheted off the rocks to her left, where the gully narrowed into a steeper ravine. When Alegado reached where she was now, he'd have a clear shot as she stumbled over hidden rocks in the creek.

Too slow. I have to go up.

She switched directions, picking up speed. The higher she went, the shallower the gully became.

Another shot fired and missed.

A swerving target was harder to hit. Soon the gully would flatten with the land and vanish into the trees. If Makalani could make it to the forest, she could turn things around.

"I ka nahele, he ali'i wau," she whisper-chanted.

In the forest, I am chief.

CHAPTER SIXTY-TWO

Flint hushed his dad. It had sounded like a gunshot, but he couldn't be sure. He rubbed the windowpane with his sleeve and smeared the dust over the glass. He should have replaced the outside bulb that had burned out last month. Between the trees hiding the moonlight and the grimy window, he couldn't see shit.

Hoʻolohe came up beside him. "No hush me, boy. I heard what you heard. Your friends are up to no good."

"They aren't my friends."

"Then why you let them squat on our land?"

"They're not squatting. They're leasing a useless area you can't even reach."

"Maybe not. But my hearing still good enough to hear the racket they make. It stay past midnight already. Go out there and tell your *tenants* to shut the hell up."

"Go back to bed. You don't understand."

Hoʻolohe scoffed. "You think I don't know what you're up to or what those men are doing on our land?"

"Then you know why I can't butt into their business. If something's going down, I don't want to get shot."

"Oh, ho! Then you admit I was right. Well, keep listening to your old dad. We could go to jail if they shoot someone on our land."

"*We?* Why would the state use taxpayer money to lock up your ass? You have one foot in the grave. If they come for either of us, it will be me."

Ho'olohe smirked as if the argument had been won. "You are such a disappointment to me."

"The feeling is mutual."

"Eh, I'm not the grown man still doing childish pranks. Bad enough you spied on da Hiapo girl when she was a kid, now you're harassing her son? Cutting his cinch, putting centipedes in his boots—what's da matter with you? When are you going to act like a man?"

Like the day Larry Hiapo died?

Flint had stood on the bed of his truck to see what was happening at the base of the gulch and saw his neighbor roping something in the pit that sounded like a bull. Although reckless, it seemed as if the old paniolo might actually pull it off. The thought had made Flint so angry that he picked up the rifle he had just used on his failed wild pig hunt. After all the stories he had heard growing up, he knew exactly what his father and his grandfather would do. Even so, he chickened out and shot into the air. Larry's horse startled and, a moment later, he slid off the saddle, seeming to stretch in midair. Before he vanished, he looked back at Flint.

Flint supposed a real man—one his father could admire—would have shot Larry Hiapo or helped him out of the pit. Instead, Flint started his engine and left the man to die.

He glared at Ho'olohe. "Nothing I do will ever be enough for you."

He grabbed the iron poker from their stone fireplace, the only source of heat in their shabby old house. "I'll go. But you stay inside, old man. We can't afford the copay if you fall and break your hip."

CHAPTER SIXTY-THREE

Makalani scrambled up the gully's final slope on hands and feet, then darted low to the tall, straight trunks. The younger trees on the edge grew slender and close. The eucalyptus forest was, indeed, more effective to keep out cattle than a fence.

But not for me.

Keeping her arms close, Makalani slipped through the trees. Her ranger uniform served as camouflage. Her sturdy work boots gave her the confidence to run. When she caught a root or a dip in the ground, she rebounded gently off the trunks, taking care not to tear off the bark. If her pursuers turned on their phone lights, she didn't want to leave a trail.

The men cursed behind her as they hit the border of trees and followed even more loudly than before. If they lived and operated on the west side of Hawai'i, they'd be used to dry, arid land, not the wild tropical jungles on Kaua'i where Makalani had grown up and hiked. Branchless trunks and tall grass were nothing compared to the undergrowth of giant ferns and tangling vines Makalani was used to. Even the foliage surrounding Tūtū's homestead was denser than this.

As she ran deeper into the eucalyptus forest, the trees became older and the trunk sizes increased. Although farther apart, their thick canopy entirely blocked out the moon. Makalani slowed to allow her eyes to adjust. The trees had spaced out, but an undergrowth of ferns and shade-loving bushes had taken over the ground. If she plowed through them, the noise would tell Alegado and Mendozas where she had gone and clear the way enough for them to gain speed.

Light flickered behind her.

Her pursuers had the advantage, so she had to be smart.

Knowing they would follow what they saw, Makalani dashed forward, creating a noticeable path. The men grumbled behind her as they hacked at the plants. They were getting closer. She had to be quick.

And silent.

Moving carefully, she lessened the damage she was causing, then backed up as quickly as she dared. She veered to the side and ducked beneath an umbrella of fronds. Although hāpuʻu ferns could grow as tall as trees, this patch only came to her waist. She crawled beneath the ferns and squirmed behind the first tree trunk she reached.

Her breath was so loud—too loud—it would give her away. They would have heard it for sure if not for the noise they made as they trudged through the brush.

“Dis sucks, brah,” Mendozas whispered to Alegado. “I say we go back and cut her off at Flint’s place.”

“And if she heads fo’ da neighbors?”

“I don’t know. Catch her at da street?”

“Nah. Da forest stay bettah. Nobody goin’ find a body in hea.”

Makalani held her breath as a hint of light traveled above the ferns to her left. A moment later, the light swept away.

After counting to five, she crawled back the way she had come. When she reached the edge of the ferns, she paused as the men argued quietly ahead.

“Her trail stops hea,” Mendozas said. “We should go back.”

“Nah,” Alegado countered. “She get mo’ careful, dass all. See da bent branches? She gotta be close.”

When the rustling sounds grew faint, Makalani emerged. She had three choices: through the forest toward Hiapo Ranch, through the forest after the men, back to the gully toward the road. She might have chosen differently with a firearm, but all she had was a knife.

Makalani slid down the gully to the pooled water and scrambled along the bank of the creek, sacrificing silence for speed. By the time she reached the path to the shack, her laboring breath and pounding heart were all she could hear.

She powered up the path, intending to snag the discarded meth-baking jug on her way. The residue and fingerprints combined with her testimony should provide enough cause for a search warrant. She and Rona could return with backup during the day. She didn't hear anything—until she fell to the ground.

Pain throbbed in her head.

Someone was talking, but she couldn't understand. She rolled onto her hip, shielding her head with one arm, and struggled through the fog. Sweatpants and slippers. Not one of her pursuers. Then who?

She tried to crawl backward and bumped into a rocky wall.

A tall man held an iron poker with two hands like a bat. "You're that ranger." He was older than her and wearing too little for the cold.

Makalani spit her bile into the dirt.

Not too old to crack me in the head.

"Stay down," he said as she tried to rise. "Why are you on my property? This isn't government land."

Auwē. This must be Flint.

He kicked her ranger boot with his slippered foot. "You can't be here without a warrant. Shit. What do I do with you now?"

Makalani leaned against the rock, trying to focus through the pain. Flint knew who she was, which likely meant those men hadn't just invaded his land on the sly. And if he was working with the meth makers, he might also have contributed to Vinnie's attack. Now he had assaulted a federal officer. Would that make him more likely to back off, or swing again and finish the job?

Better to leave him guessing than give him a reason to kill.

She pulled in her legs. "I work on Hiapo Ranch. I didn't know this wasn't their land."

As he puzzled through that logic, she kicked him hard in the knee. Flint cried out and fell back, dropping the poker as he reached for the ground. Makalani launched forward from a crouch. They grabbed the poker at the same time. As they rolled in the dirt, she could hear her father's words:

"You nevah goin' beat one pua'a if you try wrestle um in da mud."

She needed to regain her advantage over the taller, larger man.

Although ranger training included unarmed combat techniques, they hadn't spent that much time fighting on the ground. Most of what they learned was geared toward making arrests, protecting their firearm, or breaking up brawls. In a decade on the job, she never once had to wrestle for her life.

She slammed Flint's nose with her forehead. As he reacted to the pain, she torqued the poker to lock up his wrist. Although she had done this successfully many times on her feet, she didn't have the same leverage while lying on the ground. Worse yet, the longer she struggled for the poker, the less leverage she had.

"If you like keep somet'ing precious, no can grip um too tight," Pāpā would have said.

Makalani let go of the poker.

Without the resistance, Flint yanked the iron point away from her and into his throat.

CHAPTER SIXTY-FOUR

Hoʻolohe had intended to wait inside, but as the minutes ticked by, he felt a terrible sense of foreboding, a chill in his gut, as he had before the deaths of his parents and his wife.

He blew out air in a burst like a bull.

Foolish son. What had he done now?

Hoʻolohe grabbed his puffy jacket off the rack and zipped it up to his throat. October nights in Waimea got cold. Flint's jacket was still here. He hadn't even bothered to put on actual shoes. Hoʻolohe muttered as he sat to pull on his boots. His lazy son was hopeless. He should have gone himself.

Throughout Hoʻolohe's life, he was always the one to clean up the messes and finish the job, first with his father and now with his son. Why did the Reed men always give up too soon?

As he fumbled with his laces, his arthritic fingers cramped into gnarled claws. He hated how useless they had become. His hands used to be strong enough to chop trees into firewood and help clear the land—even as a child, he was uncommonly strong. He dropped out of high school to keep their ranch running when his father became too depressed to work and drowned his sorrows in cheap beer. Now these fingers that used to braid rawhide couldn't tie laces on a boot? Damn them to hell. He used to work them hard enough to blister, callous, and bleed.

He gave up the bow and tied a double knot instead. If Flint couldn't undo them later, Hoʻolohe would cut the damn things off.

He coughed out a laugh. "If I can't tie laces, how will I use a knife? No more chopping down trees or digging postholes for me."

Postholes *and* trenches.

He shook his head. Those days were long gone. He did what he did. No regrets.

Life had always been hard for his family, but their downfall became inevitable when his father sold the land. Not only did they lose their source of income, they lost their autonomy as well. They couldn't even drive to their own house without the easement Lucky Hiapo had so *generously* allowed.

Hoʻolohe snorted. "Generous with land that had always been ours!"

It put him in a rage every time he thought about Lucky and Luke chasing them up their own property that night. His father should have shot them both for trespassing. Instead, he cowered in shame over the hindquarters of beef he and Hoʻolohe had butchered off that Hiapo cow.

Hoʻolohe opened the closet and pulled out the shotgun case perched in the back. "What were we supposed to do, starve?" He removed the gun and slammed the door shut. With their dwindling cattle, they couldn't afford to butcher their own.

"Dad gave up, but I finished the job!"

Only eleven years old, Hoʻolohe had been strong enough to dig the trench in the field that tripped Lucky Hiapo's horse. His only regret was that he hadn't killed Luke.

Hoʻolohe swung open the door, as mad as he had been on that night, eighty years ago.

Mad from shame.

Mad with revenge.

Mad enough to kill.

CHAPTER SIXTY-FIVE

Makalani pressed the wound closed on the side of Flint's throat. Blood covered her hands, not from a spurting jugular—*Thank God!*—but because the man wouldn't hold still.

"Relax, Flint. It's going to be okay."

The iron point had stabbed through muscle and veins. If he kept thrashing, the embedded poker—which he still gripped—would tear into the carotid artery. Flint was a big man, but she had gravity and clarity on her side.

Makalani eased the pressure off his windpipe so he wouldn't panic, and put all her weight onto his chest instead. "Hold still."

Flint stopped resisting. Even in the moonlight, she could see he was scared.

"My name is Ranger Makalani Pahukula. You're Flint Reed, correct? Yeah, I know your name *and* what you're allowing those men to do on your land. But if you want to live to explain your reasons, you need to help me help you. Blink if you understand."

He blinked three times fast.

"Good. Now listen up. You *cannot* pull the poker out of your neck. Understand? It has to stay in place until the paramedics arrive. I'm going to get off your chest, but you need to remain still."

When she felt his body relax, she rose onto her knees, releasing the pressure from his chest and his neck. She steadied the poker with her hand to make sure it didn't move. As she did this, a vehicle rumbled and crunched up the access road beyond the trees. Had Flint called the rest of the Filipino gang?

Or maybe he called HPD!

Makalani shuddered as she imagined how it would look with Flint sprawled on the ground and her astride as if spearing him through the throat. Even so, she was afraid to move.

A shotgun racked to her right, followed by the voice of an angry old man. "Get off my son."

Makalani held out her hands in compliance—not a gang, but possibly worse. "He's hurt. I'm trying to help."

Flint's father adjusted the butt of his shotgun more securely against his shoulder. Although tall like his son and probably muscular in his youth, the man looked so frail and unsteady the gun's kick might crack a bone and knock him to the ground. Even without firing, his arms shook from holding up the weight.

"I didn't attack him, Mr. Reed. I'm a national park ranger. Your son needs medical attention. We need to call an ambulance *now*."

"Get up."

Makalani gauged the distance. Flint's father was standing about ten feet away, too far for her to charge him but far enough for a shaking old man to miss, especially when the pellets wouldn't have much distance to spread.

She rose with her weight loaded so she could leap toward the path, but as she did, the drug dealers rushed up behind her from the gulch.

Mendozas charged at Makalani.

The shotgun fired.

Alegado yelled a battle cry and fired his pistol.

Makalani fell backward, twisting her body so she wouldn't hit the poker still extended from Flint's neck.

It had all happened in an instant.

But who had been shot?

She smeared the blood up her cheek as she checked her head for the source of the pain. Shotgun pellets? A sharp rock? There might have been a gash, but she was pretty sure the blood on her hand had come from Flint's neck.

Flint rolled onto his side, still holding the iron poker in place. Yards from his reach, his father lay sprawled on the ground.

Mendozas staggered forward, one hand on his belly, the other drawing a knife. The sight of it reminded Makalani of her own. Between running for her life and getting ambushed by Flint, she hadn't had an opportunity to attack.

She flicked open her blade and lunged just as Alegado fired at the place she had been. Mendozas swiped with his knife and missed. Makalani, now on his far side, sliced his protective arm as she moved. Mendozas cursed from the new pain. When his hand slid from his belly, she scooped his arm back and planted him, face down, in the dirt.

Big mistake.

By reflexively taking him down for an arrest, she had left herself open to Alegado's attack. Worse yet, because she wasn't working as a law enforcement ranger any longer, she didn't even have cuffs.

Alegado laughed and aimed his pistol at her chest.

Makalani dove to the side, eyes on Alegado as he fired—puzzled when his face popped up as if he had been struck from behind.

His gun fired wide.

Makalani rolled as the bullet hit the shack.

Alegado stumbled and recovered with a step. Then, to Makalani's amazement, he turned into Malu's flying fist.

Malu?

Before she could ask why he was here, Alegado's partner staggered to his feet and tried to escape. Flint lay in his path still holding the poker extended from his neck. Instead of helping him, Mendozas snarled and kicked him in the head. The poker ripped from Flint's hands, tearing through his neck as it fell.

Stop Mendozas, or try to save Flint?

Makalani could only do one.

But as she lunged toward the men, Grace bolted out of the trees and tackled Mendozas into the side of the shack.

Both Malu and *Grace?*

Makalani was astounded but thankful they were here. Knowing the paniolo could handle themselves in a fight, she hurried to Flint and rolled him onto his back.

Dead eyes stared up at the moon as the last of his blood soaked into his land.

CHAPTER SIXTY-SIX

Adrenaline rushed out of Makalani as she sat back on her heels. On either side, her friends had the meth-making drug dealers planted and tied like calves ready to brand. In front of her, both Flint and his father were dead. She raised her hands, still bloody from squeezing shut Flint's wound. For the second time this year, she felt covered in death.

"E kala mai ia'u," she whispered to the Reeds. "I'm so sorry. Please forgive me. I didn't mean for you to die."

Approaching sirens were the only response she received—that and the ragged breathing of those who still lived.

"You okay?" Grace asked as Makalani rose to her feet.

Grace had tied Mendozas's hands to his ankles in front of his body. With his buck-shot belly protected, he could wait until the paramedics arrived.

Malu had tied Alegado's hands behind his back to one ankle with his face in the dirt. He had left Alegado's pistol on the ground but well out of reach.

Makalani shook her head in wonder. "Why are you guys even here?"

Malu nodded at Grace. "Because dat wahine stay one biggah pain in da ass dan you."

Sirens drowned out Grace's response as emergency vehicles drove up the access road.

"You called the police?"

"Grace did. As soon as we heard the first shot."

Smart woman.

"Well, mahalo for coming when you did. If you hadn't hit Alegado from behind, I'd have been shot, and those killers would have escaped."

Grace nodded toward the Reeds. "Did the drug dealers kill them?"

"Yeah. Alegado shot the father. Flint shouldn't have died. There was a struggle. When I released the poker, it went into his neck. I think he would have made it if Mendozas hadn't kicked him in the head. But that's not all. Alegado and Mendozas caused your grandfather's death."

Before Makalani could explain, four police officers burst through the trees, weapons drawn, their powerful flashlights illuminating the scene. When lights hit Makalani, they descended on her first. She couldn't blame them. Covered in blood, earth, and leaves, she looked like a ghoul risen from the dead.

She dropped to her knees and held her arms out to the side. "I'm a national park law enforcement ranger. There's a utility knife in my pocket, but I'm otherwise unarmed."

A stocky male officer cuffed her hands behind her back and confiscated the knife. He pulled a small wallet from her pocket. He checked her Hawaiʻi driver's license and shone his light on her uniform. "Makalani Pahukula. You work at Volcanoes?"

"No. I'm at Puʻukoholā Heiau."

"That's a national historic site, not a national park."

"I recently transferred from Oregon. My ranger ID is in the back."

After checking her credentials, the officer called to his partner and unlocked the cuffs. "She's a law enforcement ranger. I'm letting her up."

Makalani explained what had happened as officers checked the others for weapons and decided which of them were a threat and which of them needed to be questioned or detained. Once everything had been sorted, they untied the drug dealers, cuffed them properly, and led them away.

Makalani followed and found Malu and Grace waiting on the access road beside Malu's truck, blocked in by an ambulance and assorted

SUVs. Since HPD used personal vehicles rather than patrol cars, emergency lights were affixed to the roofs.

A small figure emerged from the lights.

Makalani smiled when she saw who it was. "What are you doing here?"

Detective Rona Kim shrugged. "I couldn't wind down after our call, so I drove to the Waimea office and continued to work. When I heard about shots fired, I feared it might involve you."

"I'm not sure how to take that."

Rona laughed, then nodded to Grace and Malu. "Who are they?"

"This is Larry Hiapo's granddaughter, Grace. This is Malu. He lives and works on Hiapo Ranch."

"I saw Jay Alegado and Goyo Mendozas being loaded into a car. Who are the bodies?"

"Flint Reed and his father."

"Were you involved in that?"

"To some degree. Alegado shot the father. Mendozas ultimately killed the son. They've been cooking meth in a shack on the Reeds' property and washing their jugs and equipment in the water that trickles down the gulch."

Malu overheard. "Wait. Dose guys poisoned our water and our 'āina wit' meth?"

Makalani nodded. "I'm pretty sure that's what drove Hinuhinu mad when he wandered into the gulch to drink."

"You're right," Rona said. "I didn't tell you before, but the last toxicology report I ordered showed low levels of methamphetamine in the bull's blood. The levels would have been markedly higher if we had tested urine samples or even blood samples closer to when the bull killed Larry Hiapo."

Grace joined in. "Meth would definitely have made Hinuhinu crazy enough to run wild and fall into the pit."

"Yeah," Malu said. "Violent too."

"But how could such a diluted amount intoxicate a bull?"

Malu sighed. "If dey been dumping a long time, da toxins would have built up. Cattle drink wherevah da water pools. Meth passes through da body pretty quick. Explains why he was so mellow da next day when we showed up."

A paramedic came over to check on Makalani.

She waved him off. "I'm fine. It's someone else's blood."

Rona's shoulders relaxed. "I was going to ask about that."

"No worries. Nothing a really hot shower won't fix."

As the ambulance drove off, Louie's pickup truck took its place. Kenneth and Rumiko jumped out of the passenger side and hurried to Grace.

Louie headed straight for Makalani, eyes wide at her blood-covered state. "What happened to you?"

Malu scoffed. "She caught those guys in dat aqua car dumping meth in our gulch. When Grace and me arrived, Hoʻolohe was shot dead and Flint stay on da ground wit' dakine fireplace poker sticking out of his neck."

"What da hell?"

"Yeah. Makalani stabbed one of those guys in da belly. We arrived just befo' da oddah guy try shoot her in da head."

"I only sliced his arm," Makalani said. "Hoʻolohe Reed shot him in the belly."

Rona butted in. "Was Mr. Reed trying to protect you?"

"Not exactly," Makalani said. "He thought I jabbed the poker into his son when he saw me kneeling over him with blood on my hands."

"Did you?" Rona asked.

"No. We were wrestling for it. Flint did it himself when I let it go."

Louie waved his hands. "So wait, Flint stay dead too?"

Makalani nodded. "When the drug dealer I caught making meth kicked Flint in the head, the poker ripped through his artery. The other drug dealer shot Hoʻolohe when he fired at them."

"What's this about meth?" Kenneth said, coming over with Rumiko and Grace.

While Makalani explained what she believed happened to the bull, Rumiko looked up the road toward the Reeds' house. "Did both the father and the son die?"

Makalani nodded. "I'm afraid so."

Rumiko sighed. "There was so much bad blood between their family and ours. Even so, I can't believe they meant for Larry to die. They must have been desperate to allow those men to poison the ʻāina that had once been theirs to protect."

CHAPTER SIXTY-SEVEN

Makalani kept her expression neutral as the Governor of Hawai'i spoke to the press. The state's news outlets had reported the drug bust homicides early that morning. When the Associated Press picked it up, the story broke nationwide by early afternoon with the headline, National Park Ranger Clears Meth Lab from Native Hawaiian Land.

The media attention would boost Makalani's career, but she would have felt more comfortable with an in-house ceremony at Pu'ukoholā. Then again, from the waves of anger coming from Supervisory Ranger Machado, that wouldn't have happened in a million years. She resisted a smile.

Okay, maybe this attention feels a little bit great.

After singing her praises, the governor—who had flown in from Honolulu especially for this—acknowledged the Hawai'i Island Police Department and the two detectives standing on his left. Although Detective Dan Lau had done worse than nothing, Makalani had made sure the higher-ups knew how instrumental Detective Rona Kim had been. Makalani felt lucky to have a friend like Rona on the force.

She glanced at the other friend she had made on this job, standing in the front row with her colleagues from Pu'ukoholā Heiau National Historic Site. Ranger Jamison Akaka smiled broadly. He was one of those rare, grounded people who could genuinely celebrate the advancement of others while still valuing his own talents and work. Earlier that week, he had confided that, although he enjoyed working with her at the heiau, he felt she and the National Park Service would be better served if she were in a position that made full use of her abilities.

The governor completed his acknowledgments and smiled at the press. "Any questions?"

A reporter shot up her hand. "Will Ranger Pahukula be transferred back into a law enforcement ranger position like the one she had in Oregon?"

The governor glanced at Supervisory Ranger Machado. "Well, I can't speak to that, but I imagine any of our Hawai'i National Parks would be happy to have Ranger Pahukula on their team."

He extended his hand to Makalani and smiled for the cameras as they shook.

Once the final shot had been snapped, the governor released her hand. "It was a pleasure to meet you, Ranger Pahukula. Keep up the good work."

As his handlers swooped in and whisked him off to the next gubernatorial obligation, Rona filled in the vacated space, saving Makalani from having to deal with her irritated supervisor. As nice as the governor's words had been, Makalani feared he might have harmed rather than helped her prospects at work.

"Congratulations," Rona said.

"Same to you."

Rona chuckled. "No one would have acknowledged me if you hadn't told them about my work."

Makalani shrugged. She'd been the outsider for most of her life, hanging on the fringes of established friendships and teams. She knew how hard it was to join a cohesive group. Being the only woman didn't help, especially coming in from Honolulu into a boys' club of Big Island men. "They would have figured out how good you are soon enough."

"Maybe. But would they have treated me any differently?"

Makalani winked. "Probably not."

The public acknowledgment might cause a little tension at work for Rona as well, but at least she had the governor's accolades to back her up.

As Rona left, Ranger Akaka filled her space. "Guess you found a way to use your skills after all."

Makalani thought about Larry Hiapo. "Not in the way I had hoped. But, yeah . . . I guess I did."

Ranger Akaka rested his hand on her shoulder. "No matter what we have you do at Puʻukoholā, there will always be room in your life to express who you are. Jobs are like relationships, yeah? Even the best ones won't fulfill all your hopes or welcome everything you have to give."

"Hmm. You sound like my tūtū."

"Really? Because, you know, I'm not that much older than you."

"It's the wisdom, not the years. She and my parents are always cautioning me to curb my expectations and appreciate moments, people—and jobs—as they are."

"That's a tough one."

"Right?"

He patted her shoulder. "Ka lā hiki ola. Every day is a new dawn, a chance for us to do better than before. Today's work day is basically done. Will you spend your days off at the ranch?"

"Going there now."

"Maikaʻi. Then you'll be ready for the new lessons on Sunday when you come back to us."

"Looking forward to it." And much to her surprise, she actually was.

CHAPTER SIXTY-EIGHT

The early barbecue dinner was well underway by the time Makalani arrived at the ranch. Although she had planned to change out of her ranger uniform in the bunkhouse, the smoky scent of grilling beef and sweet potatoes changed her mind. She had been too nervous to eat that day with a press conference happening at three. She could always change clothes after her growling ʻōpu had been filled.

Grace spotted her first. "ʻĀwīwī, Makalani, we saved you a steak."

When Makalani reached the grill, Grace had loaded her plate with thick slices of tri-tip, a whole sweet potato, and sides of coleslaw and rice. Makalani cracked open the ʻuala and dropped a huge chunk of chili honey butter onto its flesh. The butter melted instantly into the potato and dribbled onto the plate. "This is amazing."

"Nothing's too good for my ranger cuz."

Makalani beamed as she followed her to an empty spot on a bench. This was the first time a Hiapo other than Rosie had called her family. It made her feel as if she really belonged. But like a lot of families, this one had found yet another topic for debate.

Louie barely acknowledged her as she slid beside him on the bench. "I say we should buy da Reed property and combine it wit' ours."

Kenneth leaned back from the other side of the table. "With what money? I keep telling you we don't have the funds to shift our operations from cow-calf to grass-fed. Now you want to invest in real estate we don't need?"

"It no stay about need, brah. It stay da right t'ing to do."

Rumiko leaned forward. "What do you mean, son?"

"You saw how dey lived, Mom. Dat kuleana is ours."

"No one forced them to sell their ranch," she said.

"That's right," Kenneth agreed. "And sure as hell, no one forced them to let drug dealers cook meth in our gulch."

"Yeah, but no fo'get," Louie said, "half dat gulch belonged to dem."

Kenneth groaned. "Are you seriously defending what they did? To Dad? To the land?"

"I'm just saying . . ." Louie shook his head. "Ah hell . . . I don't know."

"I do," Kupunakāne said from the end of the table. "All dis trouble began wit' us."

Louie nodded.

"You not wrong," Kupunakāne said. "Kānaka gripe all da time about how white men stay buy up our ʻāina. And what did my faddah do? He used his white faddah-in-law's money to buy up all da grazing pasture on Reed Ranch. He nevah stop to consider how dey would feed da cattle dey kept. He just wanted mo' land fo' himself and fo' us. He nevah feel bad about it until dat night when we chased um to their house."

He looked at Louie. "Your great-grandfaddah felt just like you when he saw how dey live. Sometimes I wondah if his hewa—his guilt—made him ride ovah dat trench. He shoulda seen it, because I tell you now, it no stay dea befo'."

"You think Flint's father dug it?" Kenneth asked.

Kupunakāne nodded. "Hoʻolohe was a strong and bitter kid. When he grew up, he passed his ʻawaʻawa—his bitterness—on to his son. Both of dem die as miserable as dey live."

He looked at every member of his family. "What Louie try say is dat if we no make dis right, we goin' pass my faddah's hewa—his bad deed, his guilt—on to Grace and Vinnie."

Louie nodded. Beside him, Malu gave his shoulder a squeeze.

Makalani knew how transgressions and bad feelings could destroy a family. Not only did the Hiapos carry unresolved hewa through generations, but they had also not acknowledged or sought forgiveness for the daily harm they caused.

Kenneth sighed. "I hear what you're saying, but we still don't have the funds." He looked to his wife for confirmation.

Carolyn shook her head. As the family's accountant, she would know.

Rumiko placed a hand on Kenneth's shoulder as she rose from the bench. A huge smile bloomed across her face. "They're here."

Brian's car kicked up the dirt as he and his family approached. Everyone leaped to their feet to meet them as they parked. Rosie got out first and opened the rear passenger door for their son. When everyone saw Vinnie, they cheered.

Rumiko rushed forward to hug her grandson, careful to avoid the cast from his shoulder to his wrist. Miraculously, Vinnie had not broken a single bone in his hand. He looked like a returning veteran with the bandage wrapped around his head. The hematoma found between his skull and the outer band of his brain had been easily drained. All his surgeons predicted a full recovery.

Vinnie squirmed away from her kisses. "Grammie, stop." Then he stood tall and proudly displayed his arm.

Louie furrowed his brows as if greatly impressed. "Dass one primo cast you get dea. How you feel?"

Vinnie beamed. "Good. Kinda sore. Little bit itchy."

Louie laughed. "Well, dat part gets worse. But no worries, we get you back on Uila plenny kine soon."

"First he heals," Rosie said. "*Then* we can talk about that horse."

"Mom!"

"Mom, nothing." She pointed at Louie. "And don't encourage him."

Brian grinned as he came up from behind. "Don't mess with your mother, boy. She's tougher than them."

Rosie play-slapped his chest.

"What?" Brian gave her a hug.

Vinnie used the distraction to make his escape straight to Makalani and Grace. "Pretty cool, right? Wanna sign it? I have a pen."

Makalani laughed as Grace examined the cast with the appropriate respect. She took the pen and began drawing a rearing horse on the outside of his arm. Vinnie beamed with pride as she drew.

Malu joined Makalani to watch. "He goin' be fine."

"You think?"

"Oh, yeah. Paniolo face plenny kine danger. Dis experience goin' teach Vinnie caution and respect. Ahonui too."

Makalani nodded. "Patience would be good."

Vinnie frowned at Malu over Grace's shoulder. "The doctor said it could take six months to heal."

"Dass aurite. You stay come out bettah dan befo'."

Once again, Makalani marveled at how good Malu was with kids.

As Brian and Rosie filled dinner plates for their son and themselves, another car drove up the hill.

"Who's that?" she asked Malu.

"No idea." He turned to Louie. "You know who dat is?"

Louie shook his head. "Everybody here already."

Kenneth marched over as the driver, a local man around fifty, stepped out of the car. "This is private property. Are you lost?"

The man smiled. "Not if you're Kenneth Hiapo."

"Excuse me?"

He held out his hand. "I'm Skip Una from Oregon. We've spoken over the phone."

Kenneth glanced at the others. "Um, yeah . . . but what are you doing here?"

The man put on a grave expression Makalani didn't believe. "I heard what happened with your neighbors. I've reached out to their bank and let them know I might be willing to buy."

Kenneth grimaced. "They only died early this morning."

"True. But this is Waimea, and that's a nice piece of land."

Louie joined his brother and glared down at the man. "Why are you telling *us*?"

Skip extended his hand. "Hi. Louie, right? I'm Skip. I own Una Ranch where you guys finish your beef. I was so sorry to hear about your dad. He and I had been doing business a long time. I made him an offer for the ranch."

"So I heard."

"Kenneth and I had been discussing the same thing."

"Heard dat too."

Grace stepped forward. "You can't be serious, Dad."

"We were only talking," Kenneth said.

Skip raised his hand. "Hi. You must be Grace."

Louie scowled at his brother. "Well, you musta talked plenny kine, because dis malihini knows all of our names."

Skip smiled patiently. "I'm not a malihini. I grew up here. I came by to offer you ten percent more."

Kenneth's eyes widened with interest, but before he could respond, Kupunakāne pushed him aside. "You stay talk to da wrong Hiapo. Dis ranch still belongs to me."

"Of course," Skip said. "Everyone in town knows Luke Hiapo is still in charge. That's why I flew in from Oregon, so I could meet you in person when I offered you this life-changing deal." Skip grinned at everyone present, but when he came to Makalani in her ranger uniform, he paused.

Makalani tensed from the wrongness she felt.

This man isn't pono.

Taking advantage of his apparent concern over her uniform, she stepped forward with the authority she usually saved for work. "Mr. Una, if you are sincerely interested in making an offer on Hiapo Ranch, I suggest you go through the proper channels instead of disturbing our family dinner."

He held his hands out in surrender. "Look, clearly I came on too strong. The fact is, I have dreamed about having a ranch in Waimea since I was kid. I was a boarding student at Hawai'i Preparatory

Academy a few years before Kenneth. I only moved to Oregon because my grandfather lost his Ka'u ranch when the Department of Hawaiian Home Lands took it back."

Kupunakāne's eyes narrowed. "Una is your family name?"

"Yeah. My grandfather was Enele."

"I remembah dat guy from befo' time. Met um at a rodeo. Good paniolo. Bad horse."

Skip laughed. "Sounds about right. Grandad couldn't afford to buy quality, but he worked hard with what he had. I did the same in Oregon, and it paid off. I want to pass it to my son so I can move home."

"Your roots stay in Ka'u," Kupunakāne said.

"With Grandad, yes. But I grew up in Kona before my parents died. I fell in love with Waimea when Grandad sent me to school."

"And now you like buy my land?"

"For a fair price. Enough for *your* grandkids and *their* kids to follow their dreams."

Kupunakāne turned to his grandchildren, Kenneth, Louie, and Rosie. "Your roots grow deep in dis 'āina. If you try pull um up, da nā a'a pa'akikī—da tough roots—goin' cling to da earth and call you back. No mattah how much money you get, you goin' be like dis guy, all da time yearning to return home."

He turned to Vinnie. "When paniolo go out fo' ride, we nānā da 'āina to make sure everyt'ing stay maika'i—everyt'ing stay good—right?" He looked at everyone else. "But as kānaka maoli, we also need nānā i ke kumu—look to da source."

He paused to let that sink in. "So you tell me, my 'ohana, is dis what you want?"

One by one, the Hiapos shook their heads.

Kenneth turned to Skip. "I'm sorry you came all this way for nothing, but we're not going to sell."

Louie placed his hand on his brother's shoulder in support. "He's right. Our family grew up on dis ranch. It would be like cutting off a leg."

Rosie joined her brothers and wrapped an arm around Louie's waist. He kissed her head and hugged her to his side.

Rumiko came forward and motioned to the buffet table. "You're welcome to join us for dinner. We have plenty to share."

Skip nodded and stood awkwardly in place as Rumiko spoke with her kids. He couldn't know how unusual it was to have all three Hiapo siblings together and at peace. Even so, he knew enough to leave them alone.

Makalani reassessed her first impression of the man. Although he had barged in with a single-minded purpose, his arrogance had softened when he spoke from the heart.

What if he's like me, a kanaka who wants to come home?

She piled food onto a plate and carried it to Skip. "Hi. I'm Makalani. Come sit with me."

CHAPTER SIXTY-NINE

One Month Later

Eucalyptus chips kicked into the air as Makalani guided her chainsaw through the length of the trunk. She had already trimmed the branches for firewood and cut the log into six-foot sections. The lengthy horizontal cut required more concentration and strong, steady hands. Her wide stance supported her base. The eucalyptus scent, filling her sinuses even through the mask, kept her mind sharp.

As Makalani split the logs into rails, Grace hoisted the branches onto the UTV's bed. When it reached its capacity, she drove her load to the side of the Reeds' old house where Sue and Darius, Phil's teenage kids from branding day, unloaded the bed and stacked the branches according to size—kindling on the left and firewood on the right.

When Makalani powered off her chainsaw, the screeching buzz of another saw continued higher up the slope. It whined loudly, then paused. A new tree crashed to the ground. As Louie cut off the leafy limbs, Phil and Brian dragged them away while Rosie, Rumiko, and Carolyn raked the leaves, sawdust, and debris into piles. Once the area had been cleared enough for Kenneth's tractor, he wrapped a chain around the top of the tree and hauled the trunk to Makalani to be cut.

She lowered her mask and pulled the goggles off her head, sweaty, happy, and invigorated by the work. She wasn't the only one. All around her, the Hiapo family had finally united behind a common goal.

Grace returned with the UTV. "Time to break?"

"Almost. After we move the rails."

They loaded the planks into the truck and drove them to the clearing where Malu instructed a small group of kids, ranging from nine to eighteen, on how the horse corral would be built. With a forest full of timber to be cleared, they could save money by constructing a split-rail wood fence. Nothing would be wasted. Every resource, including the fragrant leaves and sawdust, would be saved and eventually used.

Mālama i ka ʻāina, mālama ka ʻāina iā kākou.

Care for the land, the land cares for us.

It would make Tūtū so happy to see Makalani living life as she taught.

Once Malu and the kids had mapped out the corral's dimensions in the dirt, Malu instructed the eldest teenagers on how to use the electric auger to dig the vertical postholes. He gave another teenager the manual posthole digger to clear out the dirt. With the elder kids occupied, he and the younger kids used their combined strengths to carry three split rails to each segment where they would be screwed into the grounded posts, selected and cut by Makalani from straight, slender trunks. Kupunakāne and Vinnie, with his arm in a cast, painted the bottoms of the posts with wood preserver so they wouldn't rot in the ground.

Makalani snapped photos and messaged them to the Pahukula family group chat. She had been documenting and sharing the progress since the first day of the renovation. When she flew home to Kauaʻi for Thanksgiving, she'd have wonderful stories to tell.

A pickup truck rumbled up the access road. When the driver beeped his horn, everyone stopped working. The Hiapo brothers' chainsaw and tractor engines ceased. The kids raced over as the driver emerged with a stack of pizza boxes up to his nose. Even from a distance, Makalani could see the happiness in the man's eyes.

As the kids whisked the boxes to the picnic tables, Makalani greeted the new owner of the Reeds' land. "Howzit, Skip. Thanks for bringing lunch."

He smiled broadly, looking far more comfortable than when he'd crashed the dinner at Hiapo Ranch.

"Least I could do. You guys must be starving after clearing all those trees."

Makalani chuckled. "We're getting there. The forest is really dense. By the time we're done, you'll have enough space and lumber to build a zigzag fence wherever you want."

Although Skip would retain a strip of forest between his property and the Hiapos', he planned to clear all the trees that bordered the gulch to widen his view. A stacking fence would be perfect because it didn't require any postholes and could angle between the trees. They would build it just high enough to contain the cattle he hoped to acquire.

"How's the house?" Makalani asked.

"Livable."

"Ha! That bad, huh?"

"Good enough for now. I'll rebuild before I move here for good."

"I'm happy to pitch in. I've built houses before. And if you keep providing pizza, I know a crew of kids who would be eager to help. They've been working hard. Malu says they'll have the corral up by tomorrow."

"I heard. He's already picked out a couple of horses he thinks would be great for the kids."

"I love that you're doing this."

"Me too. But it wouldn't have happened without you."

After Rumiko had invited Skip to join the family dinner he had crashed, Makalani had kept him company so he wouldn't eat alone. As he told her stories about working his grandfather's ranch and how he always dreamed of becoming part of the Waimea community, a seed of an idea began to sprout in her mind.

Louie wanted the Hiapos to buy the Reed property and make reparations for the harm his ancestors had done. Kenneth was willing but insisted they didn't have the funds. Skip had already begun negotiations with the bank to purchase the Reed property but, without adding

Hiapo land as well, it wouldn't be large enough to support a profitable cattle ranch. Makalani considered all this and came up with a plan.

"What's most important to you?" she had asked Skip. "Becoming part of the community, or earning enough to support moving back home?"

Skip considered the question carefully. "As long as my son keeps running the Oregon ranch, I'll have enough to retire. What I really want—what I've never had—is to belong."

Makalani had felt that yearning when she lived on the mainland. Although she still faced moments when she didn't quite fit in, she knew that being of service was the best way to eventually belong.

"What if you bought the Reed property and used the ranch to train a new generation of paniolo?"

Skip laughed. "I wouldn't know where to begin. I've always hired the help I needed. I haven't cowboyed since I was a kid. My strengths lie in business and livestock management."

"That's important knowledge for a modern-day paniolo to have, but I was thinking of a more hands-on, in-the-dirt kind of education. The kind that comes from actually working on a cattle ranch and participating in the daily chores and repairs."

"Is this something you would want to lead?"

"Me? No. I'm still learning the basics. But I know an experienced paniolo who has already dedicated himself to helping at-risk kids by grounding them in our Hawaiian heritage and traditions. Imagine how empowered they would feel learning to ride and care for the horses, the cattle—the *land*."

Skip mulled over the idea. "Well, if you think he'd be interested."

"Only one way to find out. Eh, Malu," she yelled. "Try come ovah hea."

Malu eyed her warily, knowing full well Makalani rarely spoke Pidgin. "Wassup?"

As she laid out her vision, Louie noticed Malu's growing excitement and came over to hear. Grace and Kenneth followed. Soon, everyone in the family had gathered around Makalani and Skip, throwing out ideas on how they could empower a new generation of paniolo, preserve old traditions, and transform the Reed property into a small but sustainable ranch.

Malu spoke to Kupunakāne in ʻolelo Hawaiʻi. Although Makalani couldn't understand everything, his meaning was clear. The children needed elder cowboys like him to share their knowledge and teach them the old ways. Kupunakāne clearly agreed, speaking with more enthusiasm than she had heard before, feeling valued and encouraged with the prospect of meaningful work. With that revitalized energy, Makalani could easily imagine him sharing and teaching into his centenarian years.

Kupunakāne looked to each member of his ʻohana for a nod of agreement before turning to Skip. "Dis plan Makalani and Malu get, stay pono work. We no get money to offer, but . . . hiki iā mākou ke kōkua . . . we can all help if dis what you want."

"Before we go any further," Skip said to everyone, "there's something I need to confess. I offered to buy the Reed property if they could pressure you into selling your ranch. Flint said he knew Rosie and could convince her to back the sale. With Rosie and Kenneth on board, I had hoped Luke and Louie would agree. I didn't know about the meth lab or that Flint would send the drug dealers to harm Rosie's boy. That said, it was obvious to me that Flint had unresolved feelings about Rosie. I used that knowledge to encourage him to act, so I am also to blame. The attack on Vinnie would not have happened if I had not pressured the Reeds."

Not only did Rosie forgive him, she had assured him it wasn't his fault. Flint had always made her uncomfortable. Since he couldn't torment her directly, he tormented her son. All those attacks on Vinnie—cutting his cinch, centipedes in his boots—must also have been him.

The family agreed.

Skip called the bank the next day, acquired the property at a discount, and gutted the Reeds' old house. Two outdoor picnic tables and a used commercial grill were the first items he bought. Now a new generation of paniolo was devouring pizzas at those very tables while the pipi kaula—the paniolo-style jerky Kupunakāne had taught them to dry—was sautéing in pans on the grill.

Makalani topped her plate of rice with pipi kaula and the leafy coconut milk lūʻau, simmering on the grill. When she joined the grown-ups' table, she found Louie and Kenneth discussing ways they might be able to keep half of their calves and bring them to market weight by grazing in their own pastures on Hiapo Ranch. The experiment would take years, but Kenneth seemed more than willing to try. Likewise, Louie was more cognizant of how much the transition to producing Hawaiʻi sustainable beef would cost.

Rosie and Brian sat down beside Makalani while their son ate pizza and talked story with the kids.

"Vinnie seems happy," Makalani said.

Rosie rolled her eyes. "Yeah, now that you guys started this program, he's going to be a paniolo for sure."

"Is that so bad? Your grandfather is teaching him the old ways. Your brothers are giving him balanced views of the new. He has empowering role models and friends. He's even learning livestock management from a ranch owner with a college degree." She leaned forward so she could see Brian as well. "You guys have taught thousands of kids. You know the temptations and obstacles they face. Can you honestly say you're worried about *him*?"

Rosie sighed. "No. Not anymore. But it still hurts to see his arm and shoulder in a cast."

Grace leaned over her plate. "Eh, I broke my leg in a rodeo and came back better than before."

Louie overheard and scoffed. "Dat was not'ing. Remembah da time when I . . ."

Makalani stopped listening and watched the joyful faces instead as Hiapo after Hiapo trumped one another with their tales. Even Rosie laughed when Vinnie came over and embellished his own adventures with comical flair.

The Hiapos were family, and this was their life.

Whether they lived on the ranch or taught chemistry in school, their paniolo history in Waimea bound them together in the same way Makalani and her ʻohana were tied to their Anahola homesteading roots.

Vinnie caught her attention as he told everyone how she had raced over the field to help him with a calf. Grace shared memories of how awkward Makalani had been on her first day. Malu gave a play-by-play of how she had fallen out of the UTV and into a ravine. And Louie jumped in with how she had sung the "Pūpū Hinuhinu" lullaby to the Charolais bull. Even Kenneth joked about how such a tall woman could always be underfoot.

His mother laughed. "I feel the same way about you!"

Kupunakāne smiled with satisfaction. "Dis is how it should be. Mālama i ka ʻohana, mālama ka ʻohana iā mākou." *Care for the family, the family cares for us.*

He winked at Makalani. "You one Hiapo now, so dat includes you."

HAWAI‘I RAGE CHARACTERS

Main Characters

Makalani Pahukula (28)—Native Hawaiian ranger at Pu‘ukoholā Heiau National Historic Site, former law enforcement national park ranger at Crater Lake National Park in Oregon, rides Rocky Road

Luke Hiapo "Kupunakāne" (97)—patriarch and owner of Hiapo Ranch

Larry Hiapo (67)—Luke's son, rides ‘Opihi

Rumiko Yanagi Hiapo (78)—Larry's wife

Kenneth Hiapo (47)—Larry and Rumiko's son

Carolyn Chen Hiapo (47)—Kenneth's wife

Grace Hiapo (19)—Kenneth and Carolyn's daughter, rides Baby

Louie Hiapo (45)—Larry and Rumiko's son, rides Auali‘i

Rosie Hiapo Pahukula (44)—Larry and Rumiko's daughter, Brian's wife

Brian Pahukula (46)—Makalani's cousin, Rosie's husband

Vinnie Hiapo (8)—Rosie and Brian's son, Makalani's cousin, rides Uila

Malu Au (46)—Hiapo Ranch paniolo

Kam (48)—Malu's Mauna Kea rancher friend

Skip Una (60s)—owner of Una Ranch in Oregon

Ho'olohe Reed (91)—Hiapos' neighbor

Flint Reed (49)—Ho'olohe's son

Rona Kim (30)—detective for Hawai'i County's West Criminal Investigations Section

Dan Lau (54)—senior detective for Hawai'i County's West Criminal Investigations Section

Jamison Akaka (36)—senior ranger at Pu'ukoholā Heiau National Historic Site

Daniel Machado (48)—supervisory ranger at Pu'ukoholā Heiau National Historic Site

Freddy Liu (30s)—bull breeder

Sharon Yee (20s)—pathologist

Jay Alegado (20s)—gang member

Goyo Mendozas (20s)—gang member

Kaua'i Characters

Ka'ahumanu (Tūtū) Pahukula (85)—Makalani's grandmother

Julia (Māmā) Manu Pahukula (57)—Makalani's mother

Kawika (Pāpā) Pahukula (59)—Makalani's father

Kaulana Pahukula Ching (54)—Makalani's aunt

Eric Ching (57)—Aunty Kaulana's husband

Solomon (23)—Kaulana and Eric's son

Sandy Hall (29)—Makalani's childhood friend and Kaua'i firefighter

Detective Shaw (40s)—Kaua'i Investigative Services Bureau detective

Kalei (20s)—paka lōlō dealer

Branding Day Helpers

Lono (54)—Hiapo Ranch handyman/cook

Phil (45)—Hiapos' paniolo friend, twin brother to Pete

Lani (45)—Phil's wife

Sue (16)—Phil and Lani's daughter

Darius (14)—Phil and Lani's son

Jaime (5)—Phil and Lani's son

Pete (45)—Phil's twin paniolo brother

Ana (17)—Pete's daughter

Tai (50s)—Hiapos' paniolo friend

Fetu (30s)—Tai's paniolo son

Alofa (30s)—Fetu's wife

Lagi (4)—Fetu and Alofa's son

Historical and Mythological Characters

Ikua Purdy—legendary National Rodeo Hall of Fame paniolo who set the steer-roping record in 1908 at the Frontier Days Rodeo in Cheyenne, Wyoming

Archie Ka'au'a—famous paniolo who competed with distinction in 1908 Frontier Days Rodeo in Cheyenne, Wyoming

Eben Low—famous paniolo who competed with distinction in 1908 Frontier Days Rodeo in Cheyenne, Wyoming

John Palmer Parker—founder of the famous Parker Ranch, married Chiefess Kipukane, granddaughter of King Kamehameha I

Ka'ahumanu—married King Kamehameha I to become Queen

Kamehameha I (also called King Kamehameha the Great)—unified Hawaiian Islands under one rule

Kapoukahi—kāula (seer) and kahuna (expert) for King Kaumuali'i who told King Kamehameha I he had to build a heiau at the

Pu'ukoholā site before he could conquer other chiefs and unite the Hawaiian Islands

Kaumuali'i—king of Kaua'i and Ni'ihau who remained acting regent even after King Kamehameha I conquered and united the Hawaiian Islands

Ke'eaumoku—uncle to King Kamehameha I and father to Queen Ka'ahumanu who killed Kaumuali'i and his entourage

Pele—goddess of volcanoes (Madame Pele, Tūtū Pele)

Poli'ahu—goddess of snow, known for compassion

GLOSSARY

This glossary uses the ʻokina [ʻ] or glottal stop and the kahakō [ō] as found in the Nā Puke Wehewehe ʻŌlelo Hawaiʻi dictionary to recognize the importance of preserving the indigenous language and the culture of Hawaiʻi. Since the ʻokina is considered a unicameral consonant letter, these words are grouped together at the start. The glossary begins with words in ʻōlelo Hawaiʻi and walaʻau kanaka—the spoken language of paniolo (Hawaiian cowboys) that often shorten or substitutes Hawaiian words. The glossary then continues with Hawaiian language phrases; Pidgin English and common non-Hawaiian local words; locations; historical and mythological figures. The definitions coincide with their usage in this novel and are not intended to be comprehensive in meaning.

Please note that although Hawaiian Pidgin English has been declared an official creole language, it is not to be confused with ʻōlelo Hawaiʻi, the native language of the Hawaiian people.

- ʻOkina that precedes vowel words creates a glottal stop when used in a sentence.
- ʻOkina between vowels designates a glottal stop in the word.
- Vowels without ʻokina between them glide together in one elongated sound.
- A kahakō over a vowel lengthens the sound and increases the stress. For example, the word kahakō stresses the final syllable

slightly with an elongated Ō. The word Kālā stresses both elongated vowels equally. Words without kahakō are usually stressed in the first syllable for short words, second syllable for medium-length words, and the second and second-to-last syllables in long words.

- Diphthongs in the Hawaiian language create subtle differences in sound and placement than a simple glide from one vowel to the next. Since this is difficult (if not impossible) to explain in text, vowel combinations are not addressed here, except to note that *au* has a more closed and forward sound than ow. Note: If an ʻokina is not present, vowels will glide within and between words in a sentence.

Vowels (nā woela)

A—(ʻā) ah

E—(ʻē) eh

I—(ʻī) ee

O—(ʻō) oh

U—(ʻū) oo

Consonants (nā koneka)

H (hē)—similar to English

K (kē)—similar to English with less air

L (ʻlā)—similar to English

M (mū)—similar to English

N (nū)—similar to English

P (pī)—similar to English with less air

W (wē)—can be pronounced as English w or softer v

ʻ (ʻokina)—glottal stop (as in "uh-oh")

ʻŌlelo Hawaiʻi Words and Walaʻau Kanaka (Paniolo Talk)

ʻae—yes

ʻaʻā—lava that burns hot and moves quickly in chunky avalanches across the land

ʻāhiu—wild (as in *hipa ʻāhiu*, wild sheep)

ʻahu ʻula—red cape (royal color usually made from feathers as in *ʻahu ʻula hulu aliʻi*)

ʻāina—land

ʻāina nui—abundant land

ʻaumakua—family or personal god, deified ancestor (*ʻaumākua*, plural)

ʻāwīwī—hurry

ʻawaʻawa—bitterness, bitter

ʻehu—reddish tinge in dark hair (as in *ʻehu wahine*), often used to describe a beautiful local woman

ʻiʻi—deep rasping tremor in the voice made while chanting

ʻili—leather

ʻohana—family

ʻōhiʻa lehua—type of flowering tree

ʻōkole—buttocks

ʻōkumu—pommel, saddle horn

ʻōlelo—language, words, often used on its own to mean the Hawaiian language

ʻōlelo Hawaiʻi—Hawaiian language

ʻōlelo noʻeau—words of wisdom, clever words, Hawaiian proverbs

ʻono—delicious

ʻOpihi—Larry's horse, named for the limpets in the ocean found clinging to the rocks

ʻōpu—belly, stomach

ʻuala—sweet potato

ʻuhane hoʻopilikia—disturbed spirit

ʻula—red

ahonui—patience

ahupuaʻa—land division that extends from the mountain to the sea

akamai—smart

akua—god (*nā akua,* plural; *ke Akua,* God)

ala moku—type of rainbow, meaning a broken path

aliʻi—chief, ruler, monarch, royalty

aliʻi nui—high chief

aloha—love, affection, hello, goodbye

aloha kakahiaka—good morning (see also *kakahiaka nō*)

auwē—expression of surprise, exasperation

haku lei—plaited or braided lei, usually flowers sewn onto a flat lei of woven leaves

hanohano—honored, dignified

haole—white person

hapa—part, portion, fragment, half

hāpai—pregnant

hāpuʻu—type of fern

hauʻoli—happy

heiau—temple, meeting place

hewa—transgression, offense, guilt, crime, wrongdoing

hinuhinu—shiny, lustrous (as in "Pūpū Hinuhinu" lullaby)

hipa—sheep (as in *hipa ʻāhiu*, wild sheep)

honi—tradition Hawaiian kiss of touching foreheads and exchanging the divine breath in us all

hoʻoponopono—the Hawaiian practice of conflict resolution and forgiveness

hūi—a greeting or call, usually from a distance (as in *Hūi!*)

huli—to turn (as in turning *huli huli* chicken on the grill)

hulu—feather, plumage

hulu manu—bird feathers, featherwork (see *nā hulu aliʻi*)

ilima—delicate orange flower used in lei making

imu—cooking pit, underground oven

ka—the (as in *ka wā kahiko*, the ancient times)

kahiko—old, ancient (see also *wā kahiko*)

kahu—reverend, minister, pastor

kahuna—priest, sorcerer, expert (*kāhuna*, plural)

kakahiaka—morning

kakahiaka nō—paniolo way of saying good morning

kākau—tattoo

kalo—taro

kanaka—human, person (short for *kanaka maoli*, Native Hawaiian; *kānaka*, plural)

kānaka maoli—true people, Native Hawaiians

kāne—man, male

kapa—fabric made from pounded bark (as in *kapa-like fabric*)

kapu—taboo, prohibition, no trespassing, keep out

kāula—prophet, seer

kaula—rope, strap

kaula 'ili—rawhide lariat

kaula 'ōpu—leather strap that secures the saddle to the horse

ke Akua—God

keiki—child, offspring (as in *pipi keiki*, meaning calf) also used in Pidgin English to mean kids

kīkepa—kapa-like fabric wrapped around the body and draped over one shoulder

kōkua—help, assistance

konohiki—headman of an ahupuaʻa land division in ancient Hawaiʻi

Kope Attack—walaʻau kanaka (paniolo talk) for when a bull rakes his target under his chest with his forelegs and then bludgeons or impales his target with his head or horns

kuleana—sacred and reciprocal responsibility

kūlolo—rich coconut cream and kalo dessert

kumu—teacher

kuni—brand

kupuna—grandparent, elder, relative, or close friend of that generation (*kūpuna*, plural)

laho—paniolo talk for bull, short for *pipi laho* (also *pipi kāne*, male cow)

lā kuni pipi—paniolo talk for branding day

lānai—patio, porch

lauhala—hala leaves used for weaving as in lauhala hats

lio—horse

lo'i—kalo/taro paddy or field

lū'au—kalo leaves simmered in coconut milk (also a Hawaiian feast)

lua—toilet, bathroom

mahalo—thank you, gratitude, thanks, praise, respect

māhele—land division (as in the *Great Māhele*)

mahiole—feathered helmet

mahiole ali'i hulu manu—royal feathered helmet

māhū—homosexual

maika'i—good

maile—fragrant vine worn as a lei

maka'āinana—commoners, people who worked the land in ancient Hawai'i

maka'ala—to pay attention

makai—toward the sea, seaside

mākaukau—ready, able, competent, skilled

makuahine—(also *makua wahine*) mother (*mākuahine,* plural) makua kāne—father (*mākua kane*, plural)

mālama—care for, to take care of, preserve, protect

mālie—calm

malihini—visitor, foreigner nonlocal, outsider

mana—supernatural or divine power

manini—poured (as in poured concrete "tofu" blocks)

manō—shark

mauka—toward the mountains, mountainside

mea oli—chanter

moe aikāne—sleep friend, referring to a homosexual relationship

moʻolelo—story

moʻopuna—grandchild or grandchildren

nā akua—gods

nā hulu aliʻi—royal featherwork

nā aʻa paʻakikī—the tough roots

nana—type of kalo (taro)

nānā—survey, notice, inspect (as in *nānā ʻāina*)

noʻeau—clever, wise (as in *ʻōlelo noʻeau*)

olakino—health (as in *olakino maikaʻi*, good health)

oli—chant that is not intended for dance

olonā—native shrub used as a base for feather capes and other crafts

pā—corral, pen, fence, wall

pā kuni—branding corral

pā pōhaku—dry-stack rock wall

paʻakikī—stubborn

pāʻina—small dinner party

pāhoehoe lava—flows like a river and dries in smooth, ropy patterns

paka lōlō—crazy weed, Hawaiian word for marijuana

pakalana—fragrant tiny green flowers

palaka—signature checkered design, introduced in the heavy twill jackets worn by sailors and adapted into work shirts by plantation workers and paniolo

paniolo—Hawaiian cowboy, derived from the Spanish word, Españolo, for the Mexican vaqueros who taught the Hawaiians how to cowboy and ride papa ku'i 'ai—poi pounding board

pāpale—hat, frequently woven from sturdy hala leaves (as in *pāpale lauhala*)

pele—lava flow, volcano, eruption (capitalized for the goddess Pele)

pīkake—Hawaiian jasmine used in lei making

pilau—stinky, bad smell

pipi—general name for cow or cattle

pipi 'ula—red cow

pipi kaula—strips of semidried beef

pipi laho—paniolo talk for bull (*laho* for short, also *pipi kāne*)

pipi wahine—cow

Pō—realm of the gods, eternity to which spirits are returned

pōhaku—rock, stone

pololei—correct

pono—righteous, good

po'o wai u—an old paniolo technique and Hawaiian rodeo event where the cowboy uses the fork in a tree while roping to help secure a cow, calf, or bull puaʻa—pig, boar

puka—hole

pule—prayer

pū ʻohe—sanded, hollow link of bamboo used to blow like a conch, more common upland

pūpū—shell (as in "Pūpū Hinuhinu" lullaby)

puʻu—hill

tī—(kī) ti plant

uepa—rawhide short hand whip

wā kahiko—ancient times (*ka wā kahiko*, the ancient times)

wahine—woman, female

walaʻau kanaka—paniolo way of speaking, paniolo talk, paniolo terms

wao akua—godly realm

wiliwili tree—coral tree

ʻŌlelo Hawaiʻi Phrases

ʻAʻole pololei.—It's not right.

ʻĀmene.—Amen.

A hiki mai no ʻoe, hiki pu no me ke aloha.—Now that you have come, love comes with you. (line from "Oli Aloha" chant)

Ala pā!—walaʻau kanaka (paniolo talk) for wake up.

Aloha e.—Love and gratitude to you.

Aloha kakahiaka.—Good morning.

Aloha mai.—Greetings.

Aloha wau iā ʻoe.—I love you.

E ʻoluʻolu, e ke Akua.—Please, God.

E ʻoluʻolu ʻoe e hele mai.—Please come.

E hana i ka hana.—Do the work.

E hoʻolohi.—Slow down.

E hoʻomanawanui.—Be patient.

E kala mai iaʻu.—I'm sorry, please forgive me.

E komo mai.—Welcome.

Hele hele.—Come, come.

Hele mai.—Come with me. Come along.

Hele ma kai.—walaʻau kanaka (paniolo talk) used to tell the cattle to go home.

Hiki iā mākou ke kōkua.—We can help.

Hoʻopilikia ka manaʻo maikaʻi ʻole i ka hana.—Hawaiian proverb (ʻōlelo noʻeau) meaning negative thoughts ruin the work.

I ka nahele, he aliʻi wau.—In the forest, I am chief.

I ka ʻōlelo no ke ola, I ka ʻōlelo no ka make.—Hawaiian proverb (ʻōlelo noʻeau) meaning in language there is life, in language there is death, and cautions us about the power of words.

I ulu nō ka lālā i ke kumu.—Hawaiian proverb (ʻōlelo noʻeau) meaning branches grow from or because of the trunk.

Iā ʻoe i ka mahalo.—Thank you to you. Gracious way of expressing thanks.

Ka lā hiki ola.—Every day is a new dawn.

Kakahiaka nō.—walaʻau kanaka (paniolo talk) for good morning.

Kōkua aku kōkua mai, pēlā ka nohona ʻohana.—Hawaiian proverb (ʻōlelo noʻeau) reminding people to treat others like family by helping and accepting help in return.

Kulikuli!—Be quiet!

Ma ka hana ka ʻike.—Hawaiian proverb (ʻōlelo noʻeau) meaning knowledge is learned by action, doing, or work.

Mahalo no kou hele ʻana mai.—Thank you for coming.

Mahalo iā mākou.—Gratitude to us.

Mahalo nui no kāu kōkua ʻana.—I appreciate your help so much.

Maikaʻi kēia.—This is good.

Maikaʻi nā mea a pau.—Everything is fine. It's all good.

Maikaʻi wau. A ʻo ʻoe?—I'm good. And you? (Common response to *Pehea ʻoe.*)

Mālama i ka ʻāina, mālama ka ʻāina iā kākou.—Care for the land, the land cares for us.

Mālama i ka ʻohana, mālama ka ʻohana iā mākou.—Care for the family, the family cares for us.

Me ka mahalo nui.—With much gratitude.

Me ke aloha nui a me ka mahalo!—With much love and respect!

Nānā ʻāina.—walaʻau kanaka (paniolo talk) for survey the land, make sure everything is okay.

Nānā i ke kumu.—Look to the source.

No hea mai ʻoe?—Where are you from?

Noʻu ka hauʻoli.—The pleasure is mine.

Noho mālie.—Be still. Stay calm.

Pehea ʻoe?—How are you?

Pehea ʻoe e ka moʻopuna?—How are you, my granddaughter?

Pili pā.—wala'au kanaka (paniolo talk) to tell cattle to *cling* to the *fence*.

Pōmaika'i mākou.—We are blessed.

Puka nānā.—wala'au kanaka (paniolo talk) to tell cattle to look for the gate (i.e., *hole*).

Welina mai iā kākou!—Welcome to all of you!

Pidgin English and Common Non-Hawaiian Words as Used/ Spelled in the Book

aurite—alright

befo' time—back in the day, before

bettah—better

braddah—brother, friend

brah—brother, friend

broke—break

buggah—a person (especially male) or sometimes a thing, especially when causing trouble

can, no can—it's possible, it's not possible

cone sushi—deep-fried tofu pocket cut on the diagonal, filled with sweet vinegared rice

coulda—could have

cuz—cousin

da—the

dakine—pronoun used in place of or preceding a noun (as in *get dakine* or *get dakine car*)

dan—than

dass—that's

dass why—that's the reason

dat—that

dea—there

dem—them

den—then

dey—they

eh—hey

evah—ever

fa'afetai—thank you (Samoan)

faddah—father

fo'—for

fo' real—are you serious, you've got to be kidding

geev—give

goin'—going to

good fun—enjoyable, fun

grind—eat

grindz—food

halmeoni—grandmother (Korean)

harabeoji—grandfather (Korean)

hea—here

howzit—greeting like hello, how is it, how are you?

junk—things of no value

jus'—just

kaukau—slang for food

latah—later

li'dat—like that

li'dis—like this

loco moco—rice, eggs, and meat served in a bowl, covered with gravy mattah—matter

mo'—more

nah—no, no way, just kidding, really? (rhymes with gnat)

nevah—never, don't, didn't

nevah mind—don't pay attention to

no need—not necessary

no worry, beef curry—don't worry

not'ing—nothing

numbah/s—number/s

o'—of

oddah—other

one—number used as an article in place of *a* (e.g., *catch one wave*)

or what—phrase tacked on at the end of a question

oughta—ought to

plenny—(also, plenny kine) plenty, lots

pissed off—angry

primo—best

remembah—remember

saimin—a mixed-cultural noodle soup originating in Hawai'i with a simple shrimp soup base whose name is drawn from the Chinese words *sai* (thin) and *min* (noodles)

shaka—hand signal for hello, thanks, howzit, formed with thumb and pinkie extended from a fist

shoots—expression with a mild meaning like *dang*

sistah—sister or affectionate word for or way to call a woman

small kine—insignificant, small

stay—used in place of *is* or *at*. Also thrown in front of a verb, as in *stay come ovah hea*

stink eye—mean look

t'ank/s—thank or thanks

t'ink/t'ought—think/thought

talk story—gossiping, passing the time, chatting, having a conversation

tita—sister or a tough woman

try—thrown in front of verbs as in *try come, try eat, try go, try wait, try get*

whatchu—what are you (as in *Whatchu goin' do?*)

whatevah/s—whatever

wit'—with

woulda—would have

yup—I agree

Locations on Hawai'i Island (Big Island)

A-Bay (Anaeho'omalu Bay)

Hale o Kapuni Heiau

Hāmākua Valley

Hawai'i Belt Road (Māmalahoa Highway)

Hawai'i Preparatory Academy (HPA)

Hāwī

Hilo

Hualālai Volcano

Ka Lua Kauka (Doctor's Pit)

Kahalu'u Beach Park

Kailua-Kona

Kailua Village

Kawaihae Bay, Port, Area

Kawaihae-Māhukona Road

Ka'u

Kahua Ranch

Kīlauea

Kohala (town, volcano, mountain)

Kohala Burger & Taco

Kohala Mountain Road (Highway 250)

Kona

Mana Road

Mauna Kea

North Kohala

Palihae Gulch

Parker Ranch

Parker Square

Pololū Valley

Ponoholo Ranch

Pu‘ukoholā Heiau National Historic Site

Queen’s North Hawai‘i Community Hospital

Saddle Road

South Kohala

Spencer Beach Park

The Fish & The Hog

Waikui Beach

Waimea / Waimea Town (Kamuela)

Waimea General Store

ACKNOWLEDGMENTS

I had just moved to Oregon for the birth of our second grandchild while doing my research for *Hawai'i Rage* and felt hopelessly distracted by my new and all-consuming tūtū life. Mahalo to my husband, eldest son, daughter-in-law, and author friends Dana Fredsti and Terry Shepherd for encouraging me to relish in the experience, guilt-free, and for assuring me that I would find my voice and momentum for writing when the time was right. They say it takes a village, and mine was a vast, interconnected web.

Mahalo to Ranger Renson T. Madarang from Pu'ukoholā Heiau National Historic Site for generously sharing his knowledge about Hawaiian history and his job. My fictional Ranger Jamison Akaka pays homage to him.

Huge mahalo to my Punahou School classmate Kim Greeley for sharing her equestrian knowledge, checking my manuscript, and introducing me to her calabash-uncle, the hall of fame paniolo Henry "Bud" Gibson! Talking story with the two of them for hours at his New Town and Country Stables on O'ahu was the highlight of my research. Any horsemanship and ranching authenticity you felt while reading *Hawai'i Rage* was likely influenced by Kim and Uncle Bud. And mahalo to Punahou friends Kahu (Reverend) Mark Haworth, who shared moving stories about his Episcopal ceremonies that inspired my fictional memorial service for Larry Hiapo, and Thad Bond, an architect and developer who offered insights on Hawaiian construction that helped me imagine the buildings on Hiapo Ranch.

Thanks to author Lyn Liao Butler who connected me to author Eric Redmond, who in turn connected me to Carolyn Wong Auweloa and her husband, Aaia Auweloa. Carolyn, formerly the USDA Resource Conservation director for the Big Island ranchers, now runs the Lahaina Community Land Trust on Maui. Aaia, who had been the head paniolo for Parker Ranch, now oversees grazing and wildlife management for the ahupuaʻa above and including Lahaina. Together, Carolyn and Aaia connected me to Richard Kaniho and his cousin Kalani Kaniho, who welcomed me onto their Hawaiian Home Lands ranch! Rumbling along the rough terrain of their Mauna Kea ʻaʻā field pastures in the front seat of Richard's UTV, listening to his stories, counting the wild sheep, getting the stink eye from his ornery cow—and wondering if we would flip into a ravine as has happened to him before!—was an adventure that will stay with me forever. Makalani's experiences on Kam's fictional Mauna Kea ranch were inspired by that priceless day.

Mahalo to Senator Tim Richards, owner of Kahua Ranch, who talked story with me over the phone about the history and challenges of ranching in Hawaiʻi today. As luck would have it, I had just taken a Naʻalapa Stables horseback riding tour of his ranch and received a wealth of information from Jackie and Darienne. I was introduced to the senator by Nicole Galase from the Hawaiʻi Cattlemen's Council—a tremendous resource for research and transcripts—which was also recommended to me by a rancher friend of Tim Harrington on Maui, who I met through my gifted equestrian/writer friend Lauren Woodard, who answered *endless* questions each and every time I called. So many connections and friends!

While on Hawaiʻi Island, I also met with Justina Wood, manager of the Paniolo Preservation Society, who recommended a book in their shop that became an important resource for me. If you'd like a real taste of modern paniolo life, do yourself (and your kids) a favor by checking out *Ka Lā Kuni Pipi: RK Branding Day* by Roberta Ku'ulei Keakealani, written in English and 'ōlelo Hawai'i.

And of course, none of this would be possible without the amazing professionals at Thomas & Mercer, Amazon Publishing. Huge thanks to my current editor, Elizabeth Agyemang, who inherited my Ranger Makalani Pahukula series with enthusiasm and joy. Both she and my former acquisition editor, Chantelle Aimeé Osman, made this book a hundred times better with their insightful editorial suggestions. Mahalo as well to my sagacious developmental editor, Wendy Muruli; my meticulous copyeditor, Sarah E.; my proofreaders, Tara and Rachel; and Miranda Gardner, our editorial coordinator who organizes them all. Huge thanks to my visionary book cover designer, Ploy Siripant; art director Jarrod Taylor; and the legion of other editors, readers, designers, marketers, and other behind-the-scenes professionals who I have yet to meet at the time of this writing but who will dedicate their expertise to make *Hawai'i Rage* the best possible and widely read book. And, as always, mahalo nui loa to my dedicated and caring literary agents, Lesley Sabga and Nicole Resciniti from The Seymour Agency. I can't thank them enough!

I love to hear from readers, so please feel free to connect with me through my website—ToriEldridge.com—and visit my *Hawai'i Rage* book club page for discussion topics, videos, recipes, and more while you're there. If you enjoyed your reading experience, please share it with others so they might enjoy it as well.

Me ka mahalo nui,
Tori

ABOUT THE AUTHOR

Photo © 2024 JLyn Portraits

Tori Eldridge is the author of *Kauaʻi Storm*, the Lily Wong mysteries, *Dance Among the Flames*, and numerous short stories. Born in Honolulu—of Hawaiian, Chinese, and Norwegian descent—Tori graduated from Punahou School with classmate Barack Obama before performing as an actress, singer, and dancer on Broadway, television, and film, and earning a fifth-degree black belt in To-Shin Do ninja martial arts. Her literary works have garnered Anthony, Lefty, and Macavity Award nominations and the 2021 Crimson Scribe for Best Book of the Year. Tori lives in Portland, Oregon, with her husband, near her precious moʻopuna (grandchildren). For more information about Tori, her book club extras, and her reading ʻohana, visit www.torieldridge.com.